Paula Stahel

Undone: A Novel of Betrayal

To Leah -
In Friendship
and
friendship!
Paula

Austin Macauley Publishers™
London • Cambridge • New York • Sharjah

Ordering Information
Quantity sales: Special discounts are available on quantity purchases by corporations, associations, and others. For details, contact the publisher at the address below.

Publisher's Cataloging-in-Publication data
Stahel, Paula
Undone: A Novel of Betrayal

ISBN 9781685627119 (Paperback)
ISBN 9781685627126 (ePub e-book)

Library of Congress Control Number: 2023914894

www.austinmacauley.com/us

First Published 2024
Austin Macauley Publishers LLC
40 Wall Street, 33rd Floor, Suite 3302
New York, NY 10005
USA

mail-usa@austinmacauley.com
+1 (646) 5125767

I have been bent and broken, but—I hope—into a better shape.

– Emily Dickinson

Chapter 1

He'd lied to her. She'd caught him in an affair, so many years after he'd sworn it would never happen again. He'd probably taken up with some chippie—thirty, forty years younger than she. Oh, she knew she wasn't as lithe and firm as she'd been all those years ago, but then, neither was he. Gil had started growing an old man's gut in the last couple of years, and had gone gray. She was proud of the fact she was still slender and didn't have to color her hair. True, things had shifted with time, but people still thought her years younger than her age. She took pride in being fit, dressing well, staying current—for herself, and also for him. She'd always wanted to make him proud. Now, she was humiliated. And angry. Angry beyond words.

In the madness brought on by her discovery, Lydia Casselberry wanted, desperately, to claw her way out of her own skin. An impossibility. But it was possible to escape from everything else. At least for a while. To think. To get away from her husband long enough to decide what she was going to do. Now that he knew she knew, he was probably using his latest trip out of town to concoct more lies, to convince her of what he wanted her to believe when he returned.

Once the idea of leaving hit, her mind calmed a bit. Where would she go? Where could she go? She didn't know. Anywhere, somewhere, nowhere. Nowhere was somewhere. It didn't matter where. She just knew she had to leave this house. It was no longer a home. It was a tomb. Stifling. Threatening. If she didn't leave, it would smother her.

She focused on the concrete. She needed solitude. Somewhere far, far away. Pacifica and the ocean beckoned. But that meant driving cross-country from Florida. And days and days of interchangeable interstates and traffic and motels and truck stops and fast-food grab-and-goes that would only add to her misery. She couldn't run back home to Mom and Dad. They were both gone, and theirs was the only other home, besides the one she shared with Gil, that had comforted her.

Wherever she went, she now wanted to leave as soon as possible. Before he returned in two days. She looked at the clock: 10:18 p.m. Too late to call

Sheldon, unless it was an emergency. *Well, this is an emergency*, she thought. She picked up the phone and dialed Sheldon Turner's number.

When he answered, she started speaking even before he'd finished saying hello. "Shel, I'm sorry to call so late. I have decided to take an immediate leave of absence. As of tomorrow. I'll turn over my classes to two of my graduate assistants. You may as well hire them as adjuncts—they're both ready. Cheryl has access to everything, so she knows what to handle in my office. I am sorry to do this, but it's necessary."

There was a pause. "Lydia, it's been obvious something's going on with you. But, taking a few days off without notice?"

"Shel, I'm not taking a few days off. I'm leaving for the rest of the term. It's either that or I resign. As of now."

"The rest …? You can't be serious. The term's hardly begun. You want a whole ten weeks' leave?"

"At least."

"At least?" he repeated. His voice told Lydia that fear had replaced his irritation. They had worked together long enough to know each other as well as siblings. A sensitive man, he'd never been able to mask emotion in his voice—something she was adept at. "Lydia, what happened? This isn't like you."

"No, it's not. Which is why you need to trust that I have to do this."

"Will you at least tell me why? Oh, god, are you sick? It isn't cancer, is it?"

Lydia clenched her teeth. *It is a cancer*, she thought, *a cancer of my soul.* "No. But I have to do this. By the end of the term, I'll know if I can come back. I'll let you know as soon as I decide."

"Holy cow, Lyd. Are you serious? You might quit? Seriously?"

Lydia's voice caught as she answered, "Right now, I don't know."

"Geeze." Exasperation and worry poured out in that one word. After another pause, Shel spoke quietly. "If there's anything—anything at all—I can do to help …"

His concern made her throat tighten. "Thanks," she whispered, "I know. But no."

"Promise you'll let us know if there is?" Now his voice was sad.

"Yes. I'm sorry. I've got to go." She knew she sounded curt but it was all she could manage without tears giving her away before she hung up.

She grabbed a tissue, pressed the wet from her eyes, and blew her nose to stop herself from breaking down in tears again. She'd managed to hold them in all day, but they had come in waves from the minute she was in the car after work. She couldn't think when she was crying, and she needed to do that now. Focus, she commanded herself. What next? Prepare. Be ready to leave in the morning. She needed to pack.

When Gil was home, his garment bag and carry-on had permanent space in their walk-in closet, sentinels at the ready to accompany him on the next of his constant trips. Lydia traveled so seldom, only once or twice a year to present at conferences, that she knew finding her luggage in the attic might require an anthropological dig. She headed past the three bedrooms where they'd raised two kids and housed uncounted guests, past their bedroom, to the end of the hall.

The door to the attic stairs hadn't been opened since she'd packed the Christmas decorations away after New Year's. Swollen by May's humidity, it didn't budge when she turned the brass knob and pulled. It seemed another personal affront, and her anger rose again. She slammed her shoulder against the tight seal once, twice, and a third time, pain jolting her and fueling her rage, before the door loosened and opened. Rubbing her shoulder with one hand, Lydia slid the other along the wall to flip on the light high overhead. No light. A furious spate of flipping yielded nothing.

It was all too much, too damned much. Clenching her fists, she screamed into the black hole above her, "Shit!" Turning away, she grabbed the door and slammed it. The swollen wood made a resounding thwack and bounced back full force against her sore shoulder. Fists clenched, her arms flailed in the air as she did a toddler-tantrum stomp and screamed, "Shit, shit, shit, shit, shit! Why is the whole damned universe against me?"

Then she drew a deep breath and exhaled. A revelation hit. She couldn't take suitcases. That would be a give-away that she'd be gone a long time. She didn't want Gil to know that. She'd take only a few changes of clothes. Those would fit into the black leather tote she used on occasion for class and administrative materials. And no one in the office would think a thing, seeing her with it. Getting that ready would take no time at all. What else did she need to do to prepare?

Her mind clearer, Lydia's steps were lighter as she headed to the kitchen. The clock now read almost eleven, about the time she began her bedtime routine. But she was too roiled up to sleep. Opening the glass-front liquor cabinet, she pulled down a bottle of Sambuca. Her hand hesitated as she reached for a small liqueur glass. Instead, she grasped a tumbler. The bottle shook slightly as she poured, almost filling the glass. *Jesus*, she thought, *if this doesn't let me get some rest tonight, nothing will.*

She dimmed the overhead light and carried the glass to the breakfast bar at the end of the room. A wall sconce cast a soft light over the farthest stool. Lydia settled herself there and stared into the clear liquid, as if it were a looking glass through which she could see the future. She took a long sip. The licorice flavor soothed her as a flash of its fire hit the back of her throat. *Damn, I wish I had a smoke*, she thought. She hadn't had a cigarette in eons but sure could use one now. Hadn't Audra tucked a partial pack into her purse after the Hopkins's party in March? She hopped from the stool and yanked open the catchall drawer. Digging through its mess, she found the hidden cigarette pack. As she grasped it, her fingers felt a hardened piece of leather below. A tactile memory hit as she drew out the curled rectangle and rusty beaded chain that held a key. Seeing it for the first time in years, her eyes filled. On it were the words her older brother had burned into the leather: Castle Berry.

The key itself was a throwback to a disappeared past. Fashioned of cast iron, it was long and slender, with a large curlicue at the end of the shank and intricate wards cut at the pin end of the stem. Clasping it in her palm, she was surprised at its warmth against her flesh. In her mind she heard a clear voice, as if the words flowed from the key itself: Come back, come back now. Slipping it into the pocket of her jeans, she drew a deep breath. She knew where she would go.

Carrying the cigarettes, matches, and her drink, Lydia went out onto the patio. *Good thing Gil isn't home*, she thought, *he'd give me holy hell.* At parties, he would glare at her when she slipped away with Audra for a smoke, and would pitch a fit when he caught her having a rare one at home. Wait a minute, Lydia interrupted herself, who gives a damn what he thinks? She inhaled long, and a buzz hit her brain. She took another sip of her drink to enhance it. *Now*, she thought, staring into the dark, *I'm ready to do some clear-headed planning.*

After her smoke, Lydia carried her glass into her home office, a cozy space off the living room. It had always been a room of her own. When they were little, Sara and James often invaded it, breaking her concentration—sometimes to her relief, other times making her long for a lock on the door. As a teen, Sara would slip in and sit, silent, in the wingback chair until Lydia looked up from whatever she was focused on. Sara did that when she needed to talk about something important, either to unburden a worry or share some teenage world-spinning news. By then, James had adopted his father's habit—he never crossed the threshold but leaned against the doorjamb as he asked a short question or carried on some discussion. That Gil never set foot in the room was another indication he had little regard for her career, which he often let her know. It had taken her years after the kids came, after he'd made his own success, to convince him that her teaching career was about more than earning money.

She pulled open the bi-fold doors that concealed file cabinets and shelves stacked with boxes and supplies. From the top shelf, she retrieved a locked metal box labeled "Mom's Legacy." She unlocked it with the key from a desk drawer, and lifted the lid. Short white mailing envelopes nearly filled the file box, and Lydia smiled as she congratulated herself. She pulled one out, opened it, and began to count the money it contained. With the fifth envelope, she knew she had more than enough to tide her over. She closed the lid, locked the file, and returned it to the shelf. *Bless you, Mom*, Lydia thought.

Her parents had raised Lydia and her brothers to be thrifty, but it was her mother who taught her a secret: Every woman needed money of her own. Her mom had stressed that on the day she and Gil announced their engagement. While he and her dad settled down to watch football—Lydia knew that was her dad's preferred setting when he was about to grill someone over a glass of scotch, as he was about to do with Gil—her mom had said, "Lydia, let's fix a cocktail and go out on the patio to talk about wedding plans." They did, for a few minutes, before her mom reached across the table to squeeze Lydia's hand. "Honey, you're going to promise to stick by Gil through ups and downs. Marriage means you stay together no matter what. That won't always be easy. But it will be right."

"Oh, Mom, we know," Lydia protested. "We've been together long enough to have had a couple of those 'downs' already."

Her mom sat back and took a sip of her drink. "Maybe. But not the kind I'm talking about. You're going to have times when you wonder if you've made a mistake."

Lydia leaned forward. "Mom, are you saying there were times when you wanted to leave Dad?"

"Honey, every married woman asks herself that at some point. More than once. And I'm sure your dad asked himself the same question—I am not always the easiest person to live with." Her mom's look also indicated, *and neither are you.* "But the secret to getting through those times is trusting yourself to get through them. That confidence is easier when you have your own pin money. Money no one else knows about. Money you'll have if something does go terribly wrong. Then you just pray, and work, to make sure that never happens. But from the very first, I want you to start squirreling money away. If he gives you fifty dollars to spend on groceries, you spend forty-eight and tuck that two dollars away somewhere."

"Gil doesn't quote-unquote give me anything, Mom. We know how we're handling the finances, and we've both got good incomes."

"Oh, I know. That's not what I mean. What I mean is, you make sure you save something for yourself every single week. No matter what. Even if it's pocket change during tight times, which there will be if you have kids. And you keep it in cash. Stash it someplace safe and secret, not in a savings account or an investment. Gil's a terrific fellow, and I'm happy for you both. I know you're going into marriage with a clear head. But I also know that having pin money to fall back on will make it much easier to work through the trying times. Knowing that cushion exists is a reassurance that no matter what happens you'll be all right."

Lydia's voice was low. "You've been keeping this a secret from Dad all these years?"

"Thirty-one years. Even with a darned fine life, I still add to my stash every single week." With a conspiratorial smile, her mom raised her glass. "A toast to your grandmother's advice to me, after your dad asked my father for my hand in marriage. I'm continuing the tradition, and expect you to do the same if you raise a daughter."

Lydia burst out laughing. "Good god. Where do you hide it?"

"I'm not telling. If I die first, now you'll know to look for it. If your dad goes first, well, I'm going to splurge even more than I already do." Her mom's eyes sparkled as she clinked her glass in solidarity against Lydia's, then her voice turned serious. "But I mean it, Lyd. If anything happens, you've got to have money of your own. Promise me?"

It was a promise Lydia was now glad she had kept. There had been lean times early in their marriage, and also when Gil had started his own business years ago, and then when the Great Recession hit. There were times when all she managed was saving quarters in an empty coffee tin on a pantry shelf. As their financial security grew, she felt occasional pangs of guilt for keeping the secret from him. But tonight she felt the import of her mother's advice as she slipped the money into a hidden compartment at the bottom of her tote. *Pin money, such an archaic term*, Lydia thought. But so appropriate, as it was now the safety pin she needed to keep her future from unraveling further. A single one-hundred-dollar bill went into her wallet. She carried the tote to the bedroom and turned to her dresser drawers and closet. Three pairs of undies, a couple of bras, four tops, a pair of jeans and sweats, and PJs half-filled it. She tossed in the last two cigarettes Audra had given her, a pair of black flats, and gathered a few cosmetics from the bath.

Glass in hand, she padded barefoot to Gil's study. From a credenza drawer she retrieved their lockbox, keyed in the combination, and pulled out the small notebook that listed numbers and passwords to their extensive list of banking, investment, and website accounts. She copied over much of the information, including Gil's black American Express card and the password for his business email, even though she knew that one by heart. That they knew each other's passwords had been a sign of the trust they had had for each other. *Or did have at one time*, she thought—*trust's been shot to kingdom come now, hasn't it?*

Lydia replaced the lockbox, then pulled out a piece of Gil's stationary. In the top drawer her fingers brushed through a collection of pens—Gil was as much of a pen snob as he was a watch snob, collecting Mont Blanc and Waterford and Aurora pens the way he amassed Rolexes and Omegas and Longines. He wore a different watch for every occasion, but the pens lay unused, just another indication of his need to always have the best for no other reason than having it. She chose one that seemed to float on her fingers for the note she was about to write.

Gazing at the memorabilia and photos around the room, mementos that froze time and happy events of the past, Lydia's eyes stopped on a small amber object half tucked behind a photo frame atop the bookcase. She rose, walked around the desk, and reached high for it. It was a delicate orb of golden crazed glass that encased a solid, silvery glass heart. She'd found it in an antique store in Florence, when she and Gil had celebrated their twentieth anniversary with a month-long trip to Italy. He'd been off somewhere on his own that afternoon, and she presented it to him as a gift at dinner that night, along with a small card on which she'd written, "No matter how much the world tries to shatter me, you are always the protector of my heart."

A sick feeling filled Lydia's stomach, then rage followed. She flung the orb across the room and screamed, "You bastard." The thin encasement shattered as it broke the glass of a framed photo. She stared at the broken glass, the tiny flakes of gold, and the intact heart scattered on the floor. "Fucking bastard," she muttered.

Lydia picked up the pen, paper, and her glass. She clicked off the desk lamp and made her way back to the patio. Fury-filled tomes raced through her mind for half an hour before she wrote four simple lines: I'm leaving. Don't try to find me. I need time to figure out whether or not I can live with this—and you. I'll let you know what I decide.

Then she sat staring into the dark until the first silver glimmering light of dawn.

***

An hour and a half later Lydia nodded at colleagues and occasional students on her way through the Education Department to her office. She paused at her assistant's desk. "Cheryl, I've got some scheduling changes to make. As soon as you get a chance, I need to talk to you."

"Sure thing." Cheryl swiveled, peering up at her. "You okay?"

"Yeah. Just tired. Didn't sleep last night." Seeing Cheryl's frown, Lydia added, "Challenging project. It's keeping me up a lot."

"Oh. Well, I hope it's at least an interesting one. As soon as I send this term's drop confirmations to registration, I'll be right in."

Lydia hit save on the open computer file as Cheryl came in, took a seat across the desk and asked, "So, what's up with schedule changes?"

"Everything. I need you to clear my schedule for the next ten weeks. Completely." Cheryl's eyes widened, though she didn't say a word. "I'm taking a leave of absence," Lydia said. "Immediately. As of today. And for the remainder of the term."

"Jesus, Lyd. Why?"

Lydia ignored the question. “As soon as we’re done here, I’m telling two of my grad assistants they’ll take over my classes, either for the term or until Shel finds a replacement. That’s up to him.”

“A replacement? What are you talking about? What’s going on?”

Lydia stared at her ring finger, knowing that if she looked at Cheryl right now, tears would start. “That family issue I’ve been dealing with the past several days.”

Cheryl leaned forward in her chair. “Is somebody sick? It isn’t you, is it? Are you dying?”

Shel had asked the same thing. “No, nobody’s dying. I’m sorry, Cheryl, I’m not ready to say anything more. For now, you’ll need to take care of everything. You have the password to my university accounts. Anything you can’t handle, and that won’t be much, you’ll know who to pass it to. Now scoot. I told Shel last night. As soon as I talk to my replacements, I’m leaving. They’ll contact you about getting the materials they’ll need.”

Cheryl sat still, staring at Lydia wordlessly.

“Now go on. I know you’re concerned. But it’s really okay. And if you’d close the door?” She reached for the phone to text her interim replacements, and didn’t look up as Cheryl left.

It was late morning by the time her two grad students had met with her. Each left surprised too, both at the announcement of her sabbatical but excited at the opportunity it gave them. As Lydia picked up her purse and tote bag to leave, she noticed her paisley shawl tossed over the easy chair across the room. It was her grown-up version of a blankie, a sheath of armor she draped herself in during difficult admin meetings or conferences with over-entitled students. Compared to what she was going through, those weren’t difficult at all. She grabbed it.

At Cheryl’s desk, she placed a hand on the woman’s shoulder. Years of working together had created a level of closeness between them. Cheryl looked up, concern and the start of tears in her eyes. “It’s going to be okay.” Lydia’s words were as much to herself as to Cheryl. “One way or another, it’s going to be okay.”

“Well, you damned well better not tell me not to worry,” Cheryl retorted, “because you know I will.”

“I know. But as the Dalai Lama said, if you can’t do anything about the problem, why worry?”

"Fat lot of good that does us who aren't the Dalai Lama," Cheryl muttered.

"It's going to be okay," Lydia repeated, walking away. "Eventually." She hoped she was right.

At the glass entry on the first floor, Lydia stopped and loudly uttered "Oh!" as if she'd forgotten something. She strode back to the student on duty at the U-shaped check-in desk. "Excuse me." Lydia lifted the lanyard with her faculty ID. "A campus phone please? I need to make a call."

Without a word, the girl set it on the high counter and turned to help a student. Lydia punched nine, waited for the dial tone, and then keyed in the cab company's number from memory. Calling Gil a taxi when he needed one was part of the sweet little send-off ritual she'd done for years, when he was leaving on extended business trips to Europe or South America. On shorter trips, he either drove or left his car at the airport. It had taken her a long time to get used to his being away for weeks several times a year, but pulling her car into the garage next to his at those times gave her some comfort. It was as if part of him was still home, that he'd soon be beside her in bed, just as their cars were beside each other, safe for another night. Gil would find her car in the garage when he pulled in after this trip, but she wouldn't be beside him in bed.

Returning the phone to the lower desk, Lydia set off at a brisk pace for the cross-campus walk to the admin building, where the cab would meet her. It was where the ride-share driver had dropped her earlier. She didn't want to risk running into someone who'd notice and maybe remember seeing her either getting out or being picked up in front of her own building. With the temperature already in the eighties, she stripped off her suit jacket and loosened a blouse button. It felt good to move with purpose after the inner turmoil of the past few days, then even better to step into the cooling air of the admin building lobby for a moment before the taxi arrived. Slipping into the backseat, she said, "Centro Ybor, please." The cabbie, a pleasant looking woman with a Haitian accent, tried to engage her in conversation but Lydia made no reply as she stared, not hearing, out the passenger window.

Ten minutes later she stepped onto the sidewalk. The stores had opened but most of the cafés and restaurants wouldn't for another half hour, so there weren't many people roaming as she walked the block to Flo Minko's. A resonant chime sent a light musical announcement of her entry. The store, popular with locals and sought out by tourists, was filled with racks of vintage clothing and hats, an eclectic mix of décor, and walls filled with the work of local artists. A dapper young man wearing a plaid bowtie looked up as he straightened a rack of garments, calling out a cheery, "Good morning."

Far from cheerful, Lydia asked, "Where's Audra?"

"Um, she's on the phone. Is there something I can help you with? A problem?"

Lydia shook her head and tried to smile. It wasn't the young man's fault she was in a bad mood, she reminded herself. "No, I just need to see Audra."

"All right. I'll let her know. May I tell her your name?"

"That's okay. I know where her office is." Walking past him, she added a lie, "She's expecting me."

At the back of the store she climbed a flight of stairs, rapped softly on an almost closed door, and slipped inside the office Audra shared with her partner, Julie. Audra was standing, half-turned away, at her desk, the phone cradled between her ear and shoulder, shuffling papers as she talked. Looking up, she shoved aside the mop of shoulder-length blonde curls that hid her face. Surprise filled her eyes at seeing Lydia. Holding up a finger for Lydia to wait, she said into the phone, "Uh-huh … okay." The spaghetti-strap dress she wore was black, covered in a floral pattern of vivid colors. Something Audra had snagged from one of the vintage clothes racks downstairs, Lydia thought, feeling again the pang of being too tall for clothes from the forties and fifties. The full, gathered skirt swirled as Audra walked around the desk to open a file folder. "Yes, I see that. But by next Tuesday, right?" After a moment's pause, she said, "Okay. We'll talk about that later. I've got to go. Bye."

Audra hung up the phone. "Good god, girl, you look like hell. What's going on? Why aren't you on campus?"

Lydia's throat clenched so hard, it hurt. She couldn't speak, only shake her head. Tears spilled down her cheeks and she raised her face toward the ceiling to get them to stop.

"Oh, honey." Audra enveloped her in a hug, then pulled back and took Lydia's hand. "This is bad. Is it about that phone number you asked me to call?"

Still unable to speak, Lydia nodded.

Audra looked toward the timepiece hung inside a bell jar on her credenza. "Listen, it's a little early for me to take a lunch break but I didn't have breakfast. Had to be here at six to call Vienna about a shipment." She bustled behind her desk and grabbed her purse. “Let’s go down to Frankie’s. We should be able to get a back booth before the old codgers show up for their Cuban sandwiches and café con leches.”

Without a word Lydia followed her down the stairs and waited at the door while Audra gave the young store clerk some instructions. Lydia heard their words, and a bit of laughter, but none of it registered in her mind. It felt as if she were in a foreign country where she didn’t know the language, or even the terrain.

Lydia was grateful Audra didn’t speak as they walked down the block. Entering Frankie’s, the clatter of plates and chatter of patrons hurt her head at first, but it was quieter at the back booth they slid into. Before they were settled, a pert waitress appeared. “Coffee, ladies?”

Lydia didn’t respond. Audra looked at her, then at the waitress. “No. Two Long Island Iced Teas. And have a heavy hand with the rum, okay?” She smiled a bit at Lydia. “I think we’re both going to need it.” Once the waitress moved away, Audra leaned back. “Okay, sweetie. I’m listening.”

Lydia knew that if she looked at Audra she’d begin to cry again. Even with her back to the room, she couldn’t let herself cry in public. She turned her face to the wall, then toward the ceiling. Both were covered in photographs and memorabilia chronicling even the most minor events in Frankie’s and Tampa’s history.

She and Audra had a lot of history here too. They’d been coming to Frankie’s for more than forty years. It had become “their” place the summer between junior and senior years in high school, when, on the last day of eleventh grade at Plant High, Lydia’s parents presented her with the keys to a shiny red VW bug. In giddy girlhood delight at the new freedom it offered—although still limited, thanks to her parents’ restrictions—they’d raced to the Colonnade to show it off to everyone hanging out at the drive-in—making Lydia, and Audra too, part of the cool kids who wouldn’t need to cadge a ride to go for fries and Cokes with an olive after school or on weekend nights. When attention died down over Lydia’s good fortune, she and Audra set off to explore, puttering down Bayshore Boulevard, through what there was of a downtown back in those days, and then got lost.

They knew they were still too close to home to be really lost, and they didn’t care—they were together and free and had wheels. All that mattered was talking a mile a minute as they wandered through neighborhoods they’d never seen. Eventually, after turning here and there and neither-knew-where, they'd stumbled into then-seedy Ybor City. The daily summer thunderstorm was building, and both were getting nervous about being caught in it on the first day in Lydia's new car. That's when they'd spotted Frankie's. Grateful for a haven, they parked and dashed into the cool, air-conditioned café to wait out the deluge. Lydia remembered how nice old Mr. Fraguela was, how he'd penciled a map on the back of a placemat with their directions home. He'd also made them call their moms, to let them know they were okay. That's when Frankie's had become their place. Lydia kept the map in the glove box long after they both knew the route by heart.

Frankie's was where they went when deep dark secrets needed to be shared over a soda, when a heart was broken, when crummy things happened that no grown-up could ever understand. *Maybe*, Lydia thought now, *life never does stop being high school*. Here she was, again carrying a deep dark secret with a sick heart, but now she was the grown-up who didn't understand.

"Where you at, girlfriend?" Audra's voice brought Lydia back to the present. Two tall glasses of iced brown liquid and a small bowl of lemon quarters were on the table. Lydia hadn't even noticed the waitress bring them.

"I ordered us pressed Cubans," Audra added.

Lydia shook her head. "I'm not hungry."

Audra leaned back against the high-cushioned booth. "When did you eat last?"

Lydia fingered the cool glass. "I don't know. Day before yesterday? I think ..."

Audra leaned forward again and reached for Lydia's hand. "Listen. Whatever it is, tell me."

Lydia's throat closed again. She nodded.

Seconds ticked by before Audra sighed. "I'm waiting. And will. Until either you spill or old Frankie comes back from the dead. Your choice."

The sigh that followed was Lydia's. "Okay." Her mouth felt as if it had been packed with dental gauze. She reached for the lemon slice garnishing her glass and bit into it. The bitter burst sent an angry shock over her tongue, and her own anger kicked in too. Lydia looked straight at Audra. "The rat bastard is having an affair."

Only the slightest surprise showed in Audra's eyes. "I wondered about that. Damn. I was hoping it was nothing more than my three a.m. worrywart brain."

Audra took a sip of her drink. "When you texted me at six-thirty that morning and asked me to call that number, I knew something not so good was up. How did you find the number?"

Lydia's mouth twisted in a sardonic smirk. "A piece of junk mail. Or so I thought. We had an admin meeting Monday night and I got home so late I left the mail on the breakfast bar to deal with in the morning. After sorting what needed to go to Gil's desk and mine, I opened the junk mail, to flatten it out before tossing it in recycling. So, there's an envelope from Verizon. No big surprise because their promotional crap came in that kind of envelope all the time. But when I opened it, I realized it looked like a bill. So I took a closer look, and it was a bill. With pages and pages of phone and text numbers. It was the monthly bill for Gil's cell. I was totally confused until I remembered our phone carrier had been bought out. His bills always go to his office, so I'd never seen them. Apparently, with the changeover the address got screwed up and it came to the house by mistake. I'm flipping through, scanning the pages while I'm trying to figure all this out, and I noticed he called me a couple of times from New Orleans."

"Wait a minute," Audra interrupted. "I'm confused. If he was on his cell, how did you know where he was calling from?"

"Because the bill is so detailed it even lists where the call originated. 'Pinged from,' as the cop shows call it."

Lydia took the first sip of her drink as the waitress returned with their food. "Enjoy," she said. "You ladies need anything else?"

"Yeah, a shotgun." Audra voice was terse. "I may need to hunt down my best friend's husband by the time we're done here."

The waitress raised splayed hands, backed up a step, and chuckled. "Oo-kay. I don't even want to know."

Grabbing the ketchup bottle and squirting a mound of it next to her French fries, Audra asked, "So? Gil does business in NOLA, doesn't he?"

"Well, yes. But not as much as he used to do. And it struck me, I didn't remember his saying anything about going there." Lydia fingered seasoning from some of her fries and tasted the sharp saltiness. Her stomach lurched, and she pushed the plate away.

Audra shoved it back. "Girl, you've got to eat something. We're not leaving here until you do."

Lydia sighed and rested her hands on her lap. "So anyway. I didn't remember his saying anything about going to New Orleans last month. Every couple of months he updates me on his trips and I put them on my calendar, so I checked it. That weekend he was supposed to be at a trade show in Atlanta from Friday through Sunday, then in Savannah for two days, then a day in Jacksonville on the way back. Thing is, the phone bill showed he wasn't in any of those places. He'd been in New Orleans the whole time. He lied to me."

Audra finished her bite and swallowed. "Okay, that's not good. But how's that mean he's having an affair?" She pointed at Lydia's plate. "I told you, eat. At least a bite, okay?"

"God." Lydia rolled her eyes. "You are such a fucker of a mother."

"Yup. Better than the other way around." Audra bit into the second half of her Cuban, grinning over the insult they'd used on each other since they were teens. "Now, back to this business. Why did that make you think Gil was cheating?"

"It didn't. Not right away." Lydia pulled her sandwich apart, picked a bit of pork loose, and chewed it as if it were rancid. "But then I noticed this one number showed up over and over again. Sometimes four, five times a day." She looked at Audra, her face hard. "Every day except weekends. Except not at all while he was on that trip."

Audra didn't have to answer. Her eyebrows did. "And that was the number you asked me to call?"

Lydia nodded and forced herself to swallow another bite of meat. "I googled it but got nothing. Just that it was a wireless number. I didn't want to take a chance on having our house phone or my cell show up on the caller ID. In case."

As Lydia picked at the sandwich, she told Audra more. How Gil had left very early, about dawn, on the Friday he supposedly had to be in Atlanta by noon. How less than five minutes after pulling out of the drive, the phone bill showed he called that number, then called it again mid-morning, and again in the afternoon—from Pensacola. "Which we all know is not on the way to Atlanta." Then there were his occasional calls to her at home, that night from Pensacola, and for the rest of the time from New Orleans. None from Atlanta or Savannah or Jax. "And he made no calls to that other number, either. Not until he'd returned to Tampa." The calls had resumed then. Except, tellingly, on weekends. "By the time I asked you to call it for me, I was certain it belonged to a woman."

"Shit." Audra's voice was quiet. "And because I got her voicemail, you got her name. What was it? Marissa? Marybelle? Something like that."

"Marielle. Needless to say, when Gil flew back from New York on Friday night, I was not all 'Hi, honey, you're *home*.'"

"Did you confront him?"

"Damn right I did. He denied it. Of course. Said I was crazy. He didn't know what I was talking about. Until I shoved the phone bill in his face and said, 'Then why don't I call this Marielle person and ask her?'" Lydia bit into a French fry as cold as her voice. "He went as white as that plate. Stammering about how it'd 'just happened,' that it hadn't been going on long. I was so mad I couldn't say another word and he just wouldn't shut up. The more he talked, the more I knew he was bullshitting me. After thirty-seven years, I know when he is. That made me madder than ever."

"Ready for another drink, ladies? Maybe some flan?" The waitress had come to check on them. Noticing Lydia had barely touched her meal, she said, "Oh, is there something wrong with the food?"

Lydia shook her head as Audra answered, "No, she's just not hungry. You can bring our checks, please."

As the waitress turned away, Audra leaned forward, reaching for Lydia's hand. "Listen, honey. You know I know what you're going through. But when I dumped Ryan for cheating, we'd only been married six years, and both of us were too young to have gotten married in the first place. But you and Gil. Geeze, you two have been married for frigging ever. Maybe what he said is true, that it hasn't been going on all that long. Maybe a marriage counselor could help?"

The waitress slipped their tabs on the table as she passed by. Lydia reached for hers and into her purse for her credit card. "Right now I don't know. Right now I don't believe a word he says. He's gone again till Friday, so I don't have to listen to his stupid excuses for the next two days. I can barely think. Until I can, I can't make any decisions."

"Good. That's smart," Audra said on the way to the cash stand. She set her purse on an empty swivel stool and handed her cash to the man at the register. As Lydia waited behind her, she took an envelope from the front pocket of her tote and pushed it silently into Audra's bag.

Outside again, Audra asked, “Want to come back to the store for a bit?”

“No thanks. I’ve got to get going. Need to get back to work.”

Audra embraced Lydia in a long hug. “Listen, if you don’t want to be alone tonight, feel free to show up at my place, okay? You don’t even have to call. I’ll get you drunk—even if it is a school night.”

Lydia managed a small smile. “Thanks, but no. I need some time alone.”

Audra squeezed Lydia’s hand. “Okay, sweetie. I understand. Now you be careful driving, okay?”

As Audra walked away, Lydia opened the Uber app she’d installed on her phone that morning, picked up her tote, and walked around the corner to wait. Once she was inside the car, the driver confirmed, “Train station, right?” She nodded as she latched her seatbelt. Then she opened her phone settings and turned off the location service.

***

Lydia’s heels on the terrazzo floor gave off an echoing staccato as she crossed the empty waiting room of Union Station. No one else was in sight, not even at the ticket window she approached. She waited. When a woman finally appeared, Lydia purchased a ticket to Jacksonville. Taking a seat at the end of a bench along a wall, she slipped off the pumps she’d worn to the office and exchanged them for the flats in her tote. She settled back to wait.

The one train daily from Tampa to Jax wouldn’t leave until five, hours away. It didn’t matter. Time was totally suspended. There was only now—massive, oppressive. She felt caught in the exact opposite of the scenario she often wished were within her power: to stop everyone and everything, so she could rush about accomplishing all that needed to be done and manage to catch up with herself. Now, everyone and everything seem to swirl around her, while she was the one pulled out of time, unable to move past the three questions that pummeled her mind: How did this happen? What was she going to do? What else didn’t she know?

She hadn’t told Audra everything, because she wasn’t yet sure what she did know. Like probably every husband who’d been caught cheating, Gil had minimized his actions when he’d realized he couldn’t lie his way out of his lies. She had been so angry that Friday night she couldn’t even scream at him the way she had screamed into the silent void of the house between her discovery and his return. For those two days, she had envisioned lashing out at him viciously, pummeling him with her fists, devastating him with her words and tears. By the time he had walked in, that fury was spent, gone as cold as a hard winter rain.

Lydia saw none of the train station's surroundings, only the relentless loop of images that flashed through her mind from that night. Slamming and locking their bedroom door against Gil, refusing him his—their—bed. Pacing, pacing, pacing until the bedroom was too small to hold her tension. Crying in a hot shower until she retched. Tossing in bed till the sheets threatened to strangle her. Stumbling, at four, past the sound of Gil's snoring in the guestroom, infuriated that he could sleep. The flash of guilt as she removed his cell phone from its charger in his office. Never once had she ever invaded his privacy. Never once had she ever considered what secrets the phone might contain. The flash of relief when she found no listing for a Marielle person in his contact list—maybe the affair was recent, as he'd said. Was it possibly forgivable? She replaced the phone in the charger. In the kitchen, her mind was a fog as she waited for coffee to brew. She carried the carafe and her mug to her office and locked the door. *Screw him*, she thought. *If he wants coffee, he can buy it on the way to the office.* She ignored Gil when he rapped, over and over again, trying to get her to open the door. She stayed there until he left for the day, not even caring that it made her late to work.

Her stony silence continued that night. She did not cook him dinner—she couldn't eat and she sure as hell wasn't going to perform any wifely attendance on him. She didn't respond when he told her he was sorry, repeating what she knew were the lies he'd told the night before. She didn't look at him when he said goodnight and told her he had a flight to New York City in the morning. That had been two days ago.

A smattering of people was milling about the station by the time the train began to board. A handful of those were there to see someone off. Lydia and her fellow passengers dispersed themselves throughout the two coach cars. That was one of the reasons she had chosen to leave on the train. If Gil were to try and find her, he'd probably check the airlines first, then maybe later with Trailways. Flying certainly would be faster, but too easy to trace, and while a bus would have carried her off hours ago it would have been crowded. She needed space as much as anonymity.

Lydia settled into a window seat at the back of the second coach. Near the front a burly young man with short blond hair blocked the aisle as he rooted through his backpack, pulling out his laptop, phone, earbuds, and a sheaf of papers. Behind him a plump, gray-haired black woman in a shapeless housedress waited, silent and patient, but the skinny, T-shirted man behind her was neither. "Dude, move it," Lydia heard him bark. The first fellow mumbled an apology and stepped out of the aisle for them to pass. Mr. T-shirt glowered and flopped himself across two seats, while the old woman wheeled her suitcase farther to the back, near Lydia.

Old woman, Lydia thought as she watched the lady arrange her belongings and herself. Lydia realized that she too was now old. Sixty-three. Sixty-three, and starting all over again. From nothing. In her twenties, it had been easy, even fun, to reinvent herself, try out different selves, try something new. The choice had been hers then. This time the choice was not, and for the first time she felt old. Old, and weary. For the first time in decades, she felt the despair of being truly alone, not knowing who she was or what to do.

As the train started, Lydia turned to her window. She'd never viewed downtown from this perspective—the image outside was both familiar and disconcerting, as if she had walked into her own living room and found the furnishings replaced and rearranged. The sensation continued as the train made its way eastward, first alongside a roadway she'd driven so often, then across rural areas and through the backside of towns and cities. Familiar, yet not. Another reminder that the world, the life, she had known had shifted off kilter on its axis.

The sun dropped and light gave sudden way to darkness, obscuring the flat land. Lydia herself disappeared into the darkness, unaware of anything until the phone in her purse pinged. She ignored it. Another ping, then another. Retrieving it, she sighed wearily, upset at herself for forgetting to turn it off, and tapped the text icon.

—I just found your note. What do you mean you are gone!

—WTF are you doing? Where ARE you?

—I'm worried sick! PLEASE tell me what's going on!

Lydia took a deep breath, then another. She tapped in, I'm OK. I promise. I'll call. In a few days. She powered the phone off before Audra could respond and slipped it back into the purse pocket. If Gil tried to call—or even if he didn't—she didn't want to know.

By the time the train reached Jacksonville and Lydia had checked into a hotel, it was after midnight. The fortitude she had run on all day was depleted. As she turned both door locks and flipped the stop latch, a shiver—not from chill—gripped her. She stumbled slightly before she reached the bed, weakness spreading through her. She sat down, dizzy, her arms steadying her body, her breath short and shallow. When the faintness passed, she went into the half-darkened bathroom, unwrapped a flimsy plastic cup, filled it with tepid water, and drank. She filled the tiny cup again, gulped it down, and filled it once more. Still shaking, she carried the cup to the bedside table and sat down again. For the first time in days, since all this began, she was overwhelmed with exhaustion. Her skin, her muscles, her bones, every cell, felt as if they were imploding, no longer able to provide a vault for her soul. With fumbling fingers, Lydia undid her clothes, slid open the bed cover and sheet, and crawled beneath them. Tears came again, as they now did every night, but this time not for long, before Hypnos claimed her.

A too-bright light flashed through Lydia's eyelids as she rolled over. Fragments of dreams burned away in the glare. Blinking, it took a second for her to remember she was in a hotel room and that she hadn't turned off the bedside lamp. The numbers on the clock radio startled her into the next level of wakefulness—she'd slept more than ten hours. She tried to remember if she'd gotten up in the night to use the bathroom. If she had, she must have done so in her sleep. Getting old was like the B-side of being a new mother: instead of a screaming infant dragging her from sleep, it was her bladder. Too quickly, Gil refilled her mind. She'd needed a night of unbroken sleep and now she needed a break from Gil's relentless presence in her head. She needed to focus.

Focus, not on the frightening future, but only on the next step ahead, she told herself, you can do that, you have to. She drank the tepid cup of water on the nightstand before heading to the bathroom. First, shower and dress. Second, check out and find a place to eat. Food. She had no interest. But Lydia knew she had to stop neglecting her body the way she had been. What bit Audra had badgered her to consume the day before was all she she'd eaten since—when? She wasn't sure.

And why, she wondered, was she punishing herself, when it was Gil she wanted to punish. *I should be punished*, her mind whispered, out of habit. *I must have done something to cause this to happen.*

It's all my fault, it's all my fault, it's all my fault clicked like the residual rhythm of the train's wheels that had brought her here as the fog of the hot shower filled the bathroom and clouded the mirror. The water cascading over her head, face, and body eased some of her tension. Random bits of dream images, like scattered puzzle pieces, made nanosecond appearances in her head. In each, she was searching for something ... Gil, insisting she was wrong, nothing had been stolen from her ... the sound of a kitten mewing, that was what she was looking for ... Gil, his back to her, refusing to help ... her opening drawers, closets, frantic ... a shoebox on the floor, lifting the lid. It wasn't a kitten inside, it was a baby, a whimpering baby she needed to scoop up, to comfort ...

By the time she dressed and dried her hair, steam was clearing from the ceiling-to-sink mirror. The image Lydia saw reflected there was like a monochromatic cutout against the white and yellow of the small room. Her dark blond hair looked lifeless. The only color on her skin was the dark circles under her eyes. Her body felt as dull as the gray tank top and darker gray drawstring cotton pants she had put on. No presence of the vibrant woman she'd projected until recently. But had that woman even been her? What had happened to the vitality, the sexuality she'd exuded through her twenties, her thirties, well into her forties. She snorted softly. That woman had been subsumed by the roles she'd played—wife, mother, teacher, professor, mentor, volunteer. Always giving herself away. Professionally, she'd become known as a powerhouse in her field. Was there any of her real self-left?

Makeup daubed on her face, and concealer around her eyes, did nothing to hide the deadness she saw in the mirror. Leaning forward to brush on a bit of mascara, she looked into the reflection of her eyes—even their dusky blue was now gray—and then stopped, her faces inches apart. *You are in there somewhere*, she thought. *You're still in there, and I have to find you. If I don't, I'll die.* A flush of heat flared through her. Staring at herself, she spoke out loud, "And I'll be damned if I let that happen."

She briskly applied lipstick, picked up her purse and bag, and cursed as she left the room when the door refused to slam behind her.

After paying the hotel bill in cash, Lydia crossed the parking lot under the intense sun and then an even more expansive lot filled with vehicles surrounding the neighboring Cracker Barrel. As she stepped into the restaurant, a rush of cool air lifted the glisten from her skin, and kitchen aromas dispelled the outside stink of asphalt and gasoline fumes. She knew she could eat, in fact wanted to. She was glad she was hungry.

She wasn't glad when the hostess informed her of a twenty-minute wait. With no desire to wander through the tchotchkes, toys, and togs in the gift shop, she went back outside. One empty rocking chair remained, in the shade. Determined to put the time to use, she sat down, pulled her cell phone from her purse, powered it on, and muted the ringer. It didn't mute the staccato of pinging that announced a spate of text messages, sixteen in all. Lydia grimaced. She had no intention of even looking at them, let alone responding. Once she was connected to the restaurant's guest Wi-Fi, she looked up her location and searched the nearest car rental services. By the time she had made arrangements to have a twenty-four-hour rental sent over, her seat in the restaurant was ready. Although barely reminiscent of the real things, Lydia appreciated the collards, cheese grits, and meatloaf. Satisfaction began to course through her body and her mind gained a modicum of clarity. Step one had been to leave Tampa. Step two was now to get out of Jacksonville. To where next, she wondered. Chattanooga, she decided. She could get there before having to stop for the night. If she didn't make it all the way, she'd be close enough to the city to return the car before it was due and to decide whether to exchange it for a long-term rental. Part of her felt silly, like an amateur actress trying to exit a dusty stage without leaving any footprints behind. What was tomorrow? What day was it today? She thought for a moment. She had left home on Wednesday—was that only yesterday? She checked the clock on her phone. It was almost time for the rental driver to arrive. She took one last drink of water, placed several dollar bills on the table, paid her tab up front, and used the ladies' room. As she stepped into the searing heat and light, her phone vibrated. The wince of tension it caused eased when she saw an unknown number on the screen. Answering, she heard a young man's pleasant voice. "Ma'am, I'm pulling into the lot now. Look for a white Acura."

"Thanks. I'm at the entrance, in a gray shirt, dark gray pants," she replied, watching him pull up and then lean across the seat to open the passenger door.

Lydia did her best to respond to the fellow's pleasantries on the ride back to the rental agency, but felt as if she'd forgotten how to engage in normal conversation. Her sadness must have been more apparent than she'd thought, as the agent who handled the paperwork went from brusque to solicitous, even walking Lydia out to the car and patiently explaining how to operate everything. The last time Lydia had rented a vehicle, the transaction was more like a hurry-up-and-wait, followed by here's-the-key-what-are-you-waiting-for-next-in-line. In her fragile state, she was grateful for the small act of kindness, and the concern in his voice when he waved and called out, "You take care of yourself now, you hear?"

The dashboard clock showed a little after one as she curved onto the highway ramp. Once away from the city, traffic lightened enough to set the cruise control and Lydia began to relax. She turned on the radio and hit the scan button, punching "set" when John Lennon's voice ripped out with, "Hold you in his arms, yeah, you can feel his disease … Come together …"

She and Gil had come together. Now it had all come apart.

She cranked up the volume and settled into the rhythm of the road and the car. Low hills and tall pines passed alongside. Some part of her mind remained on what lay ahead. The rest became entangled in scenes from the unspooling reel of her past, carrying her to what had once been happy memories of when she'd met the love of her life.

Chapter 2

"Lyd! I can't find the tickets!"

The mirror reflected the communal bathroom door swinging wide open behind her. Lydia's glance flickered away from applying deep violet shadow to her eyelid. Wild-eyed, wearing only bra and panties, her roommate gripped the door handle with one hand, the doorjamb with the other, and panted breathlessly, "I've looked *everywhere*."

Lydia stood back to admire how the eyeshadow matched the violet streaks she'd applied to her hair that morning. "Oh, for God's sake, Sue, if you've lost our tickets, I'll bury you in a snowdrift. And you haven't looked everywhere. They were in the room last night." Lydia leaned close to the mirror again and drew emerald green eyeliner above her lashes. "They didn't walk off on their own."

Sue bounced up and down on bare feet and shouted gleefully, "That's it, that's it! I stuck them inside my boots." With a giggle, she raced away. The slam of the bathroom door caused Lydia's hand to jump and streak green across her temple. *Stupid theater majors*, she thought, *all drama*. She stepped into a toilet stall for a piece of tissue and carefully erased the slash of green before layering on mascara.

She and Sue had roomed together for two years. Sometimes, like now, Lydia found her friend's histrionics irritating. Most often, Sue was a source of fun. In many ways they were opposites, which was what made the friendship work. Sue was, as Lydia's grandma Tilde would have put it, as scattered as chicken feed in a tornado, while Lydia was the levelheaded one. *Yeah, well, not tonight—I'm going to get this head pretty messed up*, she thought as she applied more mascara. The hash brownies she'd baked that afternoon were stashed in her purse. While Sue was petite, barely five-four, which was perfect for the stage, with a plushness to her body that seemed to turn men into little boys who wanted to cuddle a soft, stuffed toy, Lydia towered over her by a good five inches, her body lean and lithe, and Sue's theater friends insisted Lydia had a dancer's form. Maybe so, she thought, but she knew looks were deceiving. As much as she enjoyed rocking out at a party, like tonight, the motion she took the most pleasure in was turning the pages of a book.

The door swung open again and a man walked in. "Oh, sorry, Lyd. Shoulda knocked."

"Yeah, Don, you shoulda." Lydia looked up from gathering her cosmetics. "If I'd been standing here naked, Fran would've gone batshit on you. You two going to the ball?"

He answered from behind a closed stall door and over the sound of pee hitting the toilet bowl. "Nah. Decided to hang here and screw each other's brains out."

His giggle told Lydia he was already totally stoned. "See you tomorrow then," she said as she left the bathroom.

In their room, Sue was straightening the seams of her fishnet stockings and repositioning the hooks of her garter belt. Minuscule lace panties made the curves of her derrière look as voluptuous as the white mounds of breasts that rose out of her black corset's bodice. She flashed Lydia a grin. "So? What do you think? Got it all from a Frederick's of Hollywood catalog."

Lydia grinned back as she stepped over clothes Sue had strewn on the floor. Hanging her robe on a hook inside the closet door, she said, "I think if you're looking for trouble, you're gonna find plenty of it."

Tying the crisscross laces of her tall, high-heeled black boots, Sue asked, "Hey, are we going to have a brownie before we leave?"

Lydia nodded as she stepped into a dress and pulled it up over her pantyhose and bra. "There's one on my dresser for us to split. Finish zipping me up?"

She sucked herself in as Sue pulled the taught zipper closed. Tugging the snug skirt smooth over her hips, Lydia said, "Okay, how do I look?" Her arms were bare, as was much of her back. Wide-set straps, emphasizing the sweep of her shoulders, throat, and collarbone, led to a low-cut sweetheart neckline that revealed ample cleavage. The shimmering, cherry-red fabric clung like a second skin, and horizontal lines of almost imperceptible shirring encircled her from hips to hem, not more than half way down her thighs. "Well, is it okay?"

Sue stood still for a moment, taking it all in. "Jesus H. Christ, girl. If you don't snag some guy in that tonight, there isn't a real man on campus. You are gorgeous. Come on, let's eat. It's nine-thirty and I want to get going." She laughed as Lydia pushed her stockinged feet into a pair of clunky plush-lined boots. "Going for the hooker-in-a-coal-mine look?"

Grinning back, Lydia broke the brownie in two and handed Sue a piece.

"Only half?"

"Uh-huh," Lydia said, biting into her half. "They might be a little potent. Connie and I tried something different." Connie was a friend with an off-campus apartment where several of the girls practiced kitchen arts, many of them the illicit kind.

Licking her fingers, Sue said, "Geeze, these are the best you've made. What did you do?"

"Connie got a new blender so we decided to try grinding up the pot like flour. And we loaded the batch with hash oil."

A bark of laughter burst from Sue. "We are going to get so messed up."

Lydia's eyebrows rose mischievously. "That's the plan, darling."

They both zipped into sweatshirts, carefully covered their hairdos with the hoods, then donned long winter coats and wound warm woolen scarves around their necks. "God, don't we look like two Pillsbury dough-girls," Lydia said, slinging her purse over her shoulder and picking up the shoe bag that held the bright red stilettos she would change into at the dance.

Sue reached for the doorknob. "Yup, but nothin' says lovin' like whoever heats up our ovens." Lydia rolled her eyes, but smiled.

An arctic shock hurt their lungs and stung their noses as they stepped into the frigid February night. The walk from Woodward House and across the length of the Quad was never relished in winter. At least tonight, the sidewalks were ice-free between the mounds of white snow that had fallen earlier. Lydia was grateful, too, that the Hawk, Chicago's notorious wind, was in its nest, not cutting them cold to the bone. Except for an occasional shout or the voices of a few other students, the only sound was of their breathing and their footsteps. Squares of warm light from distant windows served in place of stars obscured by the city lights as Lydia looked up into the clear, inky sky. "How can anything so beautiful be so frigging cold," she griped. Even shoved into her coat pockets, her gloved fingertips tingled with numbness. Sue huffed a shivering response.

A murmuring rumble built as they approached the main door of Ida Noyes Hall, and exploded into a roar of partying voices, laughter, guitars, and drums as they stepped inside. It took a moment for their eyes to adjust to the brilliant light, and longer for them to warm up enough to emerge from their heavy coverings. Lydia felt a pleasant buzz begin to unfold as she stood up from the seat where she'd put on her stilettos. The wail of a tenor sax pealed through the building. *Oh yeah, I'm going to have me some fun tonight*, she thought.

Bands were playing in several of the rooms, but Lydia and Sue headed first to the main hall and pressed their way into the crush of noise and bodies. Some were so scantily clad they made Lydia feel overdressed. Others, mostly guys who hadn't bothered with costumes warranted by the annual ball, were garbed in the standard issue of boots, jeans, and tie-died T-shirts, long-sleeved flannels, or sweatshirts. The scent of cologne, sweat, and marijuana swirled as they moved through the crowd, scoping for recognizable faces.

A hand grabbed Lydia's wrist and spun her around. A face lunged forward, and she felt wet lips and a nip of teeth on the flesh of her left breast. "God. Get off me," she shouted, shoving a leather-clad girl backwards into the embrace of another girl, who licked the side of her face. The girl who'd lunged at Lydia let out a drunken laugh as Lydia glowered and pulled a tissue from her purse to wipe off the spittle. Behind her, she heard Sue mutter, "Bitch."

In the Bacchanalian atmosphere of the party, Lydia's disgust was quickly forgotten. For the next several hours, she gave herself over to the release of the music, the noise, and to being high. It was a joy to abandon worries of studying and pressure to the pulse of the dance floor, wild laughter, and the utter lightheadedness of yet another brownie. By three a.m. all the treats she'd brought were gone, shared among friends who shared tokes passed around in return. She wandered back to one of the smaller party rooms she'd been in before. The party was beginning to wind down, the crowd slowly thinning. She spotted Sue at a table with several people they both knew. A sigh of tired contentment escaped Lydia as she plopped down on a chair to join them. At least three different conversations were going on. Peter was positing an intense theory of Charlie Parker's brilliance to Leslie, who giggled every time he said "The Bird." Wayne, Annie, Bill, and Terry were trying to decide whether they had the energy to go for breakfast in their stoned conditions. And Rachel complained to Sue about the unfairness of having lost out on the role of Kate in *The Taming of the Shrew*. Probably because you'd be playing too much to type, Lydia mused privately as she heard a voice boom out her name. Ron Thornton was walking toward them, holding hands with a petite blonde she thought she recalled having seen before.

Rachel cut herself off mid-sentence, grinning and tossing her long dark hair as she wheeled around in her chair. Slinging her arm across its back, her face darkened. She raked the blonde girl down, then up again, through narrowed eyes. "Ron, how'd you like to take a *pretty* girl home tonight?"

"Shut up, Rache. Lyd, I'm glad I spotted you," Ron said. Half turning back to the remaining crowd, he shouted, "Gil, c'mere."

A man turned and held up a finger, indicating he'd heard. After saying a few more words to the people he was with, he strode over. His dark wavy hair fell almost to his shoulders. The cut was casual, but expensive-precise, Lydia noted, shaped to draw attention to both his eyes and the sharpness of his jaw. He wore a bright red corduroy shirt, its sleeves rolled halfway to his elbows, tucked into tight black jeans, and a pair of silvery, obviously expensive snakeskin boots. He was tall—very tall, Lydia realized—and moved with athletic confidence.

"Oh, Ronny," Rachel chirped. "I'd much rather go home with him over you any night." She tossed her hair again and smiled, doing her best to look seductive.

"Shut up, Rachel," Ron repeated. "Gil, this is the chick I was telling you about. From Tampa. Lydia, this is Gil, the most ruthless Monopoly cheat on campus."

"Uh-uh-uh—I don't cheat, I just compete to my advantage," Gil retorted. "Lydia, eh?" His smile was dazzling. He threw his arms wide, went down on one knee, and sang out, "Lydia oh Lydia, have you met Lydia? Lydia, the tattooed laydeee …"

Lydia let out an exasperated sigh. "Oh, for God's sake. Like I've never heard that before?" She was glad to still be a bit high. It made it easier to not grin at his physical antics—she hadn't seen that before—and to ignore the bit of flutter in her chest. "I'm going to get my boots." She lifted the strap of her purse from the back of the chair and rose. "The B.S. is getting a bit too deep here," she said, smirking.

Gil flashed her another grin as he stood. "Well, pretty Miss Lydia, you have just tattooed yourself on my heart."

Sue burst out in laughter. "You sure your name isn't Lothario?"

Gil laughed too. "Okay, fair enough. Like I haven't heard that before either."

Lydia ignored him. "See you back in our room, Sue. See you guys."

"Wait up," Gil said. "You're seriously leaving? We just met." He fell in step with her as she went into the hall and down the wide stairs. "Answer me one question?"

Her glance at him was wary. "Depends. What's the question?"

"Plant or Hillsborough?"

Hand on the banister, Lydia stopped, one foot suspended above the step below, her face turned toward him. "You're from Tampa?"

"Mm-hmm. So which is it? I know it wasn't Jefferson because I would have noticed you."

She resumed walking. "Who says it wasn't one of the other high schools?"

"Classy, smart girl like you, coming to Chicago, narrows it down. Far as I know, we may be the only two here." Gil loped beside her. "In five years here, I haven't met anyone from home before. Lucky me, when I do, it's pretty you."

They'd reached the cloakroom and she sat down on a bench to change into her boots. Lydia felt herself flush. She pretended to ignore the compliment. "Five years? What's taking you so long to graduate?"

Gil leaned against the wall. "Already did. In my first year of my master's." As Lydia stood, he moved forward, took the coat from her hands, and held it open for her. "Would you like me to walk you back to the dorm?"

Lydia shook her head as she pulled on her gloves. "No thanks."

"You sure? I'd be happy to."

"Thanks, but I've had enough of people tonight." Lydia looked up at him. "Sorry. Didn't mean that the way it sounded."

He shrugged. "Okay. Whatever. Anyway, maybe I'll see you around." He flashed a last grin and headed back toward the stairs.

Pushing her hip and shoulder against the door, Lydia moved into the cold. A light, sharp breeze off Lake Michigan stung her cheeks as she hurried down 59th and back across the Quad. She wished the wind would blow Gil's baritone voice out of her mind. She wished he weren't so damned handsome—and tall. Mostly, she wished that bastard Geoff hadn't broken up with her two weeks before Christmas. He's not a bastard, Lydia told herself. It wasn't his fault he didn't love me, even though I loved him. The six weeks since then hadn't erased the pain in her heart. She'd made a New Year's resolution: she would not date anyone, period, during the winter and spring terms, and she intended to stick to it. But Gil sure was good-looking, and charming, she thought as she snuggled into the warmth of her bed and fell into deep sleep.

Three nights later Lydia sat, her back to the dorm room wall, at the head of her bed, studying a book propped against her raised knees. Sue was out, and Foghat's "Slow Ride" blared from the turntable. Four loud knocks hit the closed room door and a voice called out, "Lyd? You in there?"

Without looking up, Lydia hollered, "Yeah."

"Man on the phone," the voice called back.

Lydia flopped the book face down on the bed and padded, stocking-footed, to the receiver dangling from the payphone on the hallway wall. Lifting it to her ear, she said, "Hello?"

"Miss Lydia," came back across the wire in a warm baritone.

"Yes. Who is this?"

"You never answered the question—Plant or Hillsborough?"

Lydia's eyebrows furrowed and she asked again, "Who is this?" She knew, but wasn't going to give him the satisfaction of knowing he'd impressed her during their short encounter Saturday night. Or that her stomach had done a bit of a flip at the sound of his voice.

"Gil. Gil Carson. I didn't think you were so stoned you'd forget me."

No, she hadn't been. Worse, she had caught herself thinking about him too many times since then. She wasn't going to let him know that either. "How'd you find me?" she asked.

"Well, it took a bit. By the time I got back upstairs Saturday night the guys you were with had split. Sunday I called Ron but he was still at his girl's place. Monday somebody told me they thought maybe you lived in Woodward. I called the main number but that didn't work because I didn't know your last name. I tried sweet-talking the girl who answered—"

I'll bet you did, Lydia thought.

"—but no way was she going to leaf through the entire directory looking for a Lydia. And I was asking every chick I ran into if they lived in your dorm. A couple did but didn't know you. I was about to set up camp outside and wait on you. Then Ron called me a few minutes ago. Voilà—Casselberry. And the dorm operator put me right through to your floor. So, when can I see you? I'd like to, you know."

Lydia's pulse quickened at the openness of his admission but she reminded herself of her New Year's resolution. She wasn't going to date. Anyone. Period. She wasn't going to take a chance on being hurt again. "I don't think so," she said, then stammered, "Not that you'd like to … just that, well, I'm really busy. Studying and all …" Her voice trailed off.

"Come on, you've got to come up for air sometime."

"I'm sorry. I'm just really, really busy. I've got to go. Someone's waiting to use the phone," she lied. She heard him sigh as she took the receiver from her ear and hung up. The sigh mixed with her mind whispering "Idiot" as she walked back to her room.

The following Monday she stopped at the student union for coffee and some reading between classes. Making notes on the narrative structure of a Somerset Maugham story, she was unaware of the hubbub around her until a quiet "Hi" came from beside her. The voice sent a shiver through her. She looked up and an involuntary smile crossed her face. She tried to quash it as she responded, "Hi."

Gil gestured at a chair. "Mind?"

Lydia shook her head. "But I'm leaving for my next class in a minute."

Gil lowered his lanky body into a seat. "Yeah. You're really busy, I know. What I don't know is, did I do something to deserve the brush-off?"

His voice was earnest, none of the glibness Lydia had heard from him both times before. She felt a touch of embarrassment, but liked that he was so forthright. She shook her head again. "No. I'm sorry. I don't mean to be rude. It's just that … well, my head's just not in a good place. I'm sorry."

"Okay." Gil leaned back in his chair. "That's a relief. Not that your head isn't in a good place—I mean, that it's not me, it's you." He looked up toward the ceiling. "Oh man, that didn't come out right either."

Lydia's smile this time was warm. "So, how do you know Ron?" Maybe changing the subject would make the conversation easier.

Gil relaxed a bit. "He and three other guys and I play Monopoly together. Game's been going on since Halloween."

"The same game? You've been playing the same game for five months?"

"Almost. Because we made up our own rules—well, I'm the one who did. There was another guy too, but we bankrupted him last week. I intend to wipe out the rest of them before summer."

Lydia laughed. "Pretty sure of yourself, eh?"

"Yup. I'm going to have it all. In that game, and in the game of life."

His words gave Lydia pause. Everyone she hung around with, all her friends, had goals that placed social improvement or creativity or intellect above money. She wasn't sure if Gil was joking or truly greedy. She hoped it wasn't the latter. She glanced up at a wall clock. "I have to go," she said, closing up her books. "My next class is in fifteen minutes."

"Mind if I walk you?"

Zipping up her parka, she shrugged. "I guess."

"You guess you mind?"

"No. I guess that'd be okay."

A light snow was falling from a gray sky that made the sun as pale as a night moon. Lydia became aware of the heavy silence between them they walked, her mind as dull as the weather as she tried to think of something to say. After a moment of increasing awkwardness, she said, "Plant High."

"I kinda thought so." Gil looked at her with a small smile. "Did you grow up in South Tampa?"

"No. Ann Arbor mostly. We only moved about four years ago. My dad taught at Michigan, then got a job at the University of South Florida."

His face was quizzical. "USF's a long ride from South Tampa."

"Yeah, but my folks wanted my brothers and me to go to Plant. We moved down the summer before I started high school."

"That's funny."

"Why?"

"Seems we've led almost parallel lives. My dad was with Upjohn in Kalamazoo, then got hired by Anheuser-Busch when I was in ninth grade."

"Seriously? My mom works in marketing at Busch Gardens."

"See? More connections. That's what I want to go into—marketing. Good money."

There it was again, Lydia thought, a focus on money. It made her feel a bit uneasy. Still, the conversation grew easier as they compared notes on growing up in Michigan, being uprooted from childhood friends and the only lives they'd known, to be thrust into the alien culture of year-round sunshine and palm trees, beaches, and grass that was painful to walk on barefoot.

Gil reached for the door handle when they arrived at the classroom building, but didn't open it. "I would like to see you again. Can I call you?"

Lydia hugged her books to her chest and stared at the ground. "Like I said, I'm really busy. But yeah, I guess."

"Great." He swung the door wide for her and smiled. "Later, then."

Gil continued to intrude on Lydia's thoughts over the following days. A glimpse of long dark curls—which always turned out to be on a girl—would catch her eye. Something said in a lecture would send her mind chasing off and the next several minutes of the professor's words went unheard. When she heard the hall phone ring in the dorm, her pulse quickened. Over the weekend, every time she returned to her room she asked Sue if there were any messages. The answer was always the same: Not that she knew of. Lydia kept telling herself it didn't matter—she wasn't going to go out with Gil, or anyone else, anyway. She had a resolution to stick to. She insisted to herself that she didn't care that he hadn't called, but she knew she was lying. By the middle of the following week, her disappointment was tinged with a bit of anger—screw him, a guy that good-looking probably had plenty of girls waiting to hear from him, and she wasn't going to be one of them. She decided she would simply stop thinking about him. She did, but she couldn't stop him from appearing in her dreams. When that happened, she felt unsettled for half the day.

Two weeks later she returned to the dorm to find a note taped on her door: "Call Gil. 584–9633." She crumpled it and threw it away. There was another one to throw away the next night when she returned from the dining hall. An hour or so later, while sitting cross-legged on her bed playing solitaire and listening to music, there was a rap at the door. "Yeah?" Lydia looked up as it opened partway.

Tasha, the dorm floor RA, stuck her head in. "Lyd. Phone. Guy says he's been trying to reach you."

Too bad, Lydia thought. She flipped three cards from the deck face-up on the bed. "Tell him I'm busy."

Tasha lowered her chin and raised her eyebrows. "Sure don't look that busy to me, girl."

"Yeah, well, when it comes to him, I am." Lydia flipped over another three cards.

"Hoo-kay." Tasha disappeared behind the closed door. A minute later she was back. She handed Lydia a slip of paper. Without looking at it, Lydia wadded the note and lobbed it at the wastebasket across the room.

Tasha pulled out the desk chair and sat down. "Girl, a man who gets under your skin like that either done you wrong or you think he's going to. Which is it?"

Lydia laid down the cards, sighed, and leaned back against her pillow. Tasha was brilliant and, combined with her South Philly street smarts, had wisdom beyond her years—plus the best B.S. detector Lydia had ever known in anyone. That Tasha plunked herself down uninvited meant Lydia might as well be straight with her. She sighed again. "Neither. Both."

"Okay. Like that makes a whole lot of sense. Which is it?"

"Oh, I don't know. He's this guy I've talked to twice. Well, three times." Lydia told how she'd met Gil, how he called her the next week, then saw her on campus, saying he wanted to see her that he'd call her again soon. "That was three weeks ago. That's not 'soon.' That's rude."

"But he got to you, right?"

"Yeah. No. Oh, I don't know." Another sigh. "I mean, he is good looking and all. But I've sworn off dating and pretty much told him that. I don't know why this is bugging me so. I don't even know anything about him. Other than he's from Tampa. That's why a friend introduced us. And he seems to have quite an ego and this big thing for money."

Tasha folded her fleshy arms across her bosom and pressed her back to the chair. "What's a white boy from the Deep South doing up here in the snow?"

Lydia bristled a bit at the implied accusation. "No. He's not like that. And he's not from the South, not really. Turns out that's another thing we have in common. Both our families moved from Michigan the year we went into high school." She realized she was defending him, without meaning to.

"You want to see him again, don't you?" Tasha said it as a statement, not a question.

Lydia swept up the playing cards and began to shuffle them. "Crap. I don't know. Yes, no … hell, I don't know."

Tasha placed her hands on her knees and leaned forward. "Well, girl, you better shit or get off the pot, as my mama says. Either take his calls or tell him to stop. Don't expect the rest of us to keep dodging him for you." She got up, reached into the wastebasket, and tossed the crumpled note back onto Lydia's bed.

At the doorway, Tasha said, "You're coming to the meeting in my room tomorrow night, right? I've got the flyers for us to distribute." A huge grin broke across her face. "Hey, you decide to see this guy, bring him along to the MLK anniversary vigil. I'll check out his ass for you."

Lydia grinned back. "His ass is fine. Believe me." Their laughter spilled from the room as Tasha disappeared down the hall. Lydia slipped the deck of cards back into its box, then smoothed out the phone message. She stared at it before wadding it up again. But instead of tossing it, she held it in her fist. After a moment, she pitched it onto her desk and picked up the book of Maugham's short stories on her bed. She was not going to call Gil, she told herself as she settled in to read. But Tash was right—the next time he phoned she would take the call.

He did call again, the next night, while she was in the planning session for the fourth anniversary vigil of Martin Luther King Junior's assassination. He called again Friday night, when she was at a movie with two girlfriends. He called twice on Saturday, but she was gone most of the day, first doing laundry, then hitting a few end-of-winter sales. Sunday morning she was in her room when she heard the phone ring, and a minute later a voice call out, "Casselberry. Man on the line."

Oh shit, she thought, *I don't want to do this, but I have to*. Maybe it wasn't even him—maybe it was her dad, she tried to tell herself, even though that wasn't likely. All of a sudden the room seemed oppressively warm. Get up, she told herself, get it over with, and get rid of him.

She lifted the dangling receiver. "Hello."

"Hey." There was a pause. "You're hard to get ahold of."

A flush went through Lydia at the sound of his subdued voice, so different from before. Still, she knew who it was at the first word—everyone in the North said 'hi,' not 'hey' like back at home. She took a deep breath. "Yeah. Well—"

"Lydia, I'm really sorry I didn't call a couple weeks ago, like I said I would."

"It's okay." Lydia's tone was cool. No, it's not, her head said. But she heard something in his voice—either fatigue or sadness. "I'm sure you've been busy too."

"Yeah. Yeah, I have been. I would like to see you. Maybe I could buy you a coffee this afternoon?"

"No. I told you, I don't want to go out with anyone. So don't take it personally, but no." She didn't care how the sound of his voice made her feel, she wasn't going to go out with anyone who thought he could leave her dangling and then waltz back into her life, assuming she'd be waiting. Which she had been, damn it. "I've got to go."

"Well, if you won't meet me for coffee, at least give me a couple of minutes to explain myself."

"There's nothing you have to explain."

"Yes, there is. That day I saw you on campus … Well, when I got back to my apartment, Brian—he's my roommate—he said my mom called. Twice. I was to call her back, ASAP. My granddad had a stroke that morning. I threw a few things in the car and made it to Grand Rapids right before her plane landed. That's why I didn't call."

"Oh. I'm sorry." Lydia could feel the heat rising in her face. Her diffidence shifted to concern. "I hope your grandfather is okay."

Gil sighed. "Yeah, I guess he is. The rest of us aren't. He died two days later."

Lydia didn't know what to say. No one she knew had died. "Wow. I'm really sorry."

"Yeah, thanks. Anyway, I got back a few days ago. I've been trying to reach you since, to let you know I hadn't bailed on you on purpose."

"Okay," she said quietly. The silence that followed felt awkward. She wished she could see his face, to help her figure out what he was thinking. "Um, well, I guess I'd better—"

"Wait," he broke in. "Can I see you again? Maybe just coffee before a class? It wouldn't have to be like a real date or anything."

Lydia hesitated, unsettled by the sound of his voice. The desire to hear more of it and be in his presence disoriented the guard she had worked hard to maintain. "Maybe. I don't know," she stammered, "but I'm—"

"Yeah, I know, you're really busy. Well, maybe I'll call you again in a couple of weeks. Maybe you won't be so busy then."

She smarted at the resignation in his words, but also admitted she was a bit pleased to have caused it.

Walking back to her room, she mentally kicked herself. *Damn, damn, damn, damn, damn, girl, why didn't you say yes?* If he did call again, she would.

***

Winter's nip had returned with dusk, but the scent of the warm April day lingered in the air. Buds were emerging on dormant bushes, and tiny yellow-green leaf-flags crept out along the naked maple branches. Forsythia had faded, and lilies-of-the-valley were sending up the first tender shoots that snow would likely cover once or twice more. For now, what snow remained was in dirty, misshapen piles, ugly monsters in the shadowed corners of buildings where the strengthening sun didn't reach.

A wet cushion of grass was springy under Lydia's feet as she moved through the crowd with a torch lighter, igniting and relighting candles held by those at the vigil for Dr. King. In front of them, the steps of Rockefeller Chapel served as a stage where a minister from a Southside church exhorted those gathered to continue carrying Dr. King's lessons of passion and compassion into the world, to never let the dream of hope die out like their candles.

Lydia smiled at those who caught her eye and shared whispered comments with those she knew. It felt good to be in the midst of so many caring people, being reminded that good could follow in the wake of one man's horrific murder, an assault on them all. She also felt good for Tasha, who had to be pleased that her hard work had drawn several hundred students and faculty to the solemn occasion.

Someone touched her arm and she turned, expecting to see a candle needing to be relit. But the candle was burning steadily in the grasp of a strong-looking hand. Lydia looked up, a smile opening across her face. "Gil."

His smile was warm too. "Hi there. I almost didn't recognize you. Even prettier than I remembered."

Lydia was glad the darkness hid the blush she felt in her cheeks. Blushing often gave away the feelings she wanted to mask, but she knew her smile had already exposed her. She didn't care. At least not right now. She was surprised, and pleased, to see him. Ignoring his compliment, she said, "I didn't expect you'd be here."

"Well, I didn't know you would be either." Nodding toward her long lighter, he asked, "You part of the organizers?"

"Um-hmm. Our RA headed it up. We've been really busy pulling it together. It's taken most of my time, on top of classes, for the past few weeks." Lydia stopped, realizing she was prattling.

"Yeah. I've been really busy, but was going to call you tomorrow. Seriously. I was. I was wondering, do you think you might want to—"

A girl in front of them turned, shushing them as the minister's voice called out, "Now let us pray."

Lydia and Gil fell silent. As they listened to the reverend's blessing, she glanced at Gil from the corner of her eye. Neither of them had their heads bowed. Gil was scanning the crowd, his face impassive. Yet when Tasha stepped to the microphone at the preacher's amen and began to sing "We Shall Overcome," they both joined in. As the song rose in volume, Gil's baritone seemed to take charge of all the male voices. Lydia looked at him in admiration.

The voices went quiet. Extinguishing the flames, a low murmuring sounded as couples and clusters of people disappeared into the night.

"Guess I better get going too," Lydia said, without moving. "I should check with Tasha, see what needs to be done."

Gil touched her arm gently again. "What I started to ask you is, would you want to go out Saturday? The guys in the Monopoly group are getting together. To celebrate the end of the game."

"You finished it? So, did you win?"

A glint of sly superiority lit Gil's eyes and grin. "Cleaned out the last one Sunday night. Told you I would."

Lydia laughed. "You are so full of yourself."

"And why wouldn't I be?" Gil spread his arms. "Brains, cunning, looks, charm?"

"Oh for God's sake. You sure can shovel the B.S.," Lydia spat. But she was also startled by her own brashness, afraid she had offended him.

Instead, he laughed loudly. "See? That's another thing I like about you. Most girls don't say what they're thinking."

And most of the time, Lydia thought, *I don't either*. What was it about this man that made her either tongue-tied or too blunt, she wondered.

"Anyway, about Saturday night. Ron is in the group, so you'll at least know him. We're going to Uno's for pizza, then get stoned and see a late movie. I'd really like it if you'd come along."

Lydia felt at a loss for words, wondering if she should accept.

"Hey, I know you said you're off dating. This wouldn't be like a real date. Well, it would," he stammered. "But not a one-on-one date. So you could tell yourself you're just going to a party."

His confidence and smile were back. Lydia returned them. "Okay. I'll go."

"Great. I'll meet you at your dorm around eight. We want to catch the eight-twenty El."

Lydia nodded. "Okay. Look, I've got to go now, help the others."

As she moved away, Gil fell in beside her. "Why don't I pitch in? And then walk you back to your dorm?"

Three guys were lifting pieces of sound equipment as Lydia and Gil climbed the chapel steps, he taking two at a time and outpacing her quick skip up each one. Tasha swung open one of the wide chapel doors for the fellows to pass through. When one asked where they were to put the equipment, Tasha said, "I'm not sure. Just set things inside for now."

"I know where they're stored," Gil called out. He hurried ahead and said, "This way."

Tasha looked at Lydia. "Who he?"

"The guy who kept calling me. The one you got on me about. His name's Gil."

Tasha turned to watch Gil as he led the others down the far-left aisle to a door and directed them inside. "You're right—he does have a nice ass. So, you decided to invite him?"

"No. I didn't know he'd be here."

"Huh. Well, that's another point in his favor. How's he know his way around here?"

"I have no idea. I didn't know he did."

Tasha scanned the now empty lawn that had been crowded moments before. A handful of those on the committee were policing for trash. "We're pretty much done here. There's a box," she pointed to a bench, "with discarded candles. Will you take that back to the dorm for me? Kyle, wait up," Tasha called out, as she headed down the chapel steps with a wave to Lydia. "Thanks, girl. Follow-up meeting, my room, seven tomorrow. See ya there."

Lydia sat down on the bench beside the box of candles. As time passed, she began to feel uncomfortable sitting alone in the dark. She looked at her watch—twenty minutes had passed. *Screw this*, she thought. She stood up and was lifting the box when a rectangle of light broke the dark as the chapel door opened. Gil and the three fellows emerged, talking and laughing. Gil split off from them and hurried toward her. Taking the box from her, he said, "Sorry that took so long. Joe was having a smoke and we had to wait for him to unlock the storage room."

"Who's Joe?" Lydia asked as they began to walk. "And how did you know where to take the stuff?"

Gil explained that he had come to know Joe, the chapel superintendent, when he'd ushered during his freshman and sophomore years. But he hadn't done it out of religious commitment. His grandfather, the one who had died recently, had been a Christian Reformed minister and had helped finance Gil's education. Church participation, along with decent grades, had been part of the criteria for his support, figuring if Gil was hearing the Lord's word on Sunday mornings he wouldn't be out all Saturday night heeding the Devil's enticements. Gil had soon discovered he could do both, by partying until dawn, hurrying home to shower and change, and then rushing to chapel. While the all-nighters were still regular occurrences and the church-going had ended long ago, he realized the value of connections he had made through meeting members of the congregation. He still ushered periodically, making a little extra cash at weddings or funerals.

When Gil turned the subject to Lydia, asking why she hadn't bowed her head during the closing prayer, she found herself speaking candidly about her own beliefs: how the ritual of attending church began to chafe in her teens as she became aware of the dogma, the hypocrisy, and the effort at control that was systemic within organized religion—essential, in fact, for sustaining itself.

Why, Lydia wondered, was she telling him all this? What was it that made her feel so open telling Gil things she didn't share with others? Lying in bed later that night, her mind replayed scenes of the evening, the surprising ease she was beginning to feel with him. She fell asleep looking forward to Saturday night.

A rush of sensual pleasure coursed through her as she stepped into the warm spring air on Saturday evening and spotted him striding toward the dorm. Her hello was shy but they fell into easy conversation again on the walk to the El. Her quiet returned as he introduced her to everyone. Ron was the only one in the group she knew, and she remembered the pretty blonde who had been with him at the February ball. The fellows carried on boisterously, and it was apparent their dates had met before, adding to Lydia's sensation of being out of place.

Aboard the crowded El car, no seats were available so Lydia wrapped an arm around a pole. Gil grasped an overhead strap close behind her and she was keenly aware of his nearness. The guys were ripping each other and mock-arguing about their months-long Monopoly game, with the sharpest barbs launched at Gil for his ruthless tactics. The girls laughed at some of the taunts between chatting with each other. Lydia formed her lips into what she hoped was a small smile, wondering if this had been a mistake. She felt like the odd man out among these people who obviously hung out together all the time. Everyone was so at ease—except for one girl, Lydia noticed, who seemed out of sorts.

Gil's breath was warm against her ear as he lowered his head close to ask, "You okay?"

Lydia nodded. She was about to say something but Gil's head snapped up and he let loose a barb in response to a comment she hadn't caught. All the others hooted back at him. Lydia told herself she'd get through the evening as best she could.

On the walk from the El to Uno's the group fell into smaller clusters moving at different paces, and the banter died down. Lydia liked the fact Gil was, like her, a fast walker, and the two of them were the first to reach the stairs leading down to the pizzeria. A line of people waiting to be seated crowded the stairwell.

"Man, this does not look good," Gil muttered. "Wait here. I'll go see how long before we can get a table." He pushed his way past the crowd and disappeared inside.

When the others straggled up to where Lydia waited and saw the line, expletives were murmured and one of the girls whined, "I told you this was a bad idea." Ron asked Lydia where Gil was, and as she started to answer he emerged from the stairwell.

"Hour and a half to get seated," Gil said as he moved beside Lydia. "So. Backup plan? Skip the movie or skip eating?"

"But I'm hungry. You promised me dinner," the peevish girl complained to her date, who rolled his eyes but said nothing. Someone suggested hitting the movie first and then an all-night diner for burgers or breakfast. The peevish girl glowered, which everyone ignored.

Lydia turned to Gil. "I know a place a few blocks from here. Brocarro's."

"Never heard of it," Gil said. "Their pizza any good?"

Lydia shot him a look and pursed her lips. Gil laughed when she said, "No. It's lousy. Comes out of a freezer box and is heated in a toaster oven. Of course it's good. And the place is pretty big so maybe we won't have a long wait."

“Hey, guys,” Gil called out. “Problem solved. New place. Everybody follow my lovely Lydia.”

Chatter trailed behind them as she led the way with Gil beside her. He interjected comments into the others’ conversations but she was unaware of what they were. His last three words—“my lovely Lydia”—lingered in her mind. He thought she was lovely. No one had ever said that about her before. And he called her his Lydia. How did he mean that? At both the chapel and Uno’s he’d taken charge in a way that showed he assumed everyone would do as he said. Part of Lydia was impressed by his natural leadership, a skill she didn’t have. But part of her wondered about the proprietary sound of “my Lydia.” She wasn’t about to be owned by anybody. Still, it was a little flattering that he already thought of her as “his” girl. She and Gil talked of nothing in particular as the group wended its way along three blocks. When she led them around a corner, Lydia pointed to a high neon sign up ahead. “Brocarro’s” was lit in green below a flashing red arrow, all framed by clear light bulbs like on an old theater marquee. The sign hung perpendicular to a solid brick wall, with no door or windows visible as they passed under it. When Gil glanced down at her with a puzzled expression, Lydia grinned. Without thinking she grabbed his hand and steered him into a narrow alley. “Um, this way, guys,” he called out, his voice a bit hesitant.

The restaurant entrance, several paces down the alley, captured everyone’s interest. Wide planks jutted from the brick building in the almost circular shape of an enormous wine cask on its side. Heavy wooden double doors mimicked the barrel lid, and sparkling lights outlined its rim. Gil and Lydia each grasped one of the long, polished brass handles and swung the doors open for everyone to pass through. Murmurs of pleasant surprise rippled through the group as they took in the surroundings. A honeycombed wall of wine bottles lined the entrance area, which was large enough to hold their group without crowding. Four ornate brocade armchairs were placed about, and the peevish girl immediately plopped down in one. A hostess stand, set next to a nook that obscured a cash register, marked the separation of the lobby from the dining area.

A dark-haired, olive-skinned waiter appeared—a fellow who looked about their age. Wiping his hands on a white towel tucked into his crisp white apron, his smile signaled pleasure over the sudden rush of patrons. “Buonasera,” came out in a thick Italian accent as he smiled at Gil and Lydia. Sweeping his arm dramatically toward the room, he grabbed two menus and said, "A table for two? Please, this way."

"Uh, no." Gil stopped him. "Not two—ten."

"Whoa! You're all together? Hang on a sec." A startled look replaced the waiter's smile and a pure Chicago voice replaced the Italian accent. He turned and scanned the room. "Wait here. I'll be right back."

Returning, the waiter grabbed a stack of menus. "Gotcha covered. C'mon, follow me." A few diners looked up as Lydia, Gil, and the others snaked behind him. Parting a heavy floor-length drape, he gestured for them to enter. "You guys are lucky. This is an extra-charge room for private parties. A group's coming in at midnight but you've got it now. No charge."

"Cool," Gil said. "Thanks."

Like the alley entrance, the spacious room was designed like the interior of a wine barrel. Chair legs scraped on the polished plank floor as the waiter began handing out thick menus. Ron spoke up. "Uh, we just want pizza. And beer."

"Easy." From a deep narrow apron pocket he pulled three long, laminated pizza menus and set them on the table. "I'll be right back with two pitchers to get you started," he added. "Anyone want something other than beer?"

Everyone but Lydia shook their heads—beer was fine. She raised her hand to signal the waiter. Again she felt like the odd man out. "Red wine for me, please. And a glass of water?"

"Sure thing." As he turned to go he said, "Nine mugs," to a teenage girl entering with two towers of water glasses. From the pockets of her short black apron, she began handing around linen-wrapped cutlery.

"Fan-cee," crowed the burly guy whose name Lydia couldn't remember. The girl moving around the table smiled when he said, "No paper napkins? Man, the laundry's not gonna like it when they see what happens to mine."

"Yeah." His girlfriend bumped her shoulder against his and looked around at the others. "Paper napkins are considered fine dining to him. His napkins come from the toilet paper roll." Amidst the laughter the girl reached up to pull her boyfriend's face to hers and gave him a smiling kiss. "That's why I love you. Creativity."

Conversations sprang up. The serving girl returned with a tray of chilled mugs and Lydia's wine, followed by the waiter with the beer. As he poured, he asked, "Decided what you want yet?"

At Lydia's left, Ron answered, "Sure. The usual, right, guys?" With nods from Gil and the other fellows, he ordered three large deep-dish pies and reeled off a list of six toppings. At the opposite side of the table, the pouting girl scrunched her back against the chair, crossed her arms over her chest, and scowled. When her date asked what was wrong now, she whined that she didn't *like* that kind of pizza, she wanted *plain* cheese, she was *hungry*. Sighs and silence rippled around the table. The waiter said he'd be happy to do that for her. She perked up, until everyone stifled laughter as he added, on his way out, "We offer those on the children's menu."

As the beer and the talk flowed, Lydia found herself drawn into the conversations by Gil's skill at including her. When the pizzas arrived, exclamations over their excellence followed the first mouthfuls—even the peevish girl was pleased. Gil hoisted his beer mug high and said, "To Lydia."

***

On the walk to the movie, Gil wrapped Lydia's hand in his and held it all the way. In the theater, he placed his arm across her shoulder and pulled her close. In the darkness, Lydia was glad the excitement she felt at his touch didn't show. Years after, she would remember that, but nothing about the movie. What she would always recall were the sensations: his fingers playing against the back of her neck under her long hair, his light musky scent, his throaty laughter when she jumped and grabbed his leg, startled by something on the screen. He'd pulled her closer then. Her body relaxed into his and she didn't care about the armrest between them pressing into her side.

But it was on their walk back from the El to her dorm that she felt a sensation she'd never experienced. The cold wind off the lake chilled the spring night and she shivered a bit in the heavy sweater that had kept her comfortable earlier. Gil wrapped his arm around her and drew her against his warmth. Since fifth grade she'd been the tallest girl in her class, towering over the boys all through junior high until, in high school, growth spurts gave many of them an inch or two on her. Some of the guys on the basketball team were much taller but she'd never dated any of them. Embraced against Gil, her head was at his shoulder. For the first time she understood how smaller girls—like her roommate Sue—felt when dating guys of even Lydia's height: delicate, protected.

In silence, they approached Woodward House. Gil stopped. He turned Lydia to him and stared, unsmiling, into her eyes. His fingers brushed her chin, and he lifted it as his lips lowered to hers. His kiss was warm, soft, tenuous. When it ended, dizziness made it hard for Lydia to open her eyes. City noises carried from the distance but all she was aware of was Gil's quickened breathing. She looked up at him, slipped her fingers into the thickness of his hair, and pulled his face to hers again. This time their kiss was hungry, deep, long, wet. Desire erupted through her, pulsating with the throb of Gil's hips as he pulled her against him. When the kiss ended, they held each other, their breath ragged. A hunger beyond what she'd ever known made it difficult to stand.

"Come up with me?" she whispered. "Stay?" Gil pulled back to look at her. She answered his unasked question. "Sue's gone this weekend." Taking his hand and staggering slightly for the first few steps, she led him through the dorm to her room.

***

Awareness and consciousness returned from both outside and in. From the brightness of the room, Lydia presumed it was late morning. Gil's body was spooned against her naked back, one arm draped over the sheet covering her hips, the other below the pillow in the crook of her neck. From the slow rhythm of his breathing, she knew he still slept. Careful not to awaken him, she moved his arm from her body, slipped off the edge of the twin bed, and into her robe. Ever so quietly she picked up her bag of toiletries from the dresser, opened the door, stepped out, and closed it behind her. The hallway was empty, the floor almost silent. A few dorm room doors were ajar, the sound of low music spilling out. Lydia moved slowly, languidly, her muscles infused with the drug-like after-effects of the night's lovemaking. Urgency caused her to quicken her pace into the bathroom, where she tossed her kit onto the counter and hastened into a stall. As her bladder emptied, her skin stung in a not-unpleasant way, and she dried herself tenderly. Washing her hands, she checked herself in the mirror. *Oh God*, she thought, *I'm glad he didn't see me like this*. Her hair was a wild, tangled mess, her eyeliner and mascara smudged in a crazed-raccoon mask. She hadn't brought her makeup but cleaned her face as well as she could after brushing her teeth. Her lips were puffy, the skin around her mouth red and raw. It had been intense.

Gil was still asleep when Lydia returned. She sat down on Sue's bed and studied him. Dark curls fell across his forehead. She noticed again how long his eyelashes were, his aquiline nose, the square strength of his jaw now shaded by dark stubble. *Oh God*, she thought again. *What if he thinks I am an absolute slut?* She was still surprised by her brazenness. Not for the utter abandon of her lovemaking—she'd enjoyed sex from the moment she lost her virginity. Not for having initiated the sex. But never before had she brought a man to her bed on their very first date. Would he think less of her for this? She knew she didn't know him. She also knew she didn't want this to be a one-night stand.

Gil's eyelids fluttered. He sighed, rolled onto his back, and rubbed a hand over his face. When his eyes opened, Lydia could tell it took a moment for him to realize he wasn't in his own bed. "Good morning," she said softly.

Gil rolled back onto his side, giving her a still-sleepy smile as he patted the bed. "Come here." She moved to sit beside him and combed the hair away from his face with her fingers. He raised himself up to give her a gentle kiss. "Sleep well?" he asked.

Lydia chuckled. "Oh, I slept very well. When I slept. You?"

He kissed her again as he uttered, "Mm-hmm. I'd be a happy man if I slept every night like last night." He stroked Lydia's breasts and his grin turned lascivious as her nipples hardened under his touch. Between light kisses that moved from the open space of her robe up her neck, he asked, "What time is it?"

"A little after ten."

"Oh shit." Gil pulled back with a startled look, swinging himself around her off the bed. "I've got to go. I'm supposed to be at the chapel in an hour. Subbing for the sound guy. I've gotta shower and change. I've gotta go." Before he finished talking, he was in his clothes. Shoes untied, he bent down to kiss Lydia's cheek. "I'll call." He was gone before she could say a word.

Lydia flopped back on the bed and inhaled the scent of their sex. She hoped he meant it, that he would call. She couldn't call him. She didn't have his phone number. He'd left it weeks before, but she'd thrown away those messages. What if he had only wanted a night with her and nothing more? She was not about to embarrass herself by chasing after him. She got up and opened the window to the air, then stripped the linens from the bed. She didn't want the room smelling of them when Sue returned.

But he did call, late that afternoon, wanting to see her that evening. Lydia's reticence had returned. She was afraid of seeming too eager, and was still wary of his intentions, perhaps even more wary of her own. She lied and told him she had a lot of studying to do. She wasn't ready to tell him the truth—that she wasn't ready to have her heart hurt again. He asked when he could see her again. She wasn't sure. He said he'd call again. He did—the next day, and the next, and the next. Unlike a few guys she'd dated, he made no reference to their night together. When they finally talked, he asked her questions, about all sorts of things, and she found her guard falling away. He told his own stories, and he made her laugh. By Thursday, girls on the floor were giving her a hard time about tying up the phone so much. When he asked to see her Friday night and Saturday, she didn't hesitate. Yes, she said. After that, Lydia and Gil were together as often as their schedules allowed. She spent almost every weekend at his apartment, even though she didn't much like his crude roommate and best friend. Brian was smarmy, with a constant smirk and only two seeming topics of conversation: sports and women—as in who he wanted to screw and why, or who he never would and why. And he ironed his jeans: who in God's name ironed their jeans? But Brian was rarely around. When he was, she did her best to ignore him and remain quiet, which Gil noticed. What, she didn't ask, did Brian say about her body when she wasn't around?

Alone with Gil, Lydia was rarely quiet. Their lovemaking was loud and passionate, their conversations even more so. She found she could say anything and everything to him. He good-naturedly argued political and philosophical issues, even those where he agreed with her. He listened with compassion and deep interest as she shared her most personal and private experiences, things she'd never shared with anyone but her best friend, Audra. Gil was just as open, often saying, "I've never told anyone this before."

***

Everything about Gil Carson was different from any other man she'd known. Even his name. Walking across campus together one afternoon she asked him about it. "I've never known anyone named Gil before. Did your parents ever tell you why they chose that?"

"Mm-hmmm. It was my mom's choice. Here's another secret. She always wanted to marry a guy with the last name of Sullivan. She was—still is—seriously into Gilbert and Sullivan operettas. I've always wondered, if I'd been a girl, would I have been named Patience, or maybe Princess Ida?"

Lydia giggled, and then was laughing outright by the time he finished. "You're lucky Grand Rapids is full of Dutch people, and not Brits."

Gil turned to her with a sly smile and raised eyebrows.

"Wait." She said, stopping. "Are you telling me the truth?"

Now it was Gil's turn to laugh, a loud guffaw. "Had you going there, didn't I? Nah, I doubt my mom's ever heard of anything other than *Pirates of Penzance*. Or maybe *H.M.S. Pinafore*. I was named after my granddad. The one who just died."

"Then why did you make up that story?" Lydia asked, puzzled.

"To see if you'd fall for it."

"Not funny." She smacked his arm. "Well, sorta ... You make up stories like that a lot?"

"Eh, sometimes. Just to see how people react."

They walked on without speaking, until Gil said, "Truth is, I didn't much like my name as a kid."

"Really? Why not? It's cool."

"Thanks. I like it now too. People remember it. Because it's different. Growing up, I thought it was an old man's name. Nobody was named Gil. It made me feel weird. The other boys had names like Mike, Kenny, Joey, or Bobby. How come I had to be the one with a weird name? Then in high school I got picked for Boy's State and there was another kid named Gil. Kind of a shock. Cool in one way, but kinda pissed me off."

"Why so?"

"Didn't like him. Total pocket-protector dork. Even carried a slide rule. I guess he was smart but he never said a word, so who knows. Total doofus. By then, I'd decided *my* name was too cool for *him*. Totally cool for me, though." Gil gave her that charming grin again. "So, how'd you get Lydia?"

Lydia smiled up at him with her eyes. "You know already."

Gil's face was as puzzled as his voice. "Huh?"

"'Lydia oh Lydia, have you met Lydia, Lydia the tattooed lady,'" she sang. Gil burst out laughing. "Seriously. My dad used to sing that to me all the time. Still does. Told me the first time he saw Groucho Marx sing it in *At the Circus* he decided if he ever had a daughter that would be her name. My mom went along with it. But you're one up on me."

"How so?"

"I *still* haven't met another Lydia."

He put an arm across her shoulder, pulled her close, and kissed the top of her head. "Well, there's only one Lydia for me. But promise, no tattoos?"

Lydia snuggled against him, glad he couldn't see her smile of happiness. "Promise."

The last six weeks of the semester sped by too fast. Both felt it. Completing papers and studying for exams became harder, Lydia's concentration slipping, her focus skittering to thoughts of Gil, of the looming months apart.

But then something puzzling happened. Lydia was alone one evening in the student union, trying to study. She became aware of someone standing near the table and looked up to see a girl she didn't recognize. The girl said, "You're seeing Gil Carson." It wasn't quite a question; and it wasn't quite an accusation. Lydia nodded her head. "Be careful." She turned and walked away. Lydia wondered who the girl was—a jilted ex? After a moment, she tried to put the words out of her mind.

Their last night together, before she left campus, they were both unusually untalkative. He surprised her by taking her to dinner at Brocarro's. Their lovemaking was intense that night. He surprised her again when he raised himself up to look at her and said, "I love you."

She didn't surprise herself—she'd known for weeks—when she admitted, "I love you too."

The summer away from Gil, working at the lodge, had been hell.

Chapter 3

"… All these places had their moments, with lovers and friends …" John Lennon's voice pulled Lydia back to the present and with deepened sadness. Those places, all those friends, were long gone from her life. Gil was the only one who shared those memories with her. And now he was gone too.

She punched the radio mute button as she hit the brakes hard. *If Dante Alighieri had lived past fifty-six*, she thought, *would he have added more circles of hell to "Inferno"?* If he'd lived in Atlanta, she was sure, one of those circles would have been the bypass. Traffic in all lanes, in each direction, ran bumper to bumper, as far ahead and behind as she could see, sometimes snaking along at forty miles an hour, often, like now, coming to a dead stop for no apparent reason.

When she'd left Jacksonville, she knew she'd hit a traffic mess here. It was even worse than she remembered. Chattanooga was supposed to be two hours away, but at this rate it would take her that long to get around the Big Peach. She was road-weary and thirsty. A short break wouldn't delay her any more than the traffic was doing.

It took a couple of miles to work her way between cars and across the lanes to an exit. As she got out at the first fast-food place she saw, her back muscles were tense and her right hip was stiff and sore—*damn arthritis, damn getting older*, she thought, making a mental note to adjust the seat when she got back in. Maybe that would help. She climbed a low berm along the parking lot and walked for a few minutes, feeling like a dog let out for a bit of exercise. When the stiffness in her hip eased, she went inside. After using the restroom, she bought two bottled waters and a small coffee. While waiting for the coffee, she drank one full bottle of water. The smell of the deep fat fryers, usually so appealing to her, now was almost nauseating. She could hear Audra admonishing her to eat—she knew her body and brain needed fuel, but she didn't care that she was again running on empty. She didn't care about anything, except making everything go away. After a gas stop, she returned to the highway.

It did take nearly two hours to reach open road—fairly open road anyway. It was late, and dark, when she reached Chattanooga and found a decent looking motel for the night.

***

Light woke her. She groaned and rolled over, yanking the second bed pillow to hide the brightness, only to have the stench of bleach assault her nostrils. She so wanted to return to oblivion—despite the awful dreams—but between the light and the odor, she knew that wouldn't happen. Propping herself up against the headboard, she rubbed her face. Her head hurt, not helped by the sun's laser beam hitting her through a gap in the drape. The cheap radio clock next to the bed read 6:15.

The sheet and blanket had slipped to her waist and exposed her bare arms and chest to the chill room air. She pulled yesterday's shirt off the end of the bed and over her head on her way to the bathroom. Enough light came from the bedroom so she didn't have to turn on the one in there, which was a relief. She hated hotel bathroom lights, always an explosion in the dark, so painful to the eyes. As she washed her hands and brushed her teeth, she studied herself in the mirror. Her dusty blue eyes and her skin still looked as dull as she felt inside. Her hair, which had not gone gray and was still its natural ash brown, spiked in odd directions, giving testament to the night's bad dreams. It needed washing. Lydia hadn't packed shampoo, and this wasn't the caliber of motel to provide such niceties. She again regretted not having packed a hairbrush. Finger-combing with wet hands, she tried to tamp her hair into a semblance of a bob—she couldn't stand the thought of looking grotesque.

Since there was no coffee to brew, she filled the plastic glass from the sink and drank. The water tasted funny, as water always does away from home. She carried a full glass to the bedside table, then rummaged through her tote for her reader's glasses, cell phone, and tablet, and climbed back into bed. With the phone in hand, she hesitated before powering it on. Except for the short call to the car rental, it had been off since she left Tampa on Wednesday. What was today? Friday? Yes. Gil wouldn't find her note until tonight. With her phone turned off, there wouldn't be any voicemail if he had tried to call, thank God, but there probably would be a slew of texts. From the stream of pings that ensued, she knew she was right. She didn't want to deal with any of them, but there they were, waiting.

First she checked the location app. She was sure she'd turned it off on all her devices but needed to reassure herself, the way she always double-checked the back door lock before she left the house. Reassured, and biting her bottom lip, she tapped the message icon. Two names showed beside the unread texts. One was Gil, a message from the day before: Hope you're ok. We'll talk tomorrow night. I'll explain. Lydia's face tightened. *Yeah, I'll bet you'll "explain,"* she thought bitterly. She stabbed the delete command, stabbed it again, then realized it responded only to gentler action. Gentle was the last thing she felt like right now.

When Gil's message disappeared, she opened Audra's, and text after text again scrolled down the screen. When they stopped, a few lines of the last one showed. Audra had sent it near midnight. It read Call me or I call the COPS!!! Lydia's fingertips brushed the screen to scroll up to Audra's first message. The texts had begun with concern and increased in intensity to near panic. Gil could go screw himself but Audra didn't deserve to be left hanging. Lydia typed a short response. I'm OK. I'll call. I promise. She hit send. Audra would be up by now, getting ready for work. Before Audra could try calling her, Lydia shut down the phone.

She needed coffee. If she showered and dressed, she could go out for some. But she realized she wasn't sure where she was, other than on the southern edge of the Chattanooga. Nothing in the sparse room provided a clue. In the otherwise empty drawer of the nightstand, she found a small pad of paper and a pen, which didn't work. When she got up to get one from her purse, she opened the drapes to allow more light, then yanked them closed. Anyone on the balcony could look in at her. She already felt too exposed to the world, as if the pain inside her were on full display for everyone to see, to pity. Sitting on the edge of the bed, she picked up the room phone and pressed the number for the front desk. It rang so long that Lydia almost hung up before an older woman's voice answered. "Could you tell me where I am," Lydia said. "I mean, what's the address here?" Lydia wrote it down, thanked the woman, and hung up.

Back under the bed covers, she opened the maps app on her tablet and typed in the information to get her bearings on where she was. Next she searched for the local office of the car rental agency. When it came up, she was surprised to see it opened earlier than she'd thought. She could already return the car, and catch a cab to a different rental company for another. Logically, she knew it was silly, that if anyone did try to track her—and that thought seemed even sillier—an investigator or the police wouldn't have much of a problem.

Then a realization struck. She was far enough from home that she didn't have to drive the rest of the way to the lodge. Settling back against the pillows, she pulled up the Chattanooga airport site, then stopped. *More silliness*, she thought. If she were traced here, the airport would be the next logical place to look. Nashville or Knoxville, which was closer? Neither, it turned out. Both had late morning flights to Detroit or Grand Rapids but, what with returning the rental car and finding a ride-share driver—no, she'd have to take a cab, so she could pay cash. She doubted she could make it on time.

What she needed right now was coffee. And food, whether she wanted it or not. Another quick search showed a number of nearby restaurants. From her tote, she pulled her last clean shirt and panties. Her slacks she didn't mind wearing several days, but she now realized she should have packed more clothes. In the shower, tears returned. The paltry stream of water made her long for her own bathroom, the home she loved, the man she'd loved. She did still love him. That's why it hurt so. He'd sworn, when she'd found out about his previous affair, that he would never hurt her like that again. She'd slowly learned to trust him again. But he'd lied. Now she wondered if there had been other affairs over the years since. Nearly four decades together—how could she walk away from that? Yet how could she stay?

That's why I'm doing this, she reminded herself as she shut off the water, so I can think things through *away* from the source of the pain.

After dressing, Lydia towel-dried her hair and tried to work it into a reasonable semblance of decency. When the hairdryer on the wall didn't work, tears sprang up again—it seemed like just one more personal insult from the universe. Then she snorted a laugh. It wasn't like she was going to run into anyone she knew, right? So, so what if her hair was a mess? *She* was a mess.

She punched the phone button for the front office again, and again waited and waited for the woman to answer. "Could I have a late check-out, please? I may stay another night but won't know for sure until later ... Two o'clock? Thanks. I'll let you know before then." She packed up her tote, carried it to the car, and half a mile away found a homey looking restaurant with enough cars in the lot to prove its local popularity.

A seat-yourself place, Lydia was slipping into a booth when the waitress, a woman slightly younger than she, appeared with a bright smile, a menu, and a pot of coffee. Lydia tried to return the smile as she turned over a mug on the table. Filling it, the waitress said, "I'll be back in a jiffy for your order." Then she leaned down a bit, conspiratorially. "But don't order the red-eye gravy. Cook we got on today always louses it up."

Lydia's smile this time was genuine. "Thanks. And when you come back, bring the coffee again, please. I'll need a refill."

"Ah, in need of octane, are we? Well, hon, this here high-test'll rev your engines good."

As she managed to eat a scrambled egg and half a slice of toast, Lydia pondered what to do. If she did make it to either Nashville or Knoxville in time for the early afternoon flight, she could be in another rental car by evening. It would be logical to fly to Detroit, but going through Grand Rapids might be smarter. Either way, paying cash for a one-way ticket and with no luggage other than her tote, and all the cash in it, could cause security problems. She was in no mood for a hassle like that.

The waitress laid the tab on the table, picked up Lydia's plate, and asked if she wanted more coffee. Lydia nodded. When the woman returned with a fresh pot, she said, "Can I ask you something?"

Lydia stopped herself from saying "You may"—this wasn't one of her students, whose grammar she would correct automatically. "Yes."

"You get your hair done around here? My gal quit and I need to find someone new." Her hair was tied back in a bit of a ponytail. "Been thinking about going short like yours. It looks good and must not need fussing. I hate fussing with my hair."

Lydia had to chuckle. "I'm sorry, but I don't live here. And my hair, I'm afraid it looks like this because I—" She stopped herself from saying "I left everything behind." "Because the motel hairdryer didn't work. A question for you. Where can I buy some clothes? My luggage got lost," Lydia lied. She wondered why she needed to make an excuse for the question, but went on. "I pretty much need to replace everything until it shows up."

Ten minutes later Lydia left the restaurant with scrawled-on napkins that gave directions to an outlet mall, the closest Target, a laundromat, and a local branch of her bank. The bank was her first stop, and she was glad to see a guard outside the door as she carried in her tote. She left with travelers' checks and several Visa cash cards. The next few hours dragged by. Shopping was her least favorite pastime. It was at the laundromat when she realized that all the clothes she'd bought, other than underwear, were either black, gray, or navy. *Apropos*, she thought—the color of mourning. When the clothes were dry, she folded and packed them in the new suitcase and carry-on. As she looked at herself in the rearview mirror, she realized she'd forgotten to buy a curling iron. But maybe the waitress was right. She was growing accustomed to the loose, tousled look.

Evening light was deepening by the time she returned to the motel. It took two trips to carry everything up to the soulless room. Once she'd dealt with her final packing, she pocketed her phone and the room key, poured a glass of scotch, and carried it and the salad she'd bought from a liquor store-deli down to a table at the pool. Almost as soon as she turned her phone on, it rang. Lydia stared at the screen for a moment, hesitating between declining or answering. She pressed the green icon.

"Where in God's name are you? You've got me scared out of my wits. I have been calling you nonstop for two days," Audra's voice spewed in a half-angry, half-frightened torrent. "And texting. I've sent a gazillion texts. I have been worried half to death. Don't you ever do this to me again, you hear? *Ever*." By the time she stopped, Audra was sobbing.

"Oh, honey. I am so sorry," Lydia apologized. "I texted you that I'd call. And I wrote you that note so you wouldn't worry."

"Well, that sure didn't work," Audra spit back. "And you better not tell me where you are, because I'm ready to come over and murder you for scaring the crap out of me."

"I'm sorry. I really am. I texted that I'd call," she repeated. "That's why I turned on the phone just now. But you beat me to it."

"Yeah, well, that's because I've been calling constantly since Wednesday afternoon." Audra's voice was angry again. "All day and half the night. Thanks to you I haven't been getting much sleep. I take that back—thanks to that damned husband of yours."

There it was. It was all Gil's fault. Lydia knew it, and also knew that she hurt because she still loved him, had always and for so long. Love, pain, grief—such inadequate words for such enormous ordeals of the soul. She'd loved him for so long. How was she supposed to stop loving him when she knew she didn't want to? Didn't want to love him anymore, but didn't want to stop loving him. The tangle of thoughts and emotions, too overwhelming to be contained in her mind, coursed through every cell of her body, and Lydia again felt the desperate wish to escape, escape her body, escape the un-relenting thoughts of Gil's betrayal.

"But then," Audra said, "I don't suppose you're sleeping well either."

"No." Lydia's voice was almost a whisper. "It's hard to fall asleep because I can't stop thinking. And when I wake up in the morning, it's all right there again. I know I have bad dreams, even though I don't remember them. I'm just so tired, Audra. I just feel so tired. And so lost."

"I know, sweetie." Silence hung for a moment before Audra asked, "So where are you? And when are you coming home?"

"I don't know. Oh, I know where I am. I don't know when I'm coming back. I'm in Tennessee right now, but tomorrow I won't be."

"*Tennessee*? When your note said you needed to get away for a while, I thought you meant someplace at the beach for a few days. What about your classes? What about Gil, does he know?"

"Gil doesn't know any more than you do. I left a note by the coffee pot. He should find it when he gets home today. He texted me. Yesterday. One text. Says he'll explain. I'm not ready for any more of his lies."

"But where are you going?"

"Away." Lydia hesitated. "Just away. I'll tell you later, when I'm there, but not now. Call it plausible deniability—I don't want Gil to find me, and if you don't know, then he can't badger it out of you. He probably thinks I'll be back Sunday, because of work, so I doubt he'd even think about calling you until next week, at least. If he does at all. I don't care if you tell him we talked. But if you don't know anything, you won't have to lie to him. And we both know you're a lousy liar."

Audra chuckled. "Has he tried to call you?"

"I have no clue. I doubt it. I told him not to."

"What about the kids? Do they know?"

"No. I'm not ready to tell them anything. I can't, not yet."

"Jesus, girl. You can't let them think you've disappeared. It'll scare them to death."

"I know. But it's not like I talk to them every day. I need some time. To figure out what to tell them." Tears burned, clouding her vision, and pain choked her throat. "I don't even know what to tell myself. I just hurt, Audra. I hurt so badly."

"I know, sweetie. I know. I wish you'd come to stay with me rather than taking off like this." Audra's consoling voice then took a startled turn. "But what about work? You've got classes on Monday."

"No, I don't. I called Shel Tuesday night, told him I needed an emergency leave of absence. For at least the term."

"At *least*? What do you mean, at least?" An edge of hysteria sharpened Audra's words. "You can't mean you're staying away all summer."

"I don't know." Lydia sighed. "I just know I need time, and I don't know how long that will take."

"Please, please don't do anything rash ... Ha, guess it's a little late for that." Audra's voice went from imploring to sardonic. "Are you just going, or do you know *where* you're going?"

"I do. Someplace I haven't been in a long time. Someplace I know I'll be alone. But I'm not going to tell you so don't ask again. Maybe I'll tell you later, but not now. I promise I'll get in touch with you every few days, okay? So please don't worry."

"Like hell I won't," Audra snapped, then she sighed too. "Please take care of yourself, okay?"

"That's what I'm trying to do."

Lydia turned off the phone. Darkness had set in and solar lights now illuminated the top of the white iron fence enclosing the pool area, giving it a festive glow. Beyond the fence, though, a barren asphalt parking lot stretched to the blank, stark side of a commercial building. *False gaiety*, Lydia thought of the lights against a barren, ugly world. Like her marriage. She had grown so accustomed to her life with Gil, she was unaware of the blight encroaching like mold, eating away at the walls of her marriage. She'd become too satisfied, too accepting, too comfortable in her own oasis. Only now, peeling back the wallpaper, did she begin to see the deterioration it hid. When had it begun?

Lydia cast her thoughts back across the sea changes that had rocked their lives when the economic storm had hit like a sudden hurricane from the Gulf. Her position at the university hadn't been impacted, but she and Gil were both overwhelmed by the financial havoc that almost destroyed his marketing firm.

His smaller clients were the first to disappear, as they tried—or failed—to save their own businesses. Gil remained, outwardly at least, confident as his firm, which had increased revenues every year since he'd started it, lost close to $1 million in contracts within the first nine months of the Great Recession. He'd reduced his staff's hours in an effort to save them from the unemployment lines, before being forced to let several people go. He worked longer hours than ever before, scouring the country and his contacts, trying to acquire new business that no longer existed.

At first, the troubles brought them closer together. No matter how late Gil returned at night after working contacts across the time zones, Lydia had something ready for him to eat if he wanted. No matter how late, they always had a cocktail together on the patio. Sometimes he shared details of the day, which always included another stress. Sometimes he stared off into the distance, and she sat silently beside him. Together they went over every expenditure, cutting to the bone to keep the business afloat. She hadn't minded giving up their monthly long weekends flying off to someplace, or dining out several times a week, or any of the luxuries that came to seem frivolous, especially when so many others were in even more dire straits. The young couples with small children on street corners selling bottled water out of coolers on ninety-degree days. The bagger she chatted with at the grocery one day, a fellow with an MBA working minimum wage to feed his family after losing a corporate management position. The foreclosure signs that popped up like dogweed throughout neighborhoods.

Lydia recalled one night when Gil had been unusually silent, eating nothing, barely touching his drink. How, when he did turn to her in the dark and speak, his voice was low and anguished. How he struggled to tell her that they would need to get by on her salary alone, otherwise it meant closing his doors. She'd been so proud of him then. Lydia knew it meant punching a new hole in the financial belt they'd already tightened until it pinched, but she agreed without hesitation. That night they had made love, with a rare tenderness, and awakened in the morning with the shy happiness that had lingered when they were new lovers decades before. The afterglow permeated the entire weekend as they brainstormed facing new challenges like two enthusiastic kids launching a new enterprise, like they had when Gil had set out to start his business eighteen years before. And they made love again and again.

When had the lovemaking stopped? When had that closeness between them evaporated?

***

Sleep was, again, elusive, so it wasn't difficult for Lydia to be waiting at the car rental lot when it opened on Saturday morning. A pleasant young Uber driver arrived soon after the return paperwork was completed, happy to have a juicy fare and happy to carry on a one-sided conversation that occasionally penetrated Lydia's thoughts on the two-hour trip to Nashville. The fellow was especially happy with the generous tip she gave him at the airport, but Lydia was not happy to be engulfed in the hubbub. The chatter was too loud, the lights too bright. Hoping to hide her emotional rawness, she slipped on her dark glasses as she made her way to the gate. Unlike the boot-strutting men and cleavage-baring women she passed, all who seemed to wear their sunglasses as a badge of cool, Lydia hid behind hers as a mask of anonymity. She wondered why she felt the need. Everyone around her was intent on their own travels, their own farewells and frustrations, each one faceless and forgotten as soon as they were out of view. Weaving her way around slow-rolling suitcases, Lydia passed familiar fast-food counters, gift stores luring end-of-vacationers with garish T-shirts and souvenirs, baristas, and bookstores, and kiosks offering every so-called amenity to ease the boredom of hours on a plane.

Then she stopped so suddenly that the man behind her banged into her carry-on, and glared at her. "Sorry," she mumbled, and headed back to a kiosk where a bored young woman leaned against the display case, focused on the phone screen in her hand. Lydia stood for a moment, waiting for an acknowledgment. "Excuse me, do you work here?" Lydia began to wonder if she'd mistaken a traveler for a disinterested salesperson.

"Sho' do. Whatchya need?" The young woman didn't look up from her screen.

"You sell cell phones?"

"Sign says."

Lydia pushed her sunglasses to the top of her head. She noticed the plastic nametag on the young woman's shirt: Chloe. "Well, Chloe, I assume you earn a commission. If you have any intention of earning one today, you might give me more attention than you're giving that device."

The sharpness of Lydia's tone caused a blush of color to rise in the young woman's dark skin. She pocketed the phone. "Sorry. Bad day. Bad week. I'm sorry."

"Same here," Lydia said, slightly taken aback by the young woman's admission. Then she made one of her own. "That's why I'm thinking maybe I should have one of these phones. I've heard about prepaid ones. Do you sell those?"

The young woman now looked at her with a spark of interest. "Don't mean no …" Chloe stopped, then began again. "I don't mean any disrespect, but if you're getting your first phone, you'd do better to choose a major carrier's plan. These," she said, indicating the wares in the case, "are pretty much to use and lose. We sell them mostly to kids thinking they'll hit the music charts in a couple of weeks, or married men in town for a couple of days. Guys who want to be found, and guys who don't."

"No. I already have a phone. I just need … want … something else for a … for a particular work project." She placed a slight emphasis on the word work, but could tell by the look on the young woman's face and the "Mm-hmm" response that Chloe had already sized her up as a married woman in search of a hookup. "Tell me, do these work anywhere? I'm headed almost to Canada, pretty much in the middle of nowhere. And do any of them allow texting?"

"Yes ma'am, you can call from anywhere there's reception. Texting costs extra. But if you get lost in the nowhere, best have your other phone on you. These don't have GPS."

"Oh, they don't?" *Excellent*, Lydia thought. "So which one would you recommend?"

Chloe unlocked the glass case, withdrew a display flip-phone, and showed Lydia how to operate its minimal features. When Lydia agreed it met her needs, the young woman opened a packaged model and activated it. "You've got two choices," she said. "You can buy a flat one hundred minutes plus a hundred texts, and then you throw it away. Or you can pre-pay monthly, re-upping for as long as you want." Chloe flashed a sly grin. "Don't sell that plan often 'round here."

Lydia cringed at the thought of how many thousands of those disposable phones ended up in the landfills. "No, I don't imagine you do. But that's what

I want. Um …" Lydia hesitated, wondering if her next question might indicate nefarious purposes. "Do you accept cash?"

Chloe responded with a short, derisive laugh and gave Lydia a knowing glance. "'Course we do. How else you think those men keep it from their ladies back home? Credit card bill could get 'em busted. 'Course, some of them too dumb—or too cocky—to care. Like my man. Kicked him to the curb last week. None of my business, but a nice lady like you shoppin' here, seems you might be havin' man troubles too."

"You're a prescient young woman," Lydia said.

"Nah, just good at reading people. Well, most people. Didn't see it comin' but am sure glad I found out before the wedding."

"I'm sorry. For us both."

Chloe's sigh was deep as she handed the bag and receipt to Lydia. "Yeah, me too. I've got nothing to do but keep on goin'." Then her face lit up again. "And hopin' for revenge."

Lydia wended her way through travelers to the security area. Her head began to throb as she approached what looked to be an interminable wait. A roving agent asked for her boarding pass, glanced at it, gave it back with one hand and pointed with the other. "Over there, please."

"Is something wrong?" Lydia asked. Was Gil already looking for her? He couldn't have found her already, could he?

"Pre-approved. Over there." The man moved on.

Thank god for small favors, Lydia thought. It had been so long since she'd flown that she'd forgotten Gil had them both cleared for the pre-approved process. "As much time as I spend in airports," he'd told her then, "I'll be damned if I spend it standing in line with fidgety kids and old people who haven't a clue." One more little thing that had gone right for her this morning. When she called him tonight, she'd have to thank him … Her stomach turned. Old habits. This wasn't a work trip where she'd be calling home to tell him about her day.

Within minutes she had cleared security, purchased a cold bottled water and a box of chocolate-covered coffee beans—another small bonus, the benefit of coffee without the aggravation of needing a bathroom every twenty minutes—and settled in at her boarding gate.

From behind her sunglasses, she studied the people around her. Young men and women in casual business garb, closed off from the world behind laptop screens; harried parents keeping tabs on children whose backpacks were nearly as large as they. Older women like herself, some with companions who might be their daughters, others alone and wearing blank looks that were neither anticipation nor apprehension—women resigned to aloneness, women who'd known grief. To know grief, one first had to know love—they were inseparable, if not constant companions.

A laugh soared above the unrelenting sounds of the terminal and Lydia turned toward it. Backs pressed against the wall of glass overlooking the tarmac, a handsome young couple leaned against each other. The girl—*She does still look like a girl*, Lydia thought—rested her head against the fellow's shoulder and stared at his left hand, which she held in both of hers. Shiny rings, probably on their way home from their honeymoon. Would their love sustain that gold shine, or would the entwined rings of their hearts corrode like brass and leave a bilious stain on their lives forever? The bride looked up, straight at Lydia, as if she knew she was being watched.

Lydia didn't move but her gaze shifted behind the newlyweds at a plane's slow approach on the sun-seared tarmac. The passengers around her hustled to line up, in anticipation of being delivered back to their old or new lives, carrying their memories with them like baggage no airline could lose. Wearily, Lydia rose to join them.

Shortly after noon, Lydia debarked into another sea of anonymous humanity in Grand Rapids, Michigan. The last leg of her flight didn't leave for two hours. She idled her way through the limited offerings in the airside, unable to find anything that appealed to her. Magazine covers blaring headlines about business or political leaders, or celebrities who were famous solely for being famous, seemed more fatuous than usual. None of the food available looked palatable, but at a ubiquitous Starbucks she ordered a bagel. The teenage clerk seemed perplexed when she insisted on a plain one with plain cream cheese and couldn't be talked into something exotic. All Lydia wanted now was comfort food, something familiar in a life that had become so strange.

From behind her, a man called out a name. Lydia wheeled, her chest tightened. The name was not hers but the voice was too similar to Gil's. A security announcement blared over the intercom. A claustrophobic tension enveloped her. Again, the overwhelming need to escape. She needed to find a way outside, to find a place where she could be alone, without the sight or sound of another human being inflicting itself on her. Two sets of glass doors whooshed behind her, cutting off the interior noises. There were still too many people around. Some distance away was an empty bench. She moved toward it quickly, afraid someone might claim it first. She sat, angling herself sideways against the rush of cars, shuttles, and people passing. Breathe, she told herself, fighting back the tears that threatened. Breathe. She closed her eyes and inhaled another deep breath. Even with the smell of vehicle exhaust, the air was so unlike the sensual humidity of Florida. A faint breeze rippled over her face and arms, as light as a child's fingers. The feel of the sun—it too was light, not searing. She breathed again and again, taking it all in. Her senses expanded. The sound of cars passing on the arrival lane receded. Her ears picked up the far-off buzz of traffic from some distant highway. Another ruffle of the breeze carried the scent of sweet water off Lake Michigan from the west. And there was another, barely discernible but immediately recognizable scent: the scent of joy, of lilacs somewhere bursting in bloom. Lydia's mind cried out a silent *Oh*. It was a scent she had long ago given up hope of ever smelling again. She wished she could find the bushes, bury her face in the tiny purple blossoms and their powerful perfume. All that surrounded her was asphalt and flat land and hustling, rushing bodies, echoing the barrenness and turmoil she felt inside. The lilacs reminded her that comfort and contentment still existed. Somewhere. It used to exist within her. Would it ever again? She inhaled, again and again, savoring the hint of sweetness. She began to feel as if she might finally be far enough away.

Chapter 4

Walking down the steps of the small plane, the late afternoon sun struck Lydia's eyes, making her wince like a suspect under a police beam in an old movie, badgering her to explain why she was there. *I don't belong anywhere*, she thought, *but screw it, I'm here*.

She headed toward the low terminal building, which was smaller than a single airside in Tampa. Chippewa International—the name imparted a cachet that exceeded the airport's actual prestige. A baggage handler rumbled a cart past, to unload the plane's cargo hold. A handful of other people tended to the needs of the travelers inside the building. Knowing it would be a while before she could retrieve her suitcase, she headed toward the sole rental car counter. The agent was engrossed in completing forms for a tall man in a hat, who she'd seen lope down the plane's steps well ahead of her. He took the pen the agent offered and signed the papers, his signature hasty and, from Lydia's distant perspective, bold. He pocketed a set of keys and reached for the strap of the long baggage tube that leaned against the counter wall. *Fishing rod*, Lydia thought, and a cherished one from the looks of the worn brown leather of the case. As he slung the strap over his shoulder and turned, his eyes met Lydia's. He was about her age, and the smile he gave her was a happy one. With a natural ease she hadn't seen since men of her father's generation, he tipped the brim of his soft brown leather hat. The same leather as that of the case he carried. Lydia's smile in return was genuine. *That*, she thought, *is a satisfied man*.

Twenty minutes later, Lydia pulled her rental car out of the airport onto the highway, heading west into the sun. Traffic was sparse, allowing her the luxury of taking her eyes off the road to absorb her surroundings. Open expanses of land, some lush green with waving grasses, some barren, would morph into dense forest, with dark pines and occasional bursts of white birch, their leaves fluttering, aspen-like, between their light and darker sides. She'd forgotten the color of this green she saw in the land, how much yellow shone through it. The grass burst with a Caribbean glow of lime, the leaves of the maples a buttery shimmer. She'd forgotten how high the maples and pines grew, as if stretching themselves as close as possible to the sun's warmth. The landscape seemed to be a needy lover, thirsty for the light, grasping as much as possible in the short months before the sun would recede and let the land be buried again by the cold tears of winter. Here, the late spring sun was seductive, drawing the world into its embrace. Here, even the shade was affectionate. At home, shade was a stark relief, a reprieve from the relentless warrior sun that seared across the summer sky. This sun, this green, were balms to Lydia's grieving soul. But the land seemed tinged with an awareness that the reprieve was temporary, that the sun too soon would withdraw its affection, that all would plunge into dormancy, buried beneath ice and snow. And she did prefer the sun of home, demanding that one stand up to its blinding light and relentless heat, to become stronger or to wither and succumb. Still, the beauty here enticed her. Yet something about it was also disturbing. The empty stretches, the wooded miles hiding their truths deep within. There were hints of people from the occasional mailboxes, sometimes at the end of a long driveway that disappeared into the trees, sometimes before a tidy home set near the road and surrounded by lawn and new flowers just beginning to show their spring colors.

The scenery filled the car windows like frames of a 3-D movie rushing past, fragile ancient film flickering images on the antique projector of her memory. Her family had traveled this route once or twice each summer, a caravan of cars on a daytrip or two from the lodge to Lake Superior. A dozen or more of them would pile out of the cars, lugging picnic supplies and blankets. Under shorts and shirts that could be peeled off if the day was warm there were bathing suits that would never be wet by the frigid water. Except for her uncle Peter, who made an annual ritual of what he called his flash-freeze, swearing it was good for the circulation. Aunt Sally's annual ritual was to stand on the shore cursing and threatening to let his body float off from the heart attack the shock was sure to bring on. Uncle Pete always egged on the younger kids to swim with him. When her little brother Phil was eight, he took up the challenge. Making a racing start down a slope and across the beach, arms outstretched like Rocky before there was a Rocky, he ran straight into the water. When it reached the top of his waistband, he screamed like a wounded rabbit and raced right back out. He hadn't lasted three seconds. The men laughed, congratulating him, while her mom had hurried to swath her shuddering son in a beach towel, Aunt Sally hurling further invectives at her crazy idiot fool of a husband.

Dripping wet, Uncle Pete strode on shore that day and wrapped an arm around his wife's shoulder. She flinched and yelled, "You are *cold*!" Planting a smooch on her cheek, he'd laughed, and said, "Yeah, but I've got one hot mama to change that." Then he called out, "Time?" One of the men hollered, "Three minutes, thirty-seven seconds." Lydia had been a toddler when he'd achieved his personal best, swimming for a full five minutes, so she didn't remember that legendary feat when the men chided him about it every year. "Not bad for an old man," Uncle Pete had said, toweling off. She had thought of him—all of them—that way then, as old. Her parents and aunts and uncles hadn't been much older than her own kids were now.

More about that day at Lake Superior came back to her. After lunch, while the men napped and the boys fought mock battles on the steep dune and the women sunned themselves and murmured lazy gossip, Lydia had set out on a solitary walk. She promised her mother to stay within sight and headed off into the silence. The shore stretched, deserted, for as far as she could see. She meandered along the water's edge, examining stones, an occasional shell, and driftwood whose whorls often seemed face-like, with eerie eyes and mouths formed as if caught in mid-shriek, grave reminders of centuries of sailors dead in the angry, icy waters. Once in a while she would step into it, never deeper than her ankles or longer than a few painful seconds, to peer at shimmering stones. The colors were iridescent under the water's sunlit gloss. When she was little she had collected the prettiest ones, wanting to take them home but always disappointed and leaving them behind when, out of their element, they dried to drab grays and browns. Up ahead a sizable log jutted from the water, a good place to sit for a while before turning back. But when she reached it, she realized it was not a tree trunk cast up from the depths. It was the end of a massive, foot-square beam thrust several feet onto the beach. A rusted iron spike protruded from one side. Lydia ran back to the grownups and soon everyone was following her to the find, the boys racing ahead yelling, "Shipwreck!" That was the summer the men made a return trip the next day, and the summer when her grandfather had stopped chiding his son for being "too book smart." It had been her father, with his degree in mechanical engineering, who'd plotted out how to winch the beam from its watery grave, up the dunes, and onto the trailer. Years later, after it had dried, it was resurrected in glory as a ceiling beam in the lodge's great room.

It was also the summer that shocked Lydia's emotions the way the icy lake waters had shocked her little brother. Her periods started, making it impossible to indulge in the refreshing coolness of Big Manitahqua Lake for days each month. Until that summer she hadn't much minded being surrounded by her brothers, her boy cousins, the boys who came to the lodge with their dads on fishing trips. Other than her cousin Carrie who'd be up for a week with Aunt Maisie and Uncle Sam, the few girls who came tended to be outdoorsy types Lydia had little in common with. It was that summer, when her body changed, that she learned loneliness, and how to make herself invisible. After completing the hours of daily chores required at the lodge, she often slipped away. Sometimes she disappeared into the woods with a book, other times she headed out to the hard road and walked for miles. Over the next several summers her sense of alienation grew. She missed having fun things to do, dances to go to, boys to flirt with who didn't disappear in a week or two, or talking to Audra for hours on end, something their constant letter writing didn't replace. It had become a bit easier after starting college, when working at the lodge became a paying job. By then, she was more comfortable with the solitude, spending long hours studying for the next year's courses, an investment that paid off with a slightly lighter workload during the fall term.

Lydia was pulled back to the present by the pinpoint appearance of a stoplight turning red far up ahead. It had turned red again by the time she approached a familiar road sign that pointed north to Falton. What wasn't familiar was the cluster of stores and businesses that boxed the intersection, new to her yet weathered enough to reveal they'd been there for years. She wondered how much the town itself had changed during all her time away. She decided she'd play tourist when she came back later to stock up on supplies, exploring the place that had once been as familiar to her as the inside of the lodge.

Supplies. A realization hit. She had no clue what, if any, would be inside the lodge. Other than maybe a few canned goods, there'd be no food, and odds were neither the water nor electric was turned on. Her brother, Thom, still recuperating from a mild heart attack, hadn't been there since hunting season. Fatigue settled on her like a shroud. The last thing she wanted to do was go into town for supplies today. All she wanted was to get to the lodge and be as alone as she'd felt this past week. She'd eaten nothing that day except the airport bagel and knew, even though she was not hungry, she needed something. She'd also need water. Coffee, too. And would there even be toilet paper? Her throat tightened. She just wanted someone to take care of everything for her. She missed her mom.

The two-lane highway swung south, signaling that she was nearing the lodge. She sighed at the thought of having to drive past it to a store in Nibic, but there was no choice. Long-forgotten landmarks began to appear along the route she had traveled so often over all those summers, until after marrying Gil. Some of the old unmarked dirt roads leading off into the woods were now asphalt and bore street signs. Other turn-offs remained unpaved, with an occasional mailbox bearing the name of people who lived or vacationed in the cottages she couldn't see. An occasional resort sign sprouted up, beckoning or rejecting travelers with vacancy or no vacancy announcements.

Ahead, sunlight swept through an area where the woods gave way to a grassy expanse that opened the vista. Lydia's heart quickened. A small gasp escaped her as the sun's rays bounced off the lake's silvery blue water. Without thinking, she stopped in the road and drew in the view like a long breath. A car coming from behind swerved around her, honking. Her senses returned and she pulled onto the shoulder to fully absorb the sight. The edge of the lake's distant side was discernable as a deep green rim of tall pines. Against them was what seemed to be a large white house, much larger than the lodge, she thought, for it to be seen across the watery miles. Not far offshore on the near side were two rowboats, their motors stilled as fishermen let the current carry them along slowly. Lydia could barely see a narrow band of yellow sand beach and behind it a handsome, deep brown log cottage. A handful of apple and cherry trees, their young leaves fluttering, dotted the slope leading to it. Nearby was tilled earth, ready for planting after the last grasp of a hard freeze that could still come. The grass that flowed around it all was leggy but appeared tended.

As her eyes took in what was nearer, Lydia was startled to see a low white building several yards ahead. It entered her vision as if appearing by magic, out of nowhere. Set alongside a wide, half-circle drive, the building was edged with orange marigolds and lilies-of-the-valley, their tiny white bells ringing out a silent welcome to the coming summer. A garish galvanized pole with a floodlight jutted up near the road. Halfway down hung a swaying sign: Clar's Corner.

Clar's Corner. That was where her mom or Grandma Tilde would run out to if they needed something but didn't want to make the three-mile trip into Nibic. A weather-beaten house then, built long before the Depression, its front half had been turned into a little general store. Outside there'd been a single gas pump and a sign that bore the Texaco star. There'd never been a sign proclaiming it Clar's Corner—everyone just called it that because it stood on a corner and the old man who owned it was named Clar.

My God, Lydia thought. Clar had retired and shuttered the store when she was seventeen. And the store hadn't been in this exact spot. With a slight rush of hope, Lydia put the car in gear and pulled into the drive. There was one other vehicle, a small SUV. The wooden screen door clapped closed behind her and a chime rang out when she stepped onto the floor mat inside. A woman dressed in a rose-colored sweater and black jeans, her dark hair tied at the back of her neck, turned to smile and say hello. Lydia nodded. Souvenirs and a postcard rack were on display in a small room behind the cash stand. She could hear someone moving about in the back of the store.

There was a sound of gentle bubbling, and a pleasant scent infused the air like incense for Lydia—the scent of a bait tank filled with shimmering minnows. A long table to her left held bins of fresh produce. Stocked shelves lined the rest of that wall, and two more ran the short length of the room. Glass coolers were at the back, beside an open door that framed a live portrait of the lake. A grateful smile crossed Lydia's face—she could purchase a few things here and not have to go into town for a day or two. As she picked up a small shopping basket, a cooler door snapped shut and a man's voice called out, "Hey, Bess? Got any Yuengling? Looks like you're out." From the front, the woman called back, "Should have some more beer in the backroom cooler, Max. I'll check."

Above one of the aisle shelves Lydia saw a hat. *The* hat. As he came around the end of the aisle, she saw that the man wasn't wearing his brown leather jacket now, but that hat Lydia recognized. As if feeling her eyes on him, he turned and looked at her. There was that generous smile.

"Well, hello again. If I'd known we were headed in the same direction, I'd have offered you a lift. They give you a good car?"

Lydia tried to return his smile. "It's fine. Yours?"

"Yup."

The woman who must've been Bess called from the front. "Got a six-pack here for you. That should last till more comes in Monday."

Once again, he tipped his hat to Lydia, then scooped up the handle of a small bait box set on the edge of the bubbling tank, and said, "Sushi. For the walleye tomorrow." Then he was gone as quickly as he had appeared.

Lydia filled her basket and emptied it twice at the counter before she had what she'd need to tide her over for a few days. The store was small and the choices limited, but she was grateful it offered more than the usual crunchy junk food and candy. The Bunny Bread logo caused Lydia to reach for a loaf with a smile, even though she knew it was to real bread what Chef Boyardee was to real spaghetti. A cooler stocked Wisconsin butter and cheeses, and she chose a half-dozen carton of eggs marked "Fresh from Hansen's Hens—Nibic," ink-stamped with that morning's date. Another cooler offered meats and a smattering of clear-wrapped perch marked as caught the day before. Knowing the electric was probably off at the lodge, she pulled a small Styrofoam cooler from a high shelf.

When she set that on the cashier's counter, the woman named Bess was busying herself at one of the souvenir displays. "Excuse me," Lydia said, drawing her attention. "Do you have ice?"

"Yes, the ice chest is outside the back door."

Lydia began to move in that direction but Bess said, "Hang on." Then she called out, "Katie."

From outside a child's voice answered, "Yes, Momma?"

"One small bag of ice, please." Bess then asked, "Ready for me to ring you up?" Lydia nodded. Bess punched in from memory the prices of the items. When she shuffled the coffee and filters to the paid side, Lydia realized a coffee maker would be useless if the electricity was off; she wondered if there'd still be an old stovetop percolator, and if she'd remember how to use it. As the last of her purchases were rung up, a little girl ran in with a bag of ice cradled across both arms. "Take it, take it, take it, Momma," she chattered. "It's *co-co-co*-cold."

Bess laughed. "Better be, right? What's ice if it's warm, Katie?"

"Water," the little girl chirped as she hopped up and down.

Bess smiled as she snapped open a brown paper bag. "Now run on to the house and tell Daddy I'm about to close up. I'll be there in about ten minutes."

"It's Saturday, right?" Katie asked.

"Um-hmm," Bess answered as she bagged Lydia's purchases.

"Payday, right, Momma? How much did I earn this week?"

"Eight dollars and seventy-five cents."

"Woo-*hoo*." Katie fist-pumped the air as she raced away.

Lydia couldn't help but laugh, and Bess grinned at her. "Child labor. What's the use of having 'em if you can't put 'em to use, right? Besides, cheap at twice the price for the lessons learned." Bess's voice was full of affection.

"True, so true," Lydia agreed.

"Mind if I put the cold stuff in the cooler and save a paper bag?"

"Not at all. Just curious—you don't use plastic?"

"Nope. We've been trying to get the township to wise up and ban them. Too many end up in the lake. Besides, they don't work at all well to kindle a fire. Your total is twenty-eight thirteen."

Lydia pulled bills from her wallet. "I'm so glad I saw your sign. You've saved me from going into town. This sure is different from the old place."

Bess looked up from the cash drawer. "You remember my great-uncle's store? Wow, hardly anyone ever does. I didn't know him well. He died when I was a kid, and we lived downstate." She handed Lydia her change. "I'm Bess Conklin. And you are?"

Lydia almost answered reflexively but caught herself. "L."

"Elle. That's a pretty name. French?"

Lydia gave Bess a half smile. "No. Um … it's just an initial. It's what I go by."

"Oh, okay. Let me help you take this to your car." Bess inverted the cooler's lid over its contents, set the ice on top, and lifted the load from the counter. Carrying the grocery bag, Lydia opened the trunk. She pushed her small suitcase aside to make room for the cooler. As Bess set it down, she asked, "Not staying long, I take it?"

"Well, I'm not sure. Yet. I may be here all summer."

"You sure travel light then." Bess laughed and looked down at the sturdy footwear she wore. "When Dave and I manage a vacation, I have a suitcase that size just for shoes. I don't get to wear pretty ones around here often."

"Tell me about it. I spent all my summers here barefoot. Hated even having to put them on to go into Nibic or Falton."

Bess looked at Lydia with sincere interest. "You grew up here?"

“No, not really. Spent every summer here, though, until I was in my twenties. It’s been decades since I’ve been back.”

“Well, welcome home, Elle. Come back any time. I’m open every day but Monday.”

Lydia started the car. As she pulled away she glanced up at the rearview mirror to see Bess shut the store door for the night.

The last mile to the lodge, even after so many years away, was intimately familiar and she drove it slowly. Familiar places remained, yet were changed. She slowed to a crawl at the sign for Pines Pointe, which had been the largest resort on this side of the lake when she was young. It had grown, and now cottages could be seen sprinkled through the woods, set far from view of the water. She passed two other long drives, now private, that once led to two small resorts whose names she couldn’t remember. When she saw the sign for the Log Cabin Resort, the property nearest the lodge, her eyes widened in disbelief. It was the last place she expected to still be in business. As kids, she and her brothers stayed away from there, creeped out by the dank, dirty cabins. Grandma Tilde had never had a good thing to say about the people who built it, calling them hillbillies—her derisive shorthand for people who didn’t know cleanliness was next to godliness because, she was sure, they had neither.

She then slowed more, inching along as she searched for the narrow drive to the lodge. Her heart quickened when she saw a small painted sign that read Castle Berry, the red letters dulled and the wood weathered by the winters and sun. She turned off the road and stopped short, blocked by a long metal crossbar padlocked to a post. She’d forgotten that Thom had installed it long ago, when winter looters began breaking into unattended properties. How the world had changed; in warm weather they’d left screened windows and doors wide open, day and night, all the summers she’d spent here. Would she ever again know that sense of safety, she wondered, here or anywhere, let alone in her marriage? She stared at the gate. She didn’t relish the idea of making several trips on foot to carry her groceries and suitcase the quarter mile to the lodge. Nor leaving her car so close to the road, announcing her presence. Then she remembered the leather key fob in her tote, that on it was a second key along with the one to the lodge door. Digging it out, relief clicked in her as the heavy lock clicked open. She swung the gate wide, drove through, then locked it again behind her.

Images flashed through her mind. Gil calling as she passed by his office, "Honey, bring me a drink?" Her, with his glass, returning with it from the kitchen. But when she walked in, it became his office at the agency. Him, naked, standing at his desk. A faceless woman laying on it, her naked legs wrapped around his hips. Gil, reaching for the bourbon Lydia held, saying a casual thanks as he thrust himself into the woman. Again, and again, and again.

Lydia's eyes opened. Her breathing was tight. She twisted, tangled in a sheet. Rough fabric scratched her arm as she sat up. She saw nothing but black, so deep that for a moment she panicked, wondering if she had gone blind, wondering if she were dead, suspended in limbo. The silence, and the darkness—no glow of a streetlight, not the merest hint of a moon—added to her momentary confusion. Then comprehension returned. In the lodge. She was in the lodge, on the sofa. With a cautious hand, she felt the end table for the base of its lamp, then fingered her way up to find the switch. A pool of yellow illuminated the space and cast deep shadows around her. She felt the echoes of memories—her childhood fear of what sinister things lurked in the shadows, in the dark of the woods. Of encountering wild animals there, of ghouls lurking behind chairs in all the lodge rooms. Of relief when daylight meant she wouldn't have to face them. Lydia leaned back, staring up at the massive ceiling beam. The demons weren't in the shadows, they were within her, crouching. Daylight would not eradicate them. She would have to face them. But not yet. She wasn't ready.

Lydia's mouth was dry, and she had to pee. She tossed the sheet aside and moved carefully, switching on table lamps along the way. In the kitchen, she poured a glass of water from the jug she'd bought and started the coffee maker, then refilled the glass of water to take to the bathroom to brush her teeth. The refrigerator growled, shocking the silence like a shadow monster come to life. Water leapt from the glass in her hand, splattering Lydia's bare foot on the cold wooden floor. Tension tightened her back and exhaustion threatened her knees as she moved, weakly reaching out a hand to steady herself on furniture.

For the past four days she'd functioned, unfocused and alone, driven by the need to escape. To escape to here, where reality would be suspended within the surreal shadows of memory, where she could suspend herself from everything. The world beyond still spun, newspapers tossed onto driveways, families readying for church, friends meeting for brunch, drunken young men waking with hangovers, women rushing through grocery shopping and laundry, children trying to forget the homework due the next day. Just weeks ago, Lydia had been happy to be part of that world, a world that had shattered, revealing the ugliness and cruelty behind its façade.

Enervation had hit full force when she'd pulled in yesterday. Her heart felt it first, as the lake and then the lodge came into view from the winter-rutted road leading toward the shore. Her vision had blurred then with tears, transposing the scene as if by an impressionist's brush. When she stopped the car, a wave of exhaustion engulfed her, like a storm wave thrust up from the lake itself. Her face, and then her hands, became wet as she leaned her head against the steering wheel, sobbing. She cried long and hard, like she hadn't in decades, like a teenage girl who'd had her heart broken. She still *was* that broken-hearted girl. And she still was the woman in love with her husband. Would she ever be able to reconcile the two?

When she'd emptied herself of tears, her field of vision and comprehension were narrowed by the rote memory of her surroundings. She vaguely remembered opening the lodge door and being overcome as the musty scent of its closed-up interior mingled with the fresh scent of woods and water. She'd unloaded the car. Found the key to the padlock on the breaker box and turned on the electricity. Kneeled down on the dock to fill a bucket of water, and used it to fill the toilet tank. She remembered her actions, automatic but devoid of feeling. She remembered collapsing on the sheet-covered couch, closing her eyes against the window light. Then nothing else.

Shivering in the cold she'd begun to feel, Lydia pulled on socks and shoes, sweatpants, a sweater, and a zippered sweatshirt. The coffee she'd started was brewed. She poured a cup, stepped out into the dark morning, and walked toward the sound of lapping water.

The remaining stars, the shimmering of a lowering quarter-moon off the silent lake, and the quiet both comforted and saddened her. She was alone, finally, totally removed from the sensory bombardment that had had her fighting to hold onto a shred of sanity after being thrust into a cosmic whirligig. She felt totally alone, as inconsequential to the swirl of life as if she'd never existed. She could die here and no one would find her until her flesh had rotted in the damp like a fallen tree. Her students would soon forget her. Her acquaintances might give an occasional passing thought to when they'd seen her last. Her family, and Audra, would be cast into a panic, and ultimately grief, after someone eventually found her shriveled, dried out body, her face contorted like a monster's Halloween mask. Maybe she should save them the gruesome discovery. Just pull a Virginia Woolf, and perhaps create a legend that would linger for years: The Lady Who Haunted the Lake. Just let her body disappear into nothingness, like her soul had done already. No, she'd want her body found. That way her suicide would haunt Gil for the rest of his life, and he'd know it was he who had driven her to it. And he'd be haunted by the lies he'd tell people to keep them from knowing the truth, that it was all his fault.

The boulder she leaned against was ice cold. A jittery shudder coursed through her and palsied the mug in her hand. The lake water would be cold, too. She was too exhausted to kill herself. Too tired of suffering to suffer drowning. Clarity struck: that it was Gil she wanted to be the one to suffer.

The morning light began to rise, illuminating the mist hovering between the lake and sky. Only the slightest, slowest laps told her the water was a still mirror to the heavens. She could see the necklace of froth gathered at the sand's edge. *Suds*, she thought—*Grandma Tilde had us kids convinced for years that those were the suds she scooped up to do laundry.*

From far off, she heard the muffled putt-putt of a trolling boat. It was as comforting a sound as the sweet *swoosh*-pause, *swoosh*-pause of the water against the shore. A fisherman whose goal would be walleye, or pike, or perch. A simple day's goal.

She straightened up, took a deep breath of the clean air. She too had a goal. It would take longer than a day. That didn't matter. She had all the time ahead of her that she needed.

For the first time in weeks, she was hungry. Starving. And she knew she was ravenous, for more than food. But for what?

***

By afternoon Lydia had polished off half the cheese and fruit she'd bought, and had succeeded in tackling the two most challenging tasks: to turn on the water and the gas. She'd never done either, but had vague memories of her grandfather's actions when there'd been a need to service those resources. Both the pump house and the valve on the gas tank were padlocked, and by the time she found the ring of outdoor keys, she had familiarized herself with the contents of every drawer on the first floor. It took her a long time to puzzle out what to do, to find the right tools, and to overcome the fear that she might blow herself up. Twice she almost called her brother for instructions but forced herself to put down the phone. She wasn't ready for Thom to know she was here. Hours later, when water sputtered and then flowed from the tap, and the flame of the gas stove flickered, she felt an immense sense of competence. She tripped through the rest of her chores lightly. Worn bed sheets were whisked off the upholstered chairs and davenports of the great room. Fresh linens went on the bed in the back bedroom—Grandma Tilde's and Grandpa George's old room, where it seemed the scent of their ghosts still lingered. Surfaces were dusted, counters wiped down, and cupboards studied to discern what dishes, pots, pans, and utensils were on hand.

As the day went on and she warmed from the sun and the physical activity, she opened windows, letting the breeze sweep out the fustiness of the closed-up lodge and the acrid odor of the bleach she'd used in cleaning, allowing in the scent of sweet clover mingled with the perfume of cedars and the lake. She then stripped out of her clothes—the ones she'd worn the day before, that she'd slept and then worked in, and showered. Tears came again, quiet tears now, flowing into the streaming water until they and the water heater were depleted.

Late in the day, while a small pot of coffee brewed, she took the utility key ring to the boathouse. Inside, Thom's sixteen-foot speedboat sat trailered. Stepping sideways between its bulk and the vacation gear stashed around it, she surveyed the clutter for what she might want to haul out later. For now, all she was interested in getting was one of the ancient Adirondack lawn chairs. She moved the items piled on the seat of the one nearest the door, and slid a cushion off the stack nearby, then noticed a folding lawn table suspended from a hook on the wall and grabbed that too. Dragging the heavy load across the soft earth of the lawn, she recalled how, when Thom was in his prime of strength, he could hoist one of the chairs without effort, turn it upside down over his head, and stride off as if it were weightless. She was out of breath by the time she'd backed her way in inches to the shore.

When she sat down with her cup of coffee, she fussed with the wood-slat table, moving it this way and that, until it was positioned just so. There was that jitteriness again, taking over—and the caffeine wasn't going to help. She leaned back and closed her eyes. Breathe, she could hear Audra intone in her mind, breathe. As calm settled over her, the tension seemed to flow downward, as if drawn to the magnet of the earth's core. She wondered what had happened to *her* core. Would it ever reset to true north?

Lydia glanced over as she reached for her coffee, and was startled by delight. Flickers of tiny star bolts seemed to burst atop the mug's iridescent sheen. Looking up, she saw sunlight dapple through cedar leaves. Branches, clad in lace-like hunter's green, seemed to be bowing, as if to her; the tree's slender trunks seemed to bow too, as if in recognition, remembering and reaching to embrace her.

The pale sun, still hours away from sunset, gave off enough warmth to counter the coolness wafting from the lake. Slipping ripples pushed against the sand at water's edge. A flock of gulls did a fly-by, skimming the lake's surface without wetting their wings. One broke away and rose, hovered like a hummingbird and then dove, pelican-like, to pluck a minnow from below.

When the birds turned to specks in her view, she scanned the horizon across the miles of water. Not far from where she sat stood the little island that she had sometimes rowed out to with a book when she wanted to be alone. Far away the Three Sisters rose against the backdrop of the shoreline that stood a mile or so beyond them. Some days, those three islands seemed close enough to swim to—a fool's endeavor. On others, like today, they seemed as elusive as a mirage. She turned slowly, taking in all that was in view. Not all of what she noticed pleased her. She was disappointed to see how much Pines Pointe Resort had expanded, having annexed the old Sandy Shores Resort beside it. The once-wooded land that had stood between the two resorts now revealed a picnic area, a playground, and basketball and tennis courts behind seven boat-lined docks thrust from the shore. She turned away, grateful for the copse of trees that still stretched along her family's land, unadulterated, in the other direction from where she sat.

Memories pulsed through her mind as she studied the lodge. Thom and Lynn had cared for it well. The vertical split logs that framed its two stories remained painted white, as their grandfather had always insisted. Grandma Tilde, however, would not have approved that the window shutters were now white too, not the Williamsburg blue she'd insisted on. Lydia sighed but understood that the additional expense and effort of painting the contrast was frivolous when inhabitants were rare and short-term.

Lydia sipped the last of her cooled coffee and let the empty cup hang loose in one hand, its weight swinging as the breeze struck its bell shape. She rose to refill it and returned carrying the fresh cup, her reading glasses, and a pen and pad of paper stamped "Cassel Consulting" across the top, the name of

Thom's environmental consulting company. Her attention turned to making a list of food and supplies she'd need for a long stay. By the time she finished, the list ran to a second sheet. She realized that, as much as she hated to admit it, a trip into Falton the next day was wiser than paying the higher prices in Nibic's stores. She took the pad inside, then dug into her tote for her phone, plus the new one she'd bought, slipping them both into the pockets of the zippered sweatshirt she pulled on to ward off the coming chill of evening. In the kitchen, she poured a slug from the almost empty small bottle of scotch—she added a stop at a liquor store to her list—into her cup before topping it off with the last of the coffee. A bit of fortitude was needed for her next tasks.

She settled back in the lawn chair and stared at her phone, hesitating before powering it on. When it lit up, so did a litany of pings and the tiny scoreboard of numbers, signaling downloads as if racking up points in a lopsided basketball game—fifty-seven emails to fourteen texts. *Shit*, she thought. The email alone was a full day's work. And today was not that day. Odds were that quite a few were from her two grad students, panicking over being thrust into their teaching roles. They'd just have to muddle along without her. She tapped the text icon. Names popped onto the screen, three of them—Audra, Gil, and Sara. Tensing, she feared Gil might have said something to their daughter, and gingerly tapped Sara's name. The message had come in an hour ago: Hey Mom Friends coming next Sat. any quick/EZ appetizer recipes U could send? Luv ya! Lydia smiled, relieved. Will do, she dictated in response. BTW, am out of town a while, and phone mostly off. Love you too. Mom.

She stared at Gil's name next, anger and ache swirling within her. She picked up her mug and grimaced at the taste of scotch mingled with the acidic, cold coffee. What was it Winston Churchill had said—something about when you're going through hell, don't stop, keep on going.

She tapped the screen. His first message was from late Friday night: Found your note. Wish you hadn't gone. Wish you'd come home. She flicked the screen as if snapping away a gnat. The second, on Saturday: Babe, I'm sorry you're upset. Trust me, it didn't mean a thing. You know I love you. We'll work this out. Hot tears stung her eyes as anger overwhelmed the ache. It was his third message, from this morning, that soured her stomach: See you when I'm back from golf this afternoon. Want to go out to dinner? We'll talk. Miss you.

She took another drink of the coffee and sneered. So, he thought she'd be back today, to their marriage and to her students. Good. Her note had worked. Tonight he'd begin to wonder—well, maybe. Tomorrow he might call her office. Once he realized she'd taken a semester's leave, then maybe he'd really start to sweat. Sooner or later he'd think to call Audra—who deserved a heads-up.

All the other texts were from Audra—a litany of short pleas, in separate bursts: RUOK? Where are you? Worried sick.

The growing intensity of Audra's messages made her ashamed of having hurt the one person who loved her unconditionally. She'd promised Audra she would get in touch today, but it was apparent from the texts that this hadn't calmed her fears. Lydia powered the phone off, then turned on the new one. Using it, a feeling of illicitness came over her, as if she were a fugitive on the run. She *was* on the run, she knew, but she also knew that running away was her only way of running toward the way out of her personal hell.

Into the phone's text box she typed JPGR @ this # and hit send. It might take Audra a while to notice the message and recognize it; that is, if she hadn't forgotten it after all these years. JPGR—their teenage code that meant a desperate "Call me!" John, Paul, George, and Ringo. They'd been besotted with the Beatles, imploring the air with sighs or cries of, depending on their hormones at the moment, "Call me, John!", "Paul, call me!"—as if their desires would result in their adoration being returned. The Fab Four's initials, passed under the puzzled gazes of classmates handing their notes across the rows of seats, was shorthand for the teenage angst that struck almost as often as their star-struck desire: It could mean anything from "The most awful thing happened, my dad/mom's gonna kill me, my life is over, my life sucks, the world hates me, I wanna *die*" to "You are *not* going to believe who stopped me at my locker and asked me to Friday's dance." Only a girlfriend's ear to whisper secrets to could right the world again, at least for a while.

Watching a sailboat float along the far horizon, Lydia knew that part still held true. It wasn't that she had much to say to Audra—nothing had changed and Audra knew everything she had to say for now. Except where she was. She just needed her best friend, not to do or say anything, but just to be nearby.

Lydia had always wondered about women who didn't have close friends. She knew a few. Some, exuding neediness, either repelled or sucked in and drained the souls of other women who tried to befriend them. Others, the ones who, deep down, despised their own gender, moved through life pushing women aside. She felt sorry for them all, for the wasteland of loneliness they created for themselves. Lonely, Lydia realized—now it was she who was lonely.

A loud, jarring ring tone startled her. Fumbling first for the volume control and then for the answer icon, she put the phone to her ear. Her voice was tentative as she answered, "Hello?"

Audra's voice, equally unsure, asked, "Lyd?"

"Yes, honey, it's me."

Audra's words came in a gush. "Oh, thank god. I have been *so* worried. I've been calling and calling and calling. And texting. *Why* isn't your phone on? And whose number is this? I've been scared half to death. *What* is going on? Where *are* you?"

By the time Audra took a breath, Lydia was chuckling. "Okay, can I get a word in edgewise now?"

"Yes but you better tell me what is going on or I'm going to go absolutely insane and—"

"I will if you'll shut up a moment," Lydia interrupted with a laugh.

Audra sighed. "Okay. I'm shutting up now. But you better start talking. Like right this minute or I'll give you an earful—"

"Then stop talking already, will you? First, I'm fine. Really." Lydia paused. "Well, fine being relative, I guess. I'm sorry you've been worried. I told you I'd get in touch today."

"I know, I know … but still. You couldn't do that like first thing this morning so I didn't go nuts all day? And whose phone *are* you calling from?"

"It's mine. A new one. A burner phone, the cop shows call it. Save this number, because it's how you can reach me. My regular one is staying off except for when I check texts. I saw yours—all eleven of them, if I counted right. Other than one message from Sara wanting a recipe, there were three from Gil."

"Three? That's all?"

"Yeah. First one was after he got home Friday. Second one said he was sorry that I was quote-unquote upset."

"He's sorry you're *upset*? *That's* his apology? Jesus."

"Yup. And, the last one suggested that after his golf game we go out to dinner and talk that we can fix this."

"Asshole. So he's expecting you home tonight?"

"Obviously. When I don't show, he might call you. If he even bothers. You've got to promise me to go all Sgt. Schultz on him, okay? You know nothing, you've heard nothing. Period. And you absolutely have to promise not to let on knowing anything about his affair, okay?"

Audra sighed again, this time dramatically. "Okay. I'll try. What I'd really like to do is give the bastard a piece of my mind."

"Don't just try. I don't want him to know that you know anything. I want him to stew. The note I left said I needed time alone for a while. I didn't say how long a while would be. Nobody but you and my staff know it's indefinite. Shoot, no one else even knows I'm gone. If he checks with my office, let him find out from them. Okay?"

"Once he does, he won't buy that I don't know anything. He'll know. Unless … unless I act like I'm pissed off you didn't tell *me*." Audra made a wry chuckle. "And then I can vent some of my anger when I see what lame-ass excuse he gives me for you taking off. But what are you doing about money? He's going to see credit card charges show up, isn't he, and find out where you are?"

"No, he won't." When she explained why, Audra's surprise turned to admiration. "If he hadn't left on another trip the day after I confronted him," Lydia said, "I might still have taken off. But those two nights alone gave me time to think past some of the pain and get smart about taking cash. Truth is, I didn't think much beyond that until I was in Chattanooga. All I knew was I had to get away from him."

"So where are you? How far away did you *go*?"

Lydia hesitated. "Far away. I won't say where. Not yet."

"Well, what *are* you going to do now?"

A sob caught in Lydia's throat. "I don't know. Not really. Not yet."

"Sweetie, that's okay. Doing nothing is doing something. As long as you're taking care of yourself, that's doing enough right now. You are taking care of yourself, aren't you?"

By the time their call ended, Audra was reassured of Lydia's safety and sanity. When they clicked off, Lydia's tears came again—soft, quiet, soothing, the way a child cries in a mother's comforting embrace. Her tears were as much in gratitude for Audra's unquestioning support as they were over the pain of what Gil had done. She cried for a long time; then, emptied, she stared mindlessly at the silent, smooth surface of the lake. After her mind cleared, thoughts began to rise like a cool haze over the water.

***

Sunlight beamed through the bedroom window, waking Lydia. Disoriented, she pushed aside the dream she had been pulled from—of Gil's tender kiss, of her struggling against him, of the invective she hurled, screaming, as she fought him off. When clarity returned, she again had to puzzle for a moment, trying to remember what day it was. Monday. A school day, a work day.

But for her it was neither, leaving her unmoored, adrift through time that had always provided a series of destinations, the steady route to and through them—the daily, hourly patterns of her life. She wondered if she'd adapt to this new form of time, which seemed nonlinear, omnipresent yet nonexistent, suspended and suspending. She'd experienced the sensation before, in the days after the death of her brother Phil, and then again before and after the deaths of her parents. It seemed odd, then, to realize that life continued to be normal, unchanged, for everyone else, and even comforting when death's duties had been faced and she too slipped back into the flow of time.

Right now there seemed no way of orienting herself to actual time. The clocks in the lodge had been unplugged before the electricity was shut off for the winter. She'd decided to leave them off for now. The sun and the moon, which cared nothing about minutes or hours or the days of the week, could carry her in their current.

Today, Lydia thought, as she had coffee and the last piece of fresh fruit, that non-clock current would take her to and from Falton for the mundane chore of purchasing supplies. Looking over her grocery list she remembered she'd promised Sara a recipe. She poured a second cup of coffee and set up her laptop on the kitchen table. When its screen lit up, so did the announcement of the day and time that was propelling everyone else forward. Lydia turned off the clock function, rebuffing its intrusion. She tapped out a recipe from memory and a note to her daughter, rereading it twice to make sure it gave no hint of her morose state of mind. Finishing her coffee, she stared through the broad window at the serenity of the lake, wondering when the storm within her would give way to calm.

Driving into Falton was jarring. Vestiges of the remembered past were juxtaposed in stark contrast with the present, creating a dissonance that made both seem out of skew. She could almost see the ghost of Andy Hardy hurrying across the spacious lawn of the old brick high school, his biggest worry whether he'd have the money to take Polly Benedict to the homecoming dance. But now sullen teens wandered the grounds, their faces obscured by hoodies, hands jammed into jeans pockets as if to ward off both the day's chill and the cold, hard future. These were the ones, she knew, doomed to never leave town, to lives of manual labor, babies too early, dreams dashed with every week's losing lottery ticket. Her heart wrenched, for herself as much as for them. For the first time, Lydia truly understood, felt in her own bones, the soul-sucking emptiness of having the future ripped away.

Blocks away she passed the Falls Hotel. In Lydia's childhood, it had been a grand but outdated remnant of the days when the railway brought the well-to-do for excursions to nearby Tahquamenon Falls. Now it gleamed, proudly restored, yet somehow seemed as out of place as a Rembrandt in a Picasso exhibit. Several storefronts along what once had been the tiny downtown retained their expansive glass windows, beckoning tourists in to explore, but the town had expanded. The old two-block section of shops, now hemmed in by utilitarian structures, seemed embarrassed by its age. The sensory experience was almost visceral, as if the softest silk and the grit of sandpaper were both rubbing against her heart.

At the corner past the Falls Hotel, she turned. Her memory of the grocery's location was correct. Less than a dozen cars were in the lot, and Lydia encountered few shoppers as she navigated the aisles. The unfamiliar puzzle of the store gave way to calm as she focused on the next item on her list. One step at a time, she told herself as she retraced her steps again and again on her scavenger hunt. She chose items without thought of appealing flavors but for simplicity and ease. Canned soups and vegetables, bread, some sauces, boxed pasta and bagged rice, slender packages of meat, and a smattering of fresh fruits and vegetables from the lackluster selection trucked up from the Lower Peninsula. As she checked out, she asked the clerk for directions to a liquor store. There, she startled herself with how much she spent. "Looks like someone's having a party I'm not invited to," the clerk joked as he filled two boxes with wine and liquor. Lydia's smile in return was wan. She felt like replying, "Yeah, real fun—pity party, for one, lasting until doomsday."

It was early afternoon when she began unloading the car's trunk, carrying in the cold foods first to the refrigerator. The sound of car wheels on the gravel drive startled her—she had locked the road gate behind her. For an instant, a sense of vulnerability weakened her legs. If harm were to come to her here, who would know? She approached the opened door with caution, ready to slam it shut if need be.

A man peered into the trunk of her car as he strode toward the steps. When he saw her behind the screen, he stopped, as wary of her as she was of him. Lydia's eye caught a flicker of movement inside his car—a child, not another man. She stepped closer to the screen. "Yes? Who are you? How did you get in here?"

He glanced at his vehicle, then turned back at her with a frown. "Those are my questions for you. No one is supposed to be here. The owner would have told me. No one is supposed to have keys but the owner and me. Now tell me how you got in here or I'll call the cops. And then I still might."

Lydia stepped onto the porch, holding the screen door open in case she needed to retreat. "I'm one of the owners."

"Yeah, right. You're not Lynn by a long shot. If anybody was expected here, I'd have known about it. Now who are you?"

Before Lydia could reply, a small body darted out of the car and came running. "Hi, lady! Daddy, that's Lady L. L is for lady! She was in the store!"

"Katie, I told you—stay in the car."

"It's okay, Daddy." The girl grinned up at him as she grabbed his hand, pumping his arm up and down as she bounced on tiptoes. "L is nice, Daddy. That's her name, just the letter L. I heard her tell Mommy. She knows Mommy now. And she even knew great-great-great-uncle Clarence." The girl stumbled over the "greats," a frown crossing her face in concentration on the number of them. "I heard her tell Mommy that too."

The man cast a glance at Lydia, then looked down at his daughter. "Really? When was that?"

"Pay day! I made lots, a whole *eight* dollars and seventy-five *cents*. I brought Lady L ice." The girl looked up and asked, "Do you remember that, Lady L?"

"You gave the lady lice?" the man interjected.

"No, *ice*," Katie shouted, and giggled.

A soft smile accompanied Lydia's light laugh in return. "That's right. I'm impressed that you heard your mother and me talking. You weren't even inside."

"Nope. I was out back. That's 'cause I got *super*-hearing. Daddy says my hearing is so good I hear cuss words from fishermen way out on their boats." The man and the girl grinned at each other, then Katie leaned toward Lydia and whispered loudly. "That's not true. I learned them from Daddy."

"Daddy's" cheeks flushed from embarrassment, and Lydia's did the same, only from her attempt to stifle outright laughter. She let the screen door slap behind her as she walked to the porch steps. "You're Bess's husband? Katie's right. I was at the store. Saturday. Before coming here. And I really am one of the owners. Thom and Lynn are my brother and sister-in-law. I didn't tell them I was coming. I'd appreciate it if you didn't either. At least not for now."

The man regarded her with silence, then gave a nod of acceptance. He walked to the steps and extended a hand. "I'm Dave Conklin. Thom has me keep an eye on the place, always notifies me before anyone comes, so I can turn on the utilities. Otherwise I come by at random times, just to make sure no one's broken in."

"Oh, I assure you I didn't break in. I can show you my keys," Lydia said going down the steps to retrieve more groceries. "I've got to finish putting things away. You're welcome to come in and see that everything is okay."

Dave reached into the trunk. "We'll help carry these things in. Katie, come give us a hand."

Inside, Lydia watched Dave as she emptied the bags they had piled on the kitchen table. From the doorway he studied the great room, then moved to the hall, glancing into the bedroom she was using and into the bath. Katie meandered, peering at photos, murmuring as if in conversation with the people in them, so long gone. When Dave returned to the kitchen, Lydia said, "Your daughter has a storyteller's heart."

Like a cat that's in one place and suddenly in another, Katie was beside her dad. "I get stories in my head all the time." Pride was in her voice before she uttered a dramatic sigh. "What is *soooo* frustrating is trying to write them down, because I can't always make my letters right."

Dave stroked his daughter's head. "Bit of dyslexia. We homeschool so she gets more attention than in a classroom with thirty other kids. Besides, who'd put a little pumpkin like this out into a forty-below wind chill to catch a bus in the dead of winter?"

Katie ducked from under her dad's hand, yanked a chair from the kitchen table, and climbed onto it on her knees. Peering into the remaining bags, she said, "And kids in my grade have one teacher. I get two. It's not so boring. But the *other* kids get to get away from *their* teachers when school is out." She shot a mock glower at her dad.

Dave laughed. "Oh yeah, you've got it so tough. There's always that bus next winter, kiddo. We're the ones who have it tough, putting up with you twenty-four seven." He turned to Lydia. "This whole area is a great classroom, though. The lake and the woods for the sciences—"

Katie interrupted. "And I get to build things on my dad's construction projects. I already know geometry, don't I, Dad? And he's teaching me computer programming too. We're making an app for a new game and I'm going to sell it for a gazillion million hundred dollars."

"She is learning geometry," Dave said, grinning, "but her concept of money and abstract theories still need some work. So, how long are you staying?"

Lydia shook her head as she closed a cupboard door. "I'm not sure. I've got some abstract theories of my own I need to work through." She reached for another grocery bag. "So, your wife said you opened the store a few years ago."

Dave raised his eyebrows at her first statement but accepted the change of subject. "Five years ago. Lost my job in IT when the economy went bad, then Bess lost her job too. And then we lost the house. We were lucky to have the property from her great-uncle. It took a while to adjust to living up here. Now neither of us would trade what we've got here to move back down below the bridge just for more money." Dave straightened himself up from the doorjamb where he'd been leaning. "Time for us to get out of your hair. I take it you got everything turned on okay? If you've got something to write on, I'll leave our number in case you need anything."

Walking them to their car, Lydia said, "There are two things you could do for me. Next time you catch an extra walleye, consider it sold?"

Dave smiled. "You got it. Cleaned, filleted, and delivered. What's the second?"

"That you promise not to say anything to Thom. Not yet, please."

Dave opened the car door and stared at her as he got in. “For now. But he’ll have questions when he sees the next electric and water bills.”

“Thanks. I promise I’ll tell him, later. And that I asked you not to.”

Dave pointed to the west and Lydia turned to look out over the lake. Charcoal gray clouds, hanging low, were rolling in. “Best get the last of your things inside. I’d say you’ve got about twenty minutes before the rain hits.”

Lydia watched them disappear around the curve of the drive. The sound of tires faded. Utter stillness engulfed her. No sound of birds, not even the water lapped at the shore. The world seemed to echo her emptiness and tension. Then a low rumble growled and a sharp, chill wind stung her skin. Lydia shuddered, her stupor broken. She lifted the last bags from the car, slammed the trunk closed, and let the screen door slap behind her.

Chapter 5

Rain cascaded through the night, the storm bellowing thunder and spitting lightning, subsiding to a steady rain and then roiling up again like the armies of the gods in battle. Turmoil tossed Lydia in bed as if she were in an oarless boat far from the haven of shore. The storm within her was worse than the one outside. When she did sleep, it was fitful—she knew this when thunder woke her, twisted in the bedclothes. When she lay awake, unable to settle her restless body, the thunder could not drown out the relentless cacophony in her mind. She hurt so. She hated Gil. She loved him. She needed him. She needed to lay her head on his chest, whisper her pain into his breath, ask him how to make the hurt go away, ask him what she should do next. She needed him to comfort her. How could she get past the fact that the one person she needed most was the one who'd hurt her the most, had betrayed her and now could not be trusted? The pillow she hugged became damp with tears.

Morning had to come sometime, she supposed. When it did, the sun did not cut through the day's gloom, and exhaustion sapped Lydia like an unbroken fever. She got up to sip water and stare blankly at the cross-whipped whitecaps on the lake, her mind distant, washed out. She returned to bed—for how long she neither knew nor cared. All she knew was the chair at the kitchen table, the glass of water, the bed, and the utter emptiness. Rain continued again through the night, quieter now, a constant drizzle. Lydia was barely aware of the hours, yet they seemed interminable. If she slept, she didn't know it. She lay staring, unseeing, into the dusk-shrouded bedroom or out at the lake, its color as dark as her soul. Sometime during the second night she was finally aware of the silence. The rain had stopped.

Memories, and questions, now cascaded through her mind. Why had she come here—to this place that for so many summers had felt like an annual prison—to find escape? She had loved summers at the lake and the lodge as a child, the seemingly endless days to swim, wander, play, and revel in Grandma Tilde's unconditional love. But the lodge also meant work, and she'd spent summers toiling alongside Grandma and her mom and various aunts from the time she could wield a broom or strip a bed, doing traditional woman's work while her brothers were tasked with learning the skills of the men's world. By the age of ten, Lydia questioned Grandpa George's decree that men never did women's work but the women were expected to pitch in with the men whenever extra hands were needed. She hid her resentment of the extra work, because Grandpa did not cotton to children questioning authority. He called his bevy of grandchildren, underfoot all summer, his "troops" and commanded them much the same way he had ordered men about during World War II. One thing Lydia remembered puzzling over was that, for someone who did not consider women equal to men, he had expected from her, his only granddaughter, what he expected from his grandsons: the ability and determination to face what needed to be done, deal with it without complaint, and do a job right the first time. His image arose in her mind. *Lord*, she thought, *he'd have my head if he could see me in bed at this hour, let alone for two days straight*.

The summer before she started junior high, she became deeply familiar with something else, just as she had the chores: isolation. She missed her friends, all home doing summer things together, going to camp, going on family vacations to places she only read about. She envied them when it came time to write that always dreaded first-week-of-school report, "What I Did on My Summer Vacation." Once, she asked her mom why she didn't get to go to camp, why their family never took a vacation. Her mom's lilting laugh let Lydia know she was being silly even before she answered with a question of her own. "How long do people come stay at the lodge?"

Puzzled, Lydia answered. "A week. Sometimes two."

"Right. Because that's all the vacation they get. And the kids who go to camp? Camp lasts a week, two at most. We are on vacation all summer, and you, my dear daughter, are at camp for three months."

Lydia hadn't quite seen it that way.

By then, she'd also learned to be reticent with the children who came to the lodge, to be cautious about forming friendships. The sadness of saying goodbye when they left was not worth abandoning herself to the quick bond of intense closeness that young girls are capable of.

Summer after summer's long nights, she longed to be with friends, to have a boyfriend, to have things to do that took her away from the always-present grown-ups. *They* went out—Thursday night was their party night at the Beers & Belts Bar in Nibic; *they* laughed and talked late into the night over fast-slapping card games. Lydia existed in suspension between childhood's blissful acceptance of the unknown and adulthood, where, she had thought, all the answers were known. *God*, she thought now, *would that were true*. If only life came with a handbook, one where she could turn to an index, look up "adultery," scan the list of subcategories, turn to the page referenced under "solutions for," follow the instructions, and the problem was fixed.

The worst summer, though, had been her final one at the lodge, how the loneliness was greater than ever before after she had tried, and failed, not to fall in love with Gil. How she wished now she had succeeded. There wouldn't be this pain. No, a voice deep within her said, there would be pain, just of another sort, as no life is without pain. She had, somehow, endured that summer before senior year away from Gil, knowing it would be her last working at the lodge. It was the end of her commitment to her grandparents. When she had been accepted into the University of Chicago, she'd screwed up her courage and phoned Grandpa George, asking for a loan to cover the cost of books and promising to get a part-time job at school to pay him back. He flat out refused. Deflated, she listened to his lecture on why no one should ever lend money to a family member. It was his ironclad rule, he said; he'd never broken it before and he sure wasn't going to start now, no matter how proud he was of her achievement. Then she endured another lecture, this one about how she'd better get rid of any notions about working, especially during her freshman year—her more-than-fulltime job was to be studying, period. "Got that?" he asked. When she mumbled a desultory, "Yes sir," he said, "Good. Then I got a proposition for you."

That summer, he hired her to be the staff at Castle Berry Lodge. Her grandmother was getting up in years, as he put it, and needed the help of someone younger. Recalling the conversation now, Lydia did some quick figuring and smirked—she was older now than her grandmother had been then. He would pay her full-time wages and offered an amount far more generous than she'd be able to earn at any other summer job. She was to be her grandmother's assistant, seven days a week, no set hours, which meant she was to be on call whenever needed. "Down time's yours to do with as you please," he had said. "As long as most of its spent getting a leg up on your studies. Do we have a deal? And bear in mind, I'll fire you if you ever slack off. Granddaughter or not."

What he was offering was the same role that had been expected of her every summer in the past. It meant four more summers of isolation but now with pay. It meant she'd earn enough to not have to take a job at school. Lydia had gushed her response. "Yes, yes, *yes*. Oh, thank you, Grandpa. I promise I'll earn every cent." Then she said something she hadn't said since she was in first grade. "I love you, Gramps."

There was an empty beat before he gruffly answered, "Yeah, okay. I expect you here the Friday after high school graduation. You will start bright and early"—he had emphasized early—"on Saturday. Now put your father on the phone. Got some things I want to tell him."

The pay had made the summers palatable, until that last one. Gil so consumed her thoughts that her grandmother often became frustrated with Lydia's mistakes. Concentrating on her reading was difficult, too. Nights were spent in longing, her body aching for his. She wrote him almost daily. His letters, sporadic, became almost a form of cruelty: her anticipation of them was constant, and there were never enough. On the daily run into Nibic's post office, she searched for his handwriting on envelopes. She tried not to hope too much, but every day when no letter came, her spirits, and her shoulders, sagged. When there was one, she nearly danced back to the car. She never opened his letters then, instead saving them to read at night, after she was alone. Tucked into her pocket, the missive would entice her for the rest of the day, throwing her into sporadic body rushes that arced through her like orgasms. But the climax never came. The letters were always too short, leaving her wanting more, no matter how often she read them to see what he might have said between the lines.

The twelve weeks of that summer had felt like twelve months. On the Friday she left for Chicago, Grandma Tilde had been upset with her for leaving without breakfast. She drove fast, as fast as she dared push her old car and the speed limit, each mile taunting her with how many more were left to go. It was rush hour when she reached Chicago. Every slow-down and stoplight frazzled her, as if they were personal affronts. Then the frustration of not being able to find a parking spot on her block, and two long treks to carry her things to the fourth-floor walk-up she'd agreed to rent, sight unseen, with a roommate she'd never met. Then the awkward introductions and the disorientation that came with being in an unfamiliar space. But it all lifted the moment she picked up the phone and called Gil. Her mouth had been desperate for the feel of his, but to hear his voice would get her through another hour or two until she could kiss him. He hadn't answered. Neither had his roommate. She called again and again and again, until disappointment and exhaustion sent her to bed in tears late that night.

In the morning she called once more, hesitation having replaced anticipation. When Gil answered, his voice, still husky from sleep, brightened at her softly spoken "Hi."

"Babe! You about to hit the road? What time do you think you'll be back? Call me as soon as you are. I want to see you."

They'd had a spat. He insisted that she wrote she'd be returning Saturday, not Friday. He swore it was an honest mix-up. Then she'd heard a voice call out his name, a girl's faint voice. When Lydia asked who was with him, he stammered—it was someone Brian had brought home, he'd never met her before, Brian was out getting bagels, she was looking for coffee cups, that's all. Something wasn't right, Lydia knew. Still, she loved him, so she believed him. She told him so. He whispered that he loved her too.

After she hung up, it dawned on her: that voice. It sounded a lot like the whiny girl who'd been in the group the night of their first date.

The whole day had dragged on like an ache she couldn't soothe. Neither spoke when she opened the door at his knock. She melted into his kiss as if her bones were dissolving. When the kiss ended, when she stopped swaying from dizziness, when she could open her eyes again, she took his hand, drew him across the apartment into her room, and closed the door. She glimpsed her new roommate watching from the kitchen and heard her murmur, "Well, I'll be damned."

Damned. That's how she felt right now. No one ever thought about red flags back then, but looking back now, she wondered if she'd ignored pink ones. The girl warning her how he went through women. The whiny voice she'd heard in the background on the phone that day. Others over the years of marriage. All dismissed. Because she'd been young, stupid, naïve, in love. Because she wanted to believe him when he said she was the only one, all he needed. Because Gil always turned on the charm until he convinced her she was wrong. Hadn't she damned herself into a hell of her own making? No, it was a hell of Gil's making.

A scream outside and a flash of a shadow across the window jolted Lydia. Her body spun to a sitting position, her feet on the chilled floor, her hands gripping the edge of the bed. It was a death scream, her primal brain knew, like the scream of a rabbit speared by a hawk's talons. She breathed, then breathed again, deeper and slower. The sudden, fear-induced tension subsided and clarity returned. She reached for the robe entangled at the foot of the bed and slipped it on. Cold tiles stung her feet as she walked into the bathroom, and she almost relished the icy sharpness—the first physical sensation she was aware of after so much wallowing and mental pain. The rabbit wasn't swift enough to escape death from the hawk. If she didn't move, she realized, there was no hope of escape from her pain. She needed to move, move fast, move hard, to exert herself to the point where she would be beyond caring about the pain.

She brushed her teeth so hard her gums bled, but the sting of the toothbrush mattered. She needed to *feel*. Setting the coffee to brew, she glanced out at the lake. Its surface was smooth and the day crystal clear. She picked up the new cell phone from the counter and turned it on. Ignoring the pings of a half-dozen texts—all from Audra, she knew—Lydia punched in the number written on a slip of paper she'd tacked to the kitchen message board. "Dave? It's … it's L. I could use a hand getting a rowboat out. And the porch furniture … In about an hour? Thanks." Before turning off the phone she texted Audra without reading her messages: I'm ok. Will b in touch. Promise.

By the time Dave drove up, Lydia had eaten, dressed, and packed a light lunch and thermos of water. She had also rooted around the boathouse and found a pair of oars she carried to the shore. Less than an hour after Dave arrived one of the bright red rowboats was secured at the dock. Lydia was casting off even before his truck had headed back down the drive.

It took a few moments of fumbling to gain the rhythm of rowing. Her back to the far shore, Lydia leaned forward pushing the raised oars, then back as she dipped and dragged them against the water's resistance. Nothing but their sound broke the stillness as she stroked hard away from shore. When her shoulder muscles ached and her lungs burned she stopped, letting the oars and the boat float, and turned her awareness outward.

She scanned the shore for the lodge, to fix its location and gauge the current's gentle flow. She was being carried outward. Aware there were no other boats to spot her if she drifted too far out, she turned and rowed closer in. She eased north past some of the small resorts she remembered—the cabins now looked to be privately owned—and houses that had cropped up between them in clearings, cut from what had seemed endless wilderness when she was young. Except at Pines Pointe, she saw no activity. She supposed that wasn't unusual, it being midweek and not yet summer season. Just as she had for most of her years here, she wondered how people made a living in the off-season. Everything here depended on tourism—the weekenders and one-weekers and two-weekers who filled cottages and the town during three short months of good weather. She supposed people now came up to cross-country ski or snowmobile. The thought of the incessant drone and roar of revving engines disturbing the winter silence made her grimace.

Rounding the tip of curved land beyond Pines Pointe, the lake became a bit alien to her. It always had been, being out of sight from the lodge and seldom traveled along either by water or car. She sat for a moment, taking in what she could of the lake's northern sweep. For some reason, the woods had never been dense along this part of the shore. Hills rose. Open meadows and lawns covered slopes around new houses, and high grasses wafted beside worn wooden steps set into long sweeps up the hillside. Where the lake curved west, the woods took up again. A smattering of houses, looking as small as Monopoly game hotels, dotted the landscape there.

She wondered about the people behind the closed doors of their homes, and in the resorts when they vacationed. What stories did they hide from the world, from the people they said they loved, from even themselves? No one, she reminded herself, lived a fairytale life. But every life was a fairytale, wasn't it? Because monsters always lurked to disrupt the happily-ever-after. She had been naïve to believe that her happily-ever-after would last forever.

She turned the boat back toward home. Rowing steadily, the rhythm became a meditation that emptied her mind. She breathed out as she lifted the oars forward, breathed in as she dropped them and leaned to pull them back. When the current changed, she drifted once in a while, letting the water carry her closer to home. The blankness of her mind now felt different from the ogre of emptiness that had engulfed her. As she neared the lodge, she changed her mind about going back to shore. Rimming the curve of the small bay past the dock was a half-mile sweep of untouched woods. She rowed along it, and gentled the boat into the shallows.

The sun had crossed its apex, allowing ribbons of light to shimmer on the pale brown sand beneath the water. Lydia felt her movements become as languid as the crystal-clear water surrounding her. For a moment, she let the oars float and trailed her hand in the bracing water. She wished it were warm enough for swimming, but knew winter's residual cold would linger at least another month. As a child the lure of immersing herself was so great that she never cared when her skin became as blue as her bathing suit. She'd dash to shore from the cold bath to shiver in a huge towel until the sun warmed her, and then back in she'd go. Age and too many years accustomed to the sultry Gulf of Mexico no longer made that experience appealing. She wondered if she'd be here long enough for the water to warm and provide the lake's baptismal grace.

She had been alone for days now but the solitude on the water was different. The howling dervishes of her primal mind were silent. Their whirl had been draining, leaden, black, and bleak. Now, there was calm. Thoughts could never be stilled, but here they flitted lightly, hovered, and then darted off like the occasional dragonfly that seemed to appear from nowhere, hang in mid-air for a moment as if studying her, and then whisk away. One landed on the collar of an oar. Without moving, Lydia turned her eyes to look at it, not wanting to scare it off before its rest was through. It shimmered iridescent blue in sunlight, deep purple when a leaf's shadow dappled from above. Undulating gently, its wings seemed like delicate lace tatted of a spider's silk. *Sewing bugs*, Lydia thought, as the old words came unbidden. She'd been so frightened of dragonflies as a child. She'd believed her uncle Frank, before she understood he was a merciless tease, when he told all the kids that sewing bugs were called that because they'd stitch up children's lips together if they talked too much. Lydia realized that old wives' tale, repeated so often as a joke, had set her to silencing herself around others. How odd, she thought—that there'd been many things that had reinforced silence in her nature, but how odd to look back and pinpoint the origin of a tendency it had taken decades to overcome. Yet, the silencing of herself had always been situational. In school, she'd always been quick to speak up in class. In front of her students, in committee meetings, or before a conference crowd, she was confident. Everywhere else she had felt people would judge her words, or, as she learned the hard way, be used against her by friends who ultimately proved they weren't friends. She'd even learned to silence herself rather than argue with Gil over most things. He always convinced her he was right, even when her niggling doubts had told her otherwise.

The dragonfly lifted, and a blue jay cried in the distance. Lydia took up the oars again. She moved along the edge of the cove, taking in the beauty of the woods. There was no sandy strip between the lake and the trees. Tangled roots, gripping the black soil, jutted like gnarled fingers into the water. The maples with their new leaves, the fully cloaked oaks, and evergreens seemed to proclaim their intention to reclaim the lake for themselves. The water, though, refused to yield to the trees' intimidation. The water was quiet and the trees safe for now, but Lydia knew how storms whipped the waves into a rage that battered and beat back the encroaching army from the land. Their war had existed for millennia, ever since the glaciers had scooped out this place like a swipe from a giant hand, leaving a space for the melting water to linger.

As Lydia rounded the next point, she had to swing the boat out to skim above a tree that had been felled like a sentry on the battlefield, to rot for decades until it too was absorbed by the lake. Just beyond was a half-moon of sandy beach. Lydia drew in a breath of delight. It was a gem of loveliness and seclusion, an ideal place to picnic solo. With a swift, strong pull on the oars, she banked the prow of the boat far enough onto shore to step out without wetting her shoes. That was when she saw the small beach was not as private as she'd thought. Remnants of a bonfire caught her eye. Approaching it, her anger began to rise. Blackened leftovers of burned wood were ringed by rocks. A charred drink can lay in the fire pit's ashes. Smashed beer cans and cigarette butts littered the ground. Rage overtook her. Another violation against her—first by her husband, now by faceless others who believed they had a right to her land.

A white plastic grocery bag, entangled on a low branch, flapped in the wind like a mocking smirk. Lydia yanked it away. She filled it, and tossed it near the boat. The rocks she scattered into the trees, then stomped the ashes and burned chunks into the earth. When she finished, winded, her shoes, pants, and hands were covered in dirt and soot.

At the back of the clearing, Lydia spotted a footpath and followed it. Behind a small stand of trees was another clearing. The ground showed vehicles had parked there, crushing the growth. Rutted marks led into the dense woods. Lydia walked the route the interlopers had snaked out between trees and brush their tires couldn't mow down. Her anger rose like the mosquitoes that swarmed from the still of the trees to her sweat, the bugs adding to her ire as she swatted the buzzing air around her face and head. When the mosquitoes got too intense Lydia gave up and retreated, long before she found the makeshift road's exit. At the beach opening, the mosquitoes left her, pushed back into their shadowy domain by the lake breeze.

Anger gave way to disgust as Lydia dumped the trash from the grocery bag into the boat and tied the bag to a sapling where it could be spotted from the water. She kicked off her shoes and waded into the icy water to loosen the prow from the shore and climb aboard. In her mind's eye, she saw the night partiers who were sneaking onto and destroying *her* land.

Every one of them had Gil's face.

***

After emptying the boat of trash and then showering, Lydia turned on the new phone and dialed Dave. Voicemail picked up, adding to her frustration. "Dave, this is L … Elle, over at the Casselberry lodge. A bunch of idiots have a party site on our land. And it looks like it's been there a long time. Call me." She clicked off and the phone's pings of downloading texts resumed. The time showed four-fifteen. *So what*, she thought, *it's five o'clock somewhere*. She was ready for a drink, but she also needed to think, and to deal with Audra's texts. After making a small pot of coffee, she filled a mug and added a generous slosh of scotch. She carried the phone and coffee to the chair outside in the shade.

Audra had texted numerous times over the past three days. Most were almost identical—she was worried, she wanted Lydia to call. Lydia wanted to, too, longing to hear her friend's voice, but she wasn't yet ready for the solicitousness she'd be subjected to. Besides, right now Audra would be busy at the store. She texted back: All ok. Call u Sun, usual time? Late Sunday afternoons were when they had their gabfests, along with a cocktail, catching up on their week, talking books, gossiping, grousing about politics—all the things that stitched their friendship into an ever-lengthening quilt of comfort. Seconds later an incoming ping: Yes! Oh yes! So worried. Whew! Lydia sent back one last text: Pls don't worry. TTYT@4. As she typed, another message from Audra popped up: BTW no word from G. Lydia frowned. They'd both expected Gil would call Audra when Lydia didn't return home before Monday. Maybe he didn't want to subject himself to Audra's anger—he'd have to know that Lydia wouldn't keep her discovery of the affair a secret from her. Maybe, she thought, maybe he just didn't give a damn that she was gone.

Before her thoughts could go further, the phone rang, startling her until she noticed the local area code. Dave. He listened without a word as she told him of the party beach, the trash she'd brought back, her aborted quest to follow the wheel ruts into the woods. "Look, I'm not against people having fun, but not when it involves trespassing. Something goes wrong, they could set fire to the whole woods. Or something happens to someone? We'd be liable."

"You're right," Dave said. "Maybe even me too, since I'm contracted with your brother. Since you know where this place is, could you meet me there tomorrow? Around ten? If you row over I'll be able to spot you from my boat."

Morning brought gray skies again but no rain, along with a wind that made rowing difficult against choppy waters. As she crested the point of the cove she noticed a speck of a white speedboat bouncing her way from the distance. Knowing no boat larger than hers could be pulled onto the beach, she held the rowboat off shore. When the speedboat appeared around the bend, it slowed. Dave waved from behind the wheel as he scanned the lake bottom for depth. He shut off the motor and tossed an anchor over the side. "Good morning," Lydia called out as she tried, unsuccessfully, to draw alongside. By her fourth attempt, Dave was laughing at her unskilled maneuvers and Lydia's embarrassment had given way to laughter as well.

"Get close enough to throw me a line," he called. Lydia scrambled over the seat to pull a coiled rope from under the prow, then struggled to maneuver near enough to sling it to him.

"Nice pitch," he hollered as he caught it and pulled her boat alongside. After wrapping it around a cleat, he said, "Now, the aft line." When the rowboat was secured alongside his, he said, "Move to the bow so I can get in without dumping us over." He lowered himself from the speedboat that sat several feet higher in the water. After they loosed the ropes, Dave took the oars and, with a few powerful strokes, drove the rowboat high enough onto the sand for them to step out. He pulled it up further before following Lydia to the fire pit she had kicked in. "Shit," he muttered, then turned to Lydia. "Sorry."

"Hey, nothing to be sorry about. That's mild compared to my reaction to what these douches are up to." Lydia waved a hand dismissively at Dave's raised eyebrows. "I spend all day around college students. Believe me, my repertoire extends well beyond George Carlin's seven words. And I know how to use them as all eight parts of speech."

Dave chuckled and shook his head. "Okay, mosquitoes are going to get thick. Did you put on repellent?" When Lydia said she'd forgotten to buy any he pulled a bottle from his jacket pocket. "Hold your breath and close your eyes." He sprayed her head, face, and neck. "Hold out your hands." More spritzes as he doused her, front and back, head to toe. "Okay. Let's see where these guys are getting in."

It took a moment for Lydia to find the narrow footpath. In the clearing, marked by tires, Dave stopped and turned his head in counterclockwise ticks. "Jesus, they must have some big parties. They can get a good dozen vehicles packed in here." He strode ahead on the rutted route with a muttered, "Bastards."

Lydia hurried to keep up with the younger man, watching her own footing closely as she stepped along the torn-up dirt—the last thing she needed was a twisted ankle or knee. She was glad she'd bought black tennis shoes in Chattanooga, because they were soon coated in muck that would leave stains no amount of scrubbing could remove. Dave, in heavy boots, moved steadily, pausing for her to catch up whenever the road took a hard angle.

Sunlight filtered over the makeshift road but the wooded dusk engulfed them on either side. Lydia kept her eyes on the ground, glancing up only when the path was smooth. The dark bark of trees firmly rooted in dark soil, the rotting corpses of fallen limbs, the decaying logs on the bog-like land, and the occasional birdcall took on a sinister air in Lydia's imagination. The farther she and Dave went, the more the route zigzagged through the incessant hordes of mosquitoes.

"Dave?"

"Um-hmm." He looked over his shoulder as he kept walking.

"Are there bears out here?"

"Probably. But unless there's a fish in your pocket, don't worry."

Crap, Lydia thought as she stumbled a bit on a dirt clump. "Probably" wasn't exactly reassuring.

With the sun obscured over the winding route, she lost her sense of direction, not knowing whether they were heading east, west, north, south. Unease tensed her shoulders. She again felt lost, abandoned, engulfed, unable to escape. *Why?* she asked herself. She wasn't alone; Dave was only steps ahead. Sooner or later—although God only knew when—they would emerge from the woods. She just had to keep going, keep going through the oppressive closeness she felt was going to smother her.

A mental flash stopped her, and she gave out a single syllable of loud laughter. Dave turned, his face quizzical. "It's nothing." Lydia fluttered a hand. He kept walking, slipping out of view around another bend.

She stood stock-still. The metaphoric absurdity was now so obvious. She had delivered herself into the heart of the hero's journey. Forced against her will, she had run—run into the unknown. And now she was literally in the deep dark woods. Going where? Forward? To what? Going back was possible, but impossible. She looked back along the path they had come. Another realization struck: that the truth of the Bible story of Lot's wife was not that she had turned into a literal pillar of salt when she looked back, but had cried herself to death, the salt of her tears corroding her soul and hardening her heart, unable to allow happiness or love into her life again. Looking back, Lydia thought, wanting what was, what had been, would devour her too. Better to find the golden key, unlock the forbidden door, and somehow use whatever was behind it to escape. She wasn't imprisoned by Gil, she was her own captor and would remain so unless she faced the truth—whatever it was, no matter how monstrous.

"Found it!" Dave's distant voice startled her. "Hey, Elle?"

"Coming," she yelled back. Her steps now firm and sure, she hurried. Long strides and two more turns between trees too large for trucks to mow down led her to spot him. A car passed behind him and he turned to wave at it as she emerged onto the gravel shoulder of the road.

"This is it," Dave said. "It might be on the Brickell property, though, not yours. I'll have to get the survey from Thom, or have the county pull it for me, to be sure."

Her back to the pavement, Lydia studied the opening. It was about six feet wide, appearing as normal as any other natural break in the wooded growth. "Good lord. How do they manage to even spot the turnoff," she marveled.

"Crafty bastards. See this?" Dave motioned with a foot. Nearby, less than a yard from the ground, a small red reflector was attached to a tree. Cars speeding by at night might not even notice it. Dave pointed up the tree. "There's another one. I suppose that's for snowmobilers to spot when the drifts are high. First thing we can do is get rid of those." He reached into a pocket, drew out a folded knife, and opened its prying blade. It took several minutes to work the nails loose. He slipped the pieces into a jacket pocket.

As he snapped the knife shut, Lydia asked, "Don't you need to be able to find this from the road again? We're so far between the lodge drive and the Brickell's, that's going to be difficult."

"Hmmm … yeah." He looked around, as if scanning for some sort of landmark. "Maybe we can find a log to drag out here. That might work."

"Hey, wait." Lydia pulled the twisted plastic grocery bag from one of her pockets. "This is what I tied at the beach site so I could spot it again."

"Perfect." Dave flapped open the bag and knotted it around a limb of a bush. "Don't want it too close to the lane or the road. For now, it'll look like a piece of litter if anyone notices."

More sure of her footing on the walk back, Lydia kept up with him. She appreciated that he wasn't garrulous, but asked him about his family and their lives, and about names and places she remembered from decades ago. Many he didn't recognize. Lydia realized the village and people she'd known had stood still in time only in her mind. It saddened her—another adjustment to make, another shift to get accustomed to. Had she really thought time would stand still here, she wondered. The places of her memory had all changed. She had, too, and now had to change again.

She told Dave of the history she knew. How the land had come down from her grandmother's father. After her grandparents died, their sons and daughters put the land in a trust so it would pass down to their kids. "Thom bought out all of our cousins," she said. "But I still own my share. I don't know why. My son and daughter barely remember the place. They're Floridians, even though they don't live there anymore. My husband never liked coming up here. In fact, the last time I was up, I brought the kids by myself. Gil's been after me to sell to Thom for years." Her mind went blank for a moment. It was the first time she'd said his name aloud since leaving Tampa.

"Sometimes," David said as their boats came into view, "we just need to hang onto something that will always mean home. I understand that now, living up here. Bess and I weren't thrilled to do it, but it was either that or live out of our car. Which we probably would have done—for a while, at least—if we hadn't had Katie. She was two years old then. This has always been her home. And it's come to mean that to Bess and me."

Home, Lydia thought as they reached the shore. She couldn't return to the comfort of her mother's embrace, or her grandmother's, but she had returned to the embrace of the land, the trees, the lake. "You're a very wise young man," Lydia said softly.

Dave glanced at his wristwatch. "Forty-five minutes." Lydia looked at him, her face questioning. "Took us forty-five minutes to walk back from the road. Means they've carved a route a good two miles long. Likely to take me most of the summer to make it impassable." Hands in his pockets, Dave studied the open space and its placement in the cove. "Okay, let's go. We'll tow your boat back to the lodge."

The chop of the water and the boat's motor made it impossible to talk without shouting so they remained quiet until slowing near the lodge dock. Tying up the rowboat, Dave scanned the western sky. The day was still overcast and a darker line was perceptible above the far shore. He looked at his watch again. "Good. Looks like Max and I will be able to do some fishing. Storm's moving in, but not till tonight."

"Boy, you've gotten that good at reading the weather?" Lydia was impressed.

He laughed as he stepped onto his boat. "Nah. Watched the weather report at breakfast. Just looks like the forecast is right for once." His hand grasped the boat key but he hesitated before turning on the motor. "Say, how'd you like to come to our fish fry Monday? It's become an annual Memorial Day thing for us. I'm sure Bess and Katie would like that. Starts around noon." He gave her a big grin. "Lasts until the beer runs out."

"Thanks. I don't know. I'll think about it." She started to head down the dock, then turned back toward his boat. "Uh, Dave," she said over the low spit of the motor, "the L. It stands for Lydia. I might as well tell you that before Thom does. But please, let's leave it as Elle, as far as everyone else is concerned?"

He smiled and gave her a nod as the boat moved into gear.

"And I will call Thom," she hollered. "Let him know I'm here, before you do. So could you wait until tomorrow to call him?"

"Will do," he yelled back over the revving motor, and waved as he steered north.

Back inside, Lydia changed into clean clothes and tossed her dirty ones, shoes included, into the washing machine. Digging through the pantry, she found a tray to carry a late lunch out to the Adirondack chair. Eating, she studied the lake, its openness hiding nothing, the opposite of the woods where she'd been, where dangers seemed to lurk, at least in the mind, because they couldn't be seen. Again her anger rose over the violation of "her" land, land she held emotional deed to. Someone—no, she corrected herself, a lot of someones—had used what was hers for their own surreptitious pleasure. *Just like that bitch who's taken up with Gil,* Lydia thought. Lydia's husband wasn't hers, but that slut hadn't given a damn about violating Lydia's rights. And Gil: he was as guilty as the beach partiers. Like them, he thought he could keep his violation—of her, the land of her body and their marriage—a secret.

But ... what if that other woman didn't know he was married? Wedding rings slipped off as easily as pants. He could be lying to her too. Still, that didn't absolve the woman in the least, as far as Lydia was concerned.

For two weeks now, Lydia had been running, as if it would do any good. Running from the beast of betrayal was impossible—it would always pursue her. She had to turn toward it, face it, and vanquish it. She wouldn't have had the guts to walk the rutted road through the woods without Dave; this, she knew, she had to do alone.

She set her tray aside and leaned back. The thin charcoal line of clouds silhouetted the horizon like the black crayon outline of a children's coloring book picture. Small whitecaps bobbed, stirred by the breeze, but the sun acted on her like a gentle massage. She closed her eyes. Her mind was a little calmer, having reached at least her first decision, and she slipped into sleep.

Chapter 6

Dusk. The sun had not set but simply shut itself off behind the deepening swath of clouds. After a day of slow warning from far off, the clouds were rising rapidly, ominous in their spread eastward like a roll of gray carpet about to cover everything below. Streaks of lightning splayed above the coil, skating across its upper edge. The wind was quickening, mercifully driving the mosquitoes back into the depth of the trees. From the pace of the clouds' approach, Lydia figured she had fifteen or twenty minutes before the rain arrived. She took a sip of her scotch and lit the last cigarette she'd brought. She wished she had something stronger to smoke—a desire she hadn't had in years. She was glad she didn't have it, and that she'd watered down her whiskey. She needed to keep a clear head. At least for now.

A check of the time on her phone showed that it was almost late enough to begin the computer work she had decided to do. In the meantime, she called Thom, telling him she was at the lodge but lying about why, saying an unexpected sabbatical was letting her work on a project and, on a whim, had decided to do it here, where she could focus without anyone bothering her. He accepted that, although she detected a tinge of concern in his voice. But that gave way to anger when she told him about the party site, that she and Dave had followed the route to the main road, that she'd asked Dave to wait on calling him so she could do it first. She had to talk Thom out of changing his holiday weekend plans and coming up right away, reminding him she wanted to focus on her work, insisting that Dave would do what was needed, that Thom could do nothing more.

She then texted with Audra, first to reassure her that she was okay. Audra still had not heard from Gil. Lydia supposed it was possible he'd been trying to call or text her, and with her regular phone shut off she wouldn't know. She didn't care enough to turn it on to see if there were messages. Or maybe he was using her absence as time to play around. But, if he didn't know when she might reappear, would he dare?

Or maybe he was on another of his constant client junkets. That, too, had widened the breach between them, the fact that he now was home only two or three days a week. He'd always traveled—usually an overnight trip or for occasional conferences, photo shoots, or tapings that took him someplace for a week. Back before the economic downturn, she'd often taken vacation days to accompany him, so they could enjoy a bit of off-time together.

That had stopped, but with the economic recovery he began traveling more often. He said it was a good thing, it meant more business, the yearslong dry spell was over, that he had to take every advantage possible, but they still couldn't afford for her to join him. Now, she grimaced as she remembered her complaints that he was home just long enough for her to launder his underwear. And that when he was home it seemed he spent all his time either at the agency, holed up in his home office dealing with a perpetual pile-up of paperwork, or playing golf. When she had told him, repeatedly, how she missed his company, he said he knew, he missed hers too, but it couldn't be helped. He said things would change when the money got better. When she suggested they take a weekend off—their monthly getaways were still a thing of the past—he always had a reason to say no. When she asked about going along on his trips, he said there was still too much debt to pay off. They never entertained anymore, either. The rare times they went out were when she pressured him to attend a university function or when one of his clients hosted an event.

Those parties he reveled in, had from his very first job. So much so that it seemed he forgot she was with him. It hurt, early in their marriage, when he'd disappear into the crowd and she would watch him laughing and chatting with one pretty woman after another. They'd argue afterward, her jealous, him insisting he was only schmoozing, networking, building business connections. She had eventually given up trying to stay at his side, and learned to wander about the room with a smile on her face, a drink in her hand, and "I'm Gil Carlson's wife" on her lips—especially with the comely young women who tried to catch his eye. But from the start he'd never made any attempt to engage in any of her functions. She learned to turn a deaf ear to his complaints of "another wasted night listening to One-Topic Wandas and Brainiac Bills." It had gotten worse in the last few years, with Gil insisting that all he wanted was "a peaceful night at home, damn it, before I have to leave again."

When he had stopped telling her where he was headed next, it took her a while to notice. When she pointed it out, he said he hadn't even realized that. He said he would do better to keep her informed. When he didn't, Lydia had to insist he give her his month's schedule, because not having it was too disruptive to her own. On occasion, later, he'd say something that made her realize his plans had changed, but that he hadn't let her know, even though he always called her every evening.

By now, the arcs of lightning over the lake were closer, and most of the lake, all of the distant shore trees, had melted into the dark beneath the star-shuttering clouds. Thunder began, and grew louder. Lydia stubbed out her cigarette and carried it and her drink toward the lodge. Hard, fat drops stung her as she reached the porch steps.

Inside, she switched on lights—one over the kitchen sink before refilling her glass with ice and another splash of scotch, and another, a bedside lamp, so she could find her tote and the laptop again. In the great room, the glow from the kitchen cast shadows ahead as she went to the rolltop desk against the far wall, where she pulled the slender chain on the green-shaded banker's lamp. Her fingers lingered on the beaded chain, slipping down its delicate links, then brushed the brass neck and circular stand. She half-felt Grandma Tilde seated in the chair, hunched over her ledger book, adding more numbers to the always-growing list of expenses, on good weeks adding to the income page. During her first college summer working at the lodge, Lydia had opened the ledger that she'd never been curious about before. Her grandmother's script and numerals recorded a skeleton history for decades, first in delicate strokes of a fountain pen, then in splotchy ballpoints. Her stomach had tightened, seeing how the sums exposed the narrow difference between the two amounts, her shock at learning how little profit resulted from her grandmother's constant effort at running the lodge.

Lydia drew a deep breath and shook her head a bit to scatter the past. Hard rain now lashed the walls and roof, thunder pounded as if it wanted in, and lightning threatened to create a portal for it to do just that. She wondered if she should wait until the storm passed to power up the laptop, knowing its battery wouldn't last through the hours of work ahead. She didn't want to lose her determination but she also didn't want a power surge to destroy her computer. Maybe, with all the improvements Thom had made, just maybe … *Yes, bingo*, Lydia thought when she noticed a black box on the floor beside a back desk leg. She recognized it as a battery backup and massive surge protector. She connected it to a wall socket, pressed the power switch, and a litany of lights began to pulse and glow on it and the nearby router. The minutes became frustrating as she watched the router's incessant blinking of "no signal."

Maybe the storm would stymie her after all. She got up to check the router's connections, and gave herself a mental dope-slap. *Duh—tech-support's first question: Is it plugged in?* Of course Thom would have disconnected the Ethernet cable. If she had turned on the TV since arriving she'd have realized that. Seconds after connecting it, the router's lights cycled into a steady signal.

The first website she brought up was the account for hers and Gil's cell phone carrier. Once in the billing history, she was surprised to see she had access to all the call logs for the past twelve months. *Good, maybe I'll find a trail there*, she thought. But the slew of pages to review brought a sigh. It looked like she'd have to work a lot of late nights, when Gil wouldn't notice the account was in use. She noticed a tiny PDF icon on the site. *Bingo again*, she thought. Ten minutes later she'd downloaded the call history and logged off the site. She'd be able to study the records at will.

Next, what next, she asked herself. *You know damned well what next*, she chided, *you just don't want to face it*. She tried to center herself with three deep breaths, opened a private window on the search engine, and typed in the name of the woman Gil was cheating with. The first spelling she tried brought nothing, but the second—Marielle Wharton—did. The majority of hits on the first page appeared connected to the same woman, with links to published business articles. After glancing through them, she scrolled back up and clicked the link to a website in the woman's name. The page header announced "The Trade Journal Journalist" beside a photo. Lydia frowned. The image was of a pleasant looking but unspectacular woman who looked to be in her fifties, her jowly face hinting that she might carry some extra weight. She'd expected to find someone much younger, much prettier, much more a threat. Maybe this wasn't the right Marielle Wharton? But a dive into the site convinced her it was. The woman's credits listed more than a score of trade publications, many connected to the businesses and industries of Gil's clients. Calling herself a journalist was a stretch, Lydia thought derisively—more like a PR whore, who spun whatever stories in any direction her clients wanted, full truth or not. Someone good at hiding what needed to be kept hidden. Delving into the handful of other web links, Lydia learned only one other salient point: the woman was married, to a Jon Wharton. *Why was that name familiar*, Lydia wondered. Another quick search and there it was: he was vice president of marketing for a major company Gil had landed as a client late last year. Lydia remembered Gil's cautious optimism in courting the account, their shared jubilation when the contract was signed. It was the largest account he'd acquired since the recession lifted, and they had celebrated over dinner out. She distinctly remembered that night—Gil was in such a good mood, he urged her to splurge on Maine lobster, something she hadn't had in years. *So*, Lydia thought, her hand cupping her mouth, *Gil's screwing this woman one way, and stuck it to her husband in another*.

The thunder and lightning had receded, gradually fading into the distance. So had Lydia's anxiety. She had been trying to hide, in ignorance. Now, she felt rising anger. Again. A glance at the clock when she returned to the kitchen told her it was after eleven. Gil would be off his computer by now, meaning she could access their bank accounts without fear he would know.

She started with the joint household and savings accounts, and with her personal checking account. Everything was as she expected. In the notebook where she'd copied information from Gil's office the night before she left, she paged to his business account numbers. She leaned back in her chair and took a sip of her drink. Passwords. She'd copied those too, and flipped through the pages to find that list. None gave any indication as to what accounts they were connected to, but as she studied them she noticed a pattern. Each began with his three initials, followed by one or more capital letters—I, L, M, V, X—either singular or in a string. It had made no sense to her crazed mind while she was hastily copying them. Now it was obvious: they were Roman numerals. Each of those letter strings was followed by various symbols, letters, or numbers. On a hunch, she leafed back to the bank account list. The last numbers of four passwords matched the final numbers of the phone account and three bank accounts she'd already accessed. Gil would be meticulous that way, she knew. Patterns, he'd always insisted, cut down on time wasted trying to remember things. Staring at the page, another pattern emerged: the letters before the numbers must stand for a bank or credit card account. As for the pattern of letters only, she'd deal with that later. She downed her drink and went to work.

The most logical place to start, she decided, was his business bank. Their personal accounts were with a regional one, but he had set up the business account with a national bank so he could handle transactions anywhere. Scanning the list, she noticed a "wf." Wells Fargo, maybe?

Google took her to the main address. Her first login attempt using his business email address as the user ID and what she thought was the password brought an error message. Lydia sat back for a moment to consider what to do. She reminded herself, what would be the most logical for him? His full name, but with or without his middle initial? Or the agency name? A host of other permutations rose to mind. She dared to make only one more try tonight. Odds were, if she failed three times, it might generate an auto-alert to him. Well, if the first one didn't work, she decided, she'd just have to wait until the next night.

She typed in his full name and took a deep breath. If it was case-sensitive or if spaces were required, she was screwed, as the list of possibilities would grow. She clicked the submit button and held her breath. A new page flashed on the screen and her eyes lit up with satisfaction. Leaning forward on one elbow, she studied it closely and navigated to the account transactions. The current month's payments and deposits went on for three screen pages, in amounts varying from moderate to surprisingly large. As she scrolled back up from the bottom she noticed something that brought her to full attention. Every Friday, there was a transfer of five hundred dollars. Two thousand a month was going where?

She opened the small notebook and copied down the letter and numbers listed after the transfers, and then downloaded all the transaction history. Better to do it now, she decided, rather than chance accessing the account again if other questions came to mind. When she completed that task, she accessed the other three accounts listed. Two she quickly dismissed. Both had substantial deposits on the first and fifteenth, which she surmised were for payroll and tax purposes. The last was the one she was most curious about, the IRA in Gil's name, showing her as co-signer and beneficiary. She had her own IRA, through the university's credit union, and always gave Gil the quarterly reports to review. She tried to remember the last time she'd seen the statement from his retirement account. She couldn't. But here it was, showing that the balance had grown steadily every month, not weekly, and not by two thousand dollars.

Lydia leaned back, still staring at the screen. Where was the money going? Two grand was a lot, when there was supposedly so much they still couldn't afford. It was too much for walking-around cash, not when he used credit cards for everything. What was Gil doing with it? Other than simply hiding it from her.

For now, she decided to concentrate on what she could answer first, the credit card accounts listed in the notebook. She and Gil each had a slew of them, and so did his company. It was tedious and time-consuming to work through them. Her cards, his personal and business cards, car rental and gas cards—*Jesus*, she thought, *is there* any *gasoline company in the country that he doesn't have an account with?* She skipped those, as well as her own, and concentrated on his business accounts. By the time she reached his corporate AmEx account, her vision was swimming and her shoulders ached. The clock on the screen told her it was almost three a.m. No wonder she was exhausted. She closed the laptop and turned off the lights.

***

The morning sun shot a spotlight into the bedroom. Lydia rolled over, burying her head in a pillow, hoping for more sleep. Her body was still tired. Her knees reminded her of the miles she'd walked in the woods yesterday. Her neck ached from being at the computer for so long. She rolled over again, trying to get comfortable. Seconds later, heaving a loud, aggrieved sigh, as if angry with the bed itself, she thrust the covers aside and sat up. Staring at the bright window, she pondered the fruitlessness of last night's efforts. She'd learned nothing. No, not quite true, she reminded herself—the downloaded phone logs might reveal something. But where was that two thousand dollars from the company going every month?

She carried her coffee and a towel outside to swab the wet from her chair. As she sat down, the cold of the wood jolted her. The roulette wheel of words spinning in her head stopped abruptly on one: email. Gil's email. Why hadn't she gone there first?

The lake water's mist was burning off. A fuzziness of fog still shaded the far shoreline behind its mohair gray drape. As a child on days like this, she had imagined the world ended there, as if the world were flat and beyond, lo, there be dragons. Beyond, confusion and uncertainty. Now, she knew, there were dragons. And she was over the edge, suspended mid-air, shrouded in her own gray mist.

Having crested the tallest trees behind her, sunlight struck a scurry of minnow fins, creating a fairy dance of sparkle at the surface of the shallow water. The school of fish moved on, taking the miniature light show with it. Lydia's gaze moved outward again, over the mirror of the lake. That old cliché: It was a mirror, reflecting the firmament above. Even as a kid she had grown tired of it, but if there was any better way to describe it, she hadn't found it. The water was so still it looked as if it could be skated across, to reach the Three Sisters re-appearing from the receding mist again like Brigadoon. Unlike that magical village, the islands, and the land beyond, were real. The lake trusted its existence behind the gray mist. She didn't know if she could, but she had to trust that she too would emerge from the fog that engulfed her.

A warbler chirped from a limb over Lydia and she looked up. What was she going to do with her day? She didn't dare go back into the accounts, not while Gil might access them. In fact, Lydia wondered, what date was it? She'd packed on a Tuesday, that she knew, and counted her movements forward from that. Friday. It was the second Friday since she'd left. Good. Gil always called it quits on office work at four on Fridays. Maybe she could get an earlier start with her computer searches. Unless he was flying home from somewhere. If he was, he always checked his email when he got back to the house. She'd have to think about taking that risk. But there were the phone records she could study. Would they prove Gil had told her the truth, that the affair hadn't been going on long? If so, maybe he meant it when he said he'd do anything to fix their marriage?

Was I a stupid coward for running away, she wondered. What if she'd stayed, stayed right in his face with her anger until they'd both come out on the other side? Lydia unzipped her jacket in the warming air. The band of gray was gone, the islands and the sweep of brilliant green pines along the far shore proved that the world had no ending edge. Reality existed, and she had to face whatever it was. And she wasn't going to do that sitting here.

Lydia left the front door open behind her and cranked the desk window out an inch or two as the computer powered up. She cut up an apple and carried it and fresh coffee back to the desk. One after another the phone log PDFs tiled open on the screen. Her work was methodical, plodding: type the first logged phone number onto a document, copy it to the search engine, find—if she could—and note who it belonged to, repeat, repeat, repeat. The vast majority were business numbers, and many soon became familiar enough to ignore. A good one-third that she searched turned up nothing, except that they were to cell phones. Some of those were repetitious too. The one that showed up most often was the one she now knew by heart, the one that pissed her off every time she saw it on the list: Marielle's.

By the time Lydia noticed the smell of coffee burning on the bottom of the pot in the kitchen, two hours had passed. She was less than halfway through the third month of phone logs. Her shoulders ached again as she lifted her arms to rub the back of her neck. She went to soak the scorched dregs of the coffee pot, thinking that at the rate she was going it could take another twenty hours to work through all fifteen months of his calls. Was the effort worth it? She had the bitch's number. Wasn't that all she needed? What else was there to know? Maybe nothing. Probably nothing. But she had to be sure. She went back to the desk.

Numbers were beginning to swim under her gaze and she began making too many errors, transposing or mistyping them as she copied them into the search field. Her neck and shoulders ached. It was time to quit. Six months down, nine to go. Lydia shut off the computer and looked at the mantle clock across the room. It took a long moment for her vision to sharpen. *Good lord*, she thought—it was going on four. No wonder her mouth felt like she'd chewed sawdust; she hadn't had anything to drink since her morning coffee. Her stiff hip made her wince as she got up. At the kitchen sink, she took long gulps of water, its iciness out of the tap sending a release of pleasure from her throat to her limbs.

She refilled the glass, carried it to the screen door, and stared outside. She'd been oblivious to the pleasantness of the day. She was tired. She needed to do something physical, but what? There was too much of a chop on the lake to trust herself out on the boat. Besides, rowing would only make her shoulders ache more. A long walk would do her good, but didn't appeal to her without mosquito repellant. Isolation was beginning to make her antsy, even though she had no desire for companionship.

That sensation of wanting to climb out of her skin was coming back, but now in a different way. Cabin fever. I need to get away from here for a while, she realized. She could go up to Clar's Corner—she could get repellant there—but wasn't in the mood for conversation with Bess or Katie. Town. She'd been at the lodge nearly a week, and she knew why she hadn't been into Nibic yet. Facing how it had changed, as it surely would have, was going to be another reminder of her lost past. She heaved a sigh. She'd been living with illusions long enough. It was time to shatter another one.

Houses now dotted much of what had been mostly tree land along the five miles into town. But woods maintained their dominance for the mile or so south of the lodge—all Casselberry property—before giving way to a scene designed at a developer's desk. Lots had been cleared. Many of the houses had been designed to look old, almost, but not quite, pulling it off. Lydia slowed the car, trying to figure out what didn't seem right. It was like running into an acquaintance who looked slightly different, but not in a good way. Lips a little too full, cheeks a little too padded, face a little too tight. Evidence of trying, but not quite succeeding, to bring what had passed back to the present. The faux log homes, oversized A-frames, and suburb-style ranch houses seemed inorganic, intrusive to their surroundings. The actual old places she recognized brought names back—that had been the Masseys, with all those kids who were so tall; the Torptons had lived there, a place to be avoided, the missus as mean as the mister. What had been the six-washer laundromat, quite modern when it opened during her teens, now boasted a sign that read "Emporium." Windows had been cut into the former front wall of the squat cinderblock building and were lined with shelves filled with china, kitchenware, and miscellany to lure both treasure hunters and scroungers. The one-room Catholic church, where kneeling space had accommodated barely two dozen worshipers, had been blended into a substantial expansion. *The year-round God business must be good*, Lydia thought, noticing a sign in its drive that directed snowmobiles to parking.

Up ahead, Lydia saw something she never expected to see here: an honest-to-god three-way stoplight, shining red at her approach. Behind it glistened a view of Little Manitahqua Lake. Two cars were waiting for the light to change. The first one blinkered a signal it would tee off to the left—that was the way to the dump, where they'd gone some nights to watch the bears. The Billingsly's old house on that corner was now a visitor's center, with a carved sign that read "Nibic—Gateway to Seney and Tahquamenon Falls." The large yard, where Mr. Billingsley had grown produce to sell and Mrs. Billingsley tended riots of flowerbeds, was paved. As she looked to the right, her eyes widened. The Jensen's store still anchored the intersection, but now sprawled as large as a steamship in port. Four gas pumps replaced the single one that had once been sufficient for the village. The split-log bait and tackle shop in front was still the rich butterscotch brown she remembered. Encircling and overpowering the building, which now seemed toy-like, were three others, metal behemoths filling space that had once been thick woods. A sign on the one facing Lydia read "Snowmobile Storage & Rent." Passing by after the light turned green, she studied the others. Bay doors were open on the two. One revealed stacked boats in storage and engines on floor stands. Pulled into a bay of the third building was a long RV, attached to a tow truck as shiny and imposing as a peacock-proud weightlifter.

Several people moved in and between the buildings and store. She wondered if any of the Jensen boys still owned the place—she knew they'd taken it over after their dad died. None of the men she saw looked even vaguely familiar. If any of the Jensens were among them, time would have changed them as much as it had changed the business. As much as it had changed her.

And as much as it had changed the rest of Nibic. Lydia was grateful that the speed limit hadn't—ten miles per hour allowed her to creep along without frustrating the driver behind her. The old post office, one of the village's first structures—where Lydia had gone so often that her mind reflexively turned the post box's lettered lock to B, and the numbered one to eleven, and saw the door swing open—had been restored as a history center. Behind it sat a more substantial, modern post office, two delivery trucks parked near the back. Places she knew, and didn't, glided past her. The Trading Post, Hanson's Grocery, the Little Lake Gifte Shoppe. Many of the resorts and summer cottages tucked in the narrow span between the town road and the Little Lake's shore remained the same. New businesses surprised her—a dockside restaurant, a sporting goods store, a women's apparel shop with windows showcasing expensive-looking outfits intended for big-city wear and high-toned summer parties. Other old places had new names. The Beer & Belts Tavern was now Doozy's Bar & Grill; a reader board out front proclaimed "Friday Nite Fish Fry—It's Always a Doozy." The handful of side streets climbing hills to her right were still dotted with pleasant houses, many now with front yard signs of invitation to come in—a ceramic studio, a bed-and-breakfast, a weaver's, sundry seasonal cottage industries. It wasn't until she'd reached the crest of the big hill that shock set in. Sug's Restaurant, so ultramodern when it was built and where she'd waited tables part-time as a teen, still thrust its glass front forward like the prow of a ship, but was now the Nibic Arts and Cultural Center. Lydia pulled into its circular drive to read the broadsheets and flyers attached to the window expanse. They announced classes, group meetings, a week-long writer's retreat, audition and rehearsal dates for two summer productions, and a notice that read "Arts & Crafts Fair—

Every Sunday July thru Labor Day." She marveled at the idea that this sleepy little village had turned into an artists' enclave.

She headed away from town, picking up speed as the road swung west and then north. This side of the lake had never become familiar to her. There was rare reason to travel beyond town, unless she and a date went out cruising—and then she'd had no interest in the scenery, not with the car windows wide open, Wolfman Jack or CKLW or WLS blasting the hottest hits into the hot summer nights from the AM radio. Dates had been rare too. It wasn't that guys around her age didn't come to the lodge, just that most showed no interest in her, and being outside of town she didn't get to know many of the local boys. The ones she did meet didn't interest her. Grandma Tilde would joke about Lydia being picky. She was. That was fine. She knew even then what she was looking for. Someone she could trust. And she had found it. She thought she had. In Gil.

A dry bitterness spread in Lydia's mouth. Thirty-seven years she'd trusted him. They hadn't all been good years, or easy years, but she'd always trusted him. Except that once. They had waited four years before getting pregnant, and she was seven months along with James when she caught Gil kissing a co-worker. He'd worked for an ad agency then, they were at the Christmas party, and she'd gone outside to get away from the boozy, cigarette-smoke-filled, people-packed event. She'd smiled when she saw a couple off in the shadows of the parking lot, passionately kissing, until they broke it off. As the man stepped back, she immediately recognized it was Gil. Before he could see her, she had fled back inside, into the bathroom, and cried. And cried and cried. By the time she composed herself enough to face people again, he was back at the party. She had stormed up to him and demanded to leave. He said he couldn't yet, it was too early. She said if he didn't take her home, she was calling a taxi. The silence in the car was as icy as a northern winter night. But inside the house, she exploded like a summer storm, yelling, crying, raging. He apologized over and over again. "It was just a mistletoe kiss, that's all," he said, raking both hands through his hair. "With no mistletoe and *your hand up her skirt*?" she screamed. She threatened to leave, except she knew she didn't know how she could. Not with a baby on the way, not without anyplace else to live. But she wasn't going to tolerate the alternative. Days later, when she was willing to speak to him again in more than monosyllables, she gave him an ultimatum: divorce or counseling. He'd do anything to mend their marriage, he promised, he loved her, he wanted them to be a family. She found a therapist that day, and they went weekly for the next two months. He changed his ways, finding a new job, coming home earlier, helping prepare for the baby, when before he'd left everything to her. And when newborn James was placed in his arms in the delivery room, seeing the love and tears in his eyes, she knew she loved and needed him. And so did their baby. But it still took a long, long time before she fully trusted him again.

Should she have? Her husband was handsome, charming. Women were everywhere in his life; she couldn't be, or watching every minute.

Lydia shook her head sharply to dislodge the thoughts. She turned the car into a long driveway, reversed, and headed back toward town.

Returning from a different direction, her attention was altered. She could see boats out on the Little Lake, the sister to the one the lodge was on. Children scampered along the shore or played in the water. Storefront signs were beginning to glimmer. There was actual traffic now, and people walked along the roadside or slammed car doors as they stepped out in parking lots. Lydia was surprised by the activity until she remembered it was the start of the Memorial Day weekend. She was far from being in a holiday mood, but she also was in no mood to go back to the lodge yet, with hours to wait before daring to access more of Gil's computer accounts. She turned on her blinker, waited for a break in the slow stream of cars, and pulled into the half-filled lot at Doozy's.

Stepping through the door, it took a beat for her eyes to adjust to the dimness. A smattering of couples and families with young children were at tables in the dining room, a room where she would feel naked being alone. To her left was an opening into a bar, filled with high tables and chairs. The back corner was set up for live music. A long bar and stools ran along the wall that separated the room from the dining area. Shelves and bottles and glasses glimmered against its mirrored backdrop, where a bartender was opening beers for two fellows seated near the entry. A young couple, holding hands across one of the tables, leaned toward each other over glasses of white wine, so deep in conversation they must have felt the rest of the world did not exist. Lydia walked to the stool at the far end of the bar, and the bartender gave her a smile.

"Hi. What'll it be?"

"A glass of ice water, please. No fruit. And a Glenlivet, rocks. Unless you don't have that? If not, well brand will do."

The man chuckled as he set the water before her. "Single-malt coming right up. But if you're willing to swill rotgut, you must be having one of those days, eh?"

"One of those lives is more like it."

Lydia drank some of the water, trying to rinse the bitterness from her mouth, before taking a sip of the smooth brown liquid the bartender placed before her. He busied himself with evening prep and Lydia was glad to be unnoticed by him or the others. She stared blankly at soundless images of sports reports bouncing across a TV screen hanging in the corner above her, aware only of the images skittering across her mind. Flashes of that Marielle Wharton woman's photo. Flashes of Gil, of little things he'd said that she had taken for his being under pressure with the business. She snorted to herself—yeah, he'd been stressed all right, what with juggling an affair on top of his business and marriage.

Lydia replaced those ugly thoughts with memories of the Nibic she had known, comparing what had been to what it now was. All the changes here seemed so sudden to her, yet, like with the rest of life, had come incrementally. Her life had changed that way, too. Real change was rarely sudden, but when it was, it shattered one's entire view of the world. It came on like the shock of a sudden act of nature—an earthquake's eruption, the spin of a tornado, the lightning strike that sets the house afire, the slow-motion nightmare of a flood. Life was one thing, then it wasn't. Normal had ceased to exist. *Adapt*, Lydia scolded herself, *I have to adapt.*

Genial greetings to someone by the men at the bar caught Lydia's ear. The mirror reflected a man exchanging back slaps and handshakes with the two fellows on stools. Again, it was the hat she recognized first. Between the bottles and glasses along the mirror, she watched him. He tossed his head back in laughter at something one of the men said. Stubble now covered his face, and the creases on it looked to be from laughter, not worry. He was solidly built, with skin color that showed he was used to outdoor activity, not cloistered in a fluorescent-lit office except for a weekly golf game.

The bartender grabbed a pint glass and began drawing a Guinness. "Where ya parkin' it, Max?" he called out. "Your usual's taken."

Lydia looked up, realizing he meant her, at this stool, since all the others were empty. The sensation of again being the interloper twinged through her; her presence had altered the course of the bar's natural order, where she was the outsider. It seemed she didn't belong anywhere, wherever she was. She flushed as she saw Max look directly at her.

"No problemo, Jer. Close enough is close enough," he said, walking toward her end of the bar. "Except when it comes to a good pint. Which someday you might learn to pour."

The bartender chuckled and made a smart retort. Lydia kept her eyes on her own glass as the men exchanged barbs in mock sarcasm. From the corner of her eye, she saw Max lay a book on the bar top. Still chatting as he sloughed off his jacket, she recognized the book's title. Sara had gushed about it last year, a literary mystery her book club had read. *A man of some intelligence then*, Lydia thought. He sat down, one stool away from her, and placed his hat on the one between them.

Returning to his duties, the bartender asked, "So, Max, you here for the fish fry? Doubt you've caught anything bigger than a three-inch perch since you were in Saturday night."

"Jerry, I will have you know there is nary a perch, walleye, nor northern pike that did not succumb to the allure of my lures this week. Dave didn't do too badly either. So don't expect a big turnout tonight. Everyone's saving their appetites for the real fish fry on Monday. As am I. Tonight I invest myself in a good mystery"—his hand tapped the book—"and some of that mystery meat this place passes off as a steak."

With that, he turned toward her, lowering his voice. "The real mystery, though, seems to be our continuing encounters. While it's not odd to soon recognize faces in a town this small, wouldn't you say it is a bit odd we keep crossing paths? Apparently the gods meant for us to meet, so let me introduce myself." He reached his right hand across his body. "Maxwell Pearson. And you are?"

Only then did Lydia look over at him. A quizzical smile showed in the tilt of his lips and eyebrows, the crinkled skin around his eyes, and the cock of his head. His hand remained steady in waiting. Lydia formed what she hoped was a polite smile as she shook it. "Yes, it does seem odd," she acknowledged, "but with the way the so-called gods have been treating me, that may not be a good thing."

His eyebrows lifted a bit more and the quizzical look remained, but his smile faded some.

"Oh, I'm sorry," Lydia said. "That sounded rude. Apparently the filter between my mind and my mouth slipped. I'm sorry. I … I'm … please, call me L."

His smile returned. "Ah, the mysterious Lady L little Katie has mentioned? She insists your name is that one letter, which intrigues her. She chatters on and on about the Lady L who holds the keys to Castle Berry. That's you?" When Lydia nodded, he asked, "There is more to the name than an initial, I assume?"

Now Lydia's eyebrows rose and her mouth pursed. "Yes. But without meaning to be rude, again, that's where I prefer to leave it. For now, at least."

Max nodded as he lifted his Guinness. "So, you've adopted anonymity. My inner Sherlock Holmes, or maybe it's all the Jimmy Buffett songs, leads me to surmise such people prefer to drink themselves away in Florida, not Michigan's upper peninsula."

With that, Lydia made a small laugh. "That only works if you're not from Florida."

"Ah, the clues begin to unfold. East or west coast? I've a winter place on Sanibel."

Instead of answering his question, Lydia said, "And that would be a clue about you. That you're from somewhere in the Midwest, not from the Northeast."

"Now, now, hasty conclusions based on incomplete evidence may lead a sleuth astray." Max raised his glass as if in toast. "The I-75 and I-95 corridors south do not influence air travel. It could be that I prefer fishing the calm Gulf waters to the Atlantic's wind and waves."

His words barely registered after "conclusions based on incomplete evidence." She knew Gil was having an affair. Wasn't that all she needed to know in deciding whether to abandon or salvage their marriage? To ride out the marital storm or throw it to the wind? Tiredness crept down her back, a leaden feeling that seeped into the muscles of her arms and legs and made her feet feel like anvils resting on the barstool brace. Whether brought on by the drink, the day, or the weight pressing on her soul, she didn't know. Why didn't matter. She wasn't in the mood for small talk. "Yes, it is calmer on our side." She reached into her purse for cash to slip under her glass and stood.

"'Our side'—another clue. Oh, you're leaving? I hope it's not because I've been intrusive."

"No. No." Lydia tried to smile but knew sadness was heavy on her face. "I don't know if it's the day, the drink, or …" she stuttered, stopping herself before she said Gil's name. "Or this … uh, project I'm, uh, up here working on." She hesitated, then said, "Thank you for introducing yourself, Max. I'm sorry I was in your spot. You can have it back now."

"Well, it's good to have met you, Katie's Lady L. I shall tell her we did, and she is right, that you are mysterious."

Lydia did her best to smile. "Oh, hardly. I'm sure the one in this book of yours will be much better."

"Possibly, but not nearly so intriguing. Say, I hope you're coming to the fish fry on Monday. I'm sure Bess and Dave have invited you. Katie would enjoy seeing you again. So would I."

Chapter 7

The insistent bleat of the kitchen stove timer woke her at night. Naps had never been her thing unless she was sick—first, she considered them a waste of good daylight; second, they usually left her more foggy than refreshed. When the timer repeated its grating noise, she rose from the sofa and padded across the cool floor to stop the buzzing. Within minutes, the computer had been fired up and a fresh coffee poured to clear her head.

The first two email accounts she opened were for Gil's corporate site—one for general business contact, the other Gil's dedicated address. She had little expectation of learning anything from the first and knew there was slim possibility of finding anything on the second, but she'd watched enough detective shows to know that Perry Mason, Monk, and Leroy Jethro Gibbs would haunt her like Dickens's Christmas ghosts if she weren't thorough. And thorough meant going through the trash, which caused her to slump when she opened both files. Hundreds and hundreds of messages had been dumped. Didn't he ever empty the trash? *Why should it surprise me*, she wondered. His taking out the trash at home was about as rare as her having lobster.

She moved on to his Gmail account. They each had one, and both knew about the other's. Her little notebook had his password.

There weren't many messages. Most had inane subject lines, others she dismissed as spam. Opening the trash, she scrolled and clicked her way through a litany of shopping pitches, male enhancement promos, "urgent" political pleas, and jokes from senders whose names she didn't know. Considering the hundreds of people he knew and she didn't, that wasn't a surprise. What was surprising was a reply to something headed "Re-Re-Fwd: I got what you want."

"Asswipe," Gil had written, "I've told you before. Do not send this shit to both gmails. This one's off limits. Use the right email, goddammit! Do it again and I'll personally break off your dick."

"But gotta admit it is funny. Take a ten-pound sack of flour to find her wet spot!"

Lydia sat up straight.

The vulgarity wasn't what shocked her—Gil could go off like that. What had Lydia's full attention were the words "both gmails."

Both?

Something else he'd kept from her. First the monthly withdrawal. That was rat number one. This was rat number two. How many more were there, unseen, waiting to be lured out?

Above Gil's note was a one-word reply, "Sorry." Below Gil's reprimand were a slew of addresses the original post had gone to. *Another idiot*, she thought, *who doesn't use bcc*—but maybe that would lead to another clue. She ignored the website link in the post to focus on the recipients. Most were people she'd never heard of, others hid the person's name, like Gil's screen name: Bluegoat. That, she knew, was for the beloved, blue 1968 GTO he'd had when they met. She gave careful attention to the ones that were obvious euphemisms—moonypie, friedLee, gatorgoat, jackovv. Her eyes hit reverse. Gatorgoat. Goat, could that be it? But why gator? Gil wasn't a University of Florida fan, or of any team; he followed sports only enough to make nice with clients. She read through the remaining addresses, then stared again at "gatorgoat."

She clicked the link at the bottom of the message and immediately wished she hadn't. A photo popped open. It was of an enormously overweight woman, naked, staring into the camera. She was seated, leaning forward, her breasts hanging like two hams resting on thighs three times as wide. Her legs were spread, one hand splaying open the lips between them, the other—. Before Lydia could shut the picture, her stomach turned in revulsion.

She lurched from the chair and stumbled into the darkness of the porch. It wasn't the porn that shocked her so, it was Gil's reaction. Bracing her hands on the railing, she leaned over it, afraid she might retch. Her breath came short and fast, and lightheadedness made her sway. Her mind compounded the dizziness as it slashed through jagged thoughts and images, fractured, jumbled, incomplete, racing through the past weeks, the past days.

She forced herself to slow her breath. She needed something to control. She couldn't control the explosion of thoughts. She loosened her hands, stretching her fingers until they tingled, and tried hard to quiet her gasps for air. As she did, her eyes began to focus on what surrounded her. Staring at the moon-silvered outlines of pines, she inhaled deeply, again and again, filling herself with their savory aroma, flavored with the spices of budding trees, herbed by wildflowers, all steeped in the heady water of the lake. She leaned against the railing and looked up into the night sky, marveling as she did every night at the sparkling black dome devoid of pollution from city lights. The stars flooding above seemed to be the size of silver dollars, so unlike the few pinpricks that managed to show above Tampa. The moon, high to the east, seemed to cast its spotlight on the Little Dipper. Straight overhead, it seemed close enough for her to reach up, grab its handle, and ladle elixir from the lake.

Not far away she found the Big Dipper. "Ursa Minor and Ursa Major," Grandpa George's memory instructed her. "Use their proper names." She remembered other constellation names and worked her memory to identify them among the quilted patterns the stars formed overhead, signaling that they held the code encrypting the secrets of the universe. She inhaled again and went back inside, knowing she needed to find the pattern that would crack the code hiding Gil's secrets—there had to be others. Grandpa's voice spoke to her again, "For every rat you see there are ten you don't."

Gil, she assumed, like most men, had an interest in pornography. She and Gil had loved—*used* to love, she corrected herself—being aroused by a good erotic movie, then nearly shattering furniture as they made love until exhausted. Gil hadn't touched her in months, and it had been months before that, and each time the sex had been so perfunctory that she was left empty, feeling as if she were no more to him than a faceless, inflatable sex doll. But the photo in that email was pure ugliness, and his reaction unlike anything she expected of him. She didn't want to believe Gil could find it funny. The fat shaming, the utter lack of respect toward another human being—how could she have lived with him all these years and never had an inkling he thought so little of women? How could she have been so oblivious to so much? He had to be hiding even more.

"For every rat you see." She'd found four now. Pretending there wouldn't be more wouldn't make it so. Right now, though, she couldn't flush them out until she knew where they were hiding: likely in the secret account. Which she had no password to.

The night air chilled her. She went inside, turned off the lights, and went to bed. Her body was exhausted and her mind numb, but sleep did not come for a long time.

***

The stars. The black dome of her mind was the universe, encompassing her, drawing her in. As if from afar, she saw herself, a tiny figure, suspended, stationary amid the nothingness. The stars, above, below, all around her, blinked on and off randomly. A handful suddenly shot across the blackness from all directions, then stopped with abrupt precision. They scattered again, more of them now, then just as quickly stilled into a new conformation. Again and again it happened, her suspended self-mystified and marveling at the kaleidoscopic patterns appearing and disappearing above, below, around her.

When all the stars had become engaged, the shape-shifting patterns began to repeat themselves. She giggled the way her child self-had done when looking for images in the clouds. There was a flower, bursting into blossom, trailing a leafed stem. As she recognized it, the stem and leaves lit up green, the petals brilliant yellow. Amazed, she let out a murmur of awe. The stars shot off again, then rearranged themselves and stopped, as if waiting, encouraging her to solve their picture puzzle. Cheshire Cat, Lydia tried, but failed, to call out. The Cheshire Cat's grin widened as first its ears and then its head and face faded, until nothing other than the grin remained, growing more and more malevolent, until it too went out in the blink of an eye.

Blackness, blackness. She couldn't see. She couldn't move. The darkness, the intense nothingness now frightened her. From the corner of her eye, she saw a wisp of silver emerge in the void. A calmness overtook her as an ethereal shape formed beside her, elongating itself into a being-like form. It did not speak yet she heard its words, as if spoken aloud: "You have what you seek." It made an arm-like sweep and the dome exploded in brilliance. In clusters the stars went dark again, leaving behind a new form. She drew back, frightened by the evil-looking reptilian shape. The stars of the beast's outline were blue, its eyes and jagged teeth burned orange.

Lydia's eyes flew open. Panic engulfed her. Pale morning light filled the bedroom, but the evil glare of the beast's eyes would not fade. She sat up, gasping for breath, and heard again, "You have what you seek."

What did those words mean? Had it been nothing more than an amazing but random dream, she wondered, or was she missing something?

***

Fog shrouded the lodge, obscuring the lake and chilling both her and her coffee as she sat at the shore. She didn't notice. Her thoughts were as amorphous as the mist wafting around her. Like a pinball, her mind bounced and careened, ricocheting from snippets of her dream to bank account numbers, to that phone number burned into her mind like a tattoo, to random snippets of the email messages. Repetitively, randomly, the fiery blue outline of the sky monster and its burning orange eyes intruded, its sinister shape emerging like a reverse Cheshire Cat, before her thoughts again shot in another direction. Then her mind went as blank as the view before her. She picked up her coffee cup and took a sip. Grimacing as she swallowed the now cold, bitter brew, she flung the cup's contents across the ground, then rose to refill it and return with a hot cup and thermos. Her head needed the caffeine to help her focus on what she would do next.

The most stymieing problem was that email account she hadn't known about. And how to get into it, or try, without his being alerted. She couldn't chance messing with that now, not when he might be on his computer. He usually was the first thing on weekends. God, she wished she had spyware on that laptop. *Wait*, she thought, *Sunday*—he had a standing golf game. That is, if he didn't have to leave for a Monday meeting somewhere. But Monday was a holiday. That was it. Tee time was ten-thirty and he wouldn't return home until around four. She'd have all that time to work.

The realization that she had a plan gave way to a sigh of frustration. Ten o'clock tomorrow morning was a long way off. What was she going to do till then? And what in god's name could that password be?

The hours dragged as she again pored over numbers from the cell phone printouts, this time working with her laptop and papers spread across the dining room table. While studying the phone numbers, she compared the origination points of his outgoing calls with where his schedule, archived on her computer calendar, said he should have been. Another troubling pattern emerged. At least once a month, always when he was away at least three nights, his calls to her were made from somewhere other than where he told her he'd be. Atlanta instead of Orlando. New York instead of Atlanta. New Orleans, Las Vegas, Biloxi, Key West. None of them places he'd told her about.

When she finished with the calendar, she went back to identifying more of the numbers he had called. There seemed to be thousands, as if he spent all day, every day on the phone. The thought made her grimace—how could anyone stay sane talking, talking, talking, or be productive without hours of solitude?

But the solitude was getting to her right now. The numbers began to blur. A headache was coming on. She kneaded her eyes and temples, and looked up at the wall clock. Its markings took several seconds to come into focus as her eyes adjusted. It was long after noon. *Good Lord*, she thought, *no wonder I'm brain-fried—I've been at this for five hours.*

Her body needed to move. She couldn't take any more of the sitting, or the silence. It was especially the silence that was getting to her. The only sounds she heard were of the lake and the birds. She wanted to hear Audra's voice but knew she would be busy at the store. It'd been two or three weeks since she had talked to her kids—that wasn't unusual, but she was in no state of mind to hold it together with either of them yet. She needed something else to do.

A phrase of Grandma Tilde's popped into her head: There is no time for boredom because there's always something to be cleaned. She headed upstairs and went to work dusting and sweeping the empty rooms, scrubbing the unused baths. When she finished, tired, she stopped to look at the door leading to the attic. *Not today*, she thought as she headed downstairs. She'd had enough of the hidden past for today.

***

Sunday morning, the clock's second hand moved at its constant steady pace, while the minute hand dragged and the hour hand seemed to stand still. Time itself seemed bent on frustrating her, refusing to let ten o'clock come. She was antsy, wandering in and out of every room, upstairs and down, and pacing the strip of sand along the shore over and over again. She'd go back to check the clock and not even ten minutes would have passed. She couldn't sit still, she couldn't focus. Part of the dream kept lunging into her mind—that long, blue reptilian shape, its flaring, blazing orange eyes. The recurring ugly image was as annoying as a "Wheels on the Bus" earworm, adding to her anxiety, her sense of spinning aimlessly.

She went inside to check the time again. Ten minutes to ten. She wheeled, pushed the screen door open wide, and strode back out. Behind her the screen slammed with a clap that echoed and snapped something inside her. She knew that if she didn't quiet her mind and body there was no way she would figure out the puzzle of his password.

Sitting down on the porch swing, she closed her eyes, and forced herself to breathe slow and long and deep. It wasn't easy. To stop the skittering thoughts she began to count the breaths. She lost track again and again as the dream reptile intruded. She would force it aside and start counting over again. Somewhere around the time she managed to make it to fifty, her tension began to ebb. The alligator shape loomed forward again, this time larger, brighter, fiercer. This time, a shock of surprise delighted her—that's what the shape was, an alligator. At the moment of realization, the gator's head rose, its menacing eyes flaring sparks of blue flame into the darkness behind her own eyes. Its head twisted, its mouth snapped and severed the head of a goat. Then it was gone.

Her eyes popped open and she stared at the pale blue water of the lake. As clearly as if spoken behind her, the dream words came again: "You have what you seek."

But what did they mean? And what exactly was she still seeking? She knew Gil had lied to her, cheated on her. All the lies, all the deceptions the computer had revealed to her over the past few days. "Rats … For every one …" That was what she still needed to know. Anger took over where there'd been anguish and tears. Now she needed to know just how much of a rat he'd been, and for how long …

Within seconds, she was at the computer. She typed "gatorgoat" into the Gmail account field and hit enter. The screen image swiped left and waited for her to type the password. The screen stared at her; she stared back. Like spinning the tumbler on a safe lock, the passwords she knew for his other accounts jumbled in her mind, sorting themselves into combinations. The patterns behind them were logical to the various account groupings. Where could she discern a pattern for the password to this one? The password to his personal email, bluegoat, was logical: 1968GTO, the year and make of the car. What would be logical to, or common between, an alligator and a goat? Gil's Goat had been blue, alligators were green. She typed "bluegreen," hit enter, and the screen jostled as if shaking its head no. "Greenblue"; again the screen mocked her with its uh-uh-uh. She knew one more try would have to be the last for the day. Her gut told her the password had to include the word blue—

that would be a pattern between these two personal accounts. If gators weren't green, what were they?

She sat for long seconds, her mind coming up blank, except for the University of Florida's teams. But with Gil's lack of interest in sports, what would connect the two? With a start, she opened a new search screen, typed in Marielle Wharton's name, and accessed the About page of her website. In the last paragraph lay the answer: the woman had a degree in communications from the University of Florida. *Well, well*, Lydia thought. So Gil must have set up the secret account to communicate privately with his mistress. Another piece of the puzzle fell into place. The university's colors were orange and blue. *How convenient*, she thought as she typed, orange&blue. Orange, the Florida Gators. Blue, his GTO.

It worked.

The inbox screen appeared, lengthening itself as messages downloaded. Some were marked as read, others not. Scanning the subject lines, it was obvious most were spam. "ASIAN BEAUTIFUL BRIDES FOR AMERICAN MEN," "Hello, Handsome, My Name is Ileana," "BANG HER WITH A BIGGER BETTER BONER!!!" and variations that went on and on down the screen. Lydia's first thought was why didn't Gil ever bother to delete the crap.

Returning to the top of the page, she began opening the messages, careful to re-mark the unread ones afterward. The first few were as she expected, pitches for sexual enhancement or pleas from "Very pretty woman would love to give American husband I know is you." Quite a few were to the same group of recipients, whose email addresses were becoming familiar. Many had links, which she ignored; others were pornographic jokes she didn't bother reading to the punch line. She reached a forwarded message telling a slew of recipients "You're gonna love this vid bit," with an attachment named "Beaver Hunt." Her mouth soured. Considering what she'd tripped across in his other account, she was certain it had nothing to do with the outdoors. She moved to the next message. It read, "Leaving soon. Won't be back from the boat till late Mon nite so radio silence till Tues. Talk then about the PPB&D invite? Hope the presentation went well and golf is good. TW—any word? Miss you."

Lydia's eyes jumped to the sender address. Orange&blue. There was a moment of puzzlement. Holy shit, she realized, they used the single account to communicate.

"TW. Any word?" Was TW a client? No, TW, would be The Wife, she realized—me. But PPB&D. What was that?

He had opened that post earlier this morning but left other new messages unread. Skipping those for now, as well as the ones that seemed obvious sales pitches, she hunted for previously opened posts sent from the orange&blue address. Some were no more than "Good morning to you," in reply to a good-morning from the other. The ones that wrenched her gut went on longer, short chats about something that had happened that day, others suggesting a good time to talk, others warning when not to call—"TH around all day." If Lydia was TW, she decided, TH must be The Husband.

She opened another, much earlier message. It was obvious Gil had told the woman that Lydia had left. "Well, at least she hasn't pulled a complete *Gone Girl* on you. Probably holed up at the beach. Either she'll be back or she's calling lawyers to find one that'll clean you out. Ha. She'll be back, you watch & to your Qs yes." Below it was his message: "She didn't say where she was or when she's coming home. That means I need to stick to schedule for now. So will you cancel the PD? And you're still coming to ORD?"

ORD—Chicago. But what was PD?

She scanned further down the page, to a message from the week before she had left. It made her sit back and stare, reading it over and over. "Hey, babe. Not sure how early I'll get out of here in the morning so no sense leaving until I call. Even if it's a late start we'll make Charleston by evening. Flying J coffee shop this time, Wildwood."

"This time." How many other times had there been? She looked at the message date, then opened her calendar to that date. Gil had told her he'd be in Jacksonville for several days, not Charleston. She opened the phone log. It confirmed he'd called her from South Carolina. And that seemed to prove the two of them had been together every time he had called home from a city other than where he said he'd be. At least once a month, he must have gone off with his little sidepiece. What about the other times, when he did call from the cities where he said he'd be? How many of those places had they been together, too?

The letters PD appeared in a smattering of the notes between them. At first, she thought it referred to a person but could find no individual or company with those initials in his contacts. Was it another code?

When she finished reading the messages between them, she fixed lunch and carried it outside but was unable to eat more than a few bites. She left the unfinished plate on the porch swing and walked the shore from one end of the property to the other, her body disassociated from her mind. She was aware of nothing but what she'd discovered—that the affair had been going on far longer than he had admitted; that between what the call logs and the emails proved, they were in touch with each other every day, sometimes multiple times; that they spent days away together every month. One question kept coming back—who, or what, was PD?

Hands stuffed into her jeans pockets, she stared across the lake. Two of the Three Sisters stood clear above the water, but the farthest island seemed to be behind gauze, as if posing a question about whether it existed or not. Lydia still had questions. She knew the answers were there—somewhere. With a glance at the sky, she turned and headed inside. From the sun's position, she figured she had at least an hour before she'd have to log out of the email account for the day.

Online again, she clicked Gil's inbox, but this time the cursor hit the small gray triangle beside it. A hidden sub-file named PD popped up, startling her. "You have what you seek," the dream message repeated again, unbidden. She clicked the file and leaned forward, her eyes widening as message after message filled the screen. A few subject lines were as simple as "Hey there." All the others were headed "P&P." The subheads on those were disturbing: Someone New 4 You, Seven New Messages Waiting, New Friend Request, Your Profile Viewed 6X This Week.

Profile? Lydia clicked that one open. "Log in to your account to see who." Below the single sentence was a link. With a long breath, Lydia tapped the touchpad. A website banner appeared, bookended by two close-up photos, one of two naked breasts, the other a woman's naked ass and crotch. The banner between them read "Pussies Pricks Boobs & Dicks." Below it, "The Place for Adult Play Dates."

The screen filled with a mash of content and lurid colors. A column titled "Welcome Our New Players" was filled with thumbnail photos—some headshots, some pornographic—above screen names that showed as links. The center of the screen announced "Upcoming Play Dates" with a list of cities and dates. Lydia stared. Play Dates: PD?

Topping the far-right column was a member login box. She typed in the gatorgoat address. As much as she wished she could use the "Forgot your password?" link, she didn't dare. *Pattern, girl, what would be the pattern*, she asked herself again. It was impossible to know what would have been logical to him. Think. They shared an email account; if the PD comments in their messages stood for Play Dates, would they both have access to this account? On a paper beside the laptop she jotted possible combos as they spooled in a steady stream from someplace in her subconscious, automatic writing that seemed to make no sense. And then a combination that did: ojm&blg—oj, orange; m, Marielle; bl, blue; g, goat, Gil. She typed it in and hit enter.

The site's homepage filled the screen again, slowly, oh so slowly, as if the limited Internet speed was teasing her before it would dash her hopes with an error message. But it didn't. A narrow banner, like an old-fashioned ticker tape, flowed leftward below the page header: "Welcome back Mar and Gil … 7 new messages … 4 PD invites … 9 new PDs in your travel cities … 6 profile views … Welcome back Mar and Gil … 7 new …" At the top of the right-hand column, the log-in box had been replaced with a drop-down menu. She clicked on "Your Public Profile." A large photo popped up at the top. A naked woman in profile, a naked man facing her, both their faces turned away from the camera. The woman's body was fleshy, her breasts droopy. Lydia didn't need to see the man's face to know who it was. One of Gil's hands groped and lifted one of the woman's breasts, his other was between her legs. One of the woman's hands cupped his testicles, pulling his erection toward her.

Lydia shut her eyes and wasn't sure she could open them again. When she did, she refused to look at the picture, instead focusing on the text below a series of filled-in fields.

Name(s): Marielle and Gil
Married: Yes but not to each other
Region: SE
Travel: Anywhere
Up for: All ways, couples, 3somes, group
Interests: Gil—hetero. Mar—hetero, bi, dyke, trans
Members: 4 yrs.

Four years. Four fucking years.

Rage and shock boiled up in Lydia like whitecaps ferocious on the lake in a storm. Numbness flattened her like the water when it became a mirror, now reflecting back the failure of her marriage, water now so clear peering into the depths of Gil's betrayal.

She logged off and slapped the laptop closed. She couldn't read any more. Not now. She pulled on a jacket, untied the boat, and rowed away from the shore. When she was so far out that the lodge seemed no bigger than a dollhouse on the shore, she anchored, curled up on the bottom of the boat, and let herself cry. When her tears ran dry, she slept under the blanket of the afternoon sun.

Chapter 8

The chilled water below the boat awakened her. Every joint, muscle, and pore ached, as if the pain of her broken heart was too immense to be contained by her body. It took a long time to uncoil herself, to row, slowly, as if her muscles had atrophied, back to shore. For the first time she felt old—old and weak and frail. And more alone than she'd ever known.

Under the steaming flow of the shower, she stood until the hot water ran out and the chill returned. Bundled like a sick child in her nightclothes and a quilt, she sat on the porch, staring, unseeing, into the evening. The moon had not yet risen and her mind was as empty as the void before her. She didn't see the bits of light from far-off cottage windows, looking like stars tossed to the ground. She wasn't aware of the waves, whose laughing rhythm infused her own cells and pulled them into harmony with the waters. When she crawled into bed, she slept the sleep of the dead. Her last thought was the hope that she would not awaken.

But hunger and a throbbing headache brought her back to consciousness in the morning. As she lay staring at the ceiling, images began to flash as if projected on it. A slideshow of all the ugliness she had uncovered the day before. She felt as if she were drowning in the images, and in her own stupidity, for having been so naïve, so trusting, so duped. Then anger returned, and grew. She wasn't the one at fault. How could Gil have done this, done it to her? What kind of a depraved man could do this, when she had loved him for nearly two-thirds of her life—and his. What kind of man?

***

Lydia rose, dressed, brushed her teeth, and went back to work. Searching for a reason to forgive Gil was no longer an option. Gathering evidence was the goal. Once she had that, she would decide how to use it.

Of course the PPB&D site provided internal messaging between members. She found that link after saving screenshots of the in-depth profile Gil and Marielle had posted. Her analytical mind now in control, emotions went unregistered as she glanced at, screen-captured, and then filed each message by date into a folder. There wasn't much to get emotional about, as few were salacious. The grossest ones had been sent, either by Gil or that woman, to the trash with no reply, which was somehow a relief. The majority of the correspondence read like appointment scheduling. In fact some referenced "business meetings," which puzzled her. Was Gil somehow involved financially in the site? But others mentioned things like "guitar lessons" and "playing Scrabble"—she'd never known Gil to play either—or "ABC Party" and other terms foreign to her.

There were others that made her skin crawl, such as the thank-you notes "for being such a fun couple." One in particular thoroughly pissed her off: "Still raw after our play week with you in Key West! LOL! Next time you come here! We show you Buenos Aires is best! Our gift! Plane tickets too! When can you come? (and come and come and come hahaha!)"

That one stopped her. It was dated in January, another time Gil was supposed to have been somewhere else, which was no surprise now. She remembered that two or three times over the past few months Gil had oh-so-casually mentioned a client might want him to attend a symposium in Buenos Aires. The first time he had brought it up, she'd been excited, urging him to let her know the dates as soon as possible so she could schedule time to go along. She'd been hurt when he rebuffed her, telling her it wasn't possible. Now she understood why. She snapped the laptop shut, slipped the new phone into her jacket pocket, and went outside.

Lydia eased herself down on the end of the dock. Ribbony shimmers of water sparkled up through the gaps between the boards. The water, lapping against the dock posts, created a rhythmic lullaby. Breathing in the lake's perfume, she leaned back against the post where the rowboat was tethered and closed her eyes, letting the sun infuse her. As her tension dissipated, her thoughts faded to some distant place at the outer edge of herself. Everything she had discovered over the past two days became devoid of emotional connection. There was certain to be more, she realized, to discover about the man she believed she'd always known, but it didn't matter. Not anymore. She'd gone looking for answers and now she had enough of them. The question was, what to do next?

After a while, the sun's heat through her jacket became uncomfortable. As she tossed it aside, the phone in its pocket clunked against the dock. That's what she wanted to do next, she thought—talk to Audra.

Audra's voice answered on the first ring but with it came disappointment. It was her voicemail message. She sighed as she waited for the beep. "Hey, girl. A lot's happened and I sure wish you were around to talk to. If you're at the store, I hope you're making tons of money. But since it's the holiday I hope you're taking a much-needed day off and having some fun. Call me back, okay? I love you."

A smattering of distant boats dotted the lake, some stationary, some in silent movement as the breeze pushed the motors' sounds toward the opposite shore. The trees behind her, the water before her, the silvery blue above seemed to hold her in a delicate bubble. She felt cocooned, looking out on a world that didn't know or care she existed. A world in which she had discovered a seediness that had been invisible to her. An alien parasite had been injected into what had once been her comfortable cocoon. It had destroyed the outer sheath but she wasn't going to let it infect her.

A shock hit: *Oh shit,* she thought, *what if that bastard gave me an STD?*

The slam of a car door brought another shock. Her body tensed, aware of her vulnerability, of being so alone. There was no other sound. And there was no alternative but to chase off whoever had intruded. Lydia grabbed her jacket with one hand and the post with her other to pull herself up. She reminded herself that the road gate was locked and only Dave had the key. As she stepped off the dock a voice called out.

"Elle? Hullo! Mysterious Lady L, wherefore art thou?"

Relief and a twinge of aggravation both slipped through her as a man—a man in a hat—came around the corner of the lodge.

"Ah, there you are."

"Oh. Max. What are you doing here?"

Max tipped his hat and flashed a smile. "Blunt and to the point. I like that in a person. I have been sent by Dave and Bess to whisk you away from your toils for a spell. The fish-fry festivities are underway, and the prime walleye fillets are going fast. Plus, Katie has been pestering us as to when you'll arrive. I entreat you. Please do not send me back alone to face their disappointment." He swept the hat from his head and bowed low.

As he rose up again, Lydia burst out laughing. "Do you *always* sound like that?"

"Like what, pray tell?"

"Like Major Charles Emerson Winchester the third."

Now Max let out a laugh. "Nah. Only when I'm trying to impress a lovely lady with how suave and chivalrous I am." Plunking his hat back on his head, off-kilter, he said, "So, please don't allow me to fail in my quest? I'll be happy to give you a lift."

Lydia sighed. "Oh, I don't know. I'm not in a partying mood. Besides, I'm not dressed for it."

"Oh? My sartorial splendor indicates this is a formal event?" He raised a hand and swept it from his shoulder downward.

Lydia laughed again. He wore a faded plaid shirt, the sleeves rolled up, open over an equally faded red T-shirt, jeans with a hole in one knee, and athletic shoes that had been, at one time, white. "Okay, you've got me there."

"Then please, accept the invitation."

Lydia looked back at the lake. Maybe it would do her good to be among people, people who couldn't see inside her head and maybe would get her out of it for a while. "All right. Let me get my keys."

"I'll be happy to drive."

"Thank you, but no. I don't know how long I'll stay, and don't want to put you out to bring me back."

Max seemed to notice the troubled look on her face. "I see."

While Lydia got her purse and locked the lodge door, Max turned his car around and waited for her to follow. She wondered if he had waited to ensure that she actually would. Minutes later, approaching Clar's Corner, she realized he had done it to be helpful. Scores of cars were parked on the land around the store. Max stretched his arm through his open window and motioned for her to follow, then turned on his blinker. He turned onto a dirt drive she hadn't noticed before, marked with a "private" sign and leading down the sloping hill to the Conklin's house. Lydia was startled by what she saw. People, picnic tables, and tables laden with food filled an area half the size of a football field that was ringed by eight cottages. Max pulled into a parking spot marked for resort guests, and she found one nearby. As she stepped out of the car she was enveloped by the sounds of voices and laughter and the scents of smoking grills and a deep fryer. Lydia stood, wondering if she should turn and leave, but Max took her elbow. "We go this way, to skirt the hoi polloi."

Lydia looked up at him, puzzled.

"Those of us staying at the resort are guests," Max said. "All others, ten dollars a head or a substantial food contribution. The line is long and will be well into the evening. Come on. We'll find Dave and Bess to let them know you're here."

Lydia stopped. "Max, I don't know. When you said fish fry, I didn't expect a festival."

Max's hand at her elbow urged her along. "Whatever you're hiding, Mysterious Lady L, it's easier to do among a hundred than a dozen."

Lydia scowled. "Who said I'm hiding anything?"

"Nobody."

"Then what makes you say something like that?" she asked.

"Let's just say I know how to read people," he said, leading her into the crowd. Several partiers glanced at them with smiles and a few called out greetings that Max returned as they wended their way past. "Ah, there's Bess. Bess!"

Bess's face lit up and she gave Lydia a welcoming hug. "I'm glad Max convinced you to come. I have to tell you, Dave was so grateful you found that party beach, but is so embarrassed that he didn't. He's been kicking himself for not being a better caretaker."

Lydia returned Bess's smile. "Oh heavens, he shouldn't be. I almost didn't see it, and I was right on top of it. Creeps can be very good at hiding things when they're up to no good." Her voice had tightened, and she was aware Max was studying her.

"Well, please tell Dave that," Bess said. "He's overseeing the cooking crew. He'll be glad you got here before the walleye runs out. And Katie will be thrilled." Bess laughed. "I'm not sure why, but you sure made an impression on her. Brings up Lady L at least once a day. Who knows where she is right now—there're so many kids around I don't even try to keep track." Something behind Lydia caught Bess's attention. "Oops, gotta go. The band's pulling in. Max, show her around. Elle, help yourself to everything. See ya in a bit."

Lydia looked at Max. "A band?"

"Mm-hmm. And they're not bad, considering they're local kids. Come on, let's get a beer, whet your appetite." As Max led the way he stopped several times to chat with people he knew. Each time he introduced her as Elle, and she let them assume what they wanted when they said, “Nice to meet you, Ellie,” or “Elle? As in Ellen?”

After filling two red party cups from one of the kegs set up under shade trees and handing her one, Max said, “Next up, getting you fed.”

Lydia let herself be steered toward a length of tables laden with potluck bowls of salads, side dishes, and desserts. She picked up a paper plate and gravitated toward the dishes familiar from the fish fries of her youth—mustardy potato salad, vinegary coleslaw, richly dark baked beans. When she returned to where Max was waiting, he looked at the small dollops she’d taken. “I … I don’t think I’m very hungry,” she murmured. “Besides, I really don’t feel I should be here.”

“Good lord, woman. There’s enough food to feed Nibic and half of Falton. And yes you should be here. Because Dave and Bess—and I,” he said looking at her, “want you here. Now, be a charming guest and enjoy our hospitality.”

“Thank you.” She smiled a bit. “I promise I’ll have more if I want, okay?”

“Up next, that fish I promised you. Come on.”

Again she followed him, and again she waited, sipping her beer, whenever he stopped to talk. After breaking away after the sixth time, her cup was half empty and she was beginning to feel the beer’s effect, she was glad the food on her plate had been cold to start with. “Is there anyone here you don’t know,” she asked.

“Well, some of them I know in passing. It’s pretty much the same crowd every year. This is for the locals and long-time Memorial Day folks who come up. The party for the tourists was yesterday, in town. David and Bess did the first one as a grand opening for the store, and so they could get to know people. It was such a hit they’ve turned it into the kickoff of the summer season. Only grumbling came from the poor souls stuck in town working, who knew what they missed. So now the party goes on well into the night, when they show up after closing shop. By then, of course, all the fish is gone so they still miss out. Dave, got another hungry one here!”

Spatula in hand, Dave looked up and waved from behind one of the grills lined up near the shore. A dozen or so men and women tended hamburgers and hot dogs, grilled fish, and the constant flow of deep-fried fish going into and out of crackling oil. “Hey, Elle, glad you made it,” Dave said. He turned toward one of the fryers and called out, “Connie. Dish up a walleye filet. Pick a good one for this gal, please.”

“Coming right up,” the woman called back.

Lydia noticed several people in line looking at her, as if wondering how she rated special treatment. The woman at the fryer lifted a large chunk of golden, breaded fish, let the hot oil drip from it, and flipped it onto a plate. Max reached for it. “This way. Since you are a first-timer, I’ll show you the ropes. Back for my shift in a few, my man,” he said to Dave.

Max craned his neck, scanning the crowd. “Picnic table over there has some space. Let’s grab a spot. This way.”

He set her fish at a place on a long picnic table where six others were chatting. “Excuse me, folks. This is Elle. I hope you’ll keep her a bit of company until my return. Elle, I’ll be back in about forty-five minutes—time for me to prove to the others how a true grill master works.”

The others nodded and said hellos. Lydia turned to Max. “Uh, thanks a lot for throwing me off the deep end,” she said, speaking so the others wouldn’t hear.

“You know how to swim just fine, I’m sure.”

Lydia smiled tentatively at her tablemates as she took off her jacket and laid it on the seat, then sat down and focused on her food as their conversation resumed. A piece of fish flaked at the touch of her fork and a warm waft of scent made her mouth water. She blew lightly on the morsel before placing it on her tongue. The burst of flavor sent a shudder through her. It was the taste of summer and freedom and breezes and the water in which the fish had lived. As she savored it, she closed her eyes and gave a silent thanks to both the lake and the fish for this bounty.

With each bite came memories. The laughter of the men around the fish-cleaning table after a good day out on the water. Her father’s patience as he taught her how to fillet a fish and release it from its skin without waste. Scales flying from perch as the boys had contests to see who was fastest—and messiest. The clatter of pans and the chatter of her grandmother, mother, and aunts bustling in the choreography women in kitchens create. She wished Gil were here to share it with her.

But then she remembered how Gil had hated coming up here, carping about how the great outdoors was anything but, until she gave up putting herself through it and stopped coming. With a jolt, she set down her fork and reached for her beer. She took a hard swallow. It tasted bitter. The beer was getting warm.

"Looks like you could use a cold one." A man at the far end of the table stood up, and Lydia realized he was speaking to her. "I'm getting one for myself. Be glad to bring you one too."

"Um, thanks, yes, that would be nice."

"Happy to. Max said your name is Elle? I'm Tony. This here's my wife, Karen." The woman he indicated smiled, and he nodded toward the others. "That's Bill, Susan, Carly, Tanya, and Sean. Anyone else ready? I can manage one more. Okay, then. Back in a flash."

"So, it's your first time here, eh?" Karen said.

Lydia nodded as she looked out over the party. The grounds were now even more crowded, and every picnic table was filled. "When I heard about the fish-fry, I didn't expect anything like this."

"Well, don't expect to get to sleep early, either," one of the other women said with a grin. "We party noisy and we party late. But I imagine you and Max do the same, every night under the sheets."

"Carly, jee-zus." Karen's voice was sharp. "For Christ's sake."

The man next to Carly glowered at her. "You're getting drunk."

"So? I'm not driving. You've got the keys. Besides, what do you think they're doing at night?"

The man reached for Carly's beer cup and pushed it out of her reach. "That's it. You're cut off."

Lydia stared at Carly with the stoniness she'd perfected over decades of dealing with smart-mouthed students. The others at the table looked down in embarrassment as Carly stared back. Lydia let the silence hang and kept her eyes locked on the woman's. Seconds ticked by before Carly's haughty grin crumbled and she looked away.

"Okay, okay. Sorry. I was only saying what everyone else is thinking. We're just glad Max has a woman again."

"I am not Max's woman." Ice tinged Lydia's words. "And I am not staying here. I have my own place down the road. As if that's any of your business."

"Oh, how nice. Where's that?" Karen said, a little too brightly, a little too eager to redirect the uncomfortable conversation.

Tony returned and set a cup of beer down by Lydia. She glanced up and said, "Thanks."

"Uh, I miss something?" he asked, seeing the look on his wife's face.

"Elle was just saying she's staying at one of the other resorts."

"That so?" Tony swung a leg over the picnic table bench to sit down. "We know you're not a local and if you're not staying at the Conklin's, how'd you wrangle an invite to this shindig?"

Lydia smiled at the simple directness of his question, so different from the Southern subtlety she'd long been accustomed to, and didn't mind answering. "Well, I used to be a semi-local, you could say. My grandparents lived up here and I spent summers on the lake. Until I graduated college. It's the first time I've been back in a long time."

"No kidding?" Carly's husband said. "Whereabouts?"

A beat of silence hung while Lydia wondered how much she wanted to divulge. *Oh, the hell with it*, she thought. "My grandparents operated a summer and hunting lodge. My dad grew up here. In fact, his granddad was one of the three men who first bought the whole lake, around the turn of the century."

"Holy cow. Three guys owned the entire Big Lake?" Tony expressed amazement as he turned to look out at it. "It's like, thirty miles around this thing."

"Wow, I never knew that," Karen said, leaning forward. "They must've made a fortune selling the land."

"Not by a long shot," Lydia said. "One of them committed suicide in the Depression. His third reverted to the state for unpaid taxes. From what I understand, the other man tried living up here for a few years but his wife couldn't stand the isolation. His kids started selling off the land around World War II—it still wasn't worth much then. My great-grandfather was the only one who stuck it out, and managed that only because he opened a lumber mill."

Bess's voice came from behind Lydia's shoulder. "I remember hearing there'd been a mill nearby. My mom told me that's why my great-uncle opened his store. Did good business because the mill workers didn't have to go into town so often. Then the mill closed and things changed for him." Bess set down a plate of food and pushed Lydia's jacket against Lydia's thigh to make room to sit.

"And count me among the ones glad you opened the store," Carly said to Bess. "It's a godsend, especially in the summer, not to have to go into Nibic unless I have to."

Bill, who looked to be about Lydia's age, asked, "So, when did your family sell off their land? Before or after the bridge?"

Lydia looked at him, aware of what he was trying to learn. Land prices had climbed after the Mackinac Bridge opened. "We didn't." She turned to Bess. "Grandpa hated shutting down the mill. He was in his sixties when a doctor told him he had a bad heart and not many years left. The doctor died about five years later. Grandpa lived another thirty and died in his sleep."

Under the ripple of laughter that followed, Lydia heard the ping of a cell phone that went ignored. When the ping repeated, Bess said, "Elle, that sounds like it's coming from your jacket."

Surprised, Lydia reached into the pocket. A red dot showed on the text icon. It had to be Audra, she knew, but now wasn't the time to respond. Resuming the conversation, she said, "My grandparents kept the lodge going until Grandpa died. I've been back only a couple of times since then."

"So where is it you're staying," Tony asked.

"Oh, at the lodge. My brother and I still own it. Well, mostly my brother. He comes up here a lot." Lydia's phone pinged again. "Excuse me. I guess I better check this. Whoever it is must think it's important."

The others' conversation veered off as she tapped the screen and read Audra's first message. Plane leaving Detroit. Land at Chippewa abt hr & half. Better b there. The second read Abt 2 turn off phone. U gonna make me walk?

Lydia stared at the screen, her mind first blank and then racing. What in the world had Audra done? She quickly typed, WTF??? and hit send. Within seconds there was a reply, a smiley face emoji followed by, Said I have to turn the phone off now.

What the hell, Audra, what the hell? Lydia thought in anger-tinged confusion. An hour and a half—that's how long it will take me to get there. She turned back to the table and interrupted the conversation. "Excuse me, I'm sorry, but I have to leave."

Polite murmurs of "Oh gosh" and "That's too bad" went up from several people as Bess said, "But you hardly got here. Katie's going to be so disappointed if you go before she sees you."

"I am sorry," Lydia repeated. "But it can't be helped. Please tell Max and Dave. And tell Dave the walleye was incredible." She glanced at the others as she rose. "It was nice to meet you all. Bye."

Cars were still coming down the drive and turning into the field to park, and Lydia had to pull aside to let several pass on her way back to the road. Until she reached the stoplight at the turnoff to Falton half an hour later, she drove without noticing anything. Her emotions bounced between pique and relief. She couldn't believe Audra had the audacity to do this. Well, yes, she could; Audra had always been one to spring things on people. But she was also grateful, because she was suddenly aware of how much she needed her friend. Tears blurred her vision for a moment as the tension of all she had been withholding was released.

When Lydia reached the airport and was about to turn into a parking lot, she saw Audra, seated outside, staring at the sky. Lydia pulled to a stop in front of the terminal and slammed the car door as she got out. Striding toward Audra, she yelled, trying to sound angry, "What the—?"

Audra flashed a sweet grin as she stood up. "Hi, sweetie. Yeah, the plane landed early. Nice, huh?"

"What the hell are you doing here?" Lydia finished.

Still smiling, Audra embraced Lydia. "What, can't a girl just want to spend some time with her best friend?"

"Don't give me that shit." Lydia drew away, tears welling in her eyes. She hugged Audra again, tight, and said, "God, I'm glad. I'm pissed, but I'm glad."

They both laughed. Audra picked up her carry-on bag and purse, which was—typical for Audra—large enough to have been disqualified as a second carry-on. Lydia took the first to deposit in the trunk.

"I'm sure glad you didn't stand me up," Audra said as she clicked the car's seatbelt. "Flying in, from what I could see, this place is in the middle of God's own nowhere. Are there even hotels up here?"

Lydia laughed—*Oh, it feels good to laugh,* she thought. "You'd be hard-pressed to find one between the Soo and Mackinac Island. Cabins, cottages, camps, and resorts, yes. But Yoopers aren't much for hotels."

"Between where and where?" Audra's face was as puzzled as her voice.

Lydia started the car, then sat back and looked at her friend. "God, I am so glad to see you. But *what* are you doing here?"

"Lyd, I couldn't stand it anymore, not knowing if you were okay."

"I texted you I—"

"Yeah, well, 'I'm okay' every few days and your rare phone calls haven't been all that reassuring. And from the looks of you, I'd say I was right—you are not okay. You lose any more weight and I'll force you into anorexia rehab." Audra reached up and lightly fingered Lydia's hair. "But I do like the new 'do. Who'da thunk all shaggy would look so cute on you?"

"Really?"

"Really. Except for looking tired, you look ten years younger without the South Tampa bob. But after all day on planes I'm feeling twenty years older. And famished. Can we please get out of here?"

On the trip back, Lydia said little. She didn't have to. Audra always was a talker, and she nattered on almost non-stop, bouncing between news from home, gossip she'd heard—some about people Lydia knew, some she'd never heard of—good store sales and lousy customers, staffing headaches and damaged shipments, or commenting on the lushness or desolation of the scenery. But not one word about Gil. Lydia knew Audra's rambling was as intentional as it was typical, and she was grateful. She wasn't ready to talk about that yet either.

"Hey, signs of civilization." Audra shifted in her seat as they approached the stoplight outside Falton. "That mean we're almost there?"

"Nope. Another half hour."

Audra groaned. "I *so* have to pee."

Lydia smiled and turned into a parking lot. "Good thing you said so now. Otherwise you'd have to go on the side of the road."

"Yeah, well, if I'd'a known I'd be out in the middle of nowhere I'd have packed my She-Wee." Audra was out of the car almost before it came to a stop in front of the convenience store, Lydia's laughter trailing behind her as she raced away.

Minutes later Audra came out, a cup of coffee in each hand, and walked to Lydia's door. Lydia rolled down the window to take one but Audra handed her both. "I'll be right back."

"*Now* where are you going?"

Striding away, Audra pointed across the parking lot. "Liquor store."

"I've got booze," Lydia yelled.

"Yeah, well, probably not enough," Audra hollered back as she kept moving.

Lydia sighed. She nestled the coffee into the console cup holders, then started the car and drove across the lot of the small strip center. When Audra reappeared, laden with two heavy bags, Lydia tapped the horn and rolled down the back window. Audra hoisted the bags through it onto the seat. "Jesus," Lydia said, "you plan to stay the summer or just get us blackout drunk?"

Sliding back into the passenger seat, Audra said, "Depends. Whatever it takes." Flashing a mischievous grin, she added, "Plus, I brought something else for us to partake of."

Concentrating on pulling back onto the two-lane, Lydia half noticed Audra reach into her bra. But she sure noticed the two baggies Audra pulled out and waved in front of the windshield. "Holy shit. You flew with joints?"

"Yup." Audra pushed the baggies in her purse. "They're a little bit smooshed but we can fix that. Now, home James. *Puh*-leeze, I'm starving. And after you feed me, we are going to talk."

Lydia chuckled as Audra opened and handed her a cup of coffee. "You *have* been talking—nonstop."

"Yeah, and I'm tired of listening to myself. So it's going to be your turn. And you *will* talk." Audra shot Lydia a sharp look as she took a sip of her coffee, then relaxed against the seat, turning her attention out the window beside her.

Silence hung between them until Lydia turned south and said, "About ten minutes more."

Audra let out a heavy sigh. "Oh, good. The coffee helped but I am pooped. It's been a long day. A long, long couple of weeks, actually." Her voice was soft.

Lydia's voice was too when she replied, "Yes. Yes it has. You have no idea."

Audra patted Lydia's knee. "I know, sweetie. But I want to know. Good Lord, what's that? A used car lot? Out here?" Audra pointed at the field packed with cars.

"That is the Conklin's Memorial Day fish-fry. That's where I was when I got your text. Max was right when he said it would be packed. It's an even bigger crowd than when we got there."

"You were at a party?" Audra's voice was as incredulous as her wide-eyed stare. "'We'? And who is this Max? Just what have you been doing up here? I'm worried sick about you, and you're already giving Gil payback with some other guy?"

Lydia glared at her best friend. "Don't even go there. Dave and Bess sent Max over to drag me there because Dave knew I wanted some walleye. It was easier to give in than to argue. I hadn't been there long, in fact I was about ten minutes away from going home when you texted."

"Well." The word was a huff. "I don't know whether I should be relieved or even more worried. You seem to be settling in quite well."

Lydia slowed the car, watching for the small Castle Berry signpost. As she turned into the tree-shrouded drive and stopped before the gate, Audra said, "Wow. How do you find this in the dark?"

"With difficulty, no doubt. I haven't tried. This is only the third time I've left."

The drive curved and opened a vista onto the lake, calm and shimmering under the evening sun. "Oh, Lyd. This is gorgeous. No wonder you wanted to come here."

Stopping the car and turning off the ignition, Lydia said, "Not so much wanted as not knowing where else to go."

Audra closed her car door and stood gazing at the lodge as Lydia opened the trunk for her baggage. Looking up, she too saw the lodge afresh, as if through Audra's eyes—the sunlight shimmering on the bright white paint and curtained windows, the wide, welcoming porch, and the wood-framed screen door that carried them both back to sweet summertime childhood memories. Closing the trunk, Lydia said, "But once I got here, I knew I needed to be. For more reasons than just Gil not being able to find me. Grab the stuff from the back seat, will you?"

Audra followed Lydia inside. "Set the booze on the long table there," Lydia said, nodding toward the left as she carried Audra's bag to the foot of the stairs. Audra slung her purse onto the sofa, scanning the great room slowly.

"Wow. This place is awesome, Lyd. I almost feel like I've stepped back into the 1940s."

Lydia smiled, filled with a sense of family pride at her friend's approval. "Thom's done a great job keeping the place up. And modernizing it. Dishwasher. Wi-Fi. Stuff our grandmother never would have approved of, even if she could have comprehended them."

"So I won't have to do laundry in an old wringer washer? My mom had one when I was little. No matter how much I begged she wouldn't let me feed clothes through it."

"I know. While boys were always being warned, 'You'll put your eye out with that BB gun,' I was told, 'You'll get your arm mangled.'"

"Oh my god, my grandmother had a Mangle," Audra countered, trailing Lydia as they carried the liquor bags into the kitchen. "Remember those? She never let me near it when she was pressing the linens. Those suckers were aptly named—they literally could mangle a person. Food!" Audra grabbed an apple from the almost empty fruit bowl on the counter. "And can I get a glass of water? I'm parched."

"Sure." Lydia drew a glass from the cupboard, filled it from the tap, and handed it to Audra.

"Ugh," Audra sputtered. "Your water tastes funny. And Jesus, it's cold. Makes my teeth hurt."

"Which is why you do not want to take a cold shower up here. And it tastes like water's supposed to, not that treated Hillsborough's Finest back home. This stuff's pure, piped from an artesian spring out in the woods. You'll get to liking it."

Audra wrinkled her nose. "We'll see about that." She bit into the apple while Lydia put the liquor away and then pulled a few things from the refrigerator. "You mind if I don't cook a proper meal? There's not much in the house."

"That's okay, just feed me, Seymour, feed me!" Audra's voice came from inside the pantry off the kitchen. "Good lord, look at all these dishes. You've got enough to serve an army."

"Yup. Back when this was a lodge we fed as many as twenty at a time when the place was full. Three times a day. And we kids were slave labor washing and drying it all," Lydia answered, filling a plate with cubes of cheese and strips of green pepper. She pulled out a cutting board to slice the last of the salami and some bread. "Got so I hated seeing those plates. Now I'm grateful to see them again. Grab a couple, will you?"

Audra returned with them. "Where can I throw this," she asked, holding up the apple core.

"Compost bin under the sink. What do you want to drink?"

"Hmmm." Audra eyed the platter Lydia was finishing. "Since we're having a continental picnic, how about opening a bottle of the red?"

"Sounds good. Wineglasses are in the pantry. Corkscrews are probably in one of the drawers."

When Audra emerged, Lydia was slipping into her light jacket. "I thought we'd eat out on the porch. It's starting to get cool, so grab a sweater." While

Audra rummaged through her bag, Lydia opened the wine. They carried everything to the porch. Audra poured the wine and lifted her glass as she handed the other to Lydia. "To us—BFFs and bad-girl goddesses to the end."

The sip Lydia took was hard to swallow through her tightened throat. She was suddenly overwhelmed by the comfort of knowing, again, what a true friend Audra was. "I still can't believe," she whispered, "that you're here. You didn't have to come."

Audra let out a long, satisfied sigh as she sank into the deep cushion of a rattan chair. "Nope, I didn't. But I had to find out if you were handing me a line of bullshit with your 'I'm okay' texts."

"Have I ever lied to you?"

"Okay, okay, okay. Then I won't lie to you either. I was scared to death. We've both had rough patches before, but *this* was drastic. I was scared to death," Audra repeated, "and *pissed*."

"I'm sorry. I kept telling you not to worry."

"Yeah, well, fat lot of good that did." Audra leaned forward to pluck a cheese cube from the platter. "Besides, I wasn't much good at the store, constantly thinking about you."

"I'm sorry," Lydia said once more.

"It's okay." She shrugged and chewed. "Gave me an excuse to take off more than three days since—what, four years ago? When the four of us went to Jamaica? And that turned out to be a real swell time, didn't it?"

Lydia couldn't help but laugh, and Audra did too. Audra had been head over heels in lust with a guy she'd been seeing for about six months. The trip to Jamaica had put an end to that when he had propositioned another woman in front of her while the four of them were at dinner. Without a word Audra had left the table, returned to their room, and locked his bags outside the door. None of them saw the guy again, and the last two days of that vacation were, to say the least, a bit tense.

"Men," Audra said in disgust as she reached for more food and sat back.

The silence of friendship hung between them as Audra continued to eat and Lydia sipped her wine. She stared out over the water, still calm and golden-flecked by the descending sun. Snippets of bird chatter and the occasional cry of a gull sounded. Then a long flock of Canada geese came into view from the south, settling on both the shore and the lake as graceful as the day itself.

Audra set her empty plate aside and picked up her wine glass. "You need to eat."

"I'm not hungry."

"No food, you'll get drunk."

Lydia's laugh was wry. "With luck."

She turned away from her friend's harsh look and reached for the wine bottle. She did want to get drunk. She'd wanted to for weeks but hadn't dared, for fear she would do something stupid, or harmful. With Audra here—Audra to protect her—maybe she would do just that, she thought. Get stinkin', pukin', plastered drunk for the first time in decades, and just for a little while make all those decades disappear, make all the pain go away.

Audra pulled a lighter and a cigarette pack from her sweater pocket, drew out two, and handed one to Lydia. "Here. We'll save the good stuff till later."

Lydia lit the cigarette and sighed in contentment as she exhaled. "Oh god, I needed this."

They sat in silence for a few minutes more, sipping their wine and smoking. Gray clouds were rising from the west, casting a filter over the sun. The lake surface darkened in a way that seemed foreboding, but laughter from a boat heading toward Pines Pointe lifted the gloom Lydia felt descending on her.

"Someone's having fun," Audra noted. "Where can I put this out?"

"Oh gosh." Lydia looked around for something to use as an ashtray. There was nothing, so she poured a bit of her wine onto her unused plate. "This'll do for now. Tomorrow I'll dig through the pantry. There used to be dozens of ashtrays. Collectors' items by now. Maybe a couple are still around."

Resettling herself with her legs tucked under her, Audra said, "So, speaking of having fun, you had some today? Tell me about this party you went to."

"Who said anything about having fun? Besides, I didn't 'went to' the party, I was dragged to it," Lydia corrected.

"Oh, yeah, right. At gunpoint?"

"Okay. More like guilted to it." Over their wine Lydia recounted the surprise of seeing the Clar's Corner name when she'd arrived, stopping there on her way to the lodge, meeting Bess and Katie, then Dave, who thought she was breaking into the lodge. She told Audra about finding the illegal party site and their trek through the woods. "When I learned they sold lake fish at the store, I asked Dave to let me know when there was some walleye. Which it turned out was today. But I had to go to the party to get it. When Dave first told me about their bash and invited me, I said thanks but no." Lydia looked at Audra. "But then Max showed up. Said he had orders to, as he put it, procure me. So I gave up arguing and gave in. But I insisted on taking my own car. I didn't want to be stuck there any longer than I had to be. I was starting to try to find a way to make an exit—I'd been there maybe an hour—when your text came in."

With a sly grin, Audra drew her sweater tighter. "Ah, again with this Max."

"Do you want to go in?" Lydia ignored Audra's comment. "It's getting a bit chilly."

"Not yet. It's too pretty out here."

"Okay. I'll get us a couple of afghans." Lydia gathered up the plates. "And another bottle of wine."

When she returned, Audra was staring at the lake with a faraway look. Placing a folded throw on Audra's lap, Lydia said, "Found us an ashtray, too."

"Mmm? Oh, good." Pulled back to the present, Audra unfolded the lap robe and snuggled beneath it. "It's so pretty here, Lyd. I can understand why you came. What I don't understand is why you don't come more often. I sure would."

"Well, it's a bit of a hike, as I think you noticed. If my brother and his wife didn't live closer—they're in Chicago and that's an all-day drive—I suppose we would have sold it years ago. Neither of us wants to do that. But I guess that'll happen after we're gone. Unless their kids take an interest. Sara and James don't have any. They haven't been up here since they were little."

"Well, I'd come up here just for the peace alone. If you ever want to invite me again, I'll be here in a heartbeat."

Lydia let out a laugh. "Invite you again? I didn't invite you this time."

Audra shrugged. "Maybe not, but you were the one who told me where you were. Figured I'd drop by, see how you're doing."

Startled, Lydia looked at Audra, whose eyes were boring into her. "What do you mean, I told you? I didn't. And I told you, I'm doing okay."

"You did. One of your texts. You said you were hiding among the yoopers. I had to look that up. Upper Peninsula. U.P. Yooper. When I did, I knew. Choosing the airport was kind of a stab in the dark, though. So," Audra said, "a fourth glass of wine, no food, total seclusion—I'd say you're not doing okay at all. Time to come clean with me, girlfriend. Now. Before you get so drunk I have to steer you to a bed."

Silent, Lydia looked out at the lake. She didn't know what to say. How to even begin. She didn't know if she could actually speak of what she'd learned about the man she thought she knew, the man she still loved and now hated in equal measure.

"So? I'm waiting. And I'll sit here all night if I have to, until you come straight with me."

Lydia's sigh was deep and tired. She set her glass down, rose, and at the screen door said, "I'll be right back."

Now it was Audra who sighed. Lydia recognized it as a sound of frustration. When she returned with her laptop, she rested it on her knees and tapped several keys. As folders flashed open on the screen, she handed the laptop to Audra. "See for yourself. This'll tell you how I'm doing."

Audra's face and voice expressed confusion. "What am I looking for?"

"Open any of them. You'll see."

As Audra began, Lydia lit another cigarette. Its orange-hot tip was the color of the setting sun. Sparrows singing a lullaby were the only sound, until Audra uttered a whispered, "Holy shit." Lydia said nothing.

Audra tapped the touchpad to open another file and whispered another expletive. She snapped the laptop closed. "I can't look at any more of this. It's sick. It makes *me* sick. What the *fuck* is going on?"

"Obviously a lot more than just an affair." Lydia put air quotes around the "just." "And obviously, it's been going on for a very, very long time."

Audra let out a long breathy, "Whoa." She set the laptop aside, then lit herself a cigarette. She shook her head. "This is mind-boggling. What are you going to do?"

"I don't know." Lydia looked her friend in the eye. "I want him dead. But after what he's done, dead's not good enough."

Chapter 9

The light through the curtains was as dull as Lydia felt. She wanted to go back to sleep—to sleep and sleep and sleep and sleep—but her bladder was an alarm clock that couldn't be ignored. She swallowed as she sat up, her mouth dry, grimacing at the wine and cigarette taste that coated her tongue. After scouring with her toothbrush, she grimaced again, this time at the haggard reflection in the mirror. Her face was puffy, dark half-moons under her eyes. Swabbing her face with a soaked washcloth and a generous amount of moisturizer did nothing to help her look or feel better. *Thank God no one but Audra will see*, she thought, *and we've both seen each other looking worse.*

Audra was at the kitchen table, laptop open, when Lydia crossed the great room. "Morning." Her voice sounded as tired as she felt.

"Morning. Coffee's ready."

"Smelled it. Thanks."

When Lydia sat down with her mug, Audra shut the laptop and looked up. "You look like hell."

Lydia's smile was half sneer. "Thanks for the confirmation. You been up long?"

"Maybe half an hour. You know, the last time we shared a bed was sleepovers in our teens? You didn't snore then."

"Ooo, sorry. The wine's fault, not mine, I'm sure. I hope I didn't keep you awake much."

"No, but this shit sure did," Audra said, pointing at the laptop.

"Tell me about it. It was bad enough when I found out about the affair. Then when I found this … Funny thing though, it was the weirdest dreams—nightmares, almost—that led me down the cyber rabbit hole to the whole truth. But I don't want to talk about it now."

Audra got up, retrieved the coffee pot, and refilled her mug. She set a potholder and the carafe on the table, and returned to the counter. "Then, to change the subject, what are we doing today? Other than getting more food in this place before we starve. Which is another reason I'm glad I came—you have got to start eating. Even if I have to force-feed you." She held up an apple and shook it at Lydia.

"Okay, okay, *Mom*."

"By the way, where do you buy stuff out here in the wilderness? I keep expecting Laura Ingalls Wilder to walk up the steps carrying eggs from the henhouse."

"It's not the wilderness, for god's sake. Did you notice there are paved roads? And flushing toilets?"

Audra sat down, placing a small bowl of apple quarters and a halved banana between them. "But after we dine on this hearty repast, you are slap out of food. Seriously. I went through the cupboards while the coffee was brewing. Everything is open-add-water-and-microwave processed food. You don't feed that brain of yours better, you're going to make some very bad decisions about this mess."

Elbow on the table, Lydia lowered her head and dragged a hand through her hair—it felt dirty. "I know. I just don't have the desire to eat, let alone cook. Or think."

"So I'll do the thinking for both of us right now. I get unpacked in a bedroom of my own, we get cleaned up, and we get food. In that order. Then can we go swimming? That lake looks so inviting."

Lydia grinned. "To a polar bear, maybe. Tell you what, though, we'll go out in the rowboat this afternoon. Floating over it is almost as good."

After rinsing out the coffee pot, mugs, and dish, they picked up Audra's bags and Lydia led the way upstairs. "Four bedrooms, your choice. Biggest one is right here, but it's farthest from the bathroom. That's at the end of the hall."

Audra opened the door and stepped in. "Oh, this is pretty. My god, look at these antiques. This furniture is gorgeous. Are all the rooms like this?" She tossed her bag onto the bed.

Lydia followed Audra and placed the bag she carried on the cedar chest set between two tall, wide windows. Opening the drapes to a view of the lake, she said, "Pretty much. The things in here were my grandparents'—actually, their parents'. The other rooms gave my brother and his wife an excuse to indulge in antique hunting in Chicago. I'll go get the sheets."

It was late morning before they were in the car. Windows rolled down, the warm day flowed through, carrying the smell of earth, decaying wood, budding trees, and blossoming wildflowers, an aroma as heady as a wine's bouquet. Audra's arm stretched out the passenger window, her fingers playing in the wind as if feeling a fine fabric. No traffic behind her, Lydia drove leisurely. She noticed things she'd missed on her earlier trip into town, like the eruption of purple irises along the bed of the creek they crossed.

"Pretty." Audra noticed them too. "Let's be bad girls and steal some on our way home."

Bad girls. Lydia and Audra had dubbed themselves the BGs long before the actual BeeGees ever had a hit. They hadn't been all that bad, although their parents would have grounded them for life if they'd found out some of the things they'd done. Like skipping school, or being part of the group—but not the part that got caught—for t.p.'ing a disliked teacher's house. Or the night Audra was sleeping over and they told their parents they were going to a dance. What they hadn't said was that the dance was in Sarasota, more than an hour away. They didn't notice the time until half an hour before their midnight curfew, but made it home in the ten-minute grace period because Audra drove her Chevy Nova at over a hundred miles an hour. They'd sweated for a week that her dad might check the odometer and bust them.

"Whatever happened to our bad-girl side?" Lydia asked as she turned at the stoplight toward town.

"Life. We were raised to be proper. Build a successful career. Have a happy marriage."

"Yeah, well, look how well that turned out, for both of us. You and Ryan split years ago, and mine is now officially fucked."

Audra reached over and patted Lydia's arm. "Hey, two out of three is still a winner. Once you get past the pain. Oh, look at all these darling shops. I wonder if I can get some ideas. Plus, then I can write this off as a business trip."

"Not today." Lydia shook her head. "You can take the car and come back. I'm not up for it."

"Deal. Now, this place has to have at least one restaurant. If I don't get lunch before we go into a grocery, I'm likely to buy the place out." Audra turned from window to window, taking in the little town as they drove. They passed Doozy's—after last night Lydia wasn't about to immerse herself in the bar smell of alcohol and cigarettes that wafted into its dining room. Not far beyond, she pulled into the parking lot of a small diner.

“This Little Piggy—that’s me!” Audra’s voice was chipper. Lydia wondered if she’d ever have an appetite for anything again.

An older man behind the cash stand greeted them with a curt, “Mornin’,” handed them each a menu and told them to sit anywhere, and went back to working a crossword puzzle. More than half the tables and booths were taken. Lydia was about to head to the far end of the room when Audra grabbed her arm and pointed. “Let’s sit there. I want to look outside.”

Three booths, two of them taken, fronted a large window. Lydia would have preferred a dark hole—maybe she should have stopped at Doozy’s, she thought, but she said nothing. A waitress clearing a nearby table called out a cheerful, “Be right there. Two coffees?”

“Please,” Audra answered as Lydia nodded silently. “And two waters, please.”

“Gotcha,” the young woman said as she carried a stack of plates away.

“I am *starving*,” Audra repeated, her attention focused on her opened menu, while Lydia ignored hers. Audra suddenly leaned low across the table between them. She stage-whispered, “Oh my god, this place sell pasties? Right on the *menu*? Let’s each get a pair. Wear them out on the rowboat.”

Lydia couldn’t help but laugh. “*Pass*-tees, dear, not pay-stees. It’s a meat and potato pie. Not like a chicken pot pie, though—shaped like a moon pie.”

“Oh.” Audra’s face fell in disappointment, then perked up again. “Hey, maybe they should sell *edible* pasties. You know, a fried egg for the boob, with bean sprout tassels.”

Lydia suppressed her giggle as the waitress, back with a coffee pot and water pitcher, said, “Um, sorry, we don’t have bean sprouts. But we do have vegetarian options.”

Audra turned an innocent smile upward. “Wise. But, since I’m not vegetarian, or Jewish, how’s your bacon?”

“All of it’s great. Five kinds—Canadian, regular, apple wood or hickory smoked, and maple syrup,” the waitress said, pulling a pencil and order pad out of her apron pocket.

“Wow. Can I get two pieces of each? Except not the Canadian, just the others?”

“Uh … sure, I guess.” The waitress’s words suggested it was an unusual request.

"And two eggs, over medium," Audra said, looking at the menu again. "Plus home fries, with onion. And toast. Rye, please." Audra slapped the menu shut and slid it across the table as the waitress turned to Lydia. "For you, ma'am?"

"Just an English muffin."

"Oh no you don't." Audra's voice was mom-sharp. She looked at the waitress. "She'll have two eggs, scrambled, home fries, and sausage links, well done. And an English muffin."

"Audra, I am not hungry."

"I don't care. You are going to eat."

The waitress silently turned away as the two women just as silently glowered at each other.

By the time they left, Audra's plates were clean and she'd ordered two enormous cinnamon rolls to go. At her unrelenting urging, Lydia managed to eat her eggs and muffin, one of the sausages, and a couple bites of the potatoes. "There now, don't you feel better already," Audra asked as she handed cash and the tab to the man on the stool. Pushing the restaurant door open, she said, "Now, groceries. And then, once more to the lake."

Stepping out of the car at the lodge, light zephyrs caressed them like cashmere under the mid-afternoon sun and cloudless sky. They opened all the downstairs windows, infusing the lodge with the sound and scent of the lake and the cocooning woods. On a kitchen counter, Audra created a still life from some of the groceries with her left eye for design. A loaf of bread and two baguettes rested between large bowls, one piled with winter-drab onions and potatoes, the other popping with the summery vividness of red apples, purple grapes, bright lemons, and limes. A bouquet of stolen iris towered in the center of the dining table—they had indeed been bad girls—and the refrigerator and cupboards were full. Lydia had given up trying to convince Audra to rein herself in at the store, and by the time they'd reached the checkout, their cart was piled high.

"Okay, you promised me we'd go out in the rowboat. I vote we do it in bathing suits. It might be too cold to swim, but it's warm enough for some sunbathing."

"If you brought one, you go ahead. I don't have one."

"Oh, yes, you do, 'cause I brought two." Audra's voice lilted with glee. "And you know it'll fit. Besides, I'm the one who'll have a fit if I don't see you in something other than black, Queen Victoria. I'll run upstairs and get it."

Audra was halfway across the great room when they heard tires on the gravel outside, then the slamming of car doors. Audra looked at Lydia with a bit of apprehension. "Should I grab something as a weapon?"

"Don't be silly," Lydia said, opening the screen door. In the drive stood a pickup truck. Extended wood-slat rails on the bed penned in beer kegs and plastic barrels marked for trash or recycling.

"Hi Lady L, hi," Katie's happy voice called out as she raced up the steps. Dave followed, and Audra approached the door. "Momma said you were at our party but I didn't get to see you. I wanted to. I would have made you a daisy necklace. Oh, hi other lady. I'm Katie."

"Hi, yourself, Miss Katie. I'm Mizz Audra." Audra turned to Lydia. "Shy child, isn't she?"

Dave laughed and tousled Katie's hair. "Yup, my daughter's a real wallflower."

"Dad-dy," Katie moaned with an eye roll. "Walls don't have flowers."

"Some walls do. On wallpaper."

"Oh! You and Momma put wallpaper in the bathroom. How come it doesn't have flowers on it? That'd be prettier than those pictures of bottles and stuff."

"Honey, you'll have to discuss decorating decisions with your mother. Now, we've interrupted Elle and her friend. Would you please explain why?"

"Yeah." Katie bounced on her toes. "We're going to the dump! Wanna come? It's a lotta fun. One time I found a—"

"Uh, honey," David interrupted, "maybe some other time. L, I come by every Saturday for trash when your brother's here. Part of my job. Thought by now you might have some to get rid of. Was going to check the cans out back if you weren't here. Special run today—actually, second run today, because of party cleanup. Sorry we didn't get a chance to chat yesterday."

"Or even say goodbye." Max leaned against the truck.

"Max, I'm really sorry." Lydia was aware of Audra's attention shifting between him and her. "I am. I had to leave right away. I'd gotten Audra's text, saying she was flying into Chippewa. I didn't know she was coming. And her plane had already landed by the time I made it there. I did ask Bess …"

"Not a problem," Dave assured her. "But Bess was worried something might've been wrong. Glad to know it was a good thing instead." He nodded to Audra with a smile.

"Well, thank you again for the walleye yesterday. It was delicious. Brought back a lot of memories."

"Now that I'm not stocking up for a fish fry, I'll bring you some next time we have a good haul. So, anything inside you want thrown away?"

"Not much. I'll get it."

"While you do that I'll get the can from out here."

Audra leaned against a porch column watching, as Lydia carried out a half-filled kitchen trash bag and two wine bottles. As she passed Audra, Lydia whispered, "They're going to think we're lushes."

"For two empty wine bottles? Get a grip."

"Less than I expected." Dave upended the minimal contents of the garbage can into another on the truck.

"Well, most of what I eat can be composted …"

"Yeah, *if* you were eating, you liar." Audra's words were too soft for anyone but Lydia to hear.

"Come on, Katie, time to go," Max called. He held the truck door open. While Dave disappeared around the corner of the lodge with the emptied garbage can, Katie climbed in, followed by Max. As Katie chattered across him, Lydia was aware of Max's profile, his eyes intent on the view out the windshield.

Dave slammed the cab door and started the ignition, calling out, "See you later."

"Bye! Bye, Lady L! And Mizz Audra. Bye!" Katie hollered, waving wildly. Max, unsmiling, gave the women a short nod.

Lydia went up the steps. Audra still leaned against the column; her arms now folded across her chest. She raised her eyebrows. "Well, that was interesting."

"What?"

"Oh, nothing." Audra followed Lydia inside. "Nothing we can't talk about later. I'm getting into a bathing suit, and so are you, and you are taking me out on that beautiful lake. Right now."

"Bring a long-sleeved shirt. It'll be cooler out on the water."

Audra said no more as she headed up the stairs. Neither of them spoke as Lydia handed Audra a small tote with water bottles, sunscreen, and repellent, then locked the lodge door. They walked to the dock after Lydia grabbed two seat cushions from the boathouse. The silence continued as they stepped into the small boat. Lydia was grateful that they did not always have to talk, but something about Audra's silence now made Lydia wonder where her friend's head was. As she rowed along the cove, she began pointing things out, naming trees she knew Audra was not familiar with, and telling little stories about the old lodge and the resorts along the shore. Audra listened but said nothing.

Lydia turned the boat out toward open water and triangulated to a point several hundred yards out from the lodge. Lifting the oars into the boat, she said, "Toss out the anchor? It's in the tip of the bow."

Still silent, Audra complied. Lydia was now certain something was behind Audra's continued quiet. "Okay, what gives?"

"Nothing." Audra turned away, reaching into the tote for the bottled waters.

"Nothing," Lydia repeated, taking the one Audra offered. "The first full word you've said since we left the lodge, and the same word you said back then. Nothing is something, and something is obviously bothering you. What?"

Audra locked eyes with Lydia as she took a swig from her bottle. Still looking at Lydia, Audra twisted the top back on. "Okay, tell me about this Max."

"Max?" She shrugged. "I don't know. He spends a few weeks a year at Dave and Bess's resort. That's about all I know."

"Max was the one who took you to that party yesterday?"

"Yeah. So? But he didn't take me. They asked him to come get me. They were busy."

"And you were perfectly fine leaving with some guy you'd just met, to supposedly go with him to someplace he said he was taking you."

"I told you; I took my own car. And it wasn't the first time we met." Lydia thought she saw an I-didn't-think-so in Audra's eyes.

Audra splayed her arms out, grasping the edges of the narrow boat, then leaned back, eyes closed, to absorb the warm sun. "I see. So, how'd you meet him?"

Shrugging again, Lydia said, "We didn't so much meet. We ran into each other a couple of times."

"You ran into each other," Audra repeated. "I thought you'd barely left this place."

"Twice. Well, before the fish fry, and today. I'd gone into Falton and town. It was nothing but coincidence."

Audra didn't need to say what Lydia had heard her say numerous times: "I don't believe in coincidence." For some reason feeling flustered, Lydia went on. "First it was at the car rental desk at the airport. He was ahead of me. Only reason I really noticed him was because he tipped his hat at me. Tipped his hat, who does that anymore?" she asked. "Then before I got to the lodge, I saw Clar's Corner and stopped for a few things. That's when I met Katie and her mom, Bess. I knew Bess's great-uncle Clar—"

"Max," Audra interrupted. "What's that got to do with Max?"

"Geeze, what is with you? It turned out Max was already in there. Kind of surprised us both. I don't remember saying anything to him but he joked that we could have rented one vehicle, not two."

"Uh-huh. Crossing paths twice isn't 'kept running into each other.' Then?"

"Then, last Friday, I went into Nibic. To confront more of the past. Before coming home, I decided to stop for a drink. And he showed up. Complete coincidence."

"Then?" Audra asked again.

"Then he said it was apparent we should introduce ourselves and told me his name. But I didn't tell him mine. I started to. Same with Bess and Katie. I just gave them my initial. For some reason, I don't want anyone to know who I am." Lydia paused, then made a small laugh. "Probably because I don't know who I am right now. I did have to tell Dave I'm Thom's sister. He was about to call the cops when he found me here. I suppose he's told Bess."

"Okay." Audra nodded. "Max. You said he took you to the party."

"Oh, for god's sake. How many times do I have to say it? He did not *take* me to the party. Dave had asked me to come over for it. I told him I couldn't, I had too much work. Then Max showed up, said Dave and Bess had sent him to get me. It was easier to go than to keep arguing. I insisted on taking my car so I could cut out. When your text came in, it gave me the perfect reason to do that."

"Don't you mean ghost Max?"

"I did not ghost. I told Bess goodbye and asked her to tell Dave, Max, and Katie I was sorry but I had to leave. What *is* it with this third degree about Max?"

"Just curious if you're as interested in him as he is in you."

"What?" Lydia spit out. "You are nuts. Why in god's name would I be interested in any man after finding out what that scumbag husband's done?"

"Yeah, but Max doesn't know that. And you took off your wedding ring. He thinks you're fair game."

"Where in the world are you coming up with this?"

"Oh, honey, it was written all over his face and body language."

"Honestly, you are nuts." But deep inside Lydia felt an uncomfortable squirming, that sensation of the beginning of awareness. "Jesus, Aud. That's the last thing I need."

"Or maybe it's exactly what you do need. Stop looking back and start moving forward."

"How? How am I supposed to do that?" Lydia's voice choked. "How am I supposed to claw my way out of this hell?"

"By *clawing* your way out. You've been pissed on. We know that. Now it's time to get pissed off."

"Oh, I am. Believe you me, I am."

"Yeah, but you're wallowing in it because you are still in love with Gil. It's time to put that anger to work for you." Audra brushed strands of wind-ruffled hair from her face. "Twenty questions. *Ladies Home Journal* first—can this marriage be saved?"

Lydia stared out at a speedboat cutting across the distant water. "No."

"Do you wish it could be?"

Still watching the boat, Lydia's answer was hesitant. "I don't know. No. And yes. Before I found out all this shit. When I thought it was just an affair … That's why I had to leave, to figure out if I could stay, after he had promised me the other time that it wouldn't happen again."

"You still loved Gil when you left?" When Lydia didn't answer, Audra asked, "You still love him?"

Lydia's eyes were hard when she looked straight into Audra's.

"Hate him?"

Lydia nodded, almost imperceptibly, as embers of anger heated within her.

"What about the other woman?"

"And the horse she rode in on."

"So what do you want?"

"Truth? I want him to suffer. And I want her dead."

"Yeah, but that's not an option. Because I do not have the time to drive up to Brooksville every week to visit you behind bars."

"Yeah, well maybe I'll get lucky and she'll die a slow, lingering death from an untreated STD."

"Oh my god." The shock of realization crossed Audra's face. "What if he's given you one?"

"Hah, I doubt it. It's been so long since he touched me I'm sure I'd have seen signs by now."

"Ooh, no. That's not good enough. You've got to get checked, and asap. As in tomorrow. There's got to be a doctor's office or medical clinic somewhere around here, and we are going to find it."

Lydia felt the squirming sensation again. "Okay."

"If you're clean, that's one less thing to think about. If you're not, you'll get treated and have more ammo for the divorce. Because there is going to be a divorce, right?"

"Oh yeah."

"And what do you want out of it?"

"I want everything. I want to leave him penniless. Homeless would be ideal. Let him go bunk with all his fuck-buddies. See how much they like him then."

"Have you heard anything from him? I haven't, and I half hoped to."

Lydia grinned. "Why? So you could tear him a new one?" Audra's smile in return was almost wicked. "If he's tried to call, I don't know it," Lydia said. "The phone's turned off. I turn it on once a day, in case one of the kids texted. There haven't been many from him. I told you about the first two. Then—get this—last Friday he said, if I was getting back did I want to go to dinner at Malio's. Like an expensive dinner was going to make it all up to me?"

"Or that discussing this in public would keep you from exploding."

"Ha. It would have been all over social media before my glass of red wine had stopped dripping off his face." Both women laughed at the idea.

"And I'd have had customers talking about it for days," Audra said. "So what about the other messages? Is he beginning to grovel?"

Lydia's laugh now was full-throated. "Oh, this is great. He wanted to know the name of the cleaners I take his things to. He needed to take his dirty laundry and pick up what was there, he was out of clean clothes. Didn't answer that one either. His problem, not mine."

"Do you suppose he's said anything to the kids?"

Lydia shook her head. "They would have gone batshit. I haven't heard from James, but that's not unusual. Sara's texted a few times, once for a recipe, the others just chit chat."

"So they don't even know you're gone?"

"Sara does. I knew if she tried to reach me at work … So I told her what I've told people up here. That I'm on a work sabbatical. But I didn't tell her where. If they talk, she'll probably tell her brother."

"When are you going to tell them? And what are you going to tell them?"

Lydia sighed. Leaning down against the edge of the boat, she slipped her hand into the cold water and stirred it, as if hoping to sweep up a handful of answers from its depths. "I don't know," she murmured. "The truth would kill them. And God knows would embarrass me. Because they'd ask the same question I've been asking myself."

"What's that?"

"How did this happen?" She sat up and looked at Audra, feeling the pain emanating from her words. "How could I not see it? How could I have been so *stupid*?"

"Are you kidding me? Stupid's got nothing to do with it. His business gave him the perfect cover for all of his little excursions. And for hiding that money. Which, by the way, will definitely work in your favor in court."

The breeze had been growing stronger and the boat began to sway, buffeted by the swells pushing against it. Lydia sighed again. "Let's go in. I'm drained. I can't talk about this anymore."

Audra pulled in the anchor as Lydia released the oars from their oarlocks. She was tired, and glad for the water's help propelling them toward shore.

Chapter 10

Shade darkened the bedroom when Lydia opened her eyes. She stared at the white bead-board ceiling as consciousness returned. Having succumbed to a nap after being out on the water was unsettling. Would she have been this worn down, she wondered, this tired—tired of life—if her marriage had imploded thirty years ago instead of now? When most of life, when a chance of happiness, still lay ahead?

The lodge was silent and empty but infused with the aroma of roasting chicken. In the kitchen, she glanced into the oven, where a pan of chicken thighs and vegetables were beginning to bubble. She eased the sink tap on, so the water flowed into a glass without disturbing the afternoon quiet, and stood at the kitchen window as she drank. Even the lake seemed to be holding its breath. A spot of bright red caught her attention near the shore. Audra was seated in one of the chairs, Lydia's computer open on her lap. Lydia refilled her glass and headed outside.

Audra looked up with a smile as Lydia approached the other chair. "Hey, you. Feel better?"

"Yeah. No," Lydia mumbled as she sat down.

"Hope you don't mind. Just checking the news." Audra closed the laptop and made space for it on the table between them. "And I sent an email to several divorced gals I know, asking about their attorneys."

"Oh, god, you didn't say why, did you?"

"No. Told them one of my good customers was asking around." Audra reached for a cigarette and then handed the pack to Lydia, who lit one too. "Do you want to fly back with me on Monday?" Audra's question was gentle. "Get this whole thing started?"

Lydia shook her head.

"You know you have to, sooner or later."

"I know. But I'm not ready yet. I still have too much to figure out. How to tell the kids. What to tell them." She paused. "And how I can make it as miserable as possible for Gil."

"That's what the attorney is for."

"I know. But I want to go in knowing what I want, then have the attorney figure out how I get it."

"Makes sense." Audra drew on her cigarette and exhaled. "So, how long are you planning to stay here?"

"I don't know. At least a few more weeks. Maybe the whole summer. Maybe forever." Audra looked over, concerned. Lydia smiled. "Oh, don't worry. I'm not sticking around here for winter. The only snow I want to see is while watching *White Christmas*."

Audra finished her cigarette and picked up the laptop. "Time for me to check the chicken."

"It looked good when I took a peek."

"Good. That mean you're hungry?"

"No. I meant it looked like it was roasting nicely."

"Well, you are going to eat. And starting tomorrow, three meals a day. I am not about to abide my best friend becoming far more becoming than I." Audra's last sentence fairly dripped from her exaggerated drawl, but then her tone sharpened. "Nor literally starve herself to death. Then Gil gets the house and your new address is R. I. P."

Lydia watched Audra walk toward the lodge, then stared at her feet. The black canvas of her shoes contrasted against the brilliant green grass. She kicked the shoes off and let the thin blades cool her soles. She reveled in the grasses' lush softness, the sensation awakening in her the young girl she'd been so long ago. How she'd loved going barefoot all summer long. But first Grandma Tilde, then Florida, had put an end to that. When she had turned nine, Grandma insisted, "You're being raised to be a lady, not a heathen, and ladies do not have feet as callused as a lumberjack's hands." The aunts and even her mother echoed Grandma Tilde's edict. Flip-flops, at least, were an acceptable compromise most times, and over the years Lydia had worn out dozens of pairs, from plain and cheap to "fancy" ones she decorated as a teen in hopes a boy would notice her lady-like feet. She'd once been young and dumb enough to think boys looked at anything but one part of a girl's body.

The grass was so very soft, so very unlike in Florida. This grass invited feet to be caressed. Walking barefoot on a Florida lawn was like stepping onto a bed of nails, with the added allure of unseen fire ant mounds. Slipping her toes through these sensuous blades reminded her of running her fingers through Gil's hair when they were young, when he wore it long, when passion was the immutable magnet that bound them.

"Cocktail time, darling." Audra set down a tray with two glasses and a small plate of pinwheel-wrapped canapés. The scent of roasting chicken lingered around her, and Lydia realized she was becoming hungry, not just for food but for flavor.

"Where'd those come from?" Lydia asked as she looked at the appetizers.

"Well, I was a busy, busy kitchen bee while you were napping." Audra raised her glass. "Where'd you go? You looked pretty far away just now."

Lydia slid her feet through the grass again. "Summers up here as a kid. God, I wish you could have been here with me. When we were teens. The families who came up were never here longer than a week or two. If there were girls my age, they'd leave about the time we started to know each other. My brothers and cousins always had each other to hang with. I was mostly lonely. You were two thousand miles away."

"I'm glad I'm here now. To see this place. You knew about stuff I put in letters to you but you were out in this big void that I couldn't imagine."

"Those letters. Man, those letters saved my sanity." Lydia grinned and reached for her drink. "Twelve-, fifteen-, twenty-page letters I'd write you. But you—lousy friend that you were—never wrote me more than five."

"Wait a minute. Sometimes I wrote on both sides of the page. Some girlfriend you are, harboring a page-count grudge for decades."

Both women laughed. "God, wouldn't it be a hoot," Lydia said, "if we still had those? To step back into who we were then?"

"Who we were then were angst-ridden adolescents, the weight of our tiny little worlds on our boney shoulders. All that's changed is the world is heavier, our flesh has sagged under its weight, and neither of us would be caught dead in a two-piece bathing suit again. So, tell me about your grandparents. What were they like?"

Lydia reminisced, trying hard to conjure through words the vibrant people they were, how summers here had been like living on the edge of wilderness. She went back through the history of the lake itself, the history her grandfather had taught her. The history that had become hers, anchoring her somehow to this place. Audra's occasional questions would lead her through another wormhole into memory.

With both their glasses and the nibble plate empty, Audra switched the light off on the past. "Time to eat, before that bird is beyond extra crispy."

Lydia left her shoes off.

***

An hour later the table had been cleared, the leftovers put away, and the kitchen cleaned. Lydia lowered the windows, leaving them open enough for a slice of the evening cool to slide through. Filmy clouds draped the dropping sun, defusing it to a buttery glow that poured through the picture window. At the far end of the great room and near the screen door, she switched lamps on low, so as not to shock the changing day. From Audra's room came the sound of humming. Something caused Lydia to stop, stand still. Her eyes took in the comfortable furnishings that filled the place, the familiar faces beaming benevolence from framed photos clustered about. Lydia was struck by how movie-like it all looked, like a scene from the thirties, where a smiling, arch-browed Bette Davis might step in with a vase of fresh flowers, chattering scripted gossip lines as she placed it on the sideboard. As the vision slipped away, Lydia let out a long sigh, a sigh of ease. A sense of contentment filled her. For the first time in weeks.

"Would you be a dear and pour us fresh drinks?" Audra's voice broke the reverie.

"Sure," Lydia called back. "Let's take them outside. I left my shoes there. The mosquitoes shouldn't be bad. Yet."

Utter silence still hung over the lake. Not a boat dotted its surface. The long-weekenders had gone, leaving the land to itself and those who belonged to it. Lydia relaxed in the chair and sighed again. "I'm full. That's the most I've eaten in weeks."

"Well, then no wonder you're getting skinny as a rail." Audra snapped the lighter and put its flame to her cigarette. "You hardly ate a thing."

"Yeah, compared to you, Miss Oink-oink."

"Hey, someone's got to set a good example. By the time I leave, I want you back in the habit of food that requires more than fingers."

"Well, tonight was a good start. Everything was delicious."

"Thank you. Next up is dessert."

"Oh, god," Lydia groaned. "I don't even have room for Jell-O."

"Mmm-mm-mm. You'll have room for this. Ta-*dah*." Audra grinned, pulling a baggie from her sweater pocket and holding it up. "*We* are gonna get high."

"Oh, sweet Jesus. I still can't believe you flew with that."

"Well, I couldn't count on a dispensary out here in the big woods."

Not much was said as the joint passed between them. What they did say came out quickly, trying not to waste the herb they'd inhaled. When the joint became too short to hold, Audra produced a bobby pin for a clip and they smoked it down to nothing. The contentment Lydia had felt in herself now spilled over into a sense of oneness with her surroundings. Everything she saw had been reinterpreted as if by the brushstrokes of Monet's hand. The grass beneath her feet was so soothing. Its softness reminded her of the baby blankets her mother crocheted for the births of James and Sara, gossamer shawls formed from delicate stitches of fine cashmere, so perfect for coddling a baby in Florida's mild winters. Her babies were grown now, Sara with her own; James—well, there was still a possibility, he and Rachel did seem serious. She needed to call the kids soon, see how they were doing. How was she going to tell them? They'd worry. Kids weren't supposed to worry about their parents. That was her job, to worry about them. Even though they didn't give her any reason to. But James was always so busy, working such long hours—was he eating right? He was a good cook. When he had the time. Did Rachel cook? She hoped they weren't eating out at restaurants all the time. It was so expensive, in New York City, and it wasn't all that healthy. She wondered what they'd eat for dinner tonight. If they ate. She wondered if Gil had eaten. She'd have had dinner on the table by now …

Audra's voice broke in. "Why in god's name are you worried about Gil? S.O.B. can go out for steak every night and die of a heart attack as far as I'm concerned. And save you the cost of the divorce."

Audra's voice caught Lydia off guard. Coming out of her haze, she looked at her friend. "What? How'd you know what I was thinking?"

"Because you weren't thinking. You have been motor-mouthing for the past fifteen minutes."

"Oh my god." Lydia giggled. "Oh my god, I just giggled."

Grinning, Audra shook her head. "You are *so* wasted."

Another giggle. "I know. And I'm getting the munchies. I know what I want—the Parmesan crackers we bought today." Lydia was out of her chair, toddling unsteady steps toward the lodge. Still grinning, Audra picked up their empty glasses and followed.

Lydia leaned against the kitchen counter, eating the crackers out of the box, while Audra poured more scotch over ice and then watered down the drinks. Lydia extended the box so Audra could grab a handful of the salty crisps. "So tell me this," Lydia asked, chewing. "When do I stop thinking about Gil all the time? When do I stop worrying about him? He sure hasn't worried about me. That seems clear."

"Probably never. Not after all the years you've been together. That's a ghost that'll never go away. But it'll start to fade. He's a big boy. He can forage for his own food."

"Ooo-ooo-*ooo*." Lydia hoisted the cracker box high, then doubled over in laughter and crackers spilled onto the floor. "I know! I'm going to order him a pizza. An extra-large—with everything he hates. And I'll charge it to him. Oh, leave those—we'll clean them up later. Come on, help me with this."

Lydia's fingers fumbled on the laptop's keyboard, making numerous mistakes as she pulled up a pizza shop near their house and navigated through the ordering page. It took them four tries, and a lot of laughter, as they added toppings until the pizza was laden. When she tapped "Payment," a new screen appeared. The first field required an email address. Lydia started to type.

"Wait a minute." Audra grasped Lydia's arm. "Make one up. You can't use yours or he could find out."

"You're right." Lydia thought for half a second. A sly grin crossed her face, and she typed.

"What's that?" Audra peered at the address.

"*That* is the email he and The Slut share, so they can communicate with each other and all their sex weirdos."

"Perfect. Maybe he'll think she sent it."

Inspiration lit Lydia's eyes. "Let's send her one, too. Maybe her husband will answer the door. I've got their address. Would you grab my notebook off the desk over there? It's got Gil's credit card numbers."

Before placing the order, Lydia added a tip, a very generous tip. She did the same with the one she sent to Gil's sidepiece. And with each of the additional five she ordered, each from a different chain, delivered to Gil at half-hour intervals. Her face was a mask of mischievous glee when she finished.

"God, this is *so* petty. And *so* much fun. Wish we could be flies on the wall at my house tonight."

Audra lifted her glass as if in a toast. "May the bad-ass bad girl just be getting started."

Laughter and chatter surrounded them like a cloud of mosquitoes as they headed back to the chairs at the shore.

***

Lydia was at the kitchen table, laptop opened and coffee cup at hand, when Audra wandered in the next morning. Lydia waited, smiling, as Audra filled a mug and sat down. "Good morning." Lydia heard the lilt in her own voice.

Still drowsy, Audra propped an elbow on the table and leaned her chin into her hand. "Mornin'. What's got you looking like a stork in a fish pond?"

"These emails. From last night. I took a chance on going into the one they use. She was totally pissed about the pizza. So is he. Turns out both of them contacted the pizza places. She doesn't believe he didn't do it—"

"Oh-oh, trouble in paradise."

"—and he's raving. Seems all those pizzas came close to a grand." Lydia chuckled. "I was so stoned I forgot I'd tipped a hundred bucks on each." Lydia got up to pour herself more coffee. "So, what do you want to do today?"

"The first thing we're doing is getting you checked at a health clinic."

Lydia's eyes went flat.

"Honey, you know you have to."

"I know. Part of me is scared. Even though I don't think I should be. It's been so damned long since we had sex."

"Still, it's a checklist item, that's all. It's time for you to start making that list and ticking things off one by one."

It was late morning by the time they arrived at the county health clinic in Falton. Audra had talked Lydia out of going to a private one, cautioning it could get back to her insurance records. The small lobby was crowded with those who obviously had no coverage. Poor mothers with restless kids ranging from well-scrubbed to near-ragamuffin. Scruffy young men and sad young women with the sallow, scabbed complexions and dead eyes of drug addicts. A couple of old men, an old woman, all who looked like despondence in the flesh. Her heart ached for those who had so little, who always would no matter how hard they worked or tried, and those who'd devastated their lives with ruinous choices to escape pain they could never run from. Two security guards, one near the entrance and the other by the door to the clinic interior, paid careful attention to one particularly agitated man, but their presence did nothing to calm Lydia's own agitation and growing revulsion. That wasn't directed at those she waited among. It was beamed on Gil. She reviled him for putting her through this, for how she felt demeaned, unclean.

Stepping into the sun more than an hour later was like being washed in a priest's blessing. Neither Audra nor Lydia spoke until they were in the car. When Lydia's hand went to move the drive stick into reverse, Audra laid hers atop it. "I'm sorry you had to do that." Her voice was a whisper.

Tears popped but didn't spill, and Lydia's face was fierce. "I have never felt so dehumanized in my life. The nurses and staff … the way most of them treated me, and all those people there. It's despicable. And I'd like nothing better than to kill that prick husband of mine for putting me through it."

"I'm sorry," Audra repeated. "But now the worst part is over."

"Half over," Lydia corrected. "The body invasion is over, not the head. The results won't be back till Friday. I have to call after two to find out."

Audra patted Lydia's hand. "Well, two days is too long to wait out here in the parking lot. Let's find someplace for lunch. Someplace with a bar. You look like you could use a drink."

Lydia wheeled out of the clinic lot and along several blocks to the main road, where she turned toward downtown. There wasn't much to choose from: a fast-food chain, a mom-and-pop diner, a closed pizza shop. She pulled into a place that didn't look half bad—enough sedans and pickups to indicate the food was decent—but before she turned off the key four motorcycles thundered in. The not-very-young men astride the behemoth machines, all dressed in black, looked hard. Loud music spilled out as they opened the front door.

"Mmm … let's not," Audra said. "Doesn't look like the kind of place it's wise to order a Pink Lady."

With the car in reverse, Lydia's brain began to slip out of the gear it had been stuck in all morning. "I know where we'll go. The Falls Hotel."

"Hotel? There's an honest to god hotel here?"

"Yup. For over a century," Lydia said, watching for an opening in the traffic. "It was old when I was a kid. Passed it when I was here last week. Still looked like it always did."

But the minute they walked in, Lydia realized that was far from true. The aged interior had been transformed into boutique elegance. A clerk behind the lobby desk smiled. "Welcome to The Falls."

"We're here for lunch." Audra indicated the restaurant area to their right.

"Go right on in. The baked trout is good today."

A short entry with two tufted leather wingback chairs and a bowl of floating roses atop an antique sideboard led into the dining room. They stopped at the hostess stand and waited as a man hastened toward them with a smile. Lydia marveled at the surroundings. To describe it as restored didn't do it justice. The hotel's history had been re-imagined; one of 1930s elegance carried forward from the Art Deco era. The room looked as if it belonged in a New York City white-shoe gentlemen's club. Custard-colored glass sconces cast a shimmering glow over the burnished walnut walls. Lydia wished her grandfather could have seen it—or maybe not. He'd have spent all his time studying the wood and boring the staff over the superb grain patterns, the level of skill needed to achieve such art. The tables were draped in creamy linen and set with an intricately folded napkin at each place. The sole modern note was a cordless miniature lamp lit in the center of each table. The room was almost empty, and quiet. Lydia could see the tops of four heads in a booth midway along the near wall. At the far end of the room, two businessmen—one with his suit jacket hung over the back of an empty chair, the cuffs of his expensive shirt rolled back, exposing an impressive watch on his left wrist—were in deep discussion.

"Good morning." The host greeted them. "Breakfast is still being served. Would you like both menus?"

Both Lydia and Audra shook their heads. "Just lunch, I think," Audra said.

"This way, please."

As he pulled out their chairs, a young woman arrived to fill their water glasses. Seconds behind her was a young man carrying a small basket. "A complementary sweet baguette, a secret recipe of our chef's. May I bring you something to drink while you consider the menu?"

"Yes, and the sooner the better," Audra said cheerfully. "Bloody Mary, salted rim, please."

“That sounds good. Make it two. And can you make mine extra spicy?”

“Certainly.” With an almost military-sharp half-bow, he headed away.

“Well, this is a much better choice than burgers, beer, and bikers.”

Lydia felt herself relax into the cushioned chair. The clinic was now a bad experience she could put out of her mind. At least until Friday. “I was here once,” she said. “The family rented the dining room for my grandparents’ fiftieth anniversary party. Grandma was mad as a wet hen—her words—when she found out the family was taking them out to dinner. ‘Waste of good money!’ she complained. ‘Why can’t we just fix a nice meal at the lodge? Why go so far from home?’ She and Grandpa didn’t know that about a hundred people had been invited. She walked in here grumbling and sour as could be.”

Lydia grinned at the recollection as she glanced up to thank the server bringing their drinks. The salt tasted sharp, cleansing, on her tongue. “Still amazes me that nobody blew the surprise. When Grandma and Grandpa came in, the whole room erupted. Grandpa burst into tears—it was literally the only time I ever saw him cry. Uncle Johnny had to catch Grandma before she fell over. Mom told me the next day she was afraid both of them would drop dead on the spot. Boy, was that a fun night. Within minutes, it was like they were newlyweds. Grandma blushing and giggling, Grandpa calling her his bride. I’d never seen them like that. I think it was the first time I realized old people still have young people inside.”

“How old were they?”

“Grandma was sixty-nine, Grandpa seventy.” Lydia looked at Audra, wide-eyed. “Jesus, they weren’t that much older than we are now.”

“Weird, isn’t it, how old ‘old’ seems until we start getting there. My head thinks I’m still in my thirties. I believe it, except when my knees and droopy boobs remind me otherwise.”

Lydia’s face had a faraway look. “Fifty years. A milestone I thought Gil and I would reach. I was so proud that our marriage was so solid, when others seemed to crumble all around us.”

The waiter returned, interrupting to take their orders. Over Audra’s protest, Lydia chose a salad, while Audra ordered the baked trout, complete with vegetables, soup, and salad. “And more of this bread, please.”

Lydia shook her head as he left. “How you can eat so much and stay thin is still beyond me.”

"Yeah, well, you make all those trips up and down the stairs in my store every day and you'll find out." Audra tore into the last piece of bread and slathered it with local honey. "Say, would you mind giving me a busman's holiday this afternoon? If we browse a bunch of the stores here, I can write this trip off—marketing research, right?"

Lydia shook her head again, amused. "Always looking for an angle."

"And why not?" As the waiter placed the cup of soup, salad, and breadbasket before her, Audra added, "Two more Bloody Marys when you bring the rest, please?"

"Um, ma'am, those drinks are pretty strong."

"Which is why we'd like another," Audra said.

"But, if you are driving ..."

"Excuse me," Lydia interrupted, sitting up straight. "Do you do this with everyone or is it because you think we're too old to know what we're doing?"

"Oh no, oh no, that's not it," the young man stammered. "It's just that the State Police office is right down the road, and tourists don't know that. I try to tell everyone." He was turning red.

"Oh, no offense taken, then." Lydia's face was still tight.

Audra gave the young man a forgiving smile. "Smart of you. But we promise to walk it off. Say, here's a question. If your favorite aunt had never been here and wanted to go shopping, what would be the best stores?"

By the time he finished listing places on Main Street and others sprinkled about town, Audra's soup cup was empty. He picked it up. "Your food should be ready any minute. I'll be right back with those drinks."

***

Early evening light and their car returned to the lodge about the same time. During lunch, and wandering through the stores, and on the drive back, Audra had kept up a steady flow of chatter, telling Lydia more about merchandising and retailing than she either needed or cared to know, and probably more gossip from home than Audra actually knew. Lydia knew why—to keep Lydia's mind off fretting about Friday's test results, which dragged on her like an invisible anchor. Now they sat in silence on the porch, sipping cocktails. The sounds of soft waves breaking, the light chirping of birds, and even the occasional far-off buzz of a motorboat, were restorative. Lydia felt her body ease, but not her mind.

"He texted again."

Audra turned her head. "Oh?" She waited, then said, "What did he say?"

"Asked if I was having a good time. Hopes I'll be back by this Friday. Again suggested dinner out. Wants to hear all about my trip."

"Are you *serious*? Like everything is hunky-dory and you're off on a lark?"

Eyebrows raised; Lydia nodded. "And then he made a joke about being ready for a real meal because he'll be eating leftover pizza till then, thanks to some weird prank." She smirked and Audra grinned.

Whiffs of cigarette smoke hung like veils before them for short seconds before dissipating like ghosts. Lydia felt haunted by ghosts, not benign ones with messages of comfort, but derisive, nasty, evil. Memories once comforting were now laced with menace, jeering at her naïveté, her trust. Somehow, somehow, if she were ever able to trust herself—or anyone else—again, she had to exorcise these demons.

"Audra. I want to hurt him." The words came out low. "I want to hurt him like he's hurt me. Shatter him. To the core. Destroy everything he's so goddamned cocksure of."

"I know you do, honey. That's why we're going to get you the best pitbull attorney in Tampa."

Lydia turned, staring at Audra. When she spoke, her voice was as hard as the look on her face. "That's not what I'm talking about. Oh, I'll get my goods but I want something no court can give me. I want my pound of flesh. I want all two hundred pounds of *his* flesh. I want to unravel his world. Completely."

Lydia could tell from Audra's gaze that her friend understood.

Audra turned away, drew on her cigarette, and exhaled. "Okay. But how?"

"All those files I downloaded. He may still be hiding more but I've got enough to more than fuck with his head. And that slut's. I'm going to take them both down."

"Jesus, you're not talking blackmail or something."

"No way," Lydia interrupted. "Besides being illegal, that's too blatant. And wouldn't give me the satisfaction I want."

Hearing herself, the demons swirling in Lydia took on new life, as allies. She had never wanted to do evil, bring anyone harm. Realizing she wanted to do exactly that to Gil shocked her. For the first time, she understood viscerally, not only intellectually, that a murderer did reside within everyone. Ideas began buzzing in her mind like a swarm of mosquitoes at her ear. “I don’t know how I’m going to do it, but I’ll find a way.”

When Audra stubbed out her cigarette, she looked at Lydia, a glint in her eye. “Gonna let me help?”

Lydia hadn’t expected that. She’d assumed her best friend would start in on 101 reasons she was crazy. “Audra, I can’t get you involved in this. It’s my fight, not yours.”

“The hell it’s not. My life’s not as upended as yours, but what Gil’s done to you has put me through the wringer too.” Audra stretched her hand, palm out, toward Lydia. “Bad-ass bad girls …”

“Together forever.” Lydia finished their oath with a smack of her hand against Audra’s.

Chapter 11

"Dave. It's L." Hearing Audra's footsteps on the stairs, she cradled the phone on her shoulder and got up to pour her friend a coffee. "Good morning to you, too ... Everything's fine. Just have a couple of questions. Any chance there's a place in town that has ink for Thom's printer?" She handed the cup to Audra with a smile. "Son of a gun, you are a real general store, aren't you? Second, where can I get some keys made? ... No, I didn't lose the lodge key. I need a, uh, personal one made." She grabbed a pencil and scribbled something on a notepad. "Thanks. Let Bess know I'll swing by this morning, okay? And say hi to Katie for me. Bye."

Plugging the cell phone into its charger, Lydia said, "Good news. Dave refills ink cartridges. And there's a semi-retired locksmith in town."

Taking the coffee, Audra asked, "A locksmith? For what?"

"I want a set of my house keys made for you. In case I need you to get something for me while I'm up here. That okay?"

"Sure." Audra sat down at the kitchen table and pushed aside scattered papers to make room for her mug. She gestured at the pages and picked one up. "What's all this? Damn, left my readers upstairs," she muttered.

Lydia pulled out a chair. "You sleep okay? You seem a little groggy."

"Yeah, well, you sound like you've been downing shots of espresso."

"I got up ..." Lydia glanced at the wall clock, "about three hours ago. Woke around four thinking about how I'm going to make this work. I decided the best place to start is with both of us going over copies of what I have. The ink ran out before I finished and it was too early call Dave. So I took a long walk and did more thinking."

"Good god. When did you become such a morning person?"

"This is the first morning in a long time," Lydia said, leaning forward over the table, "when I haven't woken up saturated by grief. Anger justified is, I've discovered, a powerful force."

"So, last night wasn't just the pot and whiskey talking."

"Nope."

"Well, let me have at least another cup of coffee—and a cigarette—before we get started."

"Oh, no rush. We'll have to put it off till afternoon. I've still got more to print first. I can't go by the locksmith's until eleven, so I'll drop the cartridges off at Bess's, go into town, and then pick up the refills on my way back. You finish waking up. I'm going to shower and start a load of coloreds. Got anything you want to throw in the wash?"

Unlike when time hung unmoving, before she dared access Gil's online accounts, the morning sped by as quickly as Lydia did through it. By ten-thirty, breakfast dishes and the kitchen were cleaned, as well as the bathrooms. The laundry was dried and put away, the great room dusted, and the papers on the kitchen table stacked into various piles. Lydia tossed a plastic baggie of ink cartridges next to her purse on the sofa and went to her room to retrieve the house keys from her tote. Looking at them as she returned, she said, "Wanna come with?"

"If you don't mind, I'll stay. Do a little reading."

"No problem." Lydia swept her arm toward the low, built-in bookcase running along two walls at the far corner of the great room, intersecting like a ship's prow. "Lord knows we've collected enough summer reading over the decades. Back in about an hour, I hope," she said, flashing a happy smile.

On the slow ride down the dirt drive, Lydia tapped the car radio's seek button several times before realizing it picked up only four stations. One carried the voice of a Bible-thumper whose words and solemnizing made her cringe. NPR and whatever was going on in the world, she couldn't care less about right now. A mellow song played on the third station and moved seamlessly into another mellow vocal. She punched the seek button again to return to the last choice. Ignoring the commercial and the announcer, she scanned the road. Her foot hit the gas at the same instant as the rollicking opening chords of a pop-country number. It wasn't Ry Cooder but it sure did have rhythm to back the singer's blues. Lydia's foot pressed harder on the gas pedal and she didn't let up until she closed the gap with a car ahead of her. Settle down, she told herself. You gotta get rhythm, she told herself, a steady rhythm. Give me the beat, boys, to free my soul, her mind sang. A woman walking alongside the road looked up and waved to the car ahead and then at Lydia's. Lydia gaily returned the greeting.

At Clar's Corner, the chime under the mat sounded as light as she felt. *God, it feels good*, she thought, *to have a purpose again, even if it is nefarious.*

"Hi, Elle." Bess came out of the little room that Lydia could see was an office. "Dave said you needed some cartridges refilled?"

"Mm-hmm." Lydia handed her the baggie. "It was quite a surprise when he said he could do this."

"Well, when word got around he'd been in IT, people started calling him their nerd in a hurry. We added the ink refill because overnight delivery isn't an option up here. Even two-day isn't guaranteed when the snow's bad."

"Listen, Bess, I owe you an apology for the way I took off from the fish-fry. And it was rude of me not to call later, to thank you and explain."

"Oh, heavens, no need. Dave told me after he stopped by your place. That a friend showed up?"

"My best friend. The text I got was from her, saying she was flying up. That was why I had to take off so fast. I didn't even know she was coming. She's, uh, helping me with my project, which is why I need the printer. Tell Dave I'll come back for these after I run an errand in town, okay?"

"Okay. Dave and Max are still out fishing. Should be back soon but if they're not, I'll take these to the house and fill them."

In town, it took a while to find the right side street and then spot the locksmith's small yard. An arrow directed her along a walk that led behind the house. Inside the shop, barely bigger than a shed, a customer leaning against the counter looked at her and then back to the old man at the key cutter, who hadn't heard the door above the noise of metal under assault. He finally looked up as he set aside the polished key and picked up another blank. He nodded. "Be a while."

The fellow standing at the counter said, "Sorry. Boss sent me in with a bunch."

"Oh. Nothing to be sorry about." The shop was so small that the only seat was the owner's stool. The metal in the key cutter began its screech and she wasn't sure the old man heard her say, "I'll wait outside."

In the car, Lydia checked text messages on her old cell phone. There was one from Gil she didn't open. Two were from Sara—one saying her recipe had been a big hit with their guests. The other said she'd called a couple of times, nothing special, just wanted to chat, and asked U OK? Couldn't leave a message. A text from James was, typically, more blunt: What's up w/phone off all the time? Tried the house. Got dad on his cell, golfing, said u antiquing for long wknd. Didn't know U were back into it. Hope it's fun. Luv.

Lydia's jaw clenched. Gil was lying to James, and probably Sara too—why not, after the way he had lied to her? She couldn't put off talking to them much longer, but still wasn't sure she could do it without making them suspicious that things weren't right.

Half an hour later, wondering if she should take a short walk to relieve the boredom, she saw the shed door open and the worker stride toward a truck, one hand dangling three sizable rings of clanking keys. He nodded at Lydia as she headed up the path.

The old man glanced up over his glasses. "Sorry 'bout the wait. What can I do you for?" Ten minutes and ten dollars later she was on her way back to Clar's Corner.

Again, Bess looked up at the sound of the tinkling bell when Lydia entered. "Hi again. Shouldn't be but another couple of minutes till your ink is ready."

"Okay. Don't let me interrupt. I'll just look around." Lydia turned toward the open room on the other side of the counter. She'd not paid it any attention when she'd been in before because it was filled with souvenirs. Walking along the counters and shelves, she noticed many were still like those the tourists had bought when she was young—miniature moccasins, shells and rocks, tiny Christmas ornaments of cabins with the letters U and P painted on the peaked roofs. And of course a rack with a few postcards, now an anachronism in a social media world. There were still shot glasses, some decorated with deer, but ashtrays were a thing of the past. Instead, Michigan-themed drinking glasses and coffee mugs abounded. The idea of getting two—one for her, one for Audra, as mementoes—appealed to her, and one of the designs caught her eye. Primitive flowers in bright colors encircled the mug's rim and base. Centered on one side in a purple field were red letters proclaiming "Goddess U.P." In between the two words were squeezed two other tiny ones: "of the." *Yup*, Lydia thought, *that's what we're going to do—goddess up. Goddess up like Freya: If you can't lay 'em, slay 'em.*

Mugs in hand, Lydia moved to the display of magnets and idly spun it. The last side was filled with key chains, and she realized it would be a good idea to get one so Audra would be able to tell Lydia's keys from her own. Most of the fobs were shaped like the Michigan mitten, others were fish or deer or snowmobiles, or reminders of Tahquamenon Falls or the long-gone

Toonerville Trolley. She settled on a snowman, generically Christmassy enough that no one in Florida would pay much attention to it.

Lydia set her purchases near the cash register. From the back of the store a man's voice—Max's—called out. "Bess. Dave asked me to bring …" He saw Lydia, and his stride hesitated a beat. "Oh. You're here."

"Thanks," Bess called from her office. "Be right there, Elle."

With a curt nod, Max placed the ink cartridges and a lumpy package wrapped in white paper on the counter and turned to leave. He'd almost reached the back door before Lydia regained her composure and hurried after him. "Max?"

He stopped, his back to her. When he turned, his face was blank. "Yes?"

"You are upset with me. And you have every right to be. I should have made a proper apology the other day. I am very sorry I had to leave the party in such a rush. The thing is, I was getting ready to leave. All the people were a bit … much … because of the stress … I really was going to find you and Dave, to thank you both. And find Katie, too. But then Audra's text came in …" Lydia realized she was rambling. "Anyway, I am sorry. It was rude of me. And I do owe you a thank-you. You went out of your way to drag me away from the lodge. It was kind of you to do that for Bess and Dave, busy as they were. I do apologize."

Max nodded. "Apology accepted. But I didn't do it solely for Dave and Bess. Enjoy your fish." Lydia stared at his back as the screen door closed behind him.

"Elle, you set?"

Still not knowing what to make of Max's comment, Lydia reached for her wallet and drew over the keychain and mugs. Bess gave her a smile. "I need to ring these up separate. Dave's business is separate from the store's. Oh, and this is a gift," she said, pointing to the white wrapped packet. "The guys had a good catch this morning, so two nice walleye fillets, for you and your friend. On the house."

"Bess, let me pay for them. Please. You don't give that away to the other customers."

"Nope. But you're not a regular customer. Dave's way of saying thanks for finding that party spot." Bess held up a hand. "So, not another word."

"Well then. Thank you, and please thank Dave—and Max—for me. But next time, I'm buying it out of the cooler and I am paying for it."

“Dave may not like that.” Bess grinned as she handed Lydia’s debit card back.

“Then we just won’t tell him, now, will we?” Lydia’s return smile was conspiratorial. “Bye.”

Minutes later Lydia opened the lodge’s screen door. In a sing-songy voice she called out, “Hi, honey, I’m *ho-o-ome*.” She set the bag with the ink cartridges on the dining table. One stack of papers there was still neat, the other spread out in smaller piles. She carried the second bag to the kitchen, where Audra was drying her hands. “That took longer than expected,” Lydia said, taking out the fish and opening the refrigerator. “Oh good, you fixed lunch. Thank you. I’m famished.” Lydia reached for the two readied plates in the refrigerator, then kneed the door closed. Placing them on the dining table she said, “I take it you didn’t find a book to read.”

“Nope. Didn’t look.”

Ice clunked into glasses, then Audra fill them with tea from a pitcher on the counter.

But something about Audra seemed off. Lydia put a hand on Audra’s arm. “You okay?”

Tears sprang into Audra’s eyes. “No. I knew it was bad … you told me it was bad, and I’d seen some of it. But, Lyd, I had no idea it was so … so *vile*.”

Lydia wrapped Audra in a hug. “Oh, honey, I should have realized you’d go through those papers. I shouldn’t have left them out. I was going to warn you before I let you see them all.”

Audra pulled away. “Huh. That wouldn’t have helped. Nothing could have prepared me. It makes me sick to my stomach.” Audra drew a deep breath. Picking up the glasses, she said, “Let’s go out on the porch. I need some air.”

This time it was Lydia who ate heartily, while Audra picked at her food. Setting the half-finished plate aside, she lit a cigarette. Exhaling, she said, “It’s a good thing I’m here.”

“Oh? Why’s that?”

“Because,” Audra said, staring at the lake, her voice low, “if I were in Tampa and knew all this, I’d take my gun and put a bullet through the bastard’s balls. Then his brain. And with luck hunt down the bitch too before the cops got me.”

“Yup. Know the feeling. It’s a damned good thing I didn’t find out at home. I might have done the same.”

Audra exhaled again. "You don't own a gun."

"So? I'd have borrowed yours."

Audra looked at Lydia. "I'd have loaned it to you."

"But then, why should they get off lightly, by being dead and all? What I want will be much better."

"It's like we've traded places," Audra said. "I totally get what's gone on inside you, and now it's like a switch has flipped in you."

"It has. Maybe I've finally hit the point where I'm no longer shocked by anything else he's done. Well, no … if there is any pedophilia, I *will* plant him under the jail. But now I know—if I'm going to get what I want, I need a plan. And I need your help. Come on, let's go inside."

Hours later Lydia shut down the laptop and Audra gathered the papers spread across the table. "You go have a smoke and I'll fix us drinks," Lydia said. "Go on now, I'll be out in a sec."

After Audra was outside, Lydia opened the bag with the mugs she'd bought, washed them, and filled them with wine. Carrying one in each hand, the message sides facing her, she stepped onto the porch. Audra's nose wrinkled. "Coffee? Thanks but no. I'm ready for something stronger."

"Uh-uh-uh, not so hasty with the assumptions there, girl. It's not the medium, it's the message." She handed a mug to Audra, who looked at it, puzzled for a second before bursting into laughter. Lydia tapped her mug to Audra's. "To us. Goddesses of the U.P. Who are seriously goddessing up!"

***

Friday morning Lydia was again up before Audra. But this time she was neither energetic nor rested. Insomnia had strangled the pre-dawn hours. The night dementors heckling her with what-ifs, how-to's, sneers of your-forgetting-somethings, you're-going-to-get-caughts, just-give-it-up-already.

Maybe I should, she thought, *but I won't.* Washing and drying the mugs from the night before, Lydia held one and stared at the "Goddess UP" emblazoned on it—the message she knew the Universe had sent on purpose—then set it down. The aroma and sound of the coffee maker as it finished followed her to the great room table. The floor was littered with papers. Separately, then together, she and Audra had brainstormed, writing down every flash of an idea, no matter how outlandish or outrageous, each on a fresh sheet of note paper. The ones Lydia now swept together and bent to pick up from the floor were the discards. She tossed them into a wastebasket. The dining room table looked like Audra's desk at the store always did, and the way Lydia's did on campus at the end of term: swarmed with papers that seemed to mock, "Good luck finding whatever you're looking for in this mess." She shoved those notes into a stack and placed it on the sideboard under the picture window. She picked up the thick file folder of Gil's email printouts and tossed it on a corner of the sideboard. That was the one thing neither of them needed or wanted to go through again.

She went to the kitchen for coffee, then sorted the other papers into order. Those they no longer needed, she cross-stacked atop the email file. Those they needed again—his business records, the financial accounts, what she had on The Slut—she piled up neatly. Seeing the clean sweep of the table made her feel a bit more in control.

Lydia refilled her mug, slipped on a jacket, and went down to the shore. The chairs were wet from the morning dew and the last wisps of lake mist. She didn't want to go back for a towel. Instead, she let the damp soak into her canvas shoes and pant hems as she walked through the beach grass on the point. She leaned against the boulder that had seemed mountain-high when she was a child, its chill growing sharp against her body. She cradled the warm mug in her hands.

How was she going to handle what would come, when news spread about the divorce? It would lead to painful questions, asked in tones of pity by people who really wanted only juicy gossip. To take the high road, to turn everything over to an attorney, to be the "good woman" responding, "We just decided it was best," might have to become her inevitable response. But sometimes the low road was the one to take. *And if it isn't*, she thought, *then to hell with it—the trek alone will be worth it.*

Her mug was empty. The damp and cold that had soaked through her shoes and jeans were beginning to hurt. Mosquitoes swirled around her like the negative thoughts skittering through her mind. Lydia went back inside.

Dry clothes and another hot coffee helped her body but did nothing for her head as she sat down to review the lists and notes from the day before. Soft sounds from the radio went unheard until two words in an announcement struck her: "Starts Friday! At two! Come on out for hours of fun!" Today was

Friday. Two o'clock. That's when she had to call the clinic. Her stomach knotted, the caffeine taste in her mouth sour.

When Audra came downstairs later, Lydia put the papers aside. She poured a mug of coffee and carried it to the sofa, where Audra sat splayed against one corner, trying to wake up. Lydia handed her the cup and sat down.

"Thanks." Audra took a sip, then nestled the mug on her lap, and gave a satisfied sigh. "Between that marvelous bed and this air, it's like I wake up every morning without any bones. I can't remember when I've slept so well. Say, I wanted to ask you about …"

They chatted, aimless and randomly, over coffee, breakfast and tidying the kitchen, and through another cup of coffee on the porch while Audra had a smoke. By ten, Lydia couldn't tolerate the distraction any longer. She stood up. "My nerves are getting to me. I've got to find something to concentrate on other than waiting for two o'clock. I'm going in to do some online research about an idea I got."

"Okay."

Lydia opened her laptop on the dining table. On the search page she typed, "how to money—" then stopped. She cleared the history and the caches, then launched a private search page. She hoped it was true these searches would be untraceable. She typed again, "how to launder money." Leaning forward, she scrolled down—hundreds of hits were listed. At the bottom of the screen were a slew of helpful, related search phrases. Lydia clicked her way through numerous articles, taking notes until the information became repetitive. She barely glanced up when Audra came inside for more coffee, but then sat back and sighed when Audra pulled out a chair at the table.

"Sometimes I can't believe how naïve I am," Lydia said. "I knew nut cases could find out how to make bombs, but I had no clue there were step-by-step instructions for this kind of stuff. There's even an article from *Business Insider*, of all things. 'The Beginner's Guide to Money Laundering.' For being an educated woman, it's amazing how much I don't know. Or how complex it is. I think I'm going to need to find an easier way."

Chin resting on a propped hand, Audra had turned toward the view of the lake. She turned to look at Lydia. "How do you eat an elephant?"

"What?"

"How do you eat an elephant?"

Still puzzled, Lydia said, "One bite at a time?"

"Right. Going after the money that way is the elephant. Bites would be dinging the accounts."

"Like how?"

"Like we dinged him with all those pizza charges. But we don't send him anything, you send stuff to other people." Audra's smile was sly. "And I'm not talking pizza."

"I'm not sure I'm following you."

"That's okay." Audra was sorting through the stack of printouts. "Just follow. Here it is … I'll read and take notes, you search."

Another pot of coffee and two cigarette breaks later, they had gathered the names and email addresses of every executive in Gil's current client list and from the last three years. Lydia had wanted to copy them to a computer document, but Audra insisted no, it could be found on her hard drive. They'd also done the same with all of Gil's current vendors, as well as the publishers, editors, and sales heads of every trade journal listed in Marielle Wharton's online portfolio.

When finished, Audra eased back and forth on the porch swing, another cigarette in hand, as Lydia paced, thinking out loud. "What I don't like about this is what it could do to the agency's employees. They're all good people. If they all lose their jobs, I'd feel awful."

"Hmmm … that's something to consider. Maybe we could give them a heads-up there might be trouble coming? Start making them wonder about him. Like text a pic of Wharton and say, 'Do you know this woman? Your boss sure does.' Or, 'Did you know your boss was in bed in Key West when he said he was in a New York client's office?'"

"Oh no. Ohhhhh no. I'm not bringing them into this that way. Besides, we don't know what they know. Or how many affairs he's had with women on his staff. That could be an open secret. Somebody's likely to tell him, and it would definitely boomerang on me."

"Yeah." Audra sighed.

"Death by paper cuts, not immolation, is what I want," Lydia said. "God, is it two o'clock *yet*?" She opened the screen door, then looked at Audra, her face tense, and held up a hand, her first two fingers entwined. Audra returned the good luck sign.

Ten long minutes later the screen door flew wide open, slamming behind Lydia with an explosive clap. Scowling, she sat down hard on the porch swing. "That son of a bitch," she roared. "God *damn* him."

"Oh honey." Audra put a hand on Lydia's knee. "They found something?"

"No. All the tests were negative."

"Jesus, don't scare me like that. I thought you were going to tell me you had full-blown AIDS." Audra's face was ashen.

"That's what I wish for *him*. I am so mad. I am so relieved but I am *so* mad. But if I'm clean, that means the asshole is too. Or was, the last time we had sex." Her rage drained, Lydia laid her head back against the cushion and closed her eyes. The warm sun and Audra's gentle rocking of the swing settled into a rhythm that replaced her tension with calm. She turned and looked at Audra. "Thank you. For being so patient with me. For putting up with me."

"You have been getting on my nerves," Audra deadpanned.

Lydia's head shot up. "I'm sorry. I feel like such a damned drama queen. I'm so sorry for taking it out on you."

"Oh for god's sake, I'm joking," Audra said. "You're only a tad worse than when Sal Masculo broke up with you junior year. Now I, of course, was the epitome of grace when Ryan walked out on our anniversary."

"Oh, yeah, right. Have I been calling you in the middle of the night, drunk, blubbering, and wailing? And I seem to remember you going off the deep end when you found out Ted Bonner was sneaking around with Sheryl Atkins right before graduation."

"God, sometimes it does feel like life is stuck in high school." Audra paused. "What is it with men that messes with our heads?"

"Do you ever think," Lydia said, "that except for sex, men really are superfluous?"

Audra's foot pushed the swing slowly. "Mmm … I don't know. But the truth is, I do like men. With definite exceptions, of course—yeah, and that list is long. Richard Nixon, Dick Cheney, Trump, to start. And that weasel of yours. All of them dicks in one way or another. But I *do* like men. I like talking to them. About politics, what's going on in Tampa, around the world. Cripes, even sports to a certain extent. I like getting their perspective. And," Audra added, "I still like an admiring glance. Rare as *that* is at our age. And oh do I miss the sex, having a man in my bed. I just don't want his shoes under it permanently."

"That's all I have. Shoes. Empty shoes. An empty marriage. Gil and I haven't had a long talk about anything in years. He's barely interested when I tell him what I've heard from the kids, and even less interested when I bring up something about work. He almost never tells me anything that's going on with him." Lydia shot Audra a knowing look. "Now I know why."

The sun struck the smooth lake at an angle that seemed to bounce Lydia's thoughts back at her off the water. "I should have made him talk to me more when the economy almost did his business in. He wouldn't. Said he didn't want me to worry more than necessary. That he'd take care of everything. He'd be fine—we'd be fine—if I just backed off. So I did. I shouldn't have. It's all my fault."

"What? Bullshit. Oh, he took care of himself, that's for damn sure. Finds some other woman to stroke his ego and his dick. That's your fault? And it's your fault he's been lying about the money and siphoning it off to wherever in god's name he's hiding it?"

"Well, is that really any different from my cash stash?"

"Big-time. I know you've always had your own mad money. If you chose to squirrel it away that was your business. His hiding money from his business is not the same thing. That's a fuck-you move. And so is all the other literal fucking around he's doing. None of that is your fault."

Tears rimmed Lydia's eyes. "Then why does it feel like it is?"

"Be*cause* ...," Audra's voice rose on the second syllable and she slapped Lydia's thigh. "Everything is *always* about *you*, you, you. Except when it's all about *me*."

Another of their lifelong jokes, and it made Lydia smile, even as the tears spilled over. Lydia retorted the next line in their script in her best stage-haughty voice. "But darling, it *is* all about me, me, me. Except when it's all about *you*."

"Damned straight." Audra slapped Lydia's leg again. "So, since it is all about me, I insist we get out of here. As bucolic as this is, I'm getting a case of cabin fever."

"Oh geeze. I don't know ..."

Audra stood up, grabbed Lydia's hands, and pulled her to her feet. "I'm not giving you a choice. We are going to put on makeup and decent clothes, and we are going to scout every tchotchke shop and boutique in that tiny tourist town up the road. March." Audra spun Lydia around and, with her hands on Lydia's shoulders, steered her inside to the bathroom.

Not long afterward Audra came lightly down the stairs, humming and slipping on a pair of splashy earrings. Lydia sat slumped on the edge of the couch, looking and feeling like a kid about to be dragged off to visit old people she didn't know in a smelly old house where there'd be no toys. Audra tsk-tsk-tsked her tongue against her teeth, signaling disapproval. "Lyd, couldn't you put on something that's not black? Or gray?"

"That's all I've got. Besides, it suits my mood."

"Understandable. But it's time to stop feeding your funk." Audra went back up the stairs, then returned and tossed a garment onto the sofa. "Here, put that on."

Petulant, Lydia did as she was told. She peeled off her black sweatshirt. The sweater she slipped over her head felt light on her shoulders, and the soft knit caressed her arms as they slid into the sleeves. It draped her, long and loose, in comfort, and wrapped her in floral art of muted blues, greens, and rose. Lydia's throat tightened. It was the first pretty thing she'd worn in … how long? She didn't know if she deserved to ever feel pretty again. Not when all she wanted was to fade into the background, fade away and become a ghost no one would notice, left to her grief and mourning.

"Much better," Audra announced. "Now let's get going."

Lydia moved through the next hours with the placidness of a dutiful daughter escorting her mother on an afternoon of errands. The smattering of gift shops that remained from the past hadn't changed much after all. The random memories that popped up as she wandered through them were banal. The new stores—some with signs stating they'd opened twelve, twenty, twenty-five years ago, so they were anything but new—held little interest for her. In some, Audra lingered, touring each aisle to study displays and striking up a conversation with the owner. In others, she spent no more than five minutes glancing around before turning to Lydia with a cheery, "Next?"

Leaving the seventh store—or eighth, Lydia wasn't sure—Audra's cheerfulness was fading. "Aren't there any places in this town that don't cater to the tight-fisted?" she asked as Lydia dug into her purse for the car keys. "Oh, wait. I want to go there. Come on."

Lydia looked up to see Audra heading toward the road, and hurried to catch up. Across the way was the boutique Lydia had noticed before, with well-dressed mannequins in the window display. Grabbing Lydia's hand as if she were a small child, Audra pulled her across the asphalt.

Stenciled in gold on the elegant oval glass of the front door were the words My Summer Closet. More elegance greeted them inside. Antique oak tables held folded items arranged under the glow of Tiffany-style lamps. Dresses on hangers were hooked over the arms of coat racks, and other items hung from racks created from old metal bed headboards. Open steamer trunks and scuffed suitcases displayed accessories. "Now *this* looks like a place," Audra whispered, "where we can do some serious damage to our credit cards. Too bad you don't have one of Gil's with you."

A smiling woman in a casual but well-cut outfit came from the back of the store carrying three long dresses by the necks of hangers, bearing them as elegantly as if she held a tray of champagne. "Good afternoon." The words conveyed a cultured tone that Lydia thought seemed as out of place in the tourist village as the store itself. Just as its name suggested, she did feel as if she'd stepped into a closet, an enormous one from a Gilded Age mansion, awaiting a lady's need of the proper outfit for the day's next engagement or an evening on the town. Just not this town. Still, Lydia had as little interest in who would shop here as she had in what was for sale. She noticed an overstuffed chair nearby and sat down. Audra was obviously going to inspect every single thing. She was going to be a while.

Audra soon shifted from casual customer chitchat to that of professional colleague with the storeowner. Lydia half-heard their words, but did smile when she heard the owner say, "I refuse to carry anything brown, plaid, or flannel. If it isn't vibrant, it isn't in my closet. If I won't wear it, I certainly won't sell it."

The lilt of Audra's laughter followed, then she called out, "Lyd, come here. You've got to see this top. It's perfect for you."

Lydia's lack of enthusiasm did nothing to deter Audra's. An hour later, carrying string-handled glossy bags back to the car, Audra said, "You're going to thank me this winter. You know how hard it is to find gorgeous sweaters in Florida. And that red sheath I made you get? I wish I could wear that color. You are so going to turn heads."

Lydia admitted to herself that the clothes Audra insisted she buy were both pretty and flattering. She doubted she'd ever wear them, though. "I don't want to turn heads," she said. "I just want to disappear, be invisible."

"Right now, I know." Audra wrapped her in a hug, then placed her hands on Lydia's shoulders and gave her a gentle shake. "But you've got to let your warrior woman out. She's ready. I've seen a lot of her peeking out this week. But honest to god, Lyd, this woe-is-me shit has got to stop. Or you're going to fuck up fucking up Gil's life. You'll be the one who gets screwed. Again. So, Morose Molly needs to go. Goddess-up, remember? Now drive, James. This Miss Daisy has one more place to visit. Let's go."

"Please, not another souvenir shop."

"No. It's an artist's gallery, on the next side street. Carmen says his work is exquisite."

"Who's Carmen?" Lydia asked, turning in the direction Audra indicated.

"The woman who owns My Summer Closet. If her eye for art is half as good as it is for clothes, I'm sure she's right. She thinks I might be able to get some of his pieces for the store. Turn up this hill. There—is that it?"

Lydia pulled in front of one of the places she'd passed on her first foray through the village. A short sidewalk and steps led to what looked like someone's home, except for the small "Gallery" sign suspended from a shepherd's hook at the edge of the front yard. The door was locked, but near the doorbell was a plaque: Gallery Visitors Please Ring Twice. Audra did, and a second later the door unlatched itself. Reaching for the door after Audra, Lydia half-whispered, "Odd to find a locked store—"

"Oh my god, I can see why. *Look* at this."

The room they stepped into wasn't just a room, it was a true gallery, a deep space that ran the full width of the house. Before the women could begin to take everything in, the click of the door lock behind them caused them to look at each other. "Not sure if that should make me feel safe, or worried," Audra murmured.

Pictures of splendorous scenic beauty, capturing the four seasons, surrounded them in a panorama. "My god, Lyd," breathed Audra, "it's like Clyde Butcher or Ansell Adams." But the images weren't only in black and white. Soft, diffused light seemed to glow from within the boundaries of each frame and mat. Lydia stepped before an image of winter so precise in detail and color that a chill wind seemed to sweep from it. Pulling her glasses from her purse, she leaned close to study it. "It may be sacrilege to say, but these are even better, Aud. And these aren't photos—they're paintings."

"Jesus, you're right." Audra's face was aglow.

Double doors in an archway opened and a silver-haired, ponytailed man came through, clicking a remote that triggered the front door to unlock again.

He nodded. “Ladies. Take your time. But not too much. Closing time is in twenty minutes. Anyone still here then is stuck for the night. And is also stuck doing the dishes.” With that, he flashed a grin.

“I’m glad you unlocked the door,” Audra said. “Had me worried maybe we’d end up served on those dishes.”

His guffaw filled the room. “Naw, take all the time you want if you’re here to spend money.” He bent down behind a counter and low music wafted through the room.

“Lincoln Mayorga. Nice.” Audra said, glancing at him.

He looked at her. “An ear for snark and an ear for music. Good on you.”

Lydia cut Audra a look, but Audra had turned back to the art.

“Locking people in isn’t meant to scare anyone,” he went on. “Well, except the lifters. I do that until I can get in here from my studio. Let me know if I can answer any questions. I don’t want to rush you too much, but I do have to be somewhere in a while.”

Lydia went back to studying the watercolors, mesmerized by the sensation of feeling that she could step into them. They seemed to be so real, as if the world she would enter would be suffused with an unreality, but one that showed reality more clearly than the actual ever could. It would be a soft place, she thought, not like the jagged cubism she felt trapped in. She turned to say something to Audra, but Audra was at the opposite end of the gallery, walking casually and giving quick glances at the works. As Lydia moved to the next image she heard Audra’s footsteps moving sharply across the wood floor. She looked up to see her approach the artist, who was leaning against the wall, arms crossed, watching Audra.

“I do have a question,” Audra said. “Actually, a proposition.”

A brow arched over one of the man’s eyes, which, like his smile, glinted with mischief.

Audra’s hand batted the air and she laughed. “Oh no, a better one than that. I do want to spend money. Only, money to make money. For both of us. How would you like to do business together?”

Lydia turned her attention back to the art, losing herself in both space and time, until Audra’s voice again brought her to the present.

“Oh my gosh. You said you have an appointment. I’m taking up too much of your time.”

"No, no, that's okay. I would have hustled you out of here if I didn't like what I'm hearing." He flashed a wide grin. "I'll still make it. Just without my dinner. So when people hear my stomach growl tonight, I'll do what we men do—blame it on a woman."

Audra's laugh was light as they exchanged cards. "Fine. Just make her worth it."

"No problem there."

Lydia caught his comment but Audra acted as if she hadn't. "Monday I fly back to Tampa. I'll contact you next week and we'll wrap up the details."

Out in the car, Audra leaned back with a satisfied sigh, then yanked the seatbelt and snapped it in place. "Now this trip *is* a legit expense. Ned's stuff is going to move faster at the store than a little lizard chased by a cat. Now," Audra repeated with more emphasis, "I am ready for a drink and a smoke. And I do not want to cook. I'm taking us out to eat. Someplace we can do all three. Um, unless that doesn't exist here?"

"I do know of one place."

Five short blocks away Lydia turned in at the "Fish Fry Friday" sign at Doozy's. Inside the fairly crowded bar, they took a high-top table next to an open, screened window lit by the slowly lowering sun. When their drinks arrived, Audra raised her glass. "To us. And to Ned. Man, I can almost smell the money I'm going to make."

Lydia shook her head as she raised her own glass. "You are something else, girlfriend."

"Seriously, his stuff is going to sell, and at good prices. All those snowbirds? All the transplants his art will remind of home? Ned's going to get more exposure in my store than he'll ever get up here."

"So it's Ned, hmm? Struck me as though Ned was as interested in you as he was in your proposition." Lydia grinned as she saw a blush creep across Audra's cheeks.

"He's not half-bad himself. But this is strictly business. Still, it was kind of nice. I haven't had a man look at me like that in ages. Except the ones who come in the store and think it'll get them huge discounts. Assholes." Audra took a drag on her cigarette, then exhaled through the window. Glancing over Lydia's head, she asked, "How many men do you know in this town?"

"Um, two. Dave and Max. Why?"

"And now Ned from the gallery. Well, two of the three are here."

Turning to look across the room, Lydia recognized Max from his hat. His back to her, he was talking to several fellows at the bar who looked familiar from her other time there. It took her half a second to see the other man, who looked like Ned but snazzier, in dark blue jeans, a crisp white shirt with the sleeves rolled up, and a purple bow tie, with his loose hair flowing. Moving between the barstools and tables, he swung a guitar case in front of him, to keep it from bumping people on his way to the riser in the back corner. "Are you sure that's him," Lydia asked. "Could be some other guy who looks like him."

"Oh, that's him all right. And he looks even better out of those paint-stained old clothes."

Lydia couldn't suppress a chuckle. "Why, mah, mah, Mizz Audra," she drawled, "Ah do b'lieve you are thinkin' 'bout that man wearin' no clothes *a*-tall." She laughed louder at the look Audra gave her, the rosiness again rising across her cheeks.

"Well, look who's here." Max was beside the table, tipping his hat. "Ladies."

Now Lydia felt her own face flush. She nodded back, wondering why she didn't know what to say.

Audra extended her hand and, as Max shook it, she said, "Funny running into someone we've met, in this megatropolis. Care to join us?"

"Thank you, no. My barstool, my Guinness, and my book await. But it would have been rude to not say hello. Are you here for the fish fry? If so, it's almost half as good as mine." His last sentence was spoken to Lydia, and again she felt herself flush.

Again, it was Audra who spoke. "Since you must know the menu, is there anything else you'd recommend to two gals in a very good mood?"

"Ah, something to celebrate, eh?"

"Yup. It's been a good day. She got her, uh, work plan nailed down and got a clean ... uh, got some positive news today. And I just made the best business find in a long time."

"Well ..." His voice pulled the word into two syllables as his eyebrows and smile rose. "Michigan again works its pure magic. As good as the local fish is, the steaks are even better. Although," he looked again at Lydia, "again not as good as mine. Now I'll leave you, before my Guinness is as flat as that bar top. Ladies, adieu." Again tipping his hat, he stepped aside and a waitress stepped into his place.

"You ready to order?"

The sounds of gentle strumming wove through the chattering voices, at first as unobtrusive as a shy girl trying to slip into a party unnoticed. Then the tempo picked up and the guitar strings rang out a funky beat. When the rhythm of talk around Lydia seemed to form a counterpoint to the plucked sound's pace, the music transformed itself again, segueing into a flamenco that soared to a crescendo. The playing stopped with a sudden finality, leaving the fading vibration of the guitar strings hanging in the room. For half a beat, the now-silent crowd's breath seemed suspended before letting itself out in appreciation and applause.

"Thank you. Thanks. Glad you liked that. I'm Ned Grambly, here for your musical pleasure—or pain." Soft sounds emanated under his touch. "From covers to crazy, anything you want to hear, let me know. Odds are I can't play it. But I will try to give you more entertainment than Jerry's flat beer and watered-down booze. And I'll try *not* to be more entertaining than the honey you're here with." He looked down at his fingers moving over the strings, then back up again. "However, if you aren't here with a honey, come see me at the break. Naw, naw, not you lugs over there at the bar. Flannel isn't my type."

Both laughter and song filled the room as Ned's baritone voice launched into a rousing rendition of a John Prine number. Audra turned to Lydia. "It's a good thing I'm leaving Monday. Before that man does me some serious damage."

"Why, Audra Farrow, I haven't seen you crush like this in decades."

"Jesus, Lyd, he's good looking. And he's at least close to our age. And an artist. And a musician. And witty. What more could a woman want?"

Lydia's snort was derisive. "This woman wants *nothing*, in or from a man. Except more than a pound of flesh from one specific rat bastard."

"I know. Speaking of which, what do we start in on tomorrow?"

Over dinner and the backdrop of music, they talked some of what they could begin over the next two days—begun cautiously, insidiously, with a restraint Lydia knew would be hard to hold—and what they might do to fill all the other hours between. But mostly they listened to the music. Lydia was grateful it filled the space around Audra, as her conversations with the shopkeepers had done earlier. She was grateful she didn't need to, as she had nothing to fill it with. She was depleted. The vast emptiness that had inhabited her on her travels north and her first two weeks at the lake again numbed her, and her tongue. She was glad Audra didn't seem to notice. Or maybe she did, and understood.

Chin propped on hand; Lydia stared at the two hands working the guitar when Audra went to the restroom. The hands caressed, cajoled, commanded the inanimate box into a living thing. Without touch, it was dead, silent. Like her. But she wasn't dead, and her thoughts couldn't be silenced. Perhaps it was the same with the guitar. Lying in the darkness of its case, did it miss the way those hands treated it, making the music it could whisper or roar? Did it long for the touch, or was it grateful for respite? An ache set in. Her life was devoid of touch, had been for so long, had disappeared so gradually she couldn't remember when it had. Touch, as necessary as the other four senses to a whole life. Without being touched in return, life had been—was—diminished. Like a person rendered colorblind, cut off from the vivid reds and greens that had disappeared but aware that others still saw them. Like Beethoven, knowing the music still existed, even though it had been stolen from him. Gil had stolen this, too, from her. It had been so gradual—how he had changed, they had changed—that she hadn't even been aware of his thievery. How could she have let it happen?

Lydia jolted back into focus. Audra was climbing onto her stool, her words midsentence. "… took so long. I ordered us a Grand Marnier. And paid the check. Oh," Audra leaned forward, her whisper conspiratorial, "and did something I've never done. I sent a drink to a man. Two men, actually."

Lydia simply stared, almost shocked, almost laughing.

"Or maybe it's only one. I sent a drink to Ned, but the one to Max is from *you*."

"Oh god, Audra, you didn't." Now there was no laughter. Mortification nibbled at her like minnows at her ankles when she stood still in the lake shallows.

"Oh yes I did. We are partners in bad-assarie, so you're in this too."

The last hum of the guitar chord fell behind words spoken, not sung. "Thanks folks. I'm taking twenty to wet my whistle and let these strings cool off. If you leave before I'm back, a reminder: tip your server well. Hell, tip *me* well."

From the floor beside the mic, Ned picked up a beer by the top of its long neck. With one step, he was off the platform and Lydia realized he was headed their way. Coming from behind Audra, he smiled at Lydia. "Came to say thanks. I understand someone at this table sent …" He stopped short as Audra turned toward him. "Well, hell-lo. So, you're a patron of the arts and of dives."

Audra's smile was what the Mona Lisa's would have been if captured after tasting her lover's kiss. With a playful shrug, she said, "And obviously so are you." Leaning back and hooking her arm over the top of her chair, she added, "Do you do everything so well?"

Lydia visored her forehead with a hand, swallowing a desire to laugh out loud at Audra's brazenness—brazenness for a Southern good girl who'd been raised right, anyway.

"Yup." He puffed out his chest and patted it. "Ned of the U.P. The U.P stands for utter perfection. That's me," he said, eliciting both rolled eyes and groans from the two women. "Um, I usually take my break out back but … uh, mind?" He pointed the bottle in his hand to the high chair beside Audra.

"No. Oh, no. Please." Audra snatched her purse from the seat and hung its strap on the back of her own.

Ned nodded to Lydia. "I didn't get your name earlier. You are …?"

"Elle." Lydia responded before Audra might answer. It seemed odd how quickly she had adapted to hiding herself. As if presenting a third version of herself, one as unknown to others as it was to herself. A blank screen for others to project on, while it hid, protected as if in a cocoon, the metamorphosis going on unseen. Shape-shifting from who she'd been to whom she didn't know. Would she emerge a butterfly, or would the larvae be consumed from the inside by bitterness, as if by some parasitic wasp?

Ned and Audra were already in conversation. Audra was back to talking business—questioning Ned on how many paintings he had on hand, how long it took to have prints made, how he preferred to ship. Lydia sat back, glad to be silent, glad to be invisible again. When the server placed their after-dinner drinks on the table, Audra reached for hers as she kept talking. Lydia smiled at the girl and said thank you. Smiling back as she turned, the girl almost bumped into Max.

"Ladies." Audra stopped talking. "And sir. I don't mean to interrupt. Your break"—he nodded to Ned—"seemed the opportune time to thank Lady L here for the drink." He lifted his glass to Lydia.

"So, you two are in the habit of sending drinks to strange men?" Ned asked.

"Nope," Audra chirped, raising her glass in mock salute. "Striking another item off our bucket lists: to someday send a drink to the most interesting guys in a bar. Ned, this is Max. Max, want to join us?"

Audra's eyes locked on Lydia's and the look between them didn't need to be spoken. G*otcha*! Audra's face proclaimed. *I could kill you*, threatened Lydia's in return.

Max swung a chair around from the table behind him, asking, "So, you've all just met?"

"Yes. No. Funniest thing." Audra said, "Lyd and I came here after leaving Ned's gallery. We had no idea he'd show up, let alone be the entertainment."

Max looked at Lydia with interest. "Lid?"

"Uh, it's a nickname. For Elle." Audra stammered, trying to cover her slip. "From high school. I'm the only one who still gets to call her that. Sorry, *Elle*."

"Oh, and where's that nickname come from," Ned asked. "That how you got your start in business, the two of you Florida girls running keys from the Keys back in the seventies?"

"Not *that* kind of lid." Audra gave his arm a joshing push. "We were good girls. Well, mostly. Now, smoke a little of it …?"

Audra, on the verge of tipsy, was veering too close to dangerous waters. Lydia jumped in. "Audra's going to sell Ned's paintings. She has a store. In Ybor City. Audra, why don't you tell Max about the store?"

The tactic, as Lydia knew it would, worked. Audra was always in her element talking about Flo Minko's, and she then talked about what a great addition Ned's work would be. "Hey, here's an idea." She grasped Ned's forearm. "Maybe you could come down this winter. We could do a meet-the-artist event. And maybe, maybe even get you a weekend gig at one of the bars. And Max, Li … uh, Elle says you winter on Sanibel. You'll have to come—we'll have a mini-reunion."

Max glanced at Lydia. She could tell he was pleased she'd remembered, and had spoken of him.

Ned pushed back his chair. "You know, that's an idea I'll seriously think on. But right now I have to think on music. Time for me to get back up there." He shook Max's hand, nodded to Lydia, and thanked Audra again for the beer.

"Aud, we should get going too," Lydia said.

"Hmm, is my company that unpleasant?"

Max's question flustered Lydia, but not for the reason its hint of haughtiness seemed to convey. "No, no—I wish we could stay for another set. It's just been a long day. A very long day."

"Well, maybe we can do this again while you're here," Max said to Audra, his voice friendly again. "Will you will be staying for some time?"

Audra swallowed the last sip of her liqueur. "Nope. Monday, goin' back to Tampa town."

"Well, safe travels then. Elle, thank you again for the drink. Perhaps you will allow me to return the favor sometime?"

"You do that, buddy boy," Audra said as she stood. "Make sure she doesn't go full Garbo, holed up in that place."

Chapter 12

New mug in hand, Lydia eased the lodge door shut behind her and stepped into the damp morning light, as soft and pearl gray as a kitten's underbelly. Dew scattered glinting crystals in the wake of her steps, in such silence she thought she heard each drop fall. Little puddles pooled in worn spots on the chairs, so Lydia went to lean against the boulder out on the point. Sipping her coffee, she stared at the water's edge, so still its ripples brushing the sand were almost imperceptible. The movement, as constant as a muted metronome, reached into her. This was what she needed, coffee and quiet, the odd juxtaposition of caffeine and meditation.

She hadn't expected to awaken so early, just as the first light tipped the trees. Audra was likely to sleep a long time. They'd stayed up late—more drinks, more smoking, more talking under the amazing stars. Well, Audra had done most of the talking, loquacious as liquor and weed always made her. Funny, Lydia thought, how a toke or two affected them in such opposite ways. Audra's natural talkativeness ratcheted up, while, unlike the other evening, Lydia tended to become as silent as a nun after vespers.

Constant, as oblivious to her as she was to the rest of the world, the water lapped a steady, subtle caress of the sand. When it stormed, the lake roared rage against the shore, threatening to overrun, overwhelm, obliterate the land from its very existence. Yet if it did, the lake too would cease to exist, absorbed by the thirsty land. Its tender motion now seemed one of gratitude, as if aware the separation between it and the land was what allowed the lake to be itself. It needed the land to shape it.

For nearly a month now Lydia had been washed away, overrun by the flood of her emotions. The onslaught, which had seemed unstoppable, was beginning—ever, so, slowly—to recede. Audra's being here helped. Audra's friendship, like sandbags deflecting the flow, had diverted the raging waters she'd been swept up in, giving her something to climb atop and save herself from drowning. This too shall pass, the Bible says, she told herself, not This has come to stay. She sighed. But it hadn't passed yet, and she had no idea when it might. She still had to scrape out the muck that had flooded her life, wash, scour, scrub it away. But the high-water mark left behind would remain a permanent stain on her memory. The lake that was her soul would come to contain itself again, albeit reshaped, with new shores redefined, stunned by the raw exposure of new shores. The self she once had been would recede and fade, soon to become unknowable to anyone who might venture near.

The last slosh of coffee in Lydia's mug was cold and somewhere a boat motor fired up, stabbing the stillness. Lydia went back inside.

There was work to do.

***

It hadn't taken long, thank god, to choose what to send in her first salvo from behind enemy lines. What had taken time was filling in the order page, over and over and over, again and again, for each and every single shipment she was making to Gil's contacts. Ship to: Name, Address, City/State/Zip. Is this a gift: Yes. Write a message (Extra $2.50): "Have fun with this! Better yet, come have fun with us!" Gift wrap: (Extra $2.50): Yes. Shipping Method: Next Day: $37.50, Expedited 2–4 days $15.75, Standard 7–10 days $8—she always clicked "Next Day." Do you want to receive email confirmation/receipt: No. Place your order. Click. Then waiting while the screen displayed, "Please don't close this page yet. We're getting your confirmation number."

Breathe, Lydia reminded herself during each of the long seconds until the confirmation flashed on the screen, along with "Thanks. We are humping on your order right now." At some point she noticed small print that read, "Orders placed weekends/holidays will ship the second following business day." Today was Saturday. Shoot, that meant the soonest deliveries would be Wednesday—it was going to be a long week. The breath she let out when she put a checkmark next to the last name on the list was one of relief. She snapped the laptop lid closed.

Reaching for the coffee pot, she stopped. It was almost ten. *The clock be damned*, she thought. She pulled a bottle of Irish whiskey from the cupboard and poured a heavy splash into the mug. And where were Audra's cigarettes? She found them out on the porch, next to the ashtray they had almost filled last night. Half a joint lay there too. *Well, why not*, she thought. She allowed herself two tokes before she carefully stubbed it out and laid it aside. The coffee tasted especially good.

She looked up at the sound of the screen door. Audra, in a robe and pajamas, her bed-head unbrushed, moved in a barely awake shuffle.

"Hey."

"Mmm," Audra grunted. She stopped at the other end of the porch swing, staring, then sat down in a chair. "Don't think I'm ready for any motion," she mumbled. "Got enough of it going on in my head."

"So I see. Why no coffee?"

"Oh I'd love some. Would you? I didn't think I could carry it without spilling."

By noon Lydia's slight buzz had worn off, and Audra was herself again. They both were restless, with nothing specific to do. Audra kept picking out a book, sitting down to read a page or two, then putting it back and wandering around before choosing another book. Lydia kept opening the laptop to stare at the screen, then closing it again, and forcing herself not to tackle tomorrow's task—too much activity would be a giveaway. Then she'd find herself in the kitchen wiping off the counters again. After the fourth time—or was it the sixth?—she slapped the dishcloth into the sink, strode across the great room and punched the screen door open with the palm of her hand. Audra was pacing the porch with a cigarette. "Grab a jacket. And your purse. We need to go do something."

"Do what?" Audra asked.

"Get away from here, that's what. Before we both go bonkers."

At the stoplight, Audra sighed over the clicking of the car's blinker. "Haven't we seen everything in this burg?" Then when Lydia turned left, not right, she asked, "Um, where are we going?"

"To play tourist," Lydia said.

An old rock number came on the radio. Lydia rolled down her window, turned up the volume on the classic rock station, and pressed the gas pedal. The years fell away on the open road: she and Audra were teens in one of their parent's cars, racing away from it-didn't-matter-what to who-cared. All that mattered was the joy of freedom, speed, and loud music. They began to sing along, voices off key, hair flying in the wind.

Miles of flat, greening rural countryside rushed by. Most of it was open, almost as barren as the interior of Florida, dotted with scrub brush instead of palmettos. An occasional "new" home squatted off the roadway. Old farmhouses and sagging barns stood off in fields. There was something tired about them all, as if the buildings, and the people inhabiting them, hadn't yet thrown off the weight of winter. As if the land knew all too well that snow could come again this early in June. But today the air was fine and the sun warm. Their voices quieted as they sang along with Bob Seeger's "Night Moves." After that, neither one said much.

The land changed after Lydia turned east onto the four-lane. It remained much the same on Lydia's side to the north, but thick stands of cedar and pine obscured the horizon on Audra's. Then, without warning, the trees disappeared. Low dunes of soft yellow sand ribboned both sides of the road, sparse tufts of lake grass sprouting like wispy patches of hair on old men's bald heads. Lydia eased her foot a bit from the gas pedal as an "ooh" of awe escaped Audra. Outside her window a lake had spilled into view. Three rows of breakers, as huge as those kicked up on the Gulf in a tropical storm, roiled white froth onto the shore, and the water raced up the sand as if trying to reach the road. Behind the surf-sized waves, calm water extended as far as their eyes could see.

"What *is* this?" Audra's voice was hushed.

"Lake Michigan."

"My god. I had no idea …"

The land changed once more, becoming rocky, a brash declaration of the primordial glaciers that had shaped this part of the Earth. A state highway sign announced the exit to St. Ignace, the last exit before the Mackinac Bridge.

"Mack-in-ack Bridge," Audra sounded out. "I think I've seen that on the news?"

"Macki*naw*," Lydia corrected. "Probably. Remember Hurricane Hugo? Back in '89? When the wind made it here, it was still so strong a car was blown off the bridge."

"Good lord."

Lydia moved into the exit lane and joined the queue of other vehicles. Soon a large sign, directing them to parking, caught Audra's eye. "Wow, Mackinac Island? The one with the hotel in all those movies? Oh my god this is so cool."

The next island ferry was beginning to load passengers and they were early enough to find seats beside an expanse of glass. As the craft made its leisurely pace, Lydia stared at the open water passing by, playing in her mind like one of Uncle Pete's old home movies on fast-forward, but all the images of her old life felt washed away, erased, leaving her interior screen as blank as the view.

She was vaguely aware of Audra, chatting away with nearby seatmates who were faceless to Lydia.

Audra went silent mid-sentence when she caught sight of the monumental bridge as the ferry cruised toward its destination. She grabbed Lydia's arm and pulled her from the seat. "Come on, I want to go outside to see this." Standing in the wind, Audra's hair flattened back, her face rosy and her mouth an open grin of awe, Lydia couldn't help but laugh. "You look like a country kid who just saw the big city at Christmas."

"This is breathtaking. Like seeing the Eiffel Tower, or the Golden Gate," Audra said, rapt with awareness. "How long is this sucker?"

"Almost a mile longer than the Skyway, and more than a hundred feet higher." Whereas the Sunshine Skyway Bridge spanned Tampa Bay like two mythical archers' bows ready to unleash arrows to the heavens, the Mackinac stood like Colossus, its girders and steel straddling the lake in testament to the twentieth-century engineering feats of Man.

Lydia wished for a moment that she had driven over it. She wished she could again hear the Gregorian chant-like sounds sent up by the thrum of the car's tires over the center-span grate. She loved the sensation that always came over her while crossing the bridges over Tampa Bay, being held safe between the above and below, between the from and the to, between the coming and the gone. A marker. The Mackinac Bridge had been such a marker all through her childhood, until she married. Two trips across every year, one marking the start of summer, the start of days and nights and weeks of time the clocks did not control, an openness that was almost disconcerting at first; the other, the coming of winter, a return to school, schedules, clocks ticking "Do this. Do that. Hurry, hurry, hurry, you're late, you're late, you're late." In these past few weeks, she'd left all that behind, that sensation—that belief—that, like the clocks, she'd been in control. It had been stripped from her as painfully as if her own skin had been flayed, as if she'd been cast naked from this bridge into the depths below, into water so cold it seared like fire. A seed of awareness took hold: as she gave up struggling, a new skin had begun to form. The flames of her anguish hadn't consumed her but were tempering something that was both as fragile yet as strong as crystal. In no longer wanting to drown, she was learning to float.

The ferry began to slow. Lydia turned and saw the island coming near. It rose mountain-like compared to the islands of Florida, yet caused the same bile to rise as whenever she'd discover another development had encroached on the beaches or barrier islands. The island's port basin, where Lydia recalled low maritime buildings, was now rimmed with boxy, bland condos draped with banners hawking summer rentals. She stared in disgust—men and their lust, their willingness to rape the land for their own greed.

"Come on, let's go." Audra bumped Lydia with her elbow, and they joined the disembarking crowd.

A flock of blue bikes stood along the pier as they walked. When she saw the "Bikes for Rent" sign, Audra said, "Don't tell me we need those to get around. No way. Not me. I haven't ridden one since my twenties."

"That makes two of us. Just keep walking."

They soon reached the edge of downtown, where storefronts set a 1950s movie scene, and garish Coney Island colors clashed with Ye Olde Shoppe-style signs hung above entrance doors. Hills, dotted with what looked like antique dollhouses, looked down on them. In the distance, the Grand Hotel gave the kingdom its castle. The sound of hooves on pavement broke through the noise of the people on the streets.

"Look." Audra pointed to a tram being pulled by a handsome horse team. "We're tourists, so let's tour."

"May as well." Lydia shrugged.

"My, your enthusiasm is underwhelming. If you are going to be an old grump, why'd you bring me here?"

"Okay, okay. I'm sorry."

Audra reached over to pat Lydia's arm. "I know, honey. But you hauled me off today to get *out* of your head. So try to do that, okay?"

"Okay. You're right." Lydia's mouth pinched into a false smile. "Fake it till I make it, right?"

Audra rolled her eyes. "Come on, Miss Sunshine. Somebody'll know where we get tickets."

The tour did brighten Lydia's mood as they were carried away from downtown. The horses' hooves clomping in steady cadence and the slight sway of the tram relaxed her until she felt at one with their rhythms. The black pavement wended higher and higher, encircling the island's hills. Pristine Victorian homes—once the massive summer "cottages" of Chicago's elite—stood on vast, manicured lawns, looking much like grande dames staring haughtily at the hoi polloi parading past.

“What was that Boopsie line from Doonesbury,” Audra asked. “Ah, ‘when men and women wore linen—and servants kept it pressed’?” Everyone within earshot, including Lydia, chuckled in agreement. Those days were long gone, as the T-shirts-and-shorts-wearing passengers attested. *Nothing does stay the same*, thought Lydia, *in my life or anyone’s.*

Returning downtown, the glass storefronts attracted oglers like sideshow barkers trying to draw crowds into the bearded lady’s tent. The air was sweet, almost cloying, from the scent of the ice cream, candy, and fudge shops that competed with those selling souvenirs, sweatshirts, and jackets galore. Not much beckoned them, but in one particular shop Audra and Lydia each splurged on several pieces of silver jewelry, and Audra’s critical eye was on constant alert for merchandising ideas.

Hungry, and ready to sit down, they chose a restaurant. At the late afternoon hour, the place was not crowded. They were shown to a booth at the front window, where the people passing by provided an ever-streaming panorama of shapes and sizes. Twirling her wineglass by its stem and looking out, Audra said, “If I ever tell anybody I’ve been here, I know just how I’ll describe it: Key West for straight, white Christians.”

***

As the ferry returned them to the mainland, the sun lowered itself behind the bridge, streaking the cream-colored spans of metal with apricot rays. Coming dusk settled a cloak over the scenery as they drove home, the lingering light a soft closing on the day. Darkness had deepened by the time Lydia slipped the key into the lodge’s door. She was glad she’d left lights on. The room was as welcoming as a mother’s embrace. They slung their purses and purchases onto the sofa.

“I’m tired,” Lydia said. “In a good way.”

“Me too. But I’m not sleepy. You?”

“Mm-mmm.”

“Good. You pour the wine; I’ll bring the smokes.”

The porch light hung behind them, an unobtrusive orb from their chairs at the shore. Before them, moonlight bounced along the light chop of waves, and emerging stars dusted the sea of space above.

“It’s been a good day.” Lydia’s sigh was relaxed. “I didn’t think it would be, this morning. I’m glad we saw the bridge and did the island. To tell the truth, I didn’t know where we were going when I took off.”

“Funny, isn’t it,” Audra said, “how sometimes you don’t know where you’re going and yet you end up in just the place you need to be.”

“God, I hope you’re right. Because right now I have no clue where I’m going, where I’ll end up, or how I’ll get there.”

“Which reminds me. I have managed to not ask this all day. Just what did you do that got you so tense before I woke up this morning?”

Lydia reached for a cigarette and lit it. “I sent gifts to Gil’s clients. Charged to his corporate credit card.”

“And what kinds of gifts?”

Lydia leaned back and exhaled deeply. “Everyone’s getting a year’s membership to the PPB&D website and service. Plus a big gift basket of sex toys.”

Audra’s howl of laughter split the night, and Lydia joined in.

***

Sunday morning came up bright, clear, and cold. So cold that when Lydia stepped out with her first cup of coffee the air shocked her. The furnace had come on every night and the mornings had been chilly, but not like this. This was winter cold. The wind stung her face and hands and the icy burn lingered after she retreated inside. She lit the gas fireplace and curled up under a throw on the sofa. As always when she stared into fire, Lydia’s consciousness shifted. The room seemed to withdraw, receding like a stage set behind a closing curtain. Thoughts, unbidden, flickered up, layered and shape-shifting like the hypnotic flames. Not really thoughts, but fragments slipping in and out, random, until they reached the one she hadn’t wanted to deal with. She tried pushing it away again, and again. It refused to give up its hold.

Sara and James. Sara and James had to be told. But what? And how? Gil had lied to James, saying she’d gone antiquing for the holiday; she’d lied to Sara, and everyone else, about being on a work sabbatical. If they hadn’t already, her son and daughter soon would talk and likely realize the deceptions. She wasn’t ready to speak to them. To have to say her words twice—and what would those words be? They’d still have to be a lie, a lie by omission, because she couldn't bear to damage them with the truth. She wasn't ready to hear the shocked silence that would follow her words. The pain in their voices as they asked the inevitable questions. And who to call first? Sara's heartbreak would spill out in wrenching tears, and Lydia knew her own would follow. James would mask his pain with anger that she was too vulnerable to deal with. But they had to be told. She sighed, tossing off the lap robe to refill her coffee, and returned to the sofa with a legal pad and pen.

Now it was the fire that receded like a stage set. Words struggled their way onto the page. Tears dropped, blurring the ink, the damp spots shredding where she slashed through something she'd written. When she finished, she turned the pad face down, curled into a corner of the sofa, and let the tears overwhelm her. When they stopped, she rewrote the letter. After the second re-write it was shorter, terser, and she moved to her grandmother's desk to copy it twice. When she sealed the envelopes addressed to Sara and to James, the pain had been replaced by anger. The anger felt better.

Rummaging through a drawer for postage stamps, Lydia became aware of sounds from the kitchen. She'd been so intent on her task she hadn't heard Audra come down. She picked up her cup from the sofa table, the coffee barely touched, and the crumpled tissues that had piled up.

"Good morning," she said. She threw the tissues in the trash and poured the cold coffee down the sink. "When did you get up?"

Audra was at the table, leafing through a magazine. "Oh, fifteen or twenty minutes. Warm mine up too, please?" Lydia carried the carafe and her own refilled mug to the table. "You looked pretty intent. I didn't want to disturb you."

"You didn't." Lydia leaned back in her chair and looked out at the lake, so gray, icy, and uninviting. "I wrote the kids."

Audra was silent for several seconds. "What did you tell them?"

"That their father was a lying, cheating, fornicating, stick-his-dick-in-any-hole scumbag rat bastard." Lydia smirked at the shock on Audra's face. "In the first version, anyway. Gil would have deserved it, but they don't. I told them something had occurred between their father and me, that I wasn't ready to explain it all yet, and that I'd gone away to think things through. And now that I have, I'm filing for divorce. I asked them to wait until the day after they get the letter, then to text me and we'll set a time for a three-way call." She drew in a long breath. "That's going to be hard. Harder than anything I've ever had to do."

"That's not true. You've already done the hardest."

"What, writing the letter to them?"

"No. Confronting the truth. You could have accepted what Gil said. You never would have known what he's been up to. But you dug. You found him out. You confronted all of that by yourself. And you survived. Talking to them won't be easy, but it won't be as hard as what you've already been through." Audra got up, brought a box of tissues back to the table, and handed one to Lydia. "What say I change my plane reservation and stay until after you talk to the kids? Julie won't be thrilled but the store will manage."

"No." Lydia shook her head. "No, you've already taken too much time away from work because of me."

"Hey, I needed this. Well, not exactly *this*, but the last time I was gone for a week it was on a business trip. You know how much fun those are."

Lydia huffed a laugh. "Oh yeah, this has been such a grand vacation for you, I'm sure."

"Well, it's a memorable one, that's for sure." Audra hoisted her coffee mug. "A toast. To us. Goddess up."

Lydia clinked her mug against Audra's. "And I'm gonna goddess right up his ass."

***

The front door opened, then closed. Audra came in, carrying the faint smell of cigarette smoke and fresh air. "God, it's cold out there."

"Still?" Lydia didn't look up from the address she was typing into the laptop.

"Still. Does summer *ever* come up here?"

"Oh, eventually. In a few weeks. For a few weeks." Lydia kept typing.

"Well, next time let's come up here when it's summer," Audra called from the kitchen while washing her hands. She came back into the dining room, drying them on a dishtowel. "How about some lunch? I'm hungry."

"Done." Lydia closed the laptop and looked at Audra. "Next time?"

"Yeah. Serious. I'd love to come back again. When things aren't so angst-ridden. Relax. Maybe do a little more sight-seeing, if there's anything else to see." Audra flicked her eyebrows. "Maybe see Ned again. Playing at the bar again, you know."

Lydia laughed. "You are so transparent. You've got the hots for that guy, don't you?"

"Mmm ..." Audra ignored the question. "So, what were you up to?"

"Part two of the plan. Gift baskets and memberships to the vendor owners and account execs. I've spent enough of his money that it'll sting. Close to ten grand."

Audra let out a low whistle. "Honey, that's not a sting, it's a sledgehammer. When does the stuff get delivered?"

"Should be Wednesday for the clients, Thursday to the vendors. Methinks Gil's going to have more than his own balls to juggle by the end of the week."

"God, wouldn't you love to be there to see it," Audra said with a bemused gaze out the window.

"Yeah. But I'm hoping"—glee crept into her voice—"a lot of the shit will blow up on email."

"Ooh, if it does, forward it to me."

"No way. With luck, this masked ISP has me covered. I'm not taking a chance forwarding anything. But I promise to tell you all."

As they sat down to lunch, Lydia asked, "What time does your plane leave tomorrow?"

"Two. It was either that or the eight-thirty a.m."

"Thank you. For both our sakes."

Across the room the phone rang, surprising them. Audra got up. "That's mine. I wonder who ..."

After Audra's hello, Lydia could hear her voice but not the words. Her mind drifted to what she could do before she'd have to talk to the kids, before the shit hit Gil's fan. It was going to be a stressful end of the week, and she wondered how she could keep herself busy till then. Tomorrow wasn't a problem, not with taking Audra to the airport and it being late afternoon by the time she would return. She needed something to fill Tuesday at least, maybe Wednesday too, to move this plan along. Marielle was going to be the next front to attack.

"That," Audra said as she returned, "was Ned. He's coming over." She grinned at Lydia as she bit into her sandwich.

"What? You invited him here?"

"He invited himself. He said he got to thinking that I might want to take some of his smaller prints back with me. I told him sure. He'll be here around four. Hmm. Long hair, artist, musician—I wonder if he tokes," Audra mused as she reached for an apple slice.

The afternoon warmed enough that, with jackets and lap robes, the women gravitated to the front porch, Audra with a book, Lydia with several ancient magazines she'd found in the attic. She'd gone up there to explore while Audra packed. Filled with boxes, footlockers, trunks, and old furniture, the attic looked like a hoarder's nightmare. Chaos threatened claustrophobia as she snaked her way through everything crammed in the huge space. Then a pleasant resolve settled over her. This was what she needed, a project to tackle, to fill the time waiting for chaos to erupt in Gil's and that woman's lives. The *Look* magazine now on her lap was filled with images of upheaval, chaotic scenes of escape, destruction, and retreat the week Vietnam was abandoned. She remembered the time clearly. In her grandparents' day, the photos would have shown the hollow-eyed stares of families escaping the ravages of the Dust Bowl. Today the long-defunct magazine would picture the fearful eyes of children and mothers streaming away from violence in Central America, the Middle East, Ukraine. All refugees, all trying to escape their own particular hells. Now, an emotional refugee herself, she better understood viscerally, not just intellectually, the immensity of their loss.

She was lucky, she knew, to have found a place of sanctuary. But all sanctuary was, in its own way, false, because the upheaval would always be with them, an invisible backpack they could never release. Turmoil was the natural order, tranquility the illusion. Life itself was constant disorder. Calm was simply a pause, a respite, a regrouping, a balancing. She'd been swept up, overwhelmed by a personal and intimate maelstrom, sucked into an internal riptide.

She had forgotten that her power was not in fighting the current but in swimming along the shore to eventual safety. Outwitting Perses, that's what she was doing now: tipping the scales back in her favor, not fighting the chaos but bending it to her will, shaping it to her needs. That's why a sense of calm had returned to her, she realized—the calm was the magic stone of her own power. Power she'd given away for so long that she had forgotten it was hers. Deluding herself into thinking chaos could be forestalled by relinquishing her power to others. To Gil, his whims and wishes. To shaping her children, her students, to mentoring them and others on how to gain their own powers while giving away hers. Reclaiming it, that's where the center of calm held. Fighting the chaos, like fighting the undertow, led to peril. Embracing the chaos, meeting it, that's where true strength lay. For the first time, she had a glimmer of understanding about how a warrior must feel in the midst of battle—not unafraid, no; but discovering the thrill of her own courage, if not to vanquish then to give herself over to the joy of battle.

Audra clapped her book shut and tossed off the lap robe. "Idiot."

Lydia looked up; eyebrows raised.

Audra laughed. "Not you, Lyd. The so-called heroine. Too stupid to live. What say we go for a walk?"

On their way back later, cold hands pocketed and faces pinked by the chill, they swung the gate open at the road for Ned's arrival. They hadn't even taken off their jackets when they heard a vehicle and stepped back outside. A battered van, as gaily decorated as a hippie-mobile, pulled to a stop, then Ned came around, calling a hello as he opened a rear door. Pulling out what looked like a salesman's sample case, he slammed the door shut and walked toward them, smiling. "I know it's not four yet. Hope you don't mind."

"No, no, come on in," Lydia answered.

"Closed up early. Decided I'd much rather see this place, and you," he said, looking at Audra as he took the steps two at a time, "than hang around the empty studio. Five customers all day. Two couples, and one teenage kid probably scoping something to rip off. One lousy twenty-five-dollar sale."

He and Audra began commiserating—complaining really—about shoplifters, the effects of the weather, whether it brought more people in looking to break up boredom or whether it kept people home. Lydia hurried to gather up all the papers from the dining room table. Piling them upside down on the sideboard, she interrupted, "Can we see what you brought? You can spread things out here."

"Great." Ned tossed his jacket on a chair and carried the case to the table. From it he pulled matted prints, two dozen in all. Lydia's and Audra's compliments were profuse as they studied each of the images and asked about them. Then the conversation between Ned and Audra turned to her selling the art. Sensing the discussion could go on for a while, Lydia took an opportunity to interrupt. "Excuse me. Why don't I fix us all drinks?"

Ned flashed a smile at Audra. "Sure. Drinks with a beautiful woman—uh, two," he corrected, glancing at Lydia. "Who'd pass that up?"

Lydia rolled her eyes at Audra, who was blushing. "Can't offer you a beer though. Sorry."

"Oh, I know," Audra piped up. "Old Fashioneds. Lyd makes great ones."

Grinning, Ned shook his head. "Yeah, I still think there's more to that nickname than you two admit."

Lydia's look at Audra was sharp as she turned toward the kitchen. "Nah. She started it to throw people off my after-school coke smuggling operation. Jesus. Why does everyone assume everyone in Florida back then dealt drugs."

"Hey, don't ruin the mystique," Audra hollered after her.

For the first time all day, the sun poured down, setting off diamond sparkles on the lake outside the picture window. They carried their drinks out to the porch to enjoy the breath of warmth returning. Ned walked to the railing, reading the horizon. "Be a gorgeous day tomorrow."

"Naturally," Audra said. "Last day of vacation, the weather's always lousy. Day I leave, it's perfect." She reached for a cigarette.

"Uh, mind?" Ned pointed at the packet as he sat down. "Haven't had one of those in a long time."

"Now I've got two people bumming from me. Good thing I am leaving, before I run out," Audra teased as she pushed the packet and lighter toward him.

"So, how did you end up in the U.S.," Lydia asked him.

"Grew up around here. Swore I'd leave and never come back." He didn't stop there, though. The casual question turned Ned into a raconteur. Through their drinks, the women sat, either mesmerized into silence or howling with laughter while he regaled them with escapades, from drug-hazed days as a supply clerk in Vietnam through years of "pucking around the U.S.," as he called it, skittering in whichever direction something propelled him. He'd work itinerant jobs, saving up enough for a stint at an artist's colony, then "puck off" to find work again when the money ran out. At the end of one tale Audra and Lydia were laughing so hard none of them heard the sound of tires on the drive.

"Oh my god, oh my god, my sides hurt." Lydia wiped tears of laughter away, then jumped at the sound of a car door slamming. All three looked up. Lydia couldn't see who had stepped out of the SUV but she recognized it and the top of the hat moving from behind the vehicle. She stood. "Max. What's he doing here?"

"Like she doesn't know," Audra muttered to Ned. "Whatever his excuse is, she's the real reason. Watch."

"Max. Hello," Lydia said. Max was carrying another white wrapped package. "This is a surprise."

He nodded to Audra and Ned. "I tried calling but no one answered, then decided to take a chance on you two being here. I thought Audra might like to discover the taste of our delectable fish while she's here. Sorry to have barged into your little party." He handed the package to Lydia and began to turn away.

"Oh, please stay," Audra urged. "You're not barging in on anything."

"Ned came by with some art for Audra to take back to her store," Lydia said. "You're welcome to join us."

He hesitated. "Thank you. If you're sure I'm not intruding."

"Good. I'll fix you a drink." Lydia carried the package to the refrigerator. By the time she returned with his drink, Max and Ned were semi-arguing over something or other. "Cheers," Max said, lifting his glass toward them, then took a sip. "Ah, an Old Fashioned. And an excellent one, too. Another of your skills, I see."

From the corner of her eye, Lydia saw Audra turn toward her with a smirk. She ignored it. The conversation picked up, as Ned and Max discussed an incident in town that led to exchanges about the latest political news from Washington. Lydia realized how out of touch she was, how little she cared, about what was happening outside her own world. She settled back, listening, as the three others traded opinions.

When Max's glass was nearly empty he said, "I think it's time to take my leave. Thank you for the drink, Elle."

"Yeah, I'd better be going too," Ned said.

"Wait. Why don't you both stay for dinner?" Lydia's suggestion surprised her as much as it did Audra. "Seriously. Please. I'd already thawed the fish I got at Bess's. With Max's contribution, there's plenty. Uh, unless you've other plans, of course. You probably do …" Her voice had begun to falter.

Audra lightly touched Ned's knee. "Yes, let's have a little dinner party. What do you say?"

"Well," Ned drawled, "does sound better than the beans and weenies waiting for me at home."

"And you too, Max?" Audra asked.

He nodded. "It would be my pleasure."

"Good." Audra stood up and reached for Ned's glass. "Then let's have another. Come on, Lyd, I'll help carry."

Lydia took Max's glass and shot Audra a look. Inside, she growled, "Jesus, Aud. That's the third time."

"I'm sorry, I'm sorry. I keep forgetting, *Elle*."

On the way back out, Lydia carried only Max's drink. As Audra handed Ned his and sat down, Lydia said, "Y'all go on talking. I'm going to get dinner started."

Through the screen door the three voices and occasional laughter reached the kitchen as Lydia cut thick slices of bread to warm in the oven and prepared a salad. She was almost finished mixing the dressing when she heard the screen door slap, and Max's voice. "Elle? Mind if I come in?"

Lydia poked her head through the kitchen doorway. "Sure. I'm in here. Can I get you something?"

His eyes were taking in the great room as he headed her way. "No, no, no. I was beginning to feel a bit like an extra player. You've quite a stunning place for your retreat."

He'd taken his hat off, and Lydia again noticed the handsome silver hair, how its slight wave and precision cut added dignity to his appearance. She capped the dressing jar and began to shake it. "Thanks. My brother and sister-in-law have taken good care of it." She turned away, biting her lip. The drinks—like Audra she was saying too much.

"Ah. Dave did say you were somehow connected to the owners. He didn't say you were family."

"I asked him not to. I haven't been up here in a long time. Just didn't think it was anyone's business."

"Understandable. But you are here for work?" Max lounged back against a counter. "Did having your friend here distract you from it?"

Lydia placed the salad bowl in the refrigerator and withdrew a package of strawberries that she emptied into a colander in the sink. "Not at all. In fact, the opposite." Wondering how to put it, she let running water cover her silence for a moment. "Audra is very familiar with my ... project, and the dilemma I had. We're in completely different fields, but her perspective actually brought quite a bit of insight. Thanks to her, things are well underway. Whether it actually works … well, that's left to be seen. But I'm feeling more confident about it now."

He reached for a strawberry and asked, "And what, may I inquire, is your field?"

"Education."

"Ah, you teach? Dave said something about you being on sabbatical. Surely school is out for the summer."

She decided to prick his assumptions. "I'm at the university," she said, stressing that word, "which is in summer session. I prefer to put my doctorate to use in the classroom, not administration."

His look was of surprised admiration. "My. The more I discover about you, the more intrigued I am about what's yet to be discovered. Shall I now address you as Dr. Elle?"

"Only if you're enrolled in a course. And in that case, it's Dr. Casselberry." He took another strawberry as she returned them to the refrigerator. Drawing out the fish, she asked, "What about you? What was your field before you went Hemingway, out hunting fish all the time?"

"Fishing is still an avocation. I haven't completely stopped working. Forensic psychology."

Oh shit, Lydia thought, her breath catching, her mind rushing—he couldn't be investigating her, he'd been staying at Bess and Dave's for years, no one knew she was coming here, he couldn't know what she was up to because she hadn't even known until a few days ago.

"I too teach," he went on, not noticing—seeming not to notice? Lydia wondered—her momentary distraction. "I taught at the University of Michigan for fifteen years. When that was no longer fulfilling or challenging, I opened my own firm. Then, after deciding to quote-unquote retire, I returned to teaching, but outside of academia. Instead, in government agencies. For which the internal politicking of academia had prepared me well."

"No doubt," Lydia said.

"Might I help by doing the fish? You're kind to invite us, and it's causing you quite a bit of work. I'd be pleased to help. Of which I am a quite capable."

"So, there's more to discover about you too? That would be nice."

"Good. Then step aside as I work my magic. However, if you'll retrieve the items I need, it will save me from creating complete disarray by searching for them myself."

Lydia gathered what he requested, and watched him as she set the table. He measured nothing as he created a marinade paste with practiced assurance. She noticed his deftness with a knife as he peeled and cut an onion into paper-thin slices. There was a newness about seeing a man at home in a kitchen. Gil's idea of helping was asking if she had the meat ready for him to put on the grill.

"Have you any panko?" Seeing the shake of her head, he suggested, "Saltines? Or even potato chips?"

"Neither. But I do have a box of Parmesan crisps. Would those do?"

"Superbly. Oh, and I'll need a few other spices."

The sound of the food processor whirring drew Audra indoors as Lydia carried wine glasses to the table. "Noisy in here. Realized what a slacker I've been. Need some help? Or saving?" Seeing Max at work, Audra looked at Lydia in surprise.

"I know. He offered. He definitely knows what he's doing. You doing okay?"

"Yes. No. Because if I weren't going home tomorrow I'd be going home with him tonight. What can I do? In here, I mean."

Lydia grinned. "Nothing. Go on back to flirting. But no PDA, hear?"

Voices and aromas swirled as they all sat down, wine was poured and glasses raised, and the food passed and served. Then silence fell as Ned, Audra, and Lydia took their first bites of the sautéed fish. The flavors, the delicacy, astonished Lydia. She'd grown up loving the taste of deep-fried walleye, but whatever Max had done took it to sublime. Almost simultaneously the three gushed their compliments, which Max brushed off before shifting the conversation, and noise and laughter again filled the room.

When bellies were filled and platters emptied, Ned said, "Elle, thank you. This has been great. But Max, don't open a restaurant in town, okay? You'd put Doozy's out of business and I'd lose my music gig."

"Doozy's—nor anyone—has no fear of that. Cooking for friends is a pleasure. For any other reason, it is a chore."

Audra pushed her chair back. "Speaking of chores, I'll clear. Take the wine bottle and your glasses and y'all get out of here."

"I'll give you a hand," Ned said, collecting dishes with the skill of someone who'd bussed many a table.

Outside, the light was softening. Lydia refilled their wine glasses and sat down, while Max gazed out at the water. "Interesting, isn't it," he said, "how seeing the lake from a position other than one's usual view alters one's perspective. Much like life." He took a chair. "Thank you. This has been most pleasant."

"I should be thanking you. The fish was superb. Where did you learn to cook like that?"

"First, from my grandmother and mother. My grandmother because she was disappointed she didn't have a granddaughter to pass her recipes down to. My mother, who told me it would impress the girls. In college, I discovered how right she was," he said with a chuckle. "My wife and I both loved cooking. We often planned vacations around restaurants or classes offered here or abroad. It's much more a pleasure cooking with someone—and for others—than alone. I don't have either opportunity often now." His eyes turned back to the lake.

So there had been a wife, Lydia thought in the silence, but she wasn't about to ask the question.

"Cynthia passed six years ago," he said, as if reading her thoughts.

"I'm sorry—" went unfinished as Ned rushed from inside and down the steps to his van. Audra came onto the porch behind him. She put down the two wine glasses she was carrying and lit a cigarette as Ned bounded back up the steps with his guitar case.

Lifting out the instrument and tuning it, he said, "A good troubadour sings for his supper, especially when the hostesses—and the cook—have been so generous." He began strumming the notes of a light, intricate piece that wafted into the fading day, and a sense of contentment settled on them all.

At the end of his third song, Ned set the guitar back in its case. Audra applauded and Lydia and Max complimented his skill. "I enjoyed it," he said. "Just as much as I've enjoyed the whole evening. But it's time to go, before I wear out my welcome."

"True." Max rose. "I expected to come by for a moment, not to impose for hours."

"If it had been an imposition, I'd have booted you all out long ago," Lydia said. "You have no idea how much I needed this."

"Me too," Audra piped. "I can't think of a better end to my stay."

Ned made his goodbyes and Audra walked with him to his van, where they disappeared from view on the driver's side. As Max put on his hat, Lydia said,

"Thank you. For the fish and for playing chef. It's been a delightful evening. I'm glad you came by."

"I am too. Perhaps you will allow me to do so again."

She hesitated a second, then nodded. "I'd like that."

She watched him go, and waved as he drove off with a toot of the horn to them all. Ned's van started up too, and Audra returned to the porch. When both sets of tail lights had disappeared the women sat down in the porch swing. Lydia emptied the last of the wine into their glasses. Waves shushed against the shore and a loon's cry came from far away. Neither spoke, letting the quiet envelop them. The setting sun infused the surroundings with a glow that melded with Lydia's own. "This turned out to be a great day, didn't it? I'd forgotten what it feels like to have fun. The only people I ever see are at work. Well, other than you. Gil and I haven't gotten together with friends for a long time. I wonder if we even have any anymore." Lydia looked at Audra with a start. "I just realized—Gil hasn't crossed my mind in hours."

Audra patted Lydia's hand. "Good. A few hours is a start. I think you need to hang out with Max more often. He seems like a good guy. You can hang out with Ned too. Some. Just not too much."

"Oh? And what does that mean?"

"I think it means I'm starting a long-distance relationship. That guy knows how to kiss."

Lydia's laughter rose to mingle with the cackle of gulls soaring overhead.

***

Mist still fingered the trees and obscured the lake horizon in the late morning as they loaded Audra's belongings into the car. The sky remained dull on the long drive to the airport, and the grayness worked its way back into Lydia's soul, unbalancing her again after the previous night's pleasure. She knew Audra needed to leave and part of her wanted her to, wanted to be alone again, but this time, she knew, the loneliness would be different. At Falton, she swung off the highway to find the post office; her fingers hesitated in releasing the letters to Sara and James. But she knew that it was time to tell them, that this was the right way, but she felt terrible about what she was about to destroy for them and fearful of how she would handle their reactions. Uneasiness crept in, over what was to ensue with the delivery of all the packages, and that the encryption she'd used might not protect her. Audra's attempts at conversation did little to keep her mind from skittering from one worry to another.

At the terminal entrance, they hugged for a long time. "I'm going to call you every night," Audra said as they stepped apart. "As much to check up on you as to keep up on what's happening."

Lydia nodded. "Text me when you're home tonight, okay?"

"Okay." Audra gave her another quick hug. "Now don't you be slipping back into that funk."

Lydia smiled. "Yes, boss." She watched Audra walk away, and when she turned back to wave, Lydia called out, "Love you."

Audra called back, "Stay bad, girl!"

Chapter 13

Tuesday dawned ensconced in fog again, this time heavy and thick, pressing against the lodge windows as if to ensure complete secrecy for Lydia. By ten, when light began to penetrate and allow outside images to emerge, she'd completed all the sex-toy orders placed in The Slut's name. She wasn't worried about being in their account on the site, figuring if either of them found it in use they'd assume the other was logged in. But she was glad to be done, to log out, to never again have to see things she couldn't unsee. She'd checked Gil's email accounts late the night before but found nothing of value to her—that, and the fact that he could be logged in now kept her from checking them again. She wasn't sure how to fill the hours ahead, without Audra to distract her.

She looked again at the text Audra had sent last night: Home safe, tired. BIG NEWS Will call after lunch. Staring at the clock wouldn't make time pass any faster. She slipped the phone and some cash into her jacket pocket and set out on foot to Clar's Corner. Walking the ribbon of road, where the trees blocked the breeze from the lake, the sun was warm. By the time Lydia reached the store, her jacket was tied around her waist. She'd get a bottled water from the cooler, and maybe Bess would have time to chat. She hoped she could learn a bit more about Max, without seeming too interested. A chink in her emotional armor had opened Sunday night, and she was curious about what Bess knew and could share. But when the bell chimed her entrance, a teenager was behind the cash register, staring intently at her cell phone. The girl said "Hi" without glancing up.

Lydia paused, then asked, as she headed back to the cooler, "Is Bess here?"

"She'll be back later this afternoon," the girl answered.

Lydia drank half the bottle of water as she carried it to the counter.

"That's all for you today?" the girl asked, looking up.

"No." Lydia reached for a small shopping basket. Picking out some fruit and produce, she said, "I didn't know Bess had any employees."

"I'm only sorta. I work weekends in the summer. Or when she takes a day off, which she almost *never* does. Sheesh. I mean, who wants to work *all* the time? I'm here 'cause they had to take Katie to the doctor."

"Is Katie sick?" Lydia felt a touch of motherly concern.

The girl's attention was still on her cell phone. "Yeah. Fever or something. Guess she threw up too."

"Oh." Lydia placed the basket on the counter. "You said 'they'?"

As the girl rang her up, she said, "Yeah. Dave always goes too. He's a good dad."

Lydia picked up the bag to leave, and said, "Tell them Lady L stopped by." The girl looked at her, curious. "Katie will know who that is. Tell them I hope she's better soon."

Closing the screen door behind her, Lydia felt another memory surface from the depths of long ago. That miserably cold January for Florida, with so many hard freezes. They were living in the little bungalow then, with no insulation and a heat pump that couldn't keep the house warm. Stomach flu went through schools like lice in September. Sara was four. Lydia held her sick body from collapsing against the toilet as she retched, smoothing the long hair away from her hot face. James, seven, came home from school, his dragging backpack scuffing the floor, and to the bathroom door. "Mom, I don't feel so good." And with that, he vomited.

It took all of her control to not do the same. James was crying, but there was no way she could get to him without stepping in the mess. She gentled Sara to a sitting position against the wall. "Stay there, sweetie. Don't move. James, honey, it's okay. It's okay"—even though it really was not—"you go lie down, and I'll be there as soon as I can, okay?" She grabbed a bath towel within reach. On hands and knees, she swabbed the floor and tossed the drenched towel in the tub. Three bath towels were sopping before the floor was clean enough to carry Sara back to her bed. Lydia took a wet washcloth into James's room, and when she touched his forehead it felt like it was on fire.

Gil, of course, was gone. It seemed he always was when something went wrong. She was almost too tired to answer the phone when it rang that night. He'd immediately launched into the excitement of his day, meeting big name sport stars on the first day of a three-day photo shoot in Miami, how the agency head had told him everyone was impressed by him. He finally stopped gushing and asked, "So, how was your day?"

She told him. He listened, concerned, until she asked, "Can you come home tomorrow? I really need you."

"Are you kidding me? No way. This account is too big to bail on. And too important to my career. Get your mom to help."

"You know damned well my parents are in Mexico. Gil, I need help. Please."

They'd had a spat. He'd finally ended the call, saying, "Do what you need to do. I've got to go. Everyone's meeting for dinner. I'll be home in three days. You'll just have to make it till then."

She had. Barely. The kids' fevers had broken the morning of his return. She hadn't slept longer than an hour at a stretch over the past days. She hadn't had a shower, because every towel they owned was filthy from cleaning up when either Sara or James—or both—couldn't make it to the toilet bowl in time or missed the basins she set by their beds. When their sheets were drenched with sweat, she changed them, then was forced to turn them around, head to foot, when those were soiled too. And they had no washer or dryer.

She'd stared at Gil through dulled eyes when he did return home. His first words to her were, "Wow. You look rough." She'd wanted to slap him, but didn't have the strength. She simply glared at him, thinking, "No shit, Sherlock."

Walking down the hall, he hollered, "Daddy's home. And he's got *preh-sents!*" He then turned to Lydia. "Tell you what, I'll watch the kids while you go do the laundry, okay?" She didn't speak to him for days.

Remembering it all, Lydia walked home to the lodge, a long, long walk.

***

The faint sound of Audra's ring tone took a moment to catch Lydia's attention. It took another moment for her to remember that the phone was still in the pocket of her jacket hanging by the door. The ringing quit before she could answer. Carrying it out to the porch she hit redial, and Audra answered almost before the dialing stopped. "Hey," Lydia said. "You sound tired."

"I am. The flights were okay but, man, eight hours on planes and in airports wore me out. Thank God everything in my suitcase is clean and I don't have to do laundry. The mail and email alone is taking me all day. But how are you? You okay?"

"Yeah. Kind of at odds and ends. There's not much else I can do from up here. The packages should start to arrive tomorrow, and I'm antsy as hell about not being able to know what happens."

"That's the big news I wanted to tell you about! You will *never* guess what I found. You know those god-awful sky mall sections in the airline magazines? Well, I was so bored I read about every single thing no one in her right mind would ever need. Or so I thought. You will *never* guess what I found," Audra repeated, excitement in her voice. She paused, almost as if she were waiting for Lydia to guess.

"Okay, then *what*?"

"Spyware." Audra's voice was conspiratorial. "Spyware you can load on Gil's phone. If you have his password. You've got that, don't you?"

"Yes, but I can already get all his data."

"Oh honey, this doesn't get the data. It gets you the *calls*. And it lets you listen in. On *every*one."

Lydia sat up straight. "Are you serious? How?"

"The ad says it routes his calls to your phone. Every time his rings, yours does too. And there's an alert to let you know when he places a call. If you pick up, neither party knows it. And there's an upgrade that lets you record everything, whether you answer or not."

The implications struck Lydia like a blinding light. "Oh. My. God. That is so illegal. But *so* what I want. Did you copy the link? Send it to me. But text it. Don't email it. And text it to this phone, not my real one."

"I'll warn you, it's not cheap."

"I don't care. Do you know what this means?"

"Yes—"

Lydia cut her off. "Hang up and send it to me right now. I've got to get this before the shit hits the fan with those deliveries."

"But wait, there's more!" Audra chirped, mimicking the TV ad pitch. "Remember I emailed some gals who'd divorced? I heard from some of them. One ranted about how her lawyer let her ex screw her, but the others gave theirs thumbs up. And two of them used the same one."

"Good. But those I don't need right away. Send them all in an email when you get a chance, okay? Now hang up and text me that link."

"Promise you'll let me know what happens?"

"Damn straight I will."

Seconds later the text came in. Lydia carefully entered the software address into a private search page on her computer. Reading the site's marketing copy made it sound like a dream come true for her. And a nightmare for Gil. It also became a nightmare for her, reading through all the agreement legalese—no way was she going to click "accept" without knowing what she was getting herself into. But she liked what she saw. She could listen to any call in real time, without either Gil or the caller knowing. Calls she didn't answer could be recorded to a secure area; once the recording was played it disappeared—permanently, unrecoverable, untraceable. Last came the laborious process of inserting the software into Gil's cell phone. And then she was done. There was nothing to do but wait. Again.

No, there was one more thing: She wanted a ring tone on her phone that would signal the calls. Choosing the right one would be fun. She fixed a drink and carried it and the phone to the porch swing. When she came across k.d. lang belting out "Your Cheatin' Heart" she smirked and hit save. As she did, a text message from Audra pinged. Forgot to tell you, left you something in dresser. You're welcome.

Lydia went upstairs to the room Audra had used, and grinned when she opened the top dresser drawers. In one was a pack of cigarettes and a baggie with two fat joints. With her drink freshened, she settled back on the porch swing and lit a cigarette. It was turning out to be a pretty good day after all, and just might get better before it was over.

Except nothing happened. The phone didn't ring. She assumed that meant Gil was traveling and his phone was turned off. She grew restless. Going upstairs earlier had reminded her the sheets were still on Audra's bed, so she laundered them. She carried the phone to the beach chair and tried to meditate. It didn't help much. She couldn't clear her mind, but she did hear her mother's voice. "A watched phone never rings," she'd say, spinning the watched pot cliché when Lydia mooned about as a teen waiting for a boy to call. She fixed dinner, but no matter how much salt she added, everything tasted flat.

She paced, window to window. When she found herself staring out over the prow shaped by the bookcases against the corner, she wondered whether there was something that might occupy her mind. The times she had tried to read, she couldn't concentrate, the words nothing but meaningless marks on the page, unable to compete with the story roaring through her head. A stab of light from a window across the room seemed to spotlight one book, illuminating its fat spine. It was the one Max had had at the bar; the one Sara urged her to read. Maybe now was the time, especially since the title reflected her state of mind: *A Ghost Between Two Worlds*. She carried it to the porch swing, and by the end of the second page time had disappeared. Mesmerized by the lyrical sentences and its unfolding mystery, the outer world ceded to the interior one.

She was three chapters in when k.d. lang's voice so startled her that the book fell to the floor. She grabbed the phone, fumbling for the volume control as lang wailed full force, "But sleep won't come—the whole night through—" She held her breath as she tapped to listen, praying this worked, praying her presence would be unknown. She came on in mid-sentence, hearing a woman saying something inane about her day, then the timber changed. "Okay, he just went out to the grill. You're in Chicago?"

Lydia's stomach soured. This wasn't a business call. This voice had to be Marielle's.

"Yeah," Gil said. "Just checked in. Thought I'd call before I go down to dinner."

"So, still no word?"

"No. And I checked with the bank again. No charges on her credit cards."

They were talking about her.

"She's got to be up to something," Marielle said.

"Yeah, well, what do you want me to do about it," Gil snapped.

Ooh, good, Lydia thought—*trouble in paradise*. And the trouble hadn't even started.

"Until I know what she knows, I'm doing nothing. I've told you that. And I've told you she doesn't know anything other than what I told her. So drop it."

"Hey, I'm sorry. I'm just worried. The longer this goes on, the more I'm afraid she'll find out who I am. My life could be screwed too, you know."

Oh, it already is, Lydia thought, *it already is*.

"Say, thanks so much for calling." The woman's voice was falsely bright again.

"He's back inside?"

"Yes, let's talk again soon. Bye!"

Lydia closed the phone and let herself breathe once more. She retrieved the book from where it had fallen, then grabbed the phone again and punched in a short text of glee to Audra before searching for the page where she'd left off.

***

She slept longer and better than she had expected to, what with the book's haunting mystery and the phone call replaying in her mind. The phone rang while she was fixing breakfast but it was a call of no consequence—Gil and a client confirming an appointment. She expected that other calls would be much the same, routine business, until much later, after the packages began to arrive. While eating, she checked his email accounts. Again, nothing of importance. With the last of the coffee, she tried reading but the building anticipation within her overrode what was building in the book. She needed something physical to do. The attic. She rinsed out her mug and headed up. Creating some sense of order out of the jumbled mess would put her nervous energy to use.

On the rare occasions the phone rang, she stopped work to listen, but Gil didn't answer and the clients left their messages on his voicemail. Early in the afternoon there was a spate of calls, all placed by Gil, checking in with his office and responding to messages. By two she was hot, tired, and dusty, and unhappy about both how little headway she'd made and the banality of the phone calls she'd heard. She decided she wasn't likely to miss anything while she took a long, hot shower.

Lydia was out on the porch swing reading when the fallout began. She clicked in on a call as Gil greeted a woman by name. The woman spit out three words. "You. Sick. Bastard." There was a beat of silence before Gil asked, "Excuse me, what?" But by then the woman had hung up. Lydia heard him mutter, "What the hell?" before he did too. A moment later another call, another woman. "You son of a bitch. I always thought you were skeevy but this is over the top. I ought to sue you for sexual harassment." Again Gil was left hanging in silence. Another call, this time a man, laughter in his voice. "Gil. I just opened the box and I am laughing my ass off. I've received some weird gifts before but this one tops them all. But don't take it the wrong way that I'll pass on the threesome with you and your wife, okay? Nothing against you and Marr—or is it Mare—swinging—"

Gil cut him off. "What are you talking about?"

"Come on, man, you know."

"I'm serious. I don't know. What are you talking about?"

"Don't shit me, man." The man laughed again. "You know damned well. Unless you were blackout drunk when you sent it."

"I've never been blackout drunk." Gil's voice was sharp. "And sent what? I didn't send you anything."

"Well, the message with all these sex toys said you did."

"Sex toys?" Gil sounded like he was choking.

"Yeah. Great selection, too. And a year's membership in something called PPB&D? Pussies, pricks, boobs and dicks—never heard of it but I'm definitely checking it out. Just not when Joyce is around." The man's laugh was loud. "She'll get a kick out of the toys but she'd kick me out if she catches me on a paid site. She's made that damned clear."

"Luke, I honest to god did not send you anything. And I don't … I don't know anyone named Marr, or Mare." *You lying asshole*, Lydia thought. "My wife's name is … Lydia."

Lydia caught the hesitation before he had said her name. Apparently, so did the man Gil was talking to. "Huh. If you say so."

"I say so. And you damn well better not say a word of this to a soul." Lydia flinched at the anger behind Gil's words. "I don't know what's going on but I am going to find out."

"Hey man, whatever. Just wanted to say thanks, not piss you off. Gotta go."

Luke clicked off before Gil shouted, "*Fuck.*"

Lydia smiled. She put down the phone and headed inside. *Time for a little bit of a toke*, she thought, *the perfect way to celebrate a job well done.*

More calls came in throughout the evening, some bewildered, some joking, most were angry. The first three or four Gil answered, his denials vehement, swearing he had no knowledge of anything, stammering his way through claims his identity must have been stolen, his computer must have been hacked, he didn't know what happened, this wasn't his doing. After that he stopped answering, as every time Lydia checked the calls were being shuttled to voicemail. By late evening, Lydia was about to quit too—the messages could be clicked through later. When the phone rang again, she gave a second thought before deciding to answer. This time, it wasn't an incoming call. It was one Gil was placing.

A woman answered. "Hello?"

"We've got to talk. Now." His voice was biting.

"Oh? Okay. Hang on." The woman's voice turned away from the phone. "Honey? One of my editors. I'm going to take this in my office." There was a stretch of silence before the sound of a door closing. "Okay. What's up?"

"Did you send anything to my clients?" Gil's voice was low, almost menacing.

"No." The word was long, drawn out. "Why?"

"My phone's been ringing for hours. Clients. Every damned one of them got a so-called gift from PPB&D. From *us*. I sure as hell didn't do it."

"Well, neither did I," Marielle snapped.

"Then who the hell did," Gil snarled.

"Jesus … If our account's been hacked, we are both in deep shit."

"I already am. I've got people threatening to sue for sexual harassment, threatening to pull their accounts if I don't prove it wasn't me—they don't believe it wasn't—and two companies have already emailed that they're terminating their contracts."

"Wow." Marielle said nothing for a minute. "You don't suppose it's someone in your office?"

Gil snorted. "Yeah, right. None of those boneheads is pissed enough at me to pull something like this."

"What are you going to do?"

"I don't know. I need to think. Right now I can't think. Jesus fucking-H Christ."

"I'd better go. Try to get some sleep."

"Yeah, right. Like that's gonna happen."

"Same here." There was a pause. "Gil, this is scary."

"Tell me something I don't know," he growled.

Lydia closed the phone and turned off the ringer. She'd heard enough for the night. And she was going to sleep very, very well.

***

As she was about to get into bed with her book, her regular phone pinged the arrival of a message. This late, she worried it was one of the kids—she doubted either had received her letter yet, but it was possible. If it were, she wasn't going to respond, but concern would plague her in the night. Then again, not knowing who the text was from would too. The screen lit up. The text was from Audra: Trying to call in. If you are up, call me. Fun day. Lydia almost hit Audra's number, then stopped. She went back to the great room for the second phone, settled herself in bed, and dialed.

"Hi, sweetie. You got my text? I'm sorry I sent it to the wrong number. I realized it the minute I hit send. I'll be more careful. But I just *have* to tell you about my day." As usual, Audra's words came out in a tumbling rush. "But first, how are you? You doing okay?"

"I'm fine. I'm better than fine. But you first. You sound tired."

"I am. I'm exhausted. First day back at the store and of course headaches there. *But*, Julie loves the prints I brought back. She'd been on board from the pics I texted her, but those barely do justice to Ned's talent. Oh, and that man also has a talent for flirty texts. What am I doing letting myself fall for a guy fifteen hundred miles away? But anyway, we had Jake clear space to hang six of them on the north wall and the minute you come through the door they leap out at you. Two of them sold this afternoon."

"That is terrific," Lydia said. "No wonder your day was good."

"So, tell me, did you get that software?"

Lydia nestled back against the pillows. It took half an hour to tell all that had happened and to answer Audra's questions as best she could before they devolved, like schoolgirls, into conjecture and imagined scenarios of what might come. By the time they hung up, they were both laughing through tears.

When Lydia turned out the bedside lamp, the tears continued, but this time from pain. She hated Gil so much, because she had loved him so much. Did she still? She wished there were someone to hold her, comfort her, but there was no one.

***

The slightest bit of daylight cast a nightlight glow outside the lodge when Lydia woke, her mind clear, her body rested. Once she'd fallen asleep, she'd slept a deep, hard, healing sleep. The comfort she longed for had come, from within. She took her coffee down to the lake and leaned against the cool boulder. The crisp air was comfortable, carrying the promise of sun-stoked warmth to come. Near her feet the lake lapped at the sand as gently as an old dog's tongue licking the hand of a beloved owner. Lydia drew a deep, relaxing breath and lifted her head to the sky, catching the last of the stars winking out one … by … one.

What was that line she'd heard years ago, she tried to recall, something a character had said on a TV show? Ah, yes: "The Universe rolls on its own. Why get out and push?" *True*, she thought, *but every once in a while it didn't hurt to give it a good shove*. Which she'd done. It was going to be interesting to see where it rolled today. Something else that needed a good shove, she decided, was that stuff in the attic. She headed back inside, invigorated and ready to tackle the mess.

By mid-afternoon, Lydia had reached two conclusions. First, sorting through and creating order from the jumble in the attic, which ran the length and breadth of the lodge, could take weeks—partly because she couldn't resist looking through everything, which either led to being washed over by memories, or puzzling over broken objects that should have been trashed. The second realization was that she should have chosen a ring tone she disliked—if she never heard "Your Cheatin' Heart" again it would be fine with her. The phone seemed to ring constantly and she'd stop picking up on every call. Tired, hot, dirty, thirsty, and hungry, in the afternoon she closed the attic door for the day. She was again disappointed she hadn't made more progress, but was deeply satisfied about the chaos now roaring through her husband's life. His outgoing calls had stopped, and he wasn't answering the incoming ones. Either he couldn't take anymore or he was on a plane. Either way, she too was ready for a break.

After showering, Lydia carried a plate of food and an iced tea down to the lake. The sweet freshness of the air cleansed the attic's mustiness from her nostrils, and the sun's wash was as pleasant as the shower had been. She leaned back in the chair, nibbling as she listened to the recorded phone messages—more anger, more outrage, more threats of pulled business or lawsuits. A couple of messages were left by men she was glad she did not know, leaving creepy jokes, but even those ended with caveats along the lines of "Fix this or it affects our account." After hearing them all, she changed the ring tone to an innocuous chime she assumed would soon become annoying too.

Except that did not happen. The ringing stopped. By evening, she realized all the packages must have been delivered and the volcanic reaction—by phone, at least—was over. Gil made no calls. Odds were, she figured, he'd locked himself either in a hotel room or in his office at home with a bottle of whiskey to stave off the panic, the way he'd done when the economy crash had swept away his clients with the force of a hurricane. There was one more phone call, late in the evening. Gil didn't answer but Lydia did. It was Marielle, screaming. "You goddamned son of a bitch, what did you do? What the fuck is going on? What the fuck did you do to me? I'm dead! Do you hear me? I don't give a shit what you say about how this happened. Goddamn you, or whoever did this, to *hell*."

Lydia let out a satisfied sigh. The packages must have started landing on the desks of Marielle's editors and clients. *Too bad, so sad, sucks to be you*, Lydia thought as she poured a scotch. She picked up her phone and called Audra to gloat over the events of the day.

Then she logged into Gil's business email account. The inbox was jammed with unread messages, almost all with similar, angry subject lines. She had no interest in reading everyone, but clicked on them randomly. Several expressed concern for Gil's mental health, two of them with actual compassion. Most seethed. Others roared with vitriol before informing him the termination clauses in their contracts were being invoked, immediately. When she noticed some of the subject lines were in response, she opened those, curious to see what Gil had replied. By the third, she realized he'd set up an auto reply—he was unable to respond at the present time, apparently his computer had been hacked, he apologized if the writer had received a package "from a website I have no knowledge of." He pleaded for patience until he got to "the bottom of this heinous crime against us all." He pledged that he would stay away from his agency "and allow my excellent staff to continue our superb service to you," and begged they not jeopardize his employees' livelihoods due to an "unfortunate circumstance" that he had not created and was not his fault.

***

Lydia's eyes popped open in the dark. The letters. Her kids had to have read them by now. Guilt knotted her.

She sat up and switched on the bedside lamp, its light stinging her eyes. The little clock next to it showed it wasn't yet five. She sat, shoulders slumped, staring at it for a moment. She didn't want to be awake this early but knew she wouldn't be able to get back to sleep. Not with this in her head. She got up and pulled on her robe. While the coffee pot burbled, she went in search of her smart phone. Powering it on and pouring a mug of coffee in the kitchen, she heard the dings of downloading texts. Her finger hesitated before she tapped the screen.

She opened Sara's first. There were four. The first one read, Mama? PLEASE CALL. The second, sent seconds later, What happened? I thought everything was okay with you and Daddy. I need to talk to you! Moments later, Tried to call, phone off, couldn't leave a mssg. PLS CALL! The last one: Daddy's not answering either. What is going on?

Mama—her daughter had picked that up in preschool and it had forever stuck; to James she had always been and would always be Mom. And Daddy—to Sara he was Dad; her grown; mature daughter only reverted to calling him that when her heart hurt. Right now, Lydia's did too. That was the torment of being a mother, she thought, knowing it was impossible to always protect your children from pain. And sometimes being the one who had to inflict it.

She opened James's text, sent late the night before. Um, the letter. Wow. That was a shock. Tried calling you both, no answers. If you get this tonight call me, ok? I'll be up another hour. This sucks. I'm really, really sorry. And worried. Love you. Both. Lydia could hear James's voice in his words, dictating the message, unlike his sister who tapped her texts out with rapid thumbs.

Lydia opened a new message, one that would go to them both. This time, like her son, she recorded her words. She told them she was sorry, that she knew the news would shock them, that the letter had been the only way she could manage to tell them, and yes she wanted to talk to them both, but at the same time, would ten the next morning work? She paused, then added, "Or figure out a good time over the weekend and let me know. But not today. I love you both. Very, very much."

Once the message was sent, she opened the laptop. She hadn't the slightest interest in whatever might be thrashing between Gil and Marielle through the shared Gmail account. Instead she turned to the websites of the attorneys Audra had sent. By the time she settled on her first choice among them, the lake outside the window was shimmering in the coming light. She picked up the phone. There'd be no one to answer at the law office at this hour but she needed to make the call now.

At the voicemail beep, she gave her name and number, then said, "Ms. Adelson, I want divorce papers sent to my husband. As soon as possible. Tomorrow, if possible. I want everything I can get in the settlement, and more.

And I have the leverage to do so. I want a pitbull attorney, and believe you are the person. Again, I want this initiated immediately. Whatever it takes. Please call me at your earliest convenience." She repeated her name and phone number, aware that her voice was sharper than she intended. *Maybe just as well,* she thought—it made it clear she knew what she wanted, and what she wanted was results.

With her regular phone in hand, she climbed to the attic. The other phone she left downstairs—the only call she was interested in answering was the attorney's. The two bare-bulb hanging lights that she flipped on cast a gloomy glow over the crowded room. A pang of memory struck as shadows painted themselves on the walls. As a child she'd been almost deathly afraid of this attic, so certain she was that monsters and ghosts lurked there. She'd long ago stopped believing in monsters, but the ghosts showed themselves in the boxes and drawers she opened. Some of the drawers were empty, and some of the box contents were of as little interest as items at a bad yard sale. But others—others unleashed waves of nostalgia as strong as if the lake had risen to sweep her away. In those moments, she was carried into her past, a past still so strong it could be the present. Pulled out of time, she again lost all track of time.

Two green, four-drawer filing cabinets were of cursory interest. She slid each drawer open and closed as she affirmed the crumbling papers inside were ancient records from the lodge and her grandfather's mill. Bending to open a box next to them, she realized the file cabinets were not pushed against the wall. Blocked behind them was an old highboy, its finish aged to near ebony, so dark it seemed to want to remain invisible. She wrestled the filing cabinets forward, making enough space to slip into and open the dresser drawers.

None of them budged on her first try, which made Lydia more determined to see if anything was inside. She tugged against the reluctant wood, swollen shut from years of disuse, careful for fear she might break off the pulls. She remembered seeing an old pocketknife in a box of fishing gear. Retrieving it, she worked its rusty blade, which she worried might snap, around the edges of the top drawer as she jostled a handle. Her arms were beginning to tire by the time it broke free. Empty. She sighed and went to work on the drawer below. It was filled with remnants of musty fabric that she set by the attic door to dispose of. The third drawer too was filled with fabric, but fabric that had been beautifully crafted. Delight overcame Lydia as she lifted embroidered christening gowns, pretty dresses and pinafores for very little girls, and buttery soft flannel pajamas for young boys. Grandma must have sewn them all, and saved them as reminders of the babies Lydia had known always as grown-ups. She folded and replaced each reverently.

At first glance, Lydia thought the bottom drawer held old bed sheets. But the way the top one was folded struck her as odd. Its corners met in a triangle at the center, as if forming an envelope. As she lifted the folds, her eyes widened. Purple velvet, the color of a queen's robe, formed a valise of some kind, a Victorian-era lady's traveling bag. The velvet puckered in gathers along what felt to Lydia's hand like a wooden dowel. Two velvet rope handles were tucked beneath, and a large clasp was formed of shimmering brocade. The clasp was closed by an oversized golden button centered in an intricately embroidered rose; petals of blood red delicately outlined in gold thread.

The valise was almost too lovely to touch. Lydia couldn't imagine such a thing belonging to her grandmother, a woman who never expressed any interest in finery. Brushing her hand across the soft nap, Lydia was surprised to feel something stiff but uneven under her touch. It was then she noticed that the satchel did not lay flat. Something was stuffed inside, probably to help preserve its shape. She gently undid the button closure, lifted the bag upright, and eased it open. Again her eyes widened. Inside was not the crumpled paper she'd expected, but paper of another kind—letters, tied in ribbon.

Lydia's fingers had just touched one of the packets when the phone rang. She scrambled up from her knees, rubbing away their stiffness. The caller ID confirmed what she'd hoped—it was the attorney's office.

She tapped the accept icon. "This is Lydia Casselberry."

"Ms. Casselberry, hello. I'm Dana Adelson. From the message you left at—what, six?—this morning, it's apparent you want to initiate divorce proceedings against your husband. And he is Gil Carson, is that correct?"

It was obvious the woman had done some quick research. "Yes," Lydia said.

"All right. But before I can begin anything on your behalf I need to ask several questions and have you complete some paperwork. Is it possible you could come in for discussion at one?"

Lydia's laugh was light. "No, I'm afraid not. I'm in the upper peninsula of Michigan."

"Oh, my gosh. Well, that complicates things."

"Not necessarily. I can complete and sign any paperwork electronically. And do a bank transfer for your retainer. Which I am prepared to send as soon as I know you can start immediately."

"Well. Okay then. I have an appointment soon but if you have time now we can go over several things, and then I'll have my assistant get additional information. Or would you prefer to call back at one?"

"No. I want you to move ahead as soon as possible." Lydia closed the clasp, picked up the valise, and carried it downstairs.

"Well, first why don't you tell me your story?"

"My story?"

"Yes. What led to this decision." Adelson's voice had the practiced, soothing tone of a therapist who was leaning back to listen. "Getting that out first might help."

Stopping on the stairs, Lydia held the phone away and looked at the screen. Maybe this Adelson woman wasn't the bulldog she was looking for after all. With the phone back at her ear she said, "My story. My husband has been living a double life. For at least the last five years, maybe longer, and has hidden a substantial amount of money. I'm not some thirty-six-year-old with two kids at home whose world has just collapsed. It has, but I'm sixty-three. The story at this point doesn't matter, and won't matter to the judge. I don't have time for that, and you don't either. What matters is my documentation. And initiating the proceedings, as in today. If you cannot do that, I'll find someone who will." Reaching the grand room, Lydia sat down on the sofa, setting the valise beside her.

"Well then," Adelson repeated. "Documentation, you say?"

"Yes. And if I retain you, I am prepared to transfer all of my files by the end of the day. Now, are you prepared to help me or should I contact the next attorney on my list?" Lydia could almost see the woman shift to sit upright, pen poised over a pad, ready to jot notes.

"Oh, I'm quite certain I can help." Lydia thought she sensed admiration in the woman's voice. "Let's get down to business."

The questions Adelson asked were succinct and lawyerly, and Lydia decided she liked this woman after all. Moving to the dining room table, she began taking notes. When Adelson was finished, her assistant came on the line, a Ms. Resta, who gathered the dry data and again went over the fees. Calculating the time needed to make herself decent and drive to Falton, Lydia said, “I’ll call you from the bank in about an hour and a half, to transfer the retainer. After I return, I’ll upload my files. Ms. Adelson will have them by the end of the day. And thank you.”

As usual, everything took longer than she anticipated, even though she was dressed, out the door, and at the bank less than an hour later. First she had to wait on the bank manager—the only one authorized to do what she wanted—who was in a lengthy meeting. Then there were the probing questions he presented as friendly but revealed his suspicions of her, someone he didn’t know, someone with a very unusual request for his bank. She did her best to remain patient. Then there were more questions, put to Ms. Adelson’s assistant when he called the phone number Lydia provided, and his insistence on verifying every answer through his computer. Though she knew he was doing his ethical due diligence, by the time the transfer was made and he offered Lydia a weak handshake and smarmy smile, she wanted to throw a question at him: Did he think she’d come all this way to launder three lousy thousand dollars of cash by sending it to a law firm at the other end of the country? She rubbed the dampness of his hand against her thigh as she left, and slammed the car door hard when she got in. And, once she passed the State Police office, she drove too fast.

After fixing a pot of strong coffee and a sandwich, she started on what the attorney needed. The number of pages seemed infinite, the details to be completed never-ending. The coffee pot was long empty and her shoulder muscles were tense when she finished hours later. As she rubbed and stretched them she looked up at the clock. It was almost six. No way would Gil be served today, let alone on a Saturday, since the court offices wouldn’t be open.

She opened his office account and pulled up his calendar. Relief washed over her as she shot one last note to Adelson, saying he was scheduled to be in his office all the following week. She poured a drink, picked up a cigarette and her phone, and went out to the porch to call Audra.

Chapter 14

She'd gone to bed drunk Friday night, not because she drank too much but because the booze and the day's exhaustion combined to hit her hard. Saturday morning started off fuzzy, which coffee was beginning to clear from her mind when the phone rang. It wasn't yet 7:30 and the wireless number, with a Tampa area code, wasn't one she recognized. She let it ring, then changed her mind just before it went to voicemail. "Hello." The word came out groggy.

"Ms. Casselberry? Dana Adelson. Did I wake you?"

"No. I'm just having a hard time getting the fog out of my brain."

Ignoring her response, Adelson went on. "I glanced at your paperwork before leaving the office yesterday, expecting it would have to be kicked back for completion. Which yours does not. Clients usually require several days to compile all the information. I need to know if the financial numbers you provided are accurate or guesstimates."

"Everything can be verified," Lydia said.

"Good. And the other non-financial files? Where did those come from?"

"When I found out my husband was having an affair, I came up here to decide whether I could forgive him. I started digging because I wanted to find out who the other woman was. That's what led me down the rabbit hole."

"Yes. I would assume that would have sealed your decision. I read through everything last night. My assistant is going into the office this morning to prepare the paperwork for filing Monday. Your husband will be served then."

"Thank you."

"You do realize, don't you, that your husband is a sociopath."

The word struck Lydia like a blunt object.

"That of course is not a clinical diagnosis, since I am not a psychotherapist and have never met your husband. I have, however, handled enough cases to recognize your husband exhibits all the traits."

"But … but, he's never been violent."

"Physically, that may be true. Sociopaths tend to employ emotional violence. Manipulating others for their own purposes. Engaging in risky behaviors to fulfill their needs, with no regard for others. By using charm to convince others of their sincerity. Using duplicitousness, as your husband obviously has in withholding information and funds from you. And in so successfully keeping his sexual escapades from you as well. You saw no indication?"

"No. No, not really. Things had changed some but I thought that was probably normal. Because we've been married so long, and because of the stress he was under when the economy crashed."

"Interesting. From what you sent me, it appears that this double life of his ramped up around the time the recession hit."

"Ramped up? What do you mean? He did have one affair, but that was years and years ago. We worked through it, and our marriage got much better." Lydia paused. "Or so I thought."

"One affair that you were aware of. I have little doubt that if you could follow a paper trail farther back, you'd find the affairs have been going on since before your marriage."

Another body blow. The memory of finding out Gil was seeing another girl over her last summer working at the lodge, when they were already talking marriage. Had he been cheating on her for all these years? "But, but," Lydia stammered again, "how could I not have seen it? How could I have been so stupid? I am *not* a stupid woman."

"Precisely. Sociopaths gravitate to the intelligent. They enjoy the challenge. By besting them, they bolster their sense of superiority. Hoodwinking the dumb is just too easy."

Lydia felt on the verge of collapse. "I … I think I need to go."

"One last thing. Nearly every woman who comes to me wants everything in the divorce. That almost never happens. With what I've seen so far in your files, in your case it almost certainly will. And I'd venture he will settle quietly and quickly, to ensure this information never comes out, as it would only further damage him."

"I need to go, Ms. Adelson." Lydia's voice was hoarse. "My son and daughter are expecting a call from me this morning, and I've got to pull myself together before then."

"Lydia—may I call you Lydia? And please, call me Dana. I'm sorry to have ripped another veil away, but I felt it necessary. Please don't be hard on yourself. You are not to blame in this. He is. I'll be back in touch in a few days. In the meantime, Ms. Resta will keep you informed of our progress."

Lydia's mind roiled under the shock of realization. Sociopath, sociopath—the word repeated itself like waves hitting the shore. How could she not have known? How could he have been so cruel—to her, who had never done anything but love him. Why?

Why—her mother had said that once Lydia learned the word "why," she never stopped using it. Why—she'd always needed to understand. She flashed on a day in third grade when she'd raised her hand and called out the question. Her teacher—Mean Mrs. Madison, all the kids called her—rebuked her with, "Why does not matter. It is what it is. Stop asking." She'd hated Mrs. Madison for humiliating her. Now Gil had too. But right now her teacher's words were true: Why didn't matter; it was what it was, and asking why wouldn't lead to an answer or change anything. She took a jacket from a peg by the door, walked down and untethered the rowboat from the dock, and set out onto the calm water.

Sometimes she stroked the oars, sometimes she drifted, aware of nothing but her thoughts. The boat bumping to a halt brought her out of her daze. It took her a second to realize she had beached on the little island, barely a mile from the shore, with no recollection of getting there. Or of what time it was. She was supposed to call the kids. She grabbed at her jacket pockets—yes, thank god, she had brought the phone. Its clock read almost ten. She slipped off her shoes, rolled up her pants, and stepped into the water to pull the boat onto the sand. Perched on its prow, she dialed her daughter first.

Sara answered before the first ring ended. "Are you okay?"

"Hello to you too, honey. I'm fine." Don't lie, a voice in her head blurted. "No, I'm not fine. I don't know how I am. But I'm okay. Let me get your brother on the line."

James answered. "Hey, Mom."

Lydia liked that he hadn't changed his Southern way for New York City's hi's and hellos. "Hey, yourself," she said, as Sara's voice overlapped, "Hey, bro."

"Hey, Sara. Okay, Mom," he said, "what's happened?"

New York City had, however, erased the Southern way of easing into discussion. She tried not to bristle at the brusqueness, knowing it masked concern. She told them she had said all she could for now in her letter. She said she'd hired an attorney and was filing for divorce. That their dad didn't know yet but would on Monday. She answered their questions as best she could. Yes, all of this seemed sudden. No, she wasn't going to say any more about what led up to it. Yes, she was certain. No, she didn't know what would happen to the house. She still had her job at the university, right? Did she need money?

"If you need any," James said, "you let me know. If you need anything, I can help. We both can, right, Sara?"

Tenderness clenched Lydia's heart.

"Yes. We know things must be tight, with business still being so bad for Daddy."

Now it was Lydia's jaw that clenched. Lying to her, lying to his children. And now she too was lying, by omission. Because she was still protecting him—no, she was protecting them.

***

Not all of her anger had been worked off on the return from the island. She stomped up the porch steps, slammed the doors behind her, and flung her jacket at the couch. It landed with a thunk, which stopped her short. The pocketed phone must have hit something, but what? She lifted the jacket. Beneath it was the valise she'd set there yesterday, forgotten. She stared at it a moment, curiosity taking over. She went to wash her hands and get a glass of water, then carried the valise out into the warm sunshine on the porch.

The threads that secured the elaborate button were frayed, and she gentled it through the buttonhole, trying to remember if she'd seen a sewing kit around so she could repair it. With the clasp again undone, she drew the dowels apart, pulled one of the packets out and untied the still-supple black ribbon around the letters it encircled. Very old letters. She lifted one and looked at the corner where a postage stamp should have been. There was a stamp, but this was of ink. Across the envelope were other faded markings. She made out the words "Passed by Censor," "Soldier's Mail," and a barely discernible date, but could make out only the month, not the year. Spidery writing addressed the envelope to Mrs. Franklin Johansen. So was the next, and the next. There were two dozen envelopes. On a few of them, she did make out the year—1918.

She opened the second packet and found more letters, the envelopes addressed to the same woman, in the same spidery penmanship. All except the last. It was a Western Union telegram, its blocky type directing it to the same woman. *Who was this Mrs. Franklin Johansen*, Lydia wondered as she drew out the telegram, and why would her grandmother have saved these?

She unfolded the small, brittle paper and read. "DEEPLY REGRET TO INFORM YOU THAT LT. FRANKLIN JOHANSEN INFANTRY DIED SUNDAY LAST STOP CAUSE INFLUENZA STOP" The telegram was dated August 23, 1918. Even more puzzled now, she replaced the telegram in its envelope and opened the letter at the top of the first stack. The paper, untouched for more than a century, unfolded stiffly, as if wanting to keep its contents private. Dated February 23, 1918, the letter read:

My Dearest Darling Missus,

The trains delivered us into New York City yesterday and such a city cannot be described as it is beyond man's ability to do so or imagine. It is also impossible to imagine how men could survive, let alone thrive amidst the noise and bustle and crowds and press of buildings so tall as to cause one to look straight up in order to see a bit of sky. If there is a tree in this city, I did not see it. We are told there is a great park where people can go to be in nature, but how can men live if not always in nature itself?

Not all feel as I do. Leave was given last night and many of the men returned drunk and telling rowdy tales of dance houses and fancy women in streets so filled with electric light as to make it seem day. I walked about a bit but returned to my bunk before dusk, too overwhelmed by what seems to me a crash of madness that deepened my loneliness and desire to be with you.

Our ship departs tomorrow, for where we do not yet know,—either England or France but surely we will be in a place of fighting too soon. I will post this now, and promise to write as often as I can but do not despair if letters are delayed in reaching you.

Please kiss our golden haired baby for me and speak of my love for her every day so she may remember me when I return. And let my love for you help keep you strong until that day.

Your loving husband,
Franklin

Mesmerized, Lydia re-read the letter before replacing it in the envelope. Who were these people, she wondered again. Whose story and history had she stumbled into? This was as intriguing as a novel; she thought as she fixed herself a drink and settled back on the porch swing to read them all.

The fourth letter answered the mystery, yet deepened it. Lydia felt as if her heart stopped when she opened it. Instead of "My Dearest Darling Missus" the salutation now read "Dear Tilde." Even though the cursive told her it had been penned by the same hand, she turned to the end, which was signed "Your loving husband, Franklin." Lydia's hand dropped with the letter onto her lap, and the screaming cackle of a crow in the silence struck her as mocking. She whipped her head around. The huge bird was perched on the porch railing, staring at her, seeming to admonish, "Oh the things in this world you do not know." It turned, lifted its wings, and flew away.

The tone of this letter, and the ones that followed it, was different. Franklin wrote of daily life and meant to be amusing but there was tension behind his words. He tried to make light of the hardships being endured. The hardship for Lydia was reading the passages where he poured out his loneliness and longing for home, for the sight of his wife's smile, for the feel of her loving embrace. Every letter ended with the same plea, to kiss their golden-haired baby and speak to her of him every day until he returned.

But he hadn't returned. The letters ended, as abruptly as the word "stop" ended a sentence in the telegram Lydia again held. Tears clouded her vision as she retied the ribbons around the letters.

Her grandmother absorbed her thoughts. The woman she'd thought she'd known had had a marriage—and a child—she'd never known about. Had anyone? Her grandmother had been so young, little more than a child herself when widowed at eighteen. But what had happened to the golden-haired child, this great-aunt Lydia had just learned of.

She returned the packets to their hiding place in the velvet valise. As she drew her hand out the back of it brushed against something stiff behind the black satin lining. There was a pocket she hadn't noticed. In it was another envelope, larger than the letters, and a faded brown. It felt padded and bore no address, but bore a name: Maarika Anja Johansen. Bits of brittle glue flaked onto Lydia's fingers as she lifted the sealed flap. From inside she removed a delicate, embroidered christening gown and two sheets of paper. The first was a birth certificate for Maarika Anja Johansen, born March 14, 1917, to Tilde and Franklin Johansen. The second was a death certificate. It too bore the name of the child. Cause of death: influenza. It was dated August 27, 1918. Four days after the telegram.

Oh sweet Jesus, oh dear Lord above. Anguish filled her. *The secrets we all carry*, she thought, staring at the paper, the neat handwriting that filled each field of the form. Stark, official facts that had shattered her grandmother's world. Did anyone, anywhere, live a life in which some devastating act beyond control did not up-end the world? Did everyone carry the shrapnel of some secret, live with a hole torn through the heart? How had her grandmother endured losing her husband and her daughter within days? Lydia had thought that what she'd discovered about Gil was almost beyond enduring, yet it paled in comparison to what her grandmother had gone through.

No, a voice inside her said, comparing tragedies is like comparing lemons and limes—outwardly different, yet to the one who bites them, both bitter. How did her grandmother not let bitterness consume her? How did she find life again, the strength to open herself to love again? What fears did she overcome to marry Grandpa George? What agonies must she have borne with the births of their children? What scars had she carried throughout her life?

Lydia stared at the porch ceiling. Each question an untold story, a story she so wished she could ask her grandmother to tell. To hear how her grandmother had made it through her wounded past might have helped Lydia make it through what lay ahead in her own future.

Lydia closed up the valise. Halfway up the attic stairs she stopped, then headed back down to her bedroom. She'd put it in the dresser, not entomb it again in the dark, swollen drawer. This was a piece of family history Thom and Lynn needed to know about, a story of resilience they all needed to share with their kids.

***

The lodge now felt too empty, yet too crowded with ghosts. The attic remained unfinished but she couldn't be up there right now, too close to the new pain haunting her. She wanted someone to talk to. The need for human interaction gripped her. Audra was still at the store. She picked up her phone and texted Call me after work? Dinnertime was hours away, maybe she could busy herself preparing a meal to cook later. Nothing in the refrigerator sparked her interest—eating had become mechanical once again. Fixing herself a fresh drink, the impromptu dinner party with Ned and Max played in her mind, how good it had felt to be pulled out of the hellish aloneness of her soul, to be engaged with others whose secrets she didn't have to carry. She knew now there must always be secrets. Secrets—they were even the plot of the book she was reading. Maybe the people alive on those pages would suffice for now.

She'd read no more than a paragraph when her second phone pinged. Eager for a text back from Audra, she picked it up. Knowing what time they could talk would give her something to look forward to. Instead, the message brought disappointment: Can't. Sorry. Going to a play. Maury's lady friend has a cold so he wants me to be his hot date. Tomorrow? Disappointed, Lydia sighed. Still, inwardly she smiled. Maury was Audra's nonagenarian neighbor, a widower who had season tickets to seemingly everything in town and often shared them with Audra in return for her kindnesses. Guess so, she texted back. Have fun.

Staring at the phone, an idea struck. She opened the contacts, where she'd stored three numbers—Audra's, Bess's store, and Dave's. She tapped the second one.

"Clar's Corner," a child's voice answered.

"Katie, hello. This is … Lady L. How are you? I heard you were sick. Are you better?"

"Hi! Yeah. Guess what? It's Saturday. And guess how much I earned this week. Twelve *whole* dollars. Mama says I got a bonus because I was an extra good worker this week. And I get something called sick pay! She says it's a beanie—a bennie—"

"A benefit," Lydia said. "That is awesome. Your mom is a good boss."

"Yeah, 'cept sometimes she gets too bossy." Katie's voice got louder on the last two words.

From the background a voice called out, "I heard that."

Lydia laughed. "Well, Katie, that is where the word comes from. Sometimes bosses have to be bossy."

"Are you a boss?"

"Yup, back home I am. Can I talk to your mom—oh, excuse me, your *boss*?"

"Sure," Katie said, then yelled, "Mom! Lady L wants to talk to you!"

Again in the background Lydia heard, "Katie, how many times have I told you, don't yell."

"See," Katie whispered into the phone. "That's her being bossy."

"Give me that. Please. Hello, Elle, what can I do for you?"

"Actually, I was calling to see if I could do something for the three of you. How'd you like to come over for dinner tonight? It'd give me a chance to cook for more than one, and give us a chance to get to know each other."

"That's so nice of you. I wish we could. But Katie's going to a sleepover, and Dave and I have dinner reservations. Today's our tenth anniversary." Her voice dropped. "And we have the whole night alone."

"Congratulations. Have fun."

"Oh, we intend to."

"Well, maybe we can get together another time."

"We'd like that. I hope you have a good evening too."

"Um, one more thing." Lydia hesitated as *Do-it, don't-do-it* seesawed in her head.

"Yes?"

Lydia hurried inside for a pen as she asked, "Uh, could you by any chance give me Max's number?"

"Sure." Bess rattled off the number from memory. "Sorry, gotta run. Beer delivery just pulled up."

Lydia pocketed the number and went outside, where she took a sip of her drink for courage. She had enough to put the number into the phone, but not enough to tap the call icon. The teenager still inside her flared up with that old fear of calling "a boy." *But you're not sixteen*, she scolded herself, *and damn it, you can do this.*

The phone rang, rang again. *If it goes to voicemail*, she thought, *I won't leave a message.* On the fourth ring, a groggy voice answered. "Mmm … h'lo?"

"Oh, I'm sorry," Lydia stuttered, "I'm sorry. I didn't mean to disturb you."

"That's okay." There was the sound of a yawn. "Nap time was almost over anyway. Who's calling, please?"

"Oh, I'm sorry," Lydia repeated, castigating herself for her nervousness. "It's Li … Elle."

"Ah, well hello." Max's voice was awake now.

"I hope you don't mind. Bess gave me your number."

"No, no, I don't mind at all." He waited a moment before prodding, "Were you calling to see if the number worked, or might there be another reason?"

"Oh, I'm sorry." Stop saying you're sorry, her mind screeched. Her words came out in a rush. "Yes. Um, I'm in the mood for some company this evening. Audra's gone, and Dave and Bess have plans, so I was wondering—"

A chuckle interrupted her. "Ah, so now you're down to the C list?"

"No, no. That's not it." Lydia wanted to smack him. "It's just, I don't know anyone else here." Now she wanted to smack herself. "I'm sorry." Again. *Get your shit together, woman.* "I was wondering, could I take you to dinner tonight? Of course, if you already have other plans ..."

"It so happens I do not. I am flattered by the invitation, and my answer is yes. Do you have a place in mind?"

"The only place in town I know is Doozy's. That'd be okay, but maybe there's another restaurant you recommend?"

"Yes, it so happens there is. A little bistro right on the lake. I'd be happy to drive. Shall we say at seven?"

"Thank you. I'd like that. I'll see you then." Lydia leaned back and rocked the porch swing, her glass in hand now, not the phone. She took a sip, thinking, *Did I just ask a man on a date?* She finished the last of her drink. It's damn well a date, girl, and you know it—she could almost hear Audra's voice scolding her—and for god's sake wear something that isn't black and doesn't look like you're going fishing. Lydia glanced at the time on the phone. She had two hours to get herself ready.

***

On work days, it took her less than half an hour to go from pajamas to shower to makeup and hair to well-dressed and out the door. Except for the shower, in the past weeks it seemed she'd lost the muscle memory that required no thought on her part. Doing her makeup, she used too much rouge and smudged the mascara, causing her to clean her face and start over again. Her sister-in-law's curling iron felt foreign in her hand, and her arm ached before she finished. Leaving the little sausage rolls of hair uncombed while she dressed, she sorted through the few clothes she had. A pair of black pants would do, but her tops now looked too casual, too sloppy. With accessories she might make one work. She had bought earrings on Mackinac Island, but had no necklace. The attic—she remembered a jewelry box in one of the drawers, its contents funky and outdated but maybe there'd be something kitschy there. She cinched her robe and headed, barefoot, up the stairs. Rummaging through the drawer it was in, she also discovered a black clutch to use instead of her bulky shoulder purse. Downstairs again, she tossed the clutch on her bed and opened the jewelry box on the dresser. She grinned when she found a strand of pop-beads—god, how she loved playing with those as a kid. She held them up to her neck in the mirror. The once white beads had yellowed, and glowed golden against the tan she'd acquired from being out so much in the late spring sun. She snapped them on, then held a black top up to her chest and grimaced at the reflection—the beads took on a sickly hue. She really wanted to wear them. Why that seemed so important, she didn't know, but they needed the contrast of something bright.

With a start, she turned to the closet. She reached for the hanger draped in a long paper bag from My Summer Closet. She slipped off the cover and held the dress at arm's length. Then she held it in front of herself and turned to the mirror. The red of the sheath shimmered; so did the beads and her tanned skin. Audra had been right to make her buy the dress—it was simple, but elegant. *Too elegant*, she wondered, *for "a little bistro" in Nibic?* Now her mother's voice was in her head: "It is always better to be overdressed than underdressed," followed by Audra's whisper of "Especially when you're looking to be undressed." "That is not happening," she snapped, her eyes blazing back at her from the mirror.

The light was going soft when she stepped out onto the porch to wait. She was glad she had her shawl, as it would be chilly later, and she'd look like a bag lady with her jacket or a sweatshirt. She wasn't thrilled with her shoes but she reminded herself that black ballet flats went with everything. Staring down at them, a thought struck, and she rushed back inside. She did have shoes, the pumps she'd taken off the day she left Tampa. They'd laid forgotten in the bottom of her tote since then. Slipping into them lifted her more than an inch, and lifted her spirits. It felt good to feel womanly again.

She tried to read as she waited, to take her thoughts off the time, though her mind was less attuned to the lyrical sentences than to listening for tires on the drive. When she heard the crunch of gravel, she set the book on the lamp table inside the door and locked the lodge. Max's car pulled to a stop as she moved to the porch steps. She hoped she didn't appear too anxious—maybe she should have waited inside, but it was too late now. She gave a small wave as he stepped out of the SUV. He wore a sport coat and tie, and a dressy black fedora now replaced the battered leather one, and had shaved. The relief of knowing she wasn't too fancy slipped like lotion over the skin of her neck and chest. Still, her smile felt dry as she walked toward the car. Max was at the passenger door before she was and swung it open. Lydia hadn't had a car door opened for her by anyone other than a valet in years, and the gesture made her feel both happy and awkward. "Hello," was all she said.

Max's smile was genuine, as was the approval she saw in his eyes. "Your hair looks nice," he said as she seated herself, and added, "And that color does well by you."

"Does it? It's new. I got it in town. Well, Audra made me get it. It's not a color I usually wear." She realized she was rambling and stopped. "Thank you."

With the start of the car, violin music poured out, mid-song, from a CD in the dash. Lydia glanced toward Max—he would be a man to appreciate classical music, she thought, unlike Gil, who always fell asleep anytime he was "forced" to attend the symphony. "Is that the 'Adagio for Strings'?"

Max's eyebrows and smile rose as he took his eyes off the road. "Ah, a woman who knows music."

"Somewhat. We have season tickets to the Florida Orchestra but we mostly give them away." She cringed as soon as she said the word "we." She was glad she'd shut up before saying "… to Gil's clients."

A warm breeze blew through Max's open window as the car turned onto the hard road. "It promises to be a pleasant evening," he said.

"Yes, the weather's been so nice." She hoped he was talking about the weather. "You can almost feel summer. It comes on so different here than at home."

"As I have the experience of knowing from my consulting jaunts into Florida this time of the year." *Jaunts*, thought Lydia, *an interesting choice of word*, one that seemed to say this was a man who approached his work with pleasure, not the blindered focus and relentless drive of an entrepreneur. She liked that. "So," he went on, "how is it you left Michigan for the Sunshine State?"

By the time she'd told the story of her family's move when she was a teen, their annual returns, and her summer work at the lodge during college they were driving through town. Not far past where the village ended, Max turned onto a side road Lydia had not noticed before. A carved wooden sign announced “DeLucca’s Ahead.” Only the violin music sounded as Lydia took in the unfamiliar drive. Max parked among the dozen or so cars in the small lot at the side of a redwood-shingled building. He casually took her elbow as he opened the bistro door for her. A young man—a very young-looking man, Lydia thought—greeted them at the host’s stand. Behind him, much of the dining room was filled. “Two?” the young man asked.

“Yes,” Max said. “Is there a table on the deck?”

“Yes sir. This way.” Wearing a white shirt, black pants, and a white towel tucked into his waistband—the ubiquitous uniform of waiters in Italian restaurants—he led them through the homelike yet elegant dining room and glass double doors framed in burnished wood. Six tables, four of them filled, were spread at discrete distances across the deck that swept out above the water. Lydia smiled at the unexpected setting.

“May we?” Max gestured toward the table next to the railing.

“Sure.” The young man pulled out a chair for Lydia, and she thanked him as he handed her the menu. “I’ll be right back with water.”

“And a basket of house bread?” Max asked with a smile.

“Yup. Uh, I mean, yes sir.”

Lydia’s own smile faded a bit as her eyes slipped down the menu, a standard list of Midwestern Italian fare: spaghetti and meatballs, chicken or eggplant Parmesan. Penne with vodka was the most exotic offering.

The young man was back almost before Lydia finished reading. “Are there any specials,” she asked.

“Yeah. Um, yes.” He flipped over his order pad and read from the back. “Tonight’s specials are chicken with salsa marinara over angel hair pasta, and something called—” He hesitated. “Oh-so-buck-oh.”

“Osso buco,” Max asked, his correction voiced as a gentle question. Lydia glanced at him, glad to know he wasn’t someone who was pompous with waitstaff.

“Yes, that’s it.” The boy then repeated, “Ah-so boo-co. I keep forgetting. I’m not quite sure what it is, to be honest. I’ve never heard of it before. It’s supposed to be good. Mrs. D made it.”

“Maggie’s here?” Max’s voice almost boomed with enthusiasm.

“Yeah, for a couple of weeks. She kinda scares me.” The waiter’s words fairly gushed out. “This is my very first job and only my second week, and she's kinda loud and makes me so nervous I'm afraid I'll drop something when I'm around her."

Max chuckled at the blurted confession. "No need to worry, my boy, no need. Maggie's a force of nature—and the more forceful, the more she likes you." Turning to Lydia, he asked, "Shall we have wine?" At her nod, he said, "Ask Gus to select a Barolo for us, please. I think I've an idea what we're likely to order, and it will pair nicely. Tell him it's for Max Pearson, and that I send my regards."

"Okay," the very young man said. "He'll serve it too. I'm not old enough."

No wonder he looked so young, Lydia realized, wondering if the boy was even eighteen. As the waiter left, she asked, "Gus? Maggie? Not exactly Italian?"

"Giuseppe DeLucca," Max replied, "and his mother, Marguerita, affectionately—and sometimes not so affectionately—known as Mrs. D. As Italian and clannish as if they'd come here from New York but they've been in the U.P. for generations. Maggie's grandfather brought his family over after he found work in the copper mines. Maggie is, to say the least, a formidable woman. No doubt she intimidates the boy. Gus can be the same, although his father softened the edges. Gus senior died, let's see, almost three years ago? Maggie comes for a few weeks whenever she can't bear to be without her grandkids. After about two days with them, she's had her fill and takes over the kitchen. I think she uses the grandchildren as an excuse to get elbow-deep in pots and pans again."

Gus arrived with a grin, bearing a bottle and wine opener in one hand and two glasses dangling by their stems in the other, and Max rose. Their handshake ended with Gus pulling Max in for the hearty, back-slapping abbraccio Lydia often saw between men hugging each other in greeting in Ybor City.

"I heard you were around," Gus said. "Took you long enough to show your face." He turned to Lydia. "And who is this, may I ask? She doesn't look like the fishing buddies you usually show up with." His smile was sly, but his face was warm and welcoming.

"This is Elle, Elle Casselberry. She's staying at her family's lodge for a while and we've made acquaintance," Max said as he resumed his seat.

Gus shook Lydia's hand. "Yeah? You related to Thom?"

"Yes, I'm his sister."

"No kidding. Didn't know he had one." Gus had opened and was pouring the wine. "He and Lynn up here too? Haven't seen them. How they doing?"

"No, they won't be coming this summer," Lydia said. "Thom had a heart attack a few months ago."

Gus looked at her, startled. "Geeze, he all right?"

"Yes, he's fine," Lydia assured him. "But the doctor, and Lynn, want him to stay close to home through the summer."

"Well, you tell him I send my regards, okay? Now, I've got to get back to the kitchen before Mama has someone in tears. You two enjoy."

Max raised his glass to Lydia, and she raised hers too. "Salud."

She savored the dusky taste of the red wine, catching first a hint of smokiness, then the hint of licorice that lingered. Unsure of how to start the conversation, she took another sip and looked toward the reddening sun over the lake. The view was almost foreign—it was still "her" lake, but she felt disoriented by its sudden unfamiliarity. Just like her life.

"The Three Sisters look so different from here," she said.

"The Three Sisters?"

"Yes. The islands. I don't know if they even have names. It's what we called them when I was growing up."

He asked her about those years. She told him about the fishermen, the hunters, and the families who came to the lodge. She told him about her grandfather's lumber mill; about the uncles and aunts who either stayed nearby or moved off; about her father, the first in the family to go to college let alone earn a PhD. Her glass was almost empty when she stopped. "Listen to me going on. I've been doing all the talking."

Max smiled, pouring her more wine. "Simply because I've been doing all the asking. And because I'm enjoying the listening."

The young waiter returned with his order pad ready. "Gus said to tell you, you should order the osso buco"—they could see he was pleased with himself for saying it correctly—"because it's about the best Mrs. D ever made. I guess that's saying something."

Max and Lydia glanced at each other and nodded. "Yes, please," Lydia said, her words mingling with Max's, "Excellent."

Over their salads, Max described how he had made the lake his summer home. He told her about his lifelong love of fishing, instilled in him by his grandmother, of all people. How, when he had earned enough to afford it, he had fished trout in pristine rivers but decided that tying flies was "too fussy to bother with." How he'd traveled to Alaska, Canada, even Iceland, to fish salmon, but while he enjoyed the people he met on those excursions, he tired of being constantly in the presence of others. "The mental intensity of my work requires solitude to balance. That's why I returned to lake fishing. Me, alone, a speck afloat in emptiness, complete silence, simply myself and my thoughts. I was very lucky to have a wife who did not begrudge my need." He looked out at the lake, a wistful shadow passing over his face. "Of course, we traveled a lot together too. I was also lucky to find her company always superb."

"Your dinners." Plates were set before them, and Lydia was spared having to find a response. They both looked up at the young man and shook their heads when he asked if there was anything else he could get them. At the first taste, Lydia's mouth responded with delight as her eyes closed. "This," she said as she lifted her fork again, "is incredible. DeLucca's would make a fortune in a big city."

As they ate, their conversation resumed. She told him she was reading the book he had with him that Friday at Doozy's, but he wouldn't say much about it, not wanting to give away what was to come. Max asked about her work, and she told him a little—teaching, faculty work, academic politics; none of it seemed all that interesting now. He told her of his career, being drawn into consulting for the legal system, how that led to his teaching skills to law enforcement and government security. "I nearly burned out before I realized there are more important riches in life than money. It was then I began giving myself as much time as I had been giving to others, which is a wealth too few realize should be sought until it's too late."

Lydia said nothing. She drank her wine and stared out at the colors cast by the descending sun over the water and shoreline. Financial gain had always been Gil's sole pursuit—*Or so I thought*, her mind said. Would things between them not have happened the way they did, she wondered, if they'd given each other more time together, time that wasn't arranged around his calendar or hers, time proscribed by others' needs? During the last hard years, why hadn't she spent some of her "pin money" to take them away somewhere, to be together and reconnect? Was it only because, she wondered, it would have revealed that she'd kept the money hidden from him? There it was again—we all have secrets.

Lydia turned and realized Max was studying her. “That,” he said as if there’d been no silence, “is when I decided I needed to rewrite my story. That part of it, anyway. What is yours?”

Lydia flicked the fingers of one hand. “Oh, I have none.”

“Ah, we all do. There are the stories we tell ourselves, and the story we tell the world. Are they the same?”

Lydia’s smile was rueful. “I used to think so.”

Before Max could probe again, heads around the deck snapped up as a woman’s voice boomed, “Maxwell.” The woman coming toward them was handsome, with striking features and a cascade of dark curls streaked with gray. She wore a sleeveless shirtwaist dress that looked retro-modern on her, its splashy floral pattern as vivid as her voice. He rose quickly with a broad smile, and the woman enveloped him in an embrace. “Still as handsome—and virile—as ever.” Her words came out in a coquettish growl.

“And you still play the vixen, Maggie.” His laughter was as loving as his eyes.

Maggie’s laugh in return was like water bubbling over stones. “If my Donatello had had any idea of what he was unleashing, he would not have gone and died, God rest his soul.” She crossed herself, then winked and turned to Lydia. “And who is this,” she asked, looking again at Max. “It’s about time you found a lady friend to squire about.”

“Maggie, this is Elle. Elle Casselberry. We recently made acquaintance and it was she who was kind enough to invite me to dine. I could think of no better place to suggest. Dinner was, as usual, excellent, and finding you here makes the evening doubly so.”

Maggie gave his arm a playful push. “Keep that up and you’ll be taking two women home tonight.”

Max invited Maggie to sit but she declined, saying she had but a minute. They exchanged short updates on their lives before Maggie said, “Time to get back to the kitchen or one of those knuckleheads will burn the marinara. I hope you have room for dessert because tiramisu is on me. Enjoy the rest of your evening.” She turned to Lydia again, saying it was a pleasure to meet her, then leaned closer and stage whispered, “He’s a keeper. Reel him in.” With a wave over her shoulder, she was gone.

The shake of Lydia’s head and her chuckle expressed her surprise. “You’re right, she is a force of nature.”

Within seconds, tiramisu and coffee were placed before them. Savoring both, the conversation meandered to food and their unusual encounters with it. Max was impressed to learn she had once eaten fruit bat. Lydia, however, was glad she'd already eaten when he told a story of a dinner in his honor in Saudi Arabia, where he'd been served the eye from the sheep's head. "I had no choice," he said. "To refuse would have been an insult. I still don't know which was worse—eating it, or having to do so without an enormous glass of scotch to wash it down. You can believe I found one as soon as I departed."

As they left, they stopped to say goodbye to Gus, who now hugged Lydia too and urged her to return. "Mama's in the kitchen, busy driving everyone nuts, but if she likes you, I do too. You impressed her."

"Me? I don't think I said a word."

"You didn't have to. She said, 'Any woman who takes a man out and pays the check is my kind of woman.'"

"Well, you can tell her she impressed me too."

"Oh," Gus said, "she already knows that. She impresses everyone, and she'll tell you so. How my father ever kept a rein on her, I don't know."

The deck outside the entrance was filled with waiting diners, most with drinks in hand. An unfamiliar sensation jolted through Lydia at the light touch of Max's hand on the small of her back as he ushered her through the crowd. She pretended not to notice, but she couldn't pretend she didn't enjoy it. When his hand dropped away, the tingling didn't, instead radiating across the skin of her back and down her legs. He was only being gracious, she told herself, it meant nothing to him. But it meant something to her—another reminder of what she hadn't noticed missing in her marriage. "Thank you," she said as he opened the car door. He didn't know that wasn't all her gratitude was directed at.

It was that time of late evening in the far north when the fading light of the sky lingers, not quite dark but dark enough that headlights and porch lights were on, lamps glowed through windows or shone inside stores, and neon-colored signs were lit. It was that time of evening where the lights made the town sparkle, and people out walking all seemed on their way to a good time. Taking it in, Lydia sighed with pleasure. "Thank you," she repeated. "It's been a lovely evening."

"That it has. Might you allow me to extend it a bit by buying you an after-dinner drink? Your friend Ned will be playing. Perhaps we could enjoy some music too?"

Lydia smiled toward his shadowed profile. "I'd like that." She wasn't quite ready to have the evening end either.

Doozy's was busy but they found a small table at the back, at the far end away from the stage. Rather than wait for the server—there seemed only one on duty—Max went for their drinks. Lydia watched him, as he first said something that made Jerry laugh while leaving the bar, then as he chatted casually with the older men and scruffy younger ones on stools nursing longnecks. She liked how easy he was with everyone he encountered, how he had no hesitation in engaging others. Jerry returned with a bottle from the back room. He poured its dark liquid into two snifters, which Max carried back to the table.

"I took the liberty of selecting an Armagnac," he said. "It's an excellent finish after wine. Perhaps you are familiar with it?"

Lydia shook her head no and lifted the glass to sample its scent. The fruity aroma intrigued her, and her eyes lit up at the taste. First there was the savory sting of plum brandy. As the sharpness faded, the redolent mingling of summer fruits—cherries, pears, hints of so many more—cascaded over her tongue, and then everything became infused with the scent of orange blossoms, the scent that had permeated Florida in the spring, before the canker and developers wrought their blight.

"Ah, good," Max said, reacting to the pleasure on her face. "Knowing you like bold reds; I thought this might appeal to you."

"It's delicious. But how is it that such a tiny town dive even has something like this?"

"Nibic attracts a stratum of sophisticates who feel no need to flaunt their wealth but still indulge themselves. Jerry, Gus, and a couple of others keep very fine selections in reserve for such occasions."

"Next up, a request." Ned had been strumming lightly and chatting to the room. "Casey. Where's Casey? Put up your hand. There she is." He pointed and heads turned. "Folks, it's Sam and Casey's seventeenth anniversary and he asked me to play this for his bride." Applause and calls of congratulations rippled through the room as Ned's fingers caressed notes from the guitar and his baritone crooned, "Chances are …"

"Ah, Johnny Mathis. Cynthia always loved his music. So did I, until …"

"Until what?"

"Until I learned he was homosexual."

Stymied for a second, Lydia recovered. "Excuse me?" Her voice was so sharp that people at the next table looked at her.

Max shrugged. "He did have a very fine voice. But as a man? To make that choice? He couldn't help being Black, but the homo thing—"

"The 'homo thing'? And he 'couldn't help being Black'? What kind of—"

"Don't get me wrong," Max cut her off. She was on the verge of such anger she didn't notice the glint in his eyes. "I hold nothing against the person that's outside their control, but choices are a different matter. And there are some gays I would count among my friends."

"Oh, I'm sure you also have some friends who are Black, and even some who are Jewish. How magnanimous of you. You're a psychologist and you are so obtuse as to believe being gay is a choice?" Lydia pulled her shawl over her shoulders and picked up her purse. "I think I'd like you to—"

Max cut her off again, this time with laughter. He raised his glass as if in toast and said, "Thank you."

"For what?" Lydia fairly spit the words.

"For having the moxie to push back. You have been so acquiescent in all of our interactions that I was becoming concerned nothing would rile you. One choice I make is not to overly invest myself in the compliant. I think there's a lot more about you I'd like to discover."

"You … you were baiting me? Why, you—"

"Ah, ah, ah." Max grinned as he shook his head. "I may very well be, but you don't know me quite well enough to call me that yet." His smile lit up his entire face, and Lydia could only shake her head and laugh as Ned closed out the song—"Well, chances are … your chances are … awfully good."

***

White birch skin seemed to grimace and black maple bark glowered as if startled by a nightmare monster's glare when the car's headlights swung onto the drive. A raccoon's eyes shone red for an instant before disappearing into the dark. Max turned off the music that had been an undercurrent to their conversation. Contentment wafted through Lydia like the night air from her open window. The evening had been far more pleasant than she'd anticipated. No moon illuminated the lodge as they approached, but the orb of the porch light did its best imitation in welcome. As the car slowed, Lydia prepared to say her goodnight. Instead, her words surprised her. "Would you like to come in for a coffee?"

Max's head tilted. "Ah, caffeine and I, this late at night …"

"There's decaf. I could make us a Black Irish Coffee."

"And that would be what," he asked as he put the car in park.

"No caf, no whip. Nothing but decaf and the Jamison's."

Max's chuckle was low and throaty. "And is there such a thing as a Lace Curtain Irish Coffee?"

"Mm-hmm. Now, that's coffee topped with fresh whipped cream, drizzled with crème de menthe, a maraschino cherry, a cinnamon stick, a sprinkling of brown sugar and chocolate shavings. So much frippery you don't even notice there's no whiskey at all."

Laughing, Max turned off the key and sat back. "Frippery. Yes, I think I prefer the unadorned. Shall we?"

She smiled back, opening the car door. "Yes, let's do."

Lydia laid her shawl and purse on a chair near the door, and clicked on another lamp as she moved toward the kitchen. "Make yourself comfortable while I start the pot." She paused and pointed to the sound system. "If you'd like any music, my brother has an extensive collection." When she returned to the room, he was flipping through the CDs. She noticed his hat set beside her belongings. She liked the look of it there, as if it said "I'm home," rather than "What's your hurry?"

"Coffee will be ready in a minute. I'm going to get into something more comfort … um, change out of this dress." She hurried away, embarrassed she'd implied something she didn't mean. *Maybe offering coffee wasn't a good idea*, she scolded herself.

Charlie Parker's saxophone infused the great room as she returned in jeans, and rolling up the sleeves of a shirt of Thom's she'd pulled from the closet. Max was studying a group of family photos, his hands clasped behind his back. Lydia's step faltered as a pang of memory struck—it was the way her grandfather had often stood. She said nothing, leaving him in contemplation until she set their cups on the coffee table.

He turned from the photos as she curled up, legs beneath her, on the sofa. "You've a lot of history here. Why is it you've not come back before?"

"How do you know I haven't?" There was a slight edge to her question.

"Dave. He said your brother never once mentioned you, and that when Dave spoke to him about your appearance in the lodge, your brother said he couldn't remember the last time you'd been here." His words were as casual as his movements as he sat down at the other end of the couch and reached for his coffee.

"Well, it's not exactly a daytrip from Tampa. And my husband and I both have careers." *My husband—shit.* The phrase she'd spoken so easily all of her married life slipped out reflexively. But the word now stung. And divulged more than she'd wanted to.

Max gave no indication of her admission. "Yes. I'm lucky in that I can conduct my business from various bases. This certainly does provide an ideal place for your sabbatical. Have you been able to accomplish a lot on your work?" At Lydia's nod, he asked, "Even with your friend's unexpected arrival?"

Lydia raked a hand through her hair. "Actually, Audra's showing up helped me put everything into focus. You see, this wasn't an actual sabbatical. Not for work anyway. Yesterday I filed divorce papers." The words were out before she could stop them, and hung in the air, mingling with the wail of Parker's horn.

"I see. This must be a very difficult time." There was neither surprise nor judgment in Max's voice.

"To say the least. Because I never saw it coming." She kept talking. Something about Max's ease and the way he'd listened all evening allowed the story to pour out. He didn't speak, even when she halted to stare into space a moment before continuing. She told him more than she'd told her children, but not everything. When she finished, she looked at him. "Do you do this with everyone you meet?"

"What's that?" His smile was gentle.

"Get them telling you things they don't tell anyone else."

"Not always. Although it is a trait that has its benefits in my profession." He took another sip of coffee. "What has it been like, returning here after all these years? Are the memories comforting or foreign?"

Grateful for his deft steering of the conversation, she told him more tales from the past. He peppered her with questions, and laughed at stories of the trouble she and her brothers and cousins got into. Then she surprised herself, with a question to him when she realized he was deflecting the conversation to her stories alone. “Tell me about your wife. That is, if it’s okay. From the little you said at our impromptu dinner party, it sounds like you loved her a lot.”

Max stared into his coffee cup, silent. She waited, wondering if she’d been too bold. “I’m sorry. I shouldn’t have asked.”

“No, no, it’s perfectly all right.” Max looked at her, his smile sad. “We did love each other, dearly. Losing her was … it was sudden. So I understand the shock of what you’re experiencing with your own loss.” He took a deep breath. “Cynthia was killed by a drunk driver. Six years ago. On her way to a court case. At eight in the morning.”

“Oh my god,” slipped from Lydia’s mouth and she reached forward to touch his knee before she could stop herself.

“You wake up on a day like any other, and then your world is ripped out from under you. So yes, I have a sense of what you’re experiencing.” Then his own words poured out, stories of their years together, the disappointment of not having children and how Cynthia channeled that loss into her work as a guardian ad litem, his rage during the trial of the man who’d walked away unscathed after taking her life. She listened, asking only the rare question. When he stopped talking, staring into something only he could see, she was silent.

“Well, listen to me,” he said finally, trying to turn a smile toward her. “You’d make a good therapist. I’ve not said a lot of these things to anyone else.”

“Thank you.”

“For what?”

“For feeling that you could.”

He glanced at his watch. “Goodness. It’s almost two in the morning. I fear I’ve kept you up far past your bedtime.” He chuckled, and stood. “I know it’s well past mine, and that I will not be meeting Dave at six to fish.”

At the door, Lydia impulsively grasped his hand. “Thank you for letting me disrupt your plans on such short notice.”

“It has been anything but a disruption. It has been a great pleasure; one I’d like to repeat. Might I return the favor with dinner next Saturday?”

"Yes. I'd like that."

Something to look forward to, she thought as he drove off. It had been a long while since she'd had anything pleasant to look forward to. She touched her cheek where he'd leaned down to kiss it.

***

Sunday passed as languidly as a canoe drifting along a shoreline on the current. She slept late, so late the sun had crossed high above her bedroom window before she woke, and she lay in bed a long time thinking about the evening before. Opening up to Max, a virtual stranger, had been cathartic. What was strange now was that she felt he was someone she could intrinsically trust. *Is this the relief Catholics feel*, she wondered, *after confession to a priest?* Max had given her a gift, she saw now: a dress rehearsal for the many tellings to come when news of the divorce rippled through her circles. Max didn't know as much as Audra, others would be told far less, and now the lines she practiced in her head, and even aloud as she drank her first coffee, began to come with ease: "Yes, Gil and I …"—no, "*we* are divorcing"; "Yes, it does seem sudden but a lot led up to it"; "No, it really is for the best"; "Yes, I'll be fine." For the first time, she believed that—that she was going to be fine. Absolutely fine. Because somehow, she realized, the anger was gone, replaced now by steely resolve. She looked at the mantra on her mug and smiled. She was goddessing up, not faking it any longer.

The ease lingered as she returned to the computer for the one task left undone. Combining a folder of documents and images to send Marielle's husband brought no more emotion than dealing with student records or office file transfers. As pages began to print, she searched through drawers in hopes Thom might have oversized envelopes on hand. She found something else instead—several thumb drives. She stopped the printer, checked until she found several that were blank, and instead copied onto one what she'd send to Mr. Cuckolded Wharton. On two others, she backed up everything she had discovered. She'd mail one to Audra and the other to her attorney, both for safekeeping.

After lunch and a long walk, Lydia returned to the attic, where she lost track of time to the past. This time she finished. She stood at the door for a moment, admiring the transformation from chaos to order. Downstairs, she was surprised to see it was well after five. She carried a drink and her book out to the porch swing and again lost herself deep inside the haunting mystery, glad to be haunted no longer by her own.

Late in the evening, Audra called. Thousands of miles apart, they shared a drink and a cigarette, as Lydia listened to Audra go on about the quick success of Ned's prints and the normal, nutty exasperations of customers and employees. She had Lydia laughing over taking Maury to the play the night before. "Everybody who didn't know about his girlfriend, he told he was using the wheelchair because I'd worn him out Friday night. Everybody who did ask about her, he told them *she* was too worn out from their antics the night before. What is it about old men getting so randy? But enough about Maury. Anything new on your end?"

Lydia lit another cigarette. "Well, I took Max to dinner last night."

***

Monday morning was so warm that she put on the swimsuit Audra had left with her and lay in the sun. When clouds began to fill the sky, she had lunch, then drove into Nibic to post her mail and shop for groceries. Standing at the post office drop box, she looked at the three envelopes. Something told her to hang on to the one meant for Marielle's husband—maybe there'd be more fallout for her to add to it. Driving past My Summer Closet toward the grocery, on a whim she decided to go in. She was pleased the owner, Carmen, remembered her, especially considering—or maybe because of—how sullen she'd been the first time. The woman even asked about Audra, too, by name. No one else was in the store, and Lydia received Carmen's full attention. Far more in the store now appealed to her, and she forced herself not to buy as much as she would have liked.

She was almost to the grocery when her phone began ringing. It was Audra's ring tone, and Lydia wondered why she'd be calling now. After pulling into a parking spot she answered. "Hey. What's up?"

"Call Gil's office," Audra said with no preamble. "Call them now. Something's happened. They've been trying to reach you at your real number for hours."

"What are you talking about?"

"It's Gil. They think a heart attack. Right after a man came in with papers—"

"The divorce papers."

"Probably. When the hospital told him they couldn't reach you, he said to have his office try me. So he's apparently not dead. The gal there that I talked to sounded real upset. No one knows for sure but she made it sound like it's bad. I think you'd better get back here, pronto."

"Holy shit." Lydia started the car. She wouldn't be needing groceries now.

Chapter 15

The drive back to the lodge gave her time to turn from reaction to action. The shock of fear for the man she'd loved disappeared the minute she remembered that this was not the man she *had* loved. As his wife, she still had legal duties. She'd perform them, that was all. For no reason other than not giving him anything to use against her in the divorce.

Walking into the lodge, she realized how much it had come to feel like home. She'd come here because she had had nowhere else to go. Now, she wasn't ready to leave. She'd run away from a home that was no longer her home, and now she was being forced away from the place that had become home. She slammed her shopping bags onto the sofa, pissed at the world for again knocking her around like a goddamn pinball just when things had stopped spinning out of control.

Standing in the middle of the great room, she wondered what to do first. *Make a list*, she thought, *sort this all out.* No, there was something else she wanted to do first. In the kitchen she poured a glass of scotch, then got out the last cigarette Audra had left. As she smoked it and sipped on the porch swing, she jotted notes. Then she picked up her phone.

On the fifth ring, a young voice answered, a voice that sounded choked. "Carson Agency."

"Hello. This is Lydia Casselberry. I under—"

"Oh, Ms. C! Oh my gosh we've been trying to reach you all day. It's awful, just awful. Something happened to Gil—to Mr. Carson. We don't know what, except the EMTs took him. I've been trying to call you all day," the young woman repeated, "but your phone's been off and your office didn't have another number and we just didn't know how to find you and we don't know what's happening."

"Slow down," Lydia said, "and take a deep breath now, okay? Are you Alisha?"

"Yes ma'am. I'm sorry, I should have told you that. Alisha Cruz. I've only been working here about three months and nothing awful like this has ever happened to me in my entire life."

"It hasn't happened to me either. So tell me what did happen."

"Oh, it was awful," Alisha repeated. Lydia could tell the young woman was crying. "Just awful, and Gil—Mr. C—is such a wonderful man. This shouldn't have happened to him, Ms. C."

"It's okay, you can call him Gil. And please, call me Lydia." She felt as if she were calming one of her over-anxious grad students in the midst of master's thesis madness. "Just start from the beginning."

"It was just awful," Alisha repeated. Lydia closed her eyes, wondering if the young woman knew another adjective—working in an ad agency, you'd think she should. "Mr. C, he started getting kinda edgy about a month ago? But things really went hinky last week, maybe Wednesday? When he got in Thursday he was real weird and he was always on the phone in his office and the door was closed and it's almost never closed and then he blocked me from his email, which I'm supposed to monitor for really important stuff in his calendar and no one in the office knew what was going on and we all got really worried ..."

Wednesday. The day the sex-toy shitstorm had hit full force. Lydia wondered how the young woman could talk so much without stopping for a breath.

"Anyway," Alisha said, "it got worse Friday and he barely spoke to any of us. God, were we *sooo* ready to get out of here that night. Only it was just as bad, worse really, today, even before this happened. Mr. C looked awful when he came in. Gray-like, like he hadn't slept? And he was closed up in his office again. And then this man showed up? About ten? And said he had to see Mr. C? He didn't have an appointment and wouldn't tell me what it was about and wouldn't leave until he saw Mr. C. So anyway, I knocked on his door and when I opened it he looked at me like he didn't know who I was. Then he told me to have the guy come in and I did and not one minute later the guy left and right after that is when we heard the crash. Trevor got there first. He was on the floor. Mr. C was, not Trevor. If he hadn't knocked over a bunch of awards when he fell, maybe we wouldn't have even found him in time. He was turning blue. It was awful, just awful. I didn't know what to do. I've never seen a person die before and I was so scared. Somebody called 911. Trevor did CPR until they got here. They wouldn't tell us anything when they left, just that they were taking him to Tampa General. Trevor called the hospital but they wouldn't tell him anything either, except that Mr. C is there. But you're his wife. They'll have to tell you. When you find out, will you let us know? Please?"

"Of course. As soon as there's anything to tell. Do you have the hospital's number?"

"Trevor does. Hang on. Let me get it." The line went silent. When Alisha picked up again, she read off the number.

"Thank you. And what's Trevor's cell number?" Trevor Bowman was head of production and had been with Gil since the agency opened. He was the one who'd now be in charge.

After Lydia read the phone numbers back, Alisha blurted, "OMG, Ms. C, I am such an awful person. All of this has been about me, about us. And I didn't even say how sorry I am for you. This must just be awful. I can't imagine … Especially not being able to be by his side. I am *so* sorry. I'm going to have my church prayer circle pray for you both. I want you to know that. We'll be praying for you."

"Thank you," Lydia said, feeling no thanks at all. Prayer wouldn't help Gil because he didn't have a prayer's chance in hell, and she sure as hell didn't need it, because if there was a God, he'd already answered hers.

She started to dial the hospital but set the phone aside and went to her computer. First she needed to know when she'd be able to get there. Looking into flights from Chippewa International, there were two a day to Detroit, the fastest route back to Tampa. She booked herself for the afternoon flight Audra had taken. Gil wasn't worth the effort of leaving the lodge before dawn to make the early one. When her schedule was confirmed, she went back to the phone.

"Tampa General information. How may I help you?"

"Hello. Could you please put me through to Mr. Gil Carson? I'm told he was admitted late this morning."

"Do you know what he was admitted for?"

"I'm sorry, no. Except that it was an emergency, that he was taken by ambulance."

"Please hold a moment." Lydia did, and took a sip of her drink.

A man's voice came on the line, but it wasn't Gil's. "CICU."

"Um, I'm trying to reach Gil Carson. Is this his room?"

"No, ma'am. This is the nurses' station, Cardiac Intensive Care Unit. What is the patient's name again, please?"

Cardiac Intensive Care, that probably meant a massive heart attack. “Carson. Gil Carson.”

“Mr. Carson is unable to receive phone calls. Try again tomorrow.”

From the brusqueness of the man’s voice, Lydia knew he was about to hang up. “Wait. Can you tell me what happened, what his condition is?”

“Sorry, I can’t divulge patient information.”

“You can divulge it to me,” Lydia said. Catching the sharpness in her voice, she changed her tone. “I’m his wife, and I need to be informed about my husband’s condition.”

“Oh. I see. Hold on while I find the attending physician. May take a moment.”

It took more than a moment. *Doctors*, she thought, *always making you wait*. Wait an hour in the waiting room, wait half an hour in the examining room, wait a week or more for test results. Waiting on the gods. Stop it, she told herself, the doctor had far more important things to do than stop for every phone call.

“Dr. Androvsky here.”

“Doctor, I’m Lydia Casselberry. My husband is Gil Carson. Can you tell me what happened?”

“Your name again, please?” Lydia repeated it. “Okay. That name is listed as emergency contact. But I can’t tell you anything without verification of identity. It would be best for you to come in. I’ll be here until seven.”

“Doctor, that’s not possible. I’m out of town, fifteen hundred miles out of town as a matter of fact, and can’t return to Tampa until late tomorrow night. I need information on my husband, and I’d like it now.”

“I see. I still can’t provide any information without verification. If you will fax in your driver’s license and your phone number, once we verify you I’ll call—”

“Wait. I could give you his Social Security and insurance card numbers. Would that work?”

“I suppose I could accept that.”

“Hang on a sec.” Lydia hurried inside to find the little notebook she’d filled with information from home. She read the numbers off.

“Yes,” the doctor said. “And your home address, and date of birth, please?” Lydia rattled off both. “Thank you. I hope you understand this is a legality, Mrs. Carson.”

"Casselberry, Lydia Casselberry," she corrected.

"Oh, sorry. Habit. Your husband sustained a major cardiac event. His current condition is critical and unstable. He's on a respirator and heavily sedated. We're monitoring the situation while we determine the appropriate course of action." His words were as dry as if he were describing a traffic route. "Once we do, we'll need your approval to proceed should he be unable to make decisions on his own behalf. What's the earliest you would be available to meet with me on Wednesday?"

"As early in the morning as you're available." They agreed to meet around eleven, after the doctor completed a scheduled surgery. Good, she thought, she wouldn't have to endure drive-time traffic downtown. "And I'll see that between now and then my phone is on at all times—except when I'm in the air," she said.

"I'll be honest with you, Mrs. … Ms. Casselberry, the situation isn't good. We're waiting on more test results, but if another incident occurs we may need to perform emergency surgery. In the event, we are unable to reach you for verbal permission—"

She cut him off. "Is there something I can email to provide that?"

"That's what I was about to suggest. I'll have one of the nurses get the address and send the form for you to complete and sign electronically. I'll see you Wednesday."

"Thank you, Doctor." After hanging up, she realized the man hadn't offered any comment of sympathy. *Surgeons*, she thought.

The kids needed to be told, she realized. But she'd call them later. She didn't want to upset them at work—there was little she could tell, and nothing they could do—but maybe Audra wouldn't mind being interrupted.

Audra answered on the first ring. "Lyd. You okay? What's going on? Hang on a minute." Her voice turned away from the phone. "I'm sorry, ma'am, this is an emergency. Julie? Can you please finish helping this customer?" Into the speaker again, Audra's words continued in a rush. "God, I've been so worried. What happened? Did you find out?" Lydia heard a door shut. "Okay, I'm in the back room. I can talk."

"Yes, you sure can." Lydia laughed. "Mind if I do now?"

"I'm sorry. I've just been so worried."

Lydia related what the doctor had told her, then what she'd learned from her call to Gil's office.

"Jesus. This is our fault. With all the shit we pulled on him."

"No. I'm not taking any responsibility and neither are you. This is his own damned fault. Right now the bastard can die, for all I care."

"Okay, okay. Please don't snap at me. I'm just really worried about you. So whatever you need me to do …"

"Can you pick me up at the airport? And can I stay at your place tomorrow night? I'm not ready to go back to the house yet."

"Of course. Let me get a pen." After Lydia gave her the flight information, they talked a while longer. Before saying goodbye, Lydia promised to stay in touch the next day by text, or to call if something drastic happened. Hanging up, the screen clock showed she should wait another hour before calling James and Sara. She walked down to the Adirondack chair, to enjoy one last late afternoon view of the lake.

***

Later, Lydia remembered the hospital was to have emailed paperwork to sign. She accessed the file, scanned through the pages of medicalese and insurancese, and filled out the required fields. After hitting send, she packed. Then she was at loose ends again.

It was after six. She fixed another drink. She might get tipsy tonight—really tipsy. And might smoke some of Audra's herb—whoops, that hit her too, what was she going to do with the leftovers? She wasn't about to fly with it, and she didn't want it left behind for Thom and Lynn to find. First, though, she needed to call the kids—they'd both be home from work now.

The first call went as Lydia expected. Sara went silent, except for wispy hics that meant she was crying, and then a long wail. "How could this happen?" she gasped. "Daddy's going to die."

Not soon enough for me, Lydia thought. "Sara, honey." Her voice was the one she used whenever Sara dissolved in tears as a child, while Lydia's hand had caressed her daughter's hair to soothe her. "Sara, honey. The doctor said nothing about his dying. There will be some more test results tomorrow, so they'll know more then. And I'll be home tomorrow night."

"I wanna be there too."

"Not yet, honey. In a few days. We need to know more first."

Sara argued before giving up and whispering, “Okay, Mommy. I love you.” Through sniffles she added, “And tell Daddy I love him too.”

Lydia had to smile as she clicked off. “Daddy,” “Mommy.” Talk about regression. But Sara always had been a daddy’s girl, one more female his charm had worked on. All of a sudden she wondered whether Gil loved Sara as much as she thought he did, or if it was another act, as false as his love for Lydia all these years.

James, too, was silent at first, but as he listened she heard taps on a keyboard. He broke in. “I’ll be in Tampa by two. What time is your flight? Where should we meet?”

“You will stay right where you are.” Lydia’s voice snapped the way it did when she’d send him to his room. She took a breath. Her children were adults, and deserved to be treated as such. “Jim, it’s too soon for you to be there. I don’t get in until late. I won’t be able to see the doctor until Wednesday morning, and for now I’m the only one allowed to see your dad. We’ll make plans after I know more. And if anything changes before then, I’ll let you know. I promise.”

James let out a sigh that sounded like his father’s. “Okay. I don’t like it, but okay.”

When they were done, she tossed the phone to the other end of the porch swing. She was tired of talking to people, tired of all the drama. Sick and tired of the month of drama she’d been through. More drama caused by goddamned Gil. She lit one of Audra’s joints. She wanted to get obliterated, not deal with more crap brought on by her husband. A buzz hit the back of her brain and a giggle leapt in her mouth. Well, she admitted with some glee, maybe she’d had a little to do with bringing on this part of it. Guilt stabbed, then anger as she reached for her drink. She wanted Gil to suffer, she wanted him dead. But was that what she wanted, to let him escape penance for his betrayal while she was left with the fallout? Having to play the grieving widow? She didn’t know what she wanted. Except to obliterate herself. She took another toke and nestled into the swing cushion.

And why, she mused, did she want to obliterate herself? She wanted to obliterate him, obliterate all the years she’d loved him, erase the memories, turn the past into the mirror-smooth lake, all the ugly detritus sunk to decompose, disappear at the bottom as if it never existed. She wanted him to rot. She hated him. She loved him, she had loved him, oh she had loved him.

But that Gil, the one she'd loved, was already dead. The man lying in a hospital bed was a man she did not know. But she had to deal with another fine mess he'd put her in.

She scanned the lake-silvered horizon, the silent woods, the comfort of the porch. She did not want to leave. This was home. She had come home again, and it had been there for her. It would wait, she realized, for her to return. She didn't know when that would be, but the lake and the lodge would always be here for her.

Thoughts came and vanished, barely noticed. Pleasantly stoned, Lydia was aware of nothing but the vibrant colors shimmering around her, punctuated by the lapping of the lake. She drew a deep breath as she came out of her trance, wondering how long she had sat there. It must have been quite some time, as the sun's orange streaks now ribboned the lake.

Inside, she turned on the CD that had ended long before she and Max finished talking Saturday night. From the fridge, she rummaged its dwindled contents for dinner. She piled her plate, her drink, and her book on a tray, then turned up the music before going back outside. She had no clue what was about to unfold for her, so she might as well lose herself in the pages of a different mystery.

***

The trouble with getting obliterated was that it led to staying up too late and feeling crappy in the morning. First, a long hot shower. Then a tall glass of cold water while the coffee brewed. The morning sun hurt her eyes but the brisk air helped as she drank the first cup. She was glad there wasn't much to do before leaving, not being able to concentrate. She washed her plate and glass from the night before, and the plate and knife from the morning's toast. She wrote a lengthy note to Dave, explaining what he needed to know, thanking him for all his help, and for all the fish. She decided she'd swing by the store on her way out to say goodbye to Bess, and maybe Katie, too. She finished packing and set the small suitcase and tote by the door, where they stood like forlorn dogs fearful of being left behind. She still didn't know what to do with the half-joint left over, until she did the one thing she didn't want to, which was flush it down the toilet. She stripped the bed and piled the sheets and towels on the washing machine, where Dave would find them. She wandered aimlessly until it was time to carry her bags to the car and lock the lodge door one last time.

As the car's wheels turned onto the gravel drive she tried to imprint the images around her in her mind—she decided she needed to buy one of Ned's pieces for her office, so the memory wouldn't be lost. At the road, she parked and got out to lock the gate she'd felt comfortable leaving open for the past couple of weeks. She had let something open in her, too. When the key clicked, she hoped she wasn't locking that part of herself up again.

At the sound of the chime inside Clar's Corner, Bess looked up. "Elle, so good to see you. I hear you and Max had a good time. And you're having dinner again this weekend?"

Oh God, Max, Lydia thought—she'd forgotten. "Uh, that was the plan," Lydia said, "but I have to call him. Things have changed. There's been an emergency. I'm flying home today. I wanted to stop in for a piece of fruit, but mostly to say goodbye."

"Oh, Elle, I am so sorry."

Lydia nodded. "Please tell Dave, and tell him there's a note on the kitchen table. And remind him to take home whatever's in the fridge and freezer, okay? You're welcome to anything in it, although there's not much."

"I will. That's kind of you. I hope everything works out okay, whatever it is. It has been so good to meet you. I'd really hoped to get to know you better. And seeing the change you've brought about in Max? I hope the two of you stay in touch. He's a good guy."

"Yes. Yes he is." Lydia handed Bess the money she owed, then gave her a quick hug. "I hope I'll be back sometime. And please give Katie a hug for me?" Her voice mingled with the jingling bell as she hurried away before Bess could say more.

The bustle of the airport, while nothing like what she knew she'd encounter in Detroit or Tampa, seemed cacophonous after the quiet of her past weeks. She returned the rental car, paying with her credit card now as there was no need to hide her whereabouts. Once she had her boarding pass tucked away, she carried her tote outside to a shaded bench and opened her phone.

On the fourth ring, Max answered. "Ah, an excuse for respite from the boredom of case file reviews. How are you? It's good of you to call."

"I'm fine. Well, no, I'm not. I mean, I am, but someone else isn't. I hate to do this. I'm at the airport. There's been an emergency, and I have to return to Tampa. Dinner Saturday is off. I'm sorry, Max. I really am."

"Ah." There was a pause. "Well, my own disappointment has no place in your worries right now, I'm sure. I do hope that, whatever the emergency is, you'll resolve it soon for the best outcome."

"Whatever that is, isn't up to me. My husband is hospitalized. It seems that after receiving the divorce filing, and, um, some other things that happened last week, he had a heart attack."

"Oh. I am sorry."

Lydia still hadn't decided if she was, but lied. "So am I. Because I'd decided to stay here all summer. It's funny—I didn't come here because I wanted to. I didn't know where else to go. Now, I don't want to leave."

"I feel the same way every summer. Until that first frost in September—or August." His voice took on a lilt. "Then I begin looking forward to winter on Sanibel."

Silence held for a moment, and she sensed they were both thinking the same thing. Lydia spoke first. "Maybe while you're there, maybe we'll be able to meet for a dinner. I've enjoyed getting to know you—a bit at least." Her words felt stilted. "I mean, I'd like that. And I hope we stay in touch."

"I would like that, too."

"Oh, I just realized … let me give you my real phone number. This one—well, it was just for this trip." As she finished, an announcement came over the airport speakers. "I've got to go. My flight's boarding. Max, thank you."

"For what?"

"Well, for tipping your hat to me that day we both landed. The world was an unwelcoming place for me then. That's when things began to change."

"Yes, yes, they did. For both of us, I suppose. You take care."

***

The Detroit airport was almost overwhelming. She felt tossed into a teeming aquarium, overcrowded by fish of all sizes and shapes, darting every which way, buffeting her as if she were swimming against the current. Even the women's bathroom was a swirl of rushing and noise. The boarding gate was crowded with strangers whose lives would intersect for the next few hours.

But across the way, the waiting area was nearly empty. She took a seat there, against a wall that would have her back. She texted Audra that her flight was on time and leaving soon. She did the same with Sara and James, again promising she'd call as soon as she'd met with the doctor the next day. Then she telephoned the hospital. The doctor, of course, was not available. The information the charge nurse gave her was minimal: Gil's condition had not improved much, although he was off the respirator; he was still lightly sedated but was speaking occasionally; the doctors were still conferring about the best course of treatment.

Lydia shut down her phone and dropped it into her tote, beside her on the floor. She remained hunched forward, freeze-tag motionless, her mind that dystopia of blankness and flashing thoughts. A loudspeaker announcement took a while to reach her awareness. Her plane was boarding. She picked up her purse and tote bag and swam back into the fray.

Three hours later she pressed her head against the tiny window. Lights beamed below and from the west. Connecting the cities, the three bridges across the dark swath of Old Tampa Bay sparkled like gem necklaces, promising the exotic, laid-back beauty of Florida. *Illusion*, she thought, *all an illusion*. Like the illusion of her marriage. The Howard Frankland Bridge appeared to be the most stunning of the strands, with headlights moving like glints off diamond facets, hiding the fact that its drive-time traffic led locals to call it the Howard Frankenstein. Had she willfully refused to pretend there was no monster under—no, *in*—her own bed?

Humidity and salty air engulfed her the moment she stepped into the jetway, embracing her home. Paul Simon's voice ran through her head, singing "Michigan seems like a dream to me now." Was confronting the monster face to face going to be a nightmare or bring relief?

Audra's headlights flashed twice as her car maneuvered into the center row of vehicles moving like a faulty conveyor belt outside of arrivals, and Lydia threaded herself through the traffic. Audra popped the trunk, hopped out to give her a quick hug and hello, then helped load the suitcase and tote. Inside the car, she handed Lydia a bottle of water. "Drink. And give me a minute so I don't miss the sign and send us to Clearwater. I hate the clusterfuck it is to get out of here."

Lydia leaned back and stared out the window. The stars were out there, she knew, but they were obscured by the cities and suburbs lit defiantly against them. The whiz of light and color coming from ahead and behind left her feeling again tossed into the pinball machine, this one designed as a psychedelic kaleidoscope. Paul Simon's lyric floated again through her head. She felt as if she hung, like a suspended bridge herself, between home and home. She was home now, home in Tampa, but it seemed as foreign to her as the lodge had when she'd arrived there.

"There," Audra said. "Out of that scrum and on our way. How was your flight? You hungry?"

"Fine. No—yeah … I dunno."

"I've a snack waiting, and wine. Unless you want to go right to bed."

"No. I'm tired but I need to decompress. The wine sounds good."

For the rest of the short drive, silence passed between them as often as words did, neither sharing anything of substance. Inside her bungalow, Audra said, "Guest room's all ready for you. Dump your stuff. Hee-eere, kitty-kitty." Samantha ballet-stepped across the Southern pine floor. "Come here, kitty. Come get some hugs," Audra oozed, scooping up the cat and heading away.

Lydia rolled her suitcase into the guest room. Unpacking her night things seemed an intimate act, as if Audra's hospitality was a personal embrace—her artistic eye had created that feeling warmly and well in the room's eclectic furnishings. Audra's whole house was that way, folding in and soothing any and everyone who entered.

When Lydia came out, Audra was in the kitchen feeding the cat. On the table were wine glasses and a plate of the salty cheese crackers they both liked to make. Lydia pulled out a chair.

"No, let's go out on the back deck," Audra said. "I'm ready for a smoke."

The night air moved around them in a warm flow. For the next hour Lydia talked, a stream of guilt, fear, conflict, uncertainty. How she wanted Gil dead but she didn't. She wanted him to pay, but if he died now she would too, knowing it was her fault.

Chapter 16

The ride-share driver pulled up near the hospital's main entrance. Lydia stepped out and into the mass of cars, valets, slow-moving people, hurrying people, all coming and going. She stood, getting her bearings. It had been almost ten years since she'd been here, since her mother had died, and the place had changed so much she hardly recognized it. Crowded in by parking garages, doctors' office buildings, and the university's medical education facility, the surrounding campus practically dwarfed the main hospital. Inside, signs directed visitors toward the East Pavilion and West Pavilion—she hadn't known the hospital now had "pavilions." Her steps hesitated, then quickened when she noticed a directory filling an expanse of wall nearby. She scanned to the C's. Did she need the Cardiothoracic ICU or the Cardiac ICU? They were on separate floors …

"Can I help you?"

The voice came from behind. Lydia turned to see a smiling, well-dressed older woman wearing a volunteer nametag at a large reception desk. "Um, yes, I hope so. My husband was admitted two days ago. He's in ICU but I don't know which one." Lydia read the woman's thoughts from her face: *And it's taken you this long to show up?* "I was out of state and couldn't get back. I'm supposed to meet with a Dr. Androvsky." Nervously, Lydia wondered why she felt a need to explain herself.

The woman's face softened and she leaned forward. "Oh, you poor dear. No wonder you look as if you didn't sleep well." *Thanks a bunch*, Lydia thought. "Well, you're here now, and I'm sure your husband will be relieved to see you." *Or not*, Lydia thought. "What's his name?" The woman typed it into her computer. "You want Cardiac ICU. It's in the West Tower, fifth floor. Follow those signs, off to the left, to the elevators. And good luck. To you both."

Lydia murmured her thanks. The way seemed direct enough but the path turned into a labyrinth. By the time she reached the elevators she'd lost her sense of direction, her body as out of sync with the outer world as her mind was. When the elevator doors closed after she stepped out on the fifth floor, she stood still in the empty corridor. She had to get her head together, she told herself, and pay attention. She had to get rid of the incessant brainworm that had plagued her since Monday night: I love him; I love him not; Don't let him die; Oh, I want him to rot, the cadence of repetition matching her steps down the hall. A sign on the CICU door stated visitors were to call on the house phone before entering. She remembered that Dr. Androvsky had mentioned there'd be one near the entrance. The beige phone, cradled in a nook in the tan wall, took a bit of searching to find. A voice answered. "This is Lydia Casselberry," she said. "I'm here to see my husband, Gil Carson. And to meet with Dr. Androvsky."

"Yes, ma'am. I'll buzz you in."

With a metallic clack, double bay doors swung outward. On either side as she entered were small rooms with windows, their interiors obscured by drawn blinds. In the center of the expansive unit, bright lights shone down on the semicircular nurses' station. Glass-fronted patient rooms, blinds partially drawn for privacy but their sliding doors open, formed a horseshoe against the exterior walls.

As she approached the desk a man looked up. "Mrs. ... Ms. Casselberry? I'm Ethan, the RN assigned to your husband days. Dr. Androvsky left a message. He'll be here within the hour." Ethan glanced down at the desk. "That was half an hour ago, so that will give you some time with Mr. Carson. He is awake, but groggy. First though, everyone entering has to scrub"—he pointed to the wash station—"before visits."

Lydia did as instructed, then was led around the circle to a room behind the nurse's monitoring area. "Wait here a moment." Ethan stopped her outside the door to 5-F.

He turned to read the medical equipment as he entered. "How are you doing, Mr. Carson? Are you up to a visit? Your wife's here. That should cheer you both up." Leaving the room, Ethan stepped past her at the door, but paused. "Ma'am? See me before you leave. I have Mr. Carson's personal things for you." He gave her a kind smile and left.

Gil lay still under a sheet and light blanket. The subdued lighting and dingy white-and-blue-patterned hospital gown he wore exaggerated his pallor. His arms lay atop the blanket that encased him from his chest down, taut and smooth like a shroud ready to be lifted over his face. Clear tubes fed into his nose, and other tubes and wires tethered him to monitors emitting low beeps, flashing blips, and numbers that held steady or blinked their way up and down a narrow range of decimals. She looked at his hands lying flaccid on the lightweight blanket. One finger was splinted. For a second, she wondered if he'd broken it when he fell, before noticing it was wired to feed information to one of the machines. Under half-closed lids, his eyes turned toward her. His face was expressionless.

"Hello, Gil," she said. She didn't know what else to say. He looked so defenseless.

"Hey." His voice was hoarse. "Thanks for coming."

She recognized a touch of snark in that sentence and it stung. "I was halfway across the country, and way out in the country. I booked a flight as soon as I could. After I got the news Monday. I got back late yesterday." She placed a hand on his. It was cool and his vulnerability shivered through her. "I'd have been here sooner if I could. Are you okay?"

His eyes hadn't left her face, but remained blank. "Depends what you mean by okay." He coughed, and she was shocked at the spasm it sent through his torso.

When he was breathing easier again, she said, "I called the kids as soon as I heard. They're both worried sick, of course. And wanted to come. I told them not to—yet—since they couldn't see you. But they'll be here as soon as that's allowed."

He nodded and closed his eyes. Just as she was beginning to think he was falling asleep, he asked, "You doing okay?"

"Yeah, I guess. Worried about you."

"Really?"

She'd been asking herself that for two days, but wondered whether his question was sarcastic or sincere. "Yes. I'm sorry this happened."

"But you're not sorry about the divorce."

"We're not talking about that now." At the edge in her voice, his eyes opened some. She couldn't tell if she read pain, sorrow, or anger in them.

"It was a shit week." His words were barely audible. "Computers. Clients. Then you hit me with that. I don't want it. I want us to work this out. What did I do to make you so mad?"

What did you do? Lydia wanted to scream back at him. What compassion she had felt sparked hotly to animosity. She glared at him. "We're not talking about—"

"Ma'am?"

Ethan's voice caused her to turn. "Dr. Androvsky is on his way up. I'll show you to a family conference room. Mr. Carson, I'll be back in a couple of minutes."

She said nothing as she left Gil's room.

Ethan ushered her into one of the small, windowed rooms near the CICU entrance. He closed the door and she sat down on a gray metal chair. The space was tiny, with two simple chairs, a desk against the wall, and a more comfortable seat for the doctor. The beige walls and the desktop were bare. Lydia hoped this wasn't going to be a long wait. She was sick and tired of always waiting. Her jaw clenched, she clasped her arms tight across her chest and crossed her legs. Her dangling foot bounced rapidly. She stared at it for a moment before noticing. Her mind snapped at her foot, and herself, to stop—*Get your shit together, girl.* She unfolded her body and rested her palms against the outside edges of the chair. She closed her eyes and took a deep breath.

Before she could take another, the door opened and a strong voice boomed in the small space. "Ms. Casselberry. Dr. Androvsky." In two strides he had flopped himself onto the chair and plopped a file on the desk. He leaned forward, elbows on his knees, hands clasped. "Glad you made it. You doing okay?"

His words were all fast, forceful, almost flippant but she could tell his question was sincere. "Under the circumstances," she said, nodding. "Knowing nothing. I want to know everything. All the details." She reached down and pulled pen and notepad from her purse.

The doctor leaned back and the chair creaked. He pulled the folder toward him, flipped it open, and glanced over the papers it held. "All right. I'm not going to sugarcoat the situation. The situation is not good. It's not dire—yet—and we hope to keep it from getting to that. Your husband has major heart disease, and apparently has had for quite some time. Has he exhibited any symptoms? Shortness of breath? Complaints of any pain?"

"Not that I know of," Lydia said. "But then, I haven't seen him in nearly a month. I've been away."

"This would have been coming on for much longer than a month. You noticed nothing?"

Lydia worked her closed mouth, thinking, shaking her head. "Well, he does have indigestion. He eats antacids like Pez candies. He insisted he'd rather do that than give up his favorite foods. There's that, and I know he's been under a lot of stress lately."

Androvsky shut the file and rocked back farther in his chair. "Your husband has very serious coronary artery disease. We've stented him but he needs a triple bypass."

"Triple?"

"Yes. Normally we would have done that by now but there are complicating factors. First, he has a low-grade infection. We can't operate until that's cleared up. Second, there's major blockage in the carotid arteries. We also have to decide what to do there. Which means we need time we don't have. The longer we wait, the greater the chance of another event. One that could kill him. As of this afternoon he'll have had forty-eight hours of antibiotics and we'll check his blood again. He should be clear, which means we could operate tomorrow morning."

"Well," Lydia said, "since he's coherent he can agree to that."

"Yes. But if an emergency arises and we need to intubate him, we want to be sure we can move immediately."

"I have the POA designating me as his medical proxy." She added, "Also his DNR."

"Good. Fax a copy of both to the desk. Ethan will give you the number. Someone will call once we know if we can perform the surgery tomorrow or if we have to wait another twenty-four hours. But I'm feeling confident. I've already booked an OR for eight a.m. You'll be able to come up to see him around five. They'll take him in for prep around six."

Lydia's made a silent snort. Gil hadn't been worth leaving the lodge at five for an early morning flight, and he sure wasn't worth a five-minute five a.m. visit. "How long will he be in surgery?"

"Three hours. Minimum. Possibly longer. I have to warn you, considering his overall condition, I'm concerned about complications during the procedure. It's likely we could encounter additional problems, and he's at high risk for bleeding. I think everything will be fine but I need you to understand the gravity of his situation." He sat forward, lifted the manila folder, and tapped its edge on the desk. "Do you have any questions for me?"

Lydia rubbed the end of her pen along her bottom lip, thinking. "No, I don't think so."

"All right." He stood, reached to shake her hand, and was gone without a goodbye.

***

The house smelled musty when she entered and disabled the security system. It wasn't the sweet lake-mingled mustiness of the lodge. This was dank, sour, a tinge of sweat, the smell of a house sealed off from life outside it. She flung open blinds and windows, not caring about the heat. The rooms weren't particularly cluttered or dirty, but they weren't exactly clean. She checked the refrigerator and dumped wilted and spoiled food into the trash. With a glass of ice water, she sat down at the breakfast bar and picked up the home phone.

When she finished talking to James and Sara, she dialed Flo Minko's. Audra answered. "Hey! You're at the house? Everything go okay at the hospital?"

"I guess. Listen, would it be okay if I stay at your place another few nights? I don't feel like being here. At least, not until the kids arrive."

"Mi casa, su casa. You've got the key. I'm off at six. What say we go someplace for a bite after? I don't feel like cooking and doubt you do either. And you can fill me in on everything then."

As she went around closing the windows against the stifling air, Lydia saved their bedroom for last. From the closet, she folded a small pile of clothes onto the bed—her lake clothes were too warm for Tampa in June. In her office she returned the unused cash from her tote to its hiding place, glad to have it locked away and relieved that she no longer needed it. For now. She tossed the extra cell phone in too, not needing that either, and the thumb drive of files she hadn't mailed. Pushing the box back into place, a realization struck. This money of hers would be considered a marital asset. She hadn't disclosed it, it hadn't even crossed her mind, when she filled out the attorney's financials. She shut the closet door, gathered up her summer clothes, and went out to her car.

On the way to dinner, Audra did her the favor of chattering on about local news and the usual customer frustrations, asking Lydia nothing about Gil until the waiter left with their dinner orders and they were alone with their wine at the patio table. Audra reached for a cigarette and, as the lighter snapped off, said, "Okay, diversionary tactics over. What happened today? What did the doctor say?"

Lydia stared at the cars and people passing on the street and sidewalk. Weariness settled on her like a blanket she wished she could toss aside. She sighed. "Gil looks like crap. Like he's aged twenty years. Like he's at death's door. Which, according to the doctor, he pretty much is. And was. Dead, that is. He was dead when the EMTs got to him. If Trevor—his production manager—hadn't done CPR, they wouldn't have managed to bring him back."

"Wow." Audra's voice was soft. "I assumed it was bad but … as much as I want the guy dead for what he did to you …"

Tears filled Lydia's eyes and she reached into her purse for a tissue. "I just feel so conflicted. Like this is all my fault."

"Bullshit," Audra snapped. "He brought this on himself."

"But if I hadn't sent all that shit to everyone he does business with … I wanted to hurt him, hurt him as much as he hurt me, not kill him. The doctor said he must have had this heart condition for a long time."

"Are you serious? You never said anything."

"Because I didn't know. But now the two and two make sense. He'd complained more about being tired. And the indigestion. I told him I was worried but he insisted it was just stress about the business."

"Ha," Audra said. "More like stress from keeping his double life afloat."

Lydia ignored her. "He needs a triple bypass. The doctor hoped to do it tomorrow, but the nurse called a while ago, said they need to wait another day. So, probably Friday. He should have had it when they took him in on Monday."

"Then why didn't they operate then?"

Lydia recapped what she'd been told. "This afternoon when the doctor was back, he saw something else he didn't like. The longer they wait, the greater the likelihood he'll have another attack, or a stroke, and either could kill him. They're pretty much in a damned-if-they-do, damned-if-they-don't position. Like me—I want him dead, but I don't want him to die."

The waiter approached with cheery words and their dinner plates. They shook their heads as he asked if they were ready for more wine, and he left them with a chipper, "Enjoy." Both simply stared at their food for a moment, as if they'd forgotten what they'd ordered. Lydia pushed her plate away.

Audra reached across the table and shoved it back. "Eat," she ordered. "I am not going to let you go back to that head-hole you were in when I got up to the lake."

Lydia glared at her. "You can be such a bitch sometimes."

"Yep," Audra plucked a morsel from her plate. "Takes one to know one. Now, eat." She stared at Lydia until Lydia did, then picked up her own fork and asked, "What have you told your kids?"

"Most everything." In between bites, Lydia shared the conversations. "They're not too happy with me," she concluded, "because I told them not to come yet. There's no reason to. There's nothing they can do, and they can't see him. And I really don't need them around to worry about on top of everything else, or have them hovering over me. Plus, I'm not ready to sleep in our bedroom again. Not yet."

"By the way, did Gil say anything about your hair?"

Lydia's fork stabbed a piece of meat. "Hell no. He never noticed it when I changed it in all the years we've been together. Why would he now?"

***

The bedside alarm went off. She didn't open her eyes as she reached out to slap the snooze button. She'd give herself ten more minutes before getting up and ready for work. But her hand slapped flatness, not the clock radio beside her bed. The alarm went off again. But it didn't sound like her alarm clock. It was her phone. Her body jolted up, her groggy mind trying to come to. Enough dawn light filtered through the blinds for her to remember that she was at Audra's, she wasn't going to her job. The phone was on the dresser. She managed to answer before it went to voicemail. Its clock said it wasn't yet four-thirty.

"Ms. Casselberry, Sharice Johnson, CICU night charge nurse. I'm sorry to wake you." The woman's voice was subdued. "Mr. Carson is being prepped for surgery. Dr. Androvsky wanted you to be notified."

"Now? Why?" Alert now, Lydia sat down on the edge of the bed. "Yesterday I was told it would be tomorrow."

"I'm afraid your husband took a downturn last night. The doctor came to check on him a few minutes ago before making rounds, and determined immediate surgery is required."

"When can I see him?"

"Not until he's moved back from recovery."

"No, I mean the doctor."

There was a pause, and Lydia thought she read the woman's unspoken question about her answer. "After the surgery. He'll meet you in the OR waiting room. As soon as you arrive, check in with the staff, and if there are any updates during surgery they'll let you know."

"What time will they start surgery?"

"Eight. Dr. A expects to be done before noon. Barring the unexpected."

Now it was Lydia who paused: "the unexpected." She wanted him dead; she didn't want him dead, she loved him, she hated him, singsonging in her thoughts.

"Ms. Casselberry?"

"I'll be there by then. If I need to be reached sooner, this is my cell, so I can be called or texted."

"All right. I'm sorry to have to start your day with this. I know it's cause for concern, but Dr. A is one of our best, and I'm sure everything will go well in his hands."

Lydia moved through the silent, darkened house to the kitchen and turned on the coffee maker. While it burbled, she used the bathroom and brushed her teeth. As quietly as possible, she opened the door to take her coffee outside. The air was not quite cool, already promising a sauna-like day ahead. Sometimes she loved the humidity, found it caressing. This would be one of the days, she could tell, when she felt it wanted to smother her. She concentrated on the sound of the waterfall in Audra's pond, and thought about the lake.

"Hey, girl. What're you doing up?"

Audra's still-sleepy voice pulled Lydia back. "Oh, I'm sorry I woke you."

"You didn't. My bladder did. I saw the kitchen light on, and the door open."

"The hospital called. Gil's going into surgery."

"Oh man. I thought you said—"

"Something happened. Apparently he took a turn for the worse last night. When the doctor saw him this morning, he ordered surgery asap."

"You going to see him before he goes under?"

Lydia shook her head. "I'll go later. They're already prepping him. And what would I say to him—good luck, or die, you bastard?"

Audra snorted a laugh. "Sorry. I'm going back to bed."

By the time Audra reappeared an hour and a half later, Lydia had showered, dressed, and was eating toast while reading the news online. She poured coffee and handed the mug to her friend, saying, "Fresh pot." Music from the local community radio station filled the kitchen along with the morning light. She glanced at the clock. Gil would be under the knife soon.

"Have you called James and Sara?"

"Not yet. I will after the surgery. If I tell them now they'd be here this afternoon, knowing them. This way, I can tell them what happens. It'll be easier on them. And on me."

"How soon are you going to the hospital?"

"In a couple of hours. No sense my sitting in a stuffy little room with a bunch of other worried people. I've got enough worries of my own. What time do you have to be at the store?"

"Not till ten. I'll be there till eight. Think you'll be back by then?"

"I intend to. If anything changes, I'll let you know."

"Mind if I turn on the morning news?" Lydia turned off the radio and Audra pressed the TV remote, then hit the mute button. "Ugh, Tammy's World," Audra grumbled. "Some people are just too spunky to tolerate this early."

At their cars later, the women hugged before driving off, Audra toward Ybor City, Lydia to her house. It was still tomb-like, silent, whatever life force that had infused it with her, Gil, and their marriage nearly dissipated. It was now a home where death hovered.

She pushed the radio button for the classical radio station and turned the volume up, way up. The "Adagio for Strings" was playing—she hadn't heard it in years, and now twice in less than a week. She smiled at her memory of the evening with Max, and questions and thoughts about him occupied her as she readied Sara's and James's rooms. After making a short list of groceries, she sorted through the accumulation of mail she had ignored the day before. Some she set aside to take to Gil's office, others were bills she'd take care of. The rest she tossed in the recycling basket that held a stack of dead papers on the way to their next life.

Next life, Lydia pondered, as she left for the hospital. None of us ever knows what's to come, even if we think we do.

The waiting room TV was on. An elderly man sat in front of it, staring at the screen. Two women, one middle-aged and the other younger, sat side by side along the back wall, and the younger one leaned over to say something to the older one as she pointed to a magazine page. Lydia picked up the room phone and gave the person who answered her name and her husband's, then took a seat and opened her book.

At first she didn't notice the time, glancing up only when doctors stepped in to speak to the women and then the man, each relieved at what they were told, all relieved to be released from the purgatory of suspension. She too felt suspended, glad to be distracted by the mystery of the past on the pages she read. But after another hour in the empty room, the present intruded. Her phone clock showed it was well past the time the surgery should have concluded. Another half-hour passed. She picked up the room phone again, but there was still no update from OR. This wasn't, she knew, a case of no news being good news. Unable to read any more, she paced the small space, wishing there were a window so she could at least see outside, not feel so trapped, her life once again suspended by Gil.

The wall phone rang, causing her to jump, and rang again before she reached it. "Yes? Hello?"

"Is this Ms. Casselberry?"

"Yes."

"Your husband is out of surgery. Dr. Androvsky will see you as soon as he's scrubbed up."

"Did everything go okay? Why did it take so long?"

"I'm sorry, that's all Dr. Androvsky said. He'll tell you more. Your husband is in recovery."

Lydia hung up the phone. Recovery—he had survived. Relief, disappointment, and anger all swept through her with the force of a dam bursting, waters raging for dominance. She paced, wanting to run. To Gil's side. Away again, as far as she could get. Back to the woman who had loved her husband in that all-consuming, unfathomable way the word love can never express. Away, to escape the responsibilities she was now burdened with. Her jaw clenched so hard her teeth hurt, and she paced.

Through the screaming in her mind she heard the turn of the door handle. "Good news." Androvsky's voice was soft, yet still forceful. His OR mask hung like a baby's bib at the neck of his operating greens. Lydia lowered herself into a chair as he continued. "We did encounter complications, but nothing we weren't prepared for."

Androvsky sat down like a man who'd been on his feet for too long, stretching his legs in the air and pedaling his feet, then crossing his ankles and relaxing. He was a good communicator, Lydia thought as she listened—he assumed her ability to understand the medical terminology just as easily as the layman's terms that wove through his explanation. "Still, your husband is not out of the woods yet. The next twenty-four to forty-eight hours are crucial. Because we hadn't eradicated the infection before surgery, and because of the complications, he'll be heavily sedated. If you want to see him in recovery—for a moment," he stressed, "we can mask and gown you. Then you can come back again this evening after six. He'll be in the surgical ICU, and aware by then."

Lydia had been alternating looking into Androvsky's eyes and staring at the wall behind him as he spoke. She looked at him now and shook her head. "No. I'll wait to see him later. I need to go … to get out of here," she stammered. "Tomorrow. I'll see him tomorrow. I have to call our son and daughter. They don't know …"

Androvsky nodded and stood, and Lydia did too. "Of course. Assure them that their father is fine. They won't be able to visit until the forty-eight hours has passed. We'll talk again tomorrow."

Lydia shook his hand. "Thank you."

She sat back down for a moment, thinking over Androvsky's words. When she picked up her purse and book, she was tired. Drained by the tension of waiting. Burdened by the conflict of emotions swirling inside her. She needed to be outside, outside in the air. The channel—that's where she'd go. She'd find a place to sit, to watch boats pass, to think. She needed to be away from people. Head down, she ignored everyone who passed in the hall, growing more irritated with every moment. She cursed the slow-moving elevator, and cursed the claustrophobia in its too-crowded space. She cursed the long, long, *long* walk to get outside. When the sliding glass door shut behind her she stopped short and cursed again. Blackened giants of clouds filled the eastern sky, slashed by bolts of lightning, the goddesses Astrape and Bronte on the verge of unleashing a full-blown tantrum on all below. She knew that by the time she left the parking garage the rain would be blinding. She loved the intense summer storms, watching the clouds create shape-shifting mountains above the flat land, the humbling sense of privilege at being safe and dry while the furious wind and rain lashed everything in its path. *But the damned timing!* she thought. She wasn't going to drive in what was about to come. She was stuck, again, damn it, and would have to wait it out in the lobby. She turned and stomped back inside.

In the hallway to the main entrance, she passed another exit door as a group of young hospital workers came in with fast food bags and drinks. It was then she remembered something she had glimpsed the day before—a covered courtyard next to a Mickey D's. It seemed incongruous to offer unhealthy fast food at a place where people came to regain their health. She veered through the door they'd entered, bought a coffee, and took a table in the courtyard where she'd be protected from the coming rain. There was no view of nature, which she desperately needed, here where buildings hemmed her in, but at least she could see sky. She popped the lid off the cup to let the coffee cool, then reached for her phone and dialed James.

He answered on the first ring, his voice worried. "Mom? Is Dad okay? You were going to call this morning. Why didn't you?"

"Your dad's okay but things changed overnight. Now take a deep breath, and listen." She could see him, his hand rubbing his forehead in agitation. "I just left the doctor. They had to do surgery this morning. Your dad's in recovery right now. The doctor decided it couldn't wait until tomorrow. It took a lot longer than expected but, considering, he said it went well. The next forty-eight hours are critical, though." A deafening thunderclap erupted, and hard-driving rain blasted the roof above.

"Holy cow, what was that? Are you there?"

"Thunder. And rain." Lydia spoke loudly. "I'm outside the hospital. Will you call your sister? The two of you make plans to come down Saturday." She paused and covered the speaker as another roar of thunder blasted overhead. "If everything is okay, you should be able to see him then." Another explosion went off above her. "Listen, we'll talk more later. Call your sister, okay? I love you."

"I love you, too. And tell dad I love him too?"

"Bye, honey," Lydia practically shouted. She still wasn't ready to say the word love to Gil, not even for her son.

The storm had passed by the time she finished her coffee, and the windshield needed no more than the intermittent wipers as she drove off. The rain had ended by the time she swung into a grocery store parking lot—she'd fix a dinner for Audra, and make enough to put in the freezer as a thank-you for taking her in. Cook, that's what she needed to do now, to Zen out in Audra's kitchen.

As the blade of the chef's knife slashed through a bell pepper, she envisioned it slashing through Gil's chest. She wanted to cut his heart out, the way he'd cut out hers. Her face tightened as the blade moved faster, chopping, chopping, chopping too close to her fingers. She jumped when it nicked the tip of a fingernail. Shaken, she walked away from the counter.

Fixing a drink, the tears came—a cocktail of anger, relief, fear, and exhaustion. She took the glass out to the deck's shade. The storm-cleared air was thick and humid, but at least a bit cooler. She sat for a long time, empty, depleted, as her mind cleared from its own storm, before going back to work. When the kitchen was cleaned and dinner was ready for finishing later, she flicked on the TV. The local news was well underway.

The realization of the time made her hit the mute button and hurry for her phone. She should have called Gil's office. She'd told Trevor she'd let them know if anything changed, and she'd forgotten. There were several rings before Alisha's voice came on, not in person but on a recorded greeting. Two flashes went through Lydia's mind: *They're gone; thank god I don't have to hear how wonderful, what a miracle it was that her prayer circle worked.* Her attention returned to the message as staff extensions were listed. She tapped in Trevor's, prepared to leave a voicemail. He answered, surprising her. "Trevor, it's Lydia. Lydia Casselberry."

"Hey, good to hear from you. How's Gil?" His voice was tired.

"He took a turn last night. They had to do surgery this morning. It went okay. I haven't seen him, and won't know more until tomorrow."

"Wow." There was a stretch of silence.

"Trevor, what's going on over there?" When he didn't answer, she pressed. "All Gil told me is something happened that put him under a lot of stress. You must know something."

He exhaled audibly. "I honest to god don't, and that's got me pretty damned stressed out too. All I know is some shit hit the fan—sorry, I'm just really tired—something bad started about a week ago and the phone rang nonstop for days. Clients are bailing. Vendors either won't take my calls or badger me with questions I can't answer. Everyone around here is tense, and they don't know half of what I do. Which is basically nothing. And I only found out what I do know because, after the EMTs took him, I knew I'd better deal with his email. To clear his schedule." He paused. "Either my boss is more fucked up than I ever knew or somebody's seriously fucking with this agency." He paused again. "Sorry. I need to watch my mouth."

"What do you mean?" Lydia hoped her tone conveyed wifely, concerned surprise. She listened to what he told her, noting what he glossed over or omitted, either because he was unaware or shielding her from what he thought she didn't need to hear. "So you have no idea how or why all this happened?"

"None. I mean, we didn't tank any jobs. At least, not that I know of. We've been doing good work. The clients were all happy. Gil's been steadily signing more. Everything was actually improving. In fact, last month he told me to start looking for another designer and a copywriter, plus an assistant for myself because of the workload. Two months ago he gave me a raise and promoted me to VP. Now we're going under and I don't know if I should tell everybody to find new jobs. I don't know if I can keep the doors open past tomorrow."

She hadn't wanted to hurt anyone other than Gil. Again, guilt stabbed her. Be honest, her mind snapped at her, you knew damn well this could happen. "Trevor, do you think you could run the agency?"

He sighed. "Yeah. Pretty much. Ninety percent of it, I guess. But I'm not authorized to make payments, not even payroll. Which is due tomorrow. And I've no clue what to do about whatever mess we've got with these clients."

"Well, if nothing else, I think you should contact them all."

"And tell them what?"

"That Gil has had major heart surgery, and he will be out indefinitely. That as VP, you are now in charge. That you've only now become aware of an apparent computer hack that compromised their relationship with Gil. That whatever it was, it was separate from the agency's work. That you hope you'll be able to repair what's happened." She stopped, and when he said nothing she went on. "It won't be easy, but it's the truth. I am now putting you in charge, authorizing you to do whatever you need to save your jobs. Including arranging bank authorization to get you added to the accounts."

There was weariness in his voice when he did speak. "You can get Gil to do that?"

"I don't need to. Gil is currently incapacitated, and I have his power of attorney. It's my decision."

"Wow. Are you sure?"

"What's the alternative? Lock up and tell everyone they're fired? You've been Gil's right hand since day one. You can do this. It won't be easy," she repeated. "Do it for the others, for yourself. For the agency." She couldn't bring herself to say, "... and for Gil." She laughed slightly. "God, I sound like a locker room coach. From what little you and Gil have told me, it's possible it could be some sort of a hack." She stopped, then feigned concern. "Wait. Did they get into the bank accounts?"

"No. I don't think so. As soon as I got the gist of something being up, I contacted the bank and credit cards. Everything is okay. So far. I did put a freeze on all the accounts, except the one I use in case of emergency."

"That's another reason we need to get your name on the accounts. You need to monitor things, just in case." Red meat dropped along a diversionary path, one she wanted to lead away from her. "So call the bank first thing in the morning, set up an appointment for us, and text me what time and where. But now, you go home. Start thinking about what needs to be done. Just don't do it at the office. It'll help you get a fresh perspective. And get some sleep tonight."

"Yes, *boss*." She could hear the smile in his voice.

Over their late dinner, she and Audra exchanged news of their day. Afterward, Audra had shipment orders to check on the computer, so Lydia carried her wine glass out to the deck and phoned Sara. Though James had relayed everything he'd been told, Sara asked all the questions over again and was frustrated that Lydia did not know more. "I want to come tomorrow," Sara insisted. "I want to see Daddy."

"I know." Lydia sighed, then tried to soothe. "But you can't, not until Saturday at least. That's why I told James you should fly in then." Sara cajoled, entreating to come sooner, but Lydia remained adamant.

When their call ended, the front she had put up for her daughter crumbled. The weight of all that had happened that day pressed on her like layers of lead aprons in the dentist's chair. For some time she sat, unable to move, staring into the night.

There were no stars.

Chapter 17

In the morning, she and Audra drifted or rushed past each other as they each prepared to leave. A text pinged as Lydia walked toward the hospital from the parking garage. Trevor had set the bank appointment for ten-thirty. That gave her an hour before she'd have to head out. At the nurses' station on the surgical CICU, she introduced herself to the charge nurse.

"Your husband had a good night. The doctor saw him earlier and won't be back till afternoon rounds. He's still heavily sedated, so he's very groggy, but you can see him. We do have to gown and mask you after you scrub, because of the infection."

When she entered his room, machines crowded the space around Gil's bed. A visitor's chair was shoved into a corner, blocked by the equipment. Lydia stood at the foot of the bed and looked at Gil, laid out as still as a corpse. The shallow rise and fall of his chest and the rising, falling lines on machine screens were all that proved otherwise. She said his name, once. He didn't respond. It was obvious he was too far under, that she didn't need to be here. At the front desk she told the nurse she'd be back in the afternoon, to please let Gil know when he woke.

She sat, pondering what to do next, before starting the car. It was too soon to go to the bank. There wasn't enough time, or any reason, to go by her house or to Audra's. She turned the ignition. Flo Minko's. It was near the bank branch where she was to meet Trevor. She had time to look at Ned's prints, choose one to buy.

As Lydia entered the store, Audra called out a cheerful, "Good morning." When she turned and recognized Lydia, she frowned. "What are you doing here?"

"Gee, is that how you greet all your customers? Nice to see you too."

"I just saw you. An hour ago. I thought you were at the hospital."

"I was. He's totally out of it. I wasn't going to stand there and watch him sleep."

"So he's okay? How's he look?"

"He's okay so far, from what I was told. His color's better than last time I saw him. But, Jesus, he looks old. Like he's got 10 years on your friend Maury."

"Whoa. Not good."

"Anyway, I'm meeting Gil's VP at the bank in a while. Thought I'd come by, maybe pick out one of Ned's prints. And I *am* paying retail." Audra had been right—the print display grabbed attention the minute anyone entered. Lydia moved toward it. Woodland scenes depicted the seasons. There was none with a lake.

"Well, you know how to ruin a surprise."

Lydia looked over her shoulder at Audra. "What?"

"A shipment from Ned arrived. He emailed me—I saw it last night—and said there's something in it for you. I was going to open the box later and bring whatever's in it to you tonight. So let's go do that now."

Lydia followed Audra into the storeroom. Audra shuffled a large box on the floor to an open space, and carefully sliced a knife through the sealing tape. Inside were two or three dozen prints standing on edge, each separated by heavy tissue paper. Audra pulled them from the box in groups and stacked them against a leg of a worktable. The last one was thicker than the others, and completely wrapped. A label sealing the tissue had "Elle" scrawled on it. Audra pushed aside table clutter and laid it there. "His email said you have to open it. But we had to be together when you did."

Puzzled, Lydia glanced at Audra, who raised her hands, palms up. "Seriously. I have no clue. Open it, will you?"

Lydia peeled away the label and folded back the paper. Audra leaned in, whispering, "Oh. My. God."

It wasn't a print; it was an original framed watercolor. Of the lake, and the lodge. Tears sprang to Lydia's eyes.

"Oh, my god, look." Audra jutted a finger at the porch. "Is that us? That's us! It *is*. Who ever thought we'd be in a painting?" In fact, it was the four of them on the evening they'd spent together—Ned seated with his guitar, Max in his battered brown leather hat, and Audra gesturing with a cigarette from the porch swing. Lydia was standing, turned sideways from the others, leaning against a porch column with her arms folded across her waist and staring out at the lake. She knew she hadn't done that that night, yet he'd captured perfectly the separateness she had felt.

"This is unbelievable," Lydia whispered, staring at it. "And you had no idea?"

"None. But now something makes sense. When you were in the kitchen with Max that night, Ned took a bunch of pictures on his phone. But I didn't know he was going to do this."

Lydia lifted the painting to hold at an angle. Beneath it, what they thought was a backboard revealed another copy, a print, unframed but matted. Tucked into a corner was a scrawled note: *One for you too, Aud. Something to remember me by.*

Lydia looked at her friend with a grin. "'Aud'? Seems like things are getting chummy between you two." She turned back to the picture. "Boy, he sure flattered us."

"Speak for yourself. I always look that good."

"Ha. You wish." Lydia bumped her shoulder against Audra's, laughter lilting from them both. It felt good to laugh, Lydia thought, realizing she hadn't since her dinner with Max.

The store's back door opened and the young man Lydia had seen the day she'd left town came in with two coffees. "Sorry I'm late. Had to wait on a fresh pot. Frankie's is slammed for some reason."

"No problem," Audra said. "Jake, this is my friend Lydia."

He smiled and nodded, setting the coffee too close to the pictures for Lydia's comfort. "Here, you can have one of these. I'll go back for one later."

"Oh no, thanks. I'm not here to visit." She pulled her phone from her purse to check the time. "In fact, I've got to go."

Audra was re-wrapping Ned's gifts. "I'll bring these home tonight. Jake, would you take these up to my office? And be extra careful."

As he carried the pictures upstairs, Audra walked Lydia to the front door and gave her a hug. "Good luck with the rest of the day. I'll be home around six-thirty. If you're there, you're there. If you're not, I won't worry. Too much."

Walking the two blocks to the bank, the mid-morning heat seared Lydia's skin, making her already dread the walk back to her car. Inside the first set of doors, a bath of chilled air washed over her. She stopped a second to drink it in, and tousled her hair off the back of her neck, enjoying the cool against its dampness. Opening the second set of doors, she noticed Trevor, standing, staring at his phone screen. When she spoke his name, he glanced up and smiled. She smiled in return as she shook his hand.

"Nice to see you again," he said. "Sorry all this happened, that you had to cut your beach trip short."

"Beach trip?"

"Yeah. Gil said you were up in the Panhandle for a while with girlfriends. Sorry this interrupted your fun."

Fun, Lydia thought, *and more lies*. She scanned the bank lobby and offices, choosing not to answer him. Everyone was busy with customers. "Looks like it'll be a few minutes," she said. "We may as well sit. So, did you get any rest last night?"

"Some. A bit more than in the past few days. But I'm still pretty fried. How is he? Did you tell him about doing this?"

Lydia shook her head. "He was still out when I went up this morning. He's doing about as well as can be expected."

A woman about Trevor's age, in her early forties, walked up, introduced herself as the bank manager, and invited them to her office. As Lydia followed, she thought back to when being forty-something felt on the cusp of getting old—how young it now seemed.

The paperwork took quite a while, first because of the manager's questions, then because of her scrutinizing the accounts and verification of Lydia's power of attorney. There were multiple forms to sign, copies to print. An hour later, the woman shook their hands and wished Lydia's husband a speedy recovery.

Outside, under the shade of the door awning, Trevor grasped Lydia's hand. "I want to thank you. I don't know if I can turn things around, but I'm going to do my damnedest. Gil did his through the recession, and I owe it to him. I know I'm not the man he is, and don't know if I can. At least now we can get paid while I try. Thank you."

"I wouldn't have done it if I didn't think you had a chance. Whatever happened was not of your doing. Listen, can I buy you lunch? A burger all the way and Frankie's onion rings sound pretty good to me right now."

"Thanks, but no. I want to get back, tell them the news. *And* release our paychecks. Knowing they have jobs next week is going to be a huge relief to everyone."

On impulse, she reached out and hugged Trevor. "You can do this. I have faith in you." Stepping back, she added, "Just concentrate on the clients. It sounds like whatever happened has calmed down, so don't waste time on that. You've got too much else to focus on."

He gave a heavy sigh. "Boy, that's the truth. Tell Gil we're all thinking of him. And to call me when he's up to it, okay?" He turned toward the parking lot, and Lydia set out for her car.

She swung the car door open wide, staying behind it as a shield from the blast of heat that spewed out. She'd been lucky enough to park under a bit of shade, but the seat still stung through her slacks as she turned the ignition, rolled down her window, and cranked the air conditioner fan to high. More heat blasted from the vents. She sat waiting, wondering. Contrary to what she'd said to Trevor, she wasn't hungry. She also had no appetite for going back to the hospital. Not yet. Androvsky wouldn't be back until after three, and she wasn't about to sit with Gil until then. Cool air began to flow around her. She rolled up the window, put the car in gear, and headed to the grocery near her house. With the kids coming, she might as well replenish the fridge.

Gil was awake and alert when she returned to his room. He looked at her appreciatively. He clucked his tongue, then said, "That's how you dress when your man is taking you out to shake some bones?"

She smiled, but it was a rueful one. That stinking charm of his. It was what had made her fall in love with him in the first place. She didn't love him now—no, she wasn't *in* love with him now—but he had lived, and she didn't see how she could abandon him, at least until he'd recovered. "You," she said, "are lucky your bones aren't rattling in a coffin."

"So I hear tell. I don't remember any of it." He lay his head back and looked at the ceiling. "Last I remember is that guy showing up in my office on Monday. Nurse told me it's Friday. Weird." His eyes turned to her, leaning against the wall by the door. "When did you get back?"

"I was here Wednesday. We talked. You don't remember?" He shook his head. "I came by this morning but you were asleep. So I left to do some business"—she wasn't going to tell him what—"and picked up some groceries. The kids will be here tomorrow."

Their conversation meandered, stumbled almost, as if between two strangers forced side by side at a banquet table. Gil said nothing about what had happened the previous week, and didn't mention the divorce papers. Lydia wasn't ready to tell him she was calling the lawyer Monday, to put things on hold—for now.

When Dr. Androvsky arrived, his visit was short, perfunctory. Gil was doing well; barring any further complications, he'd be moved out of surgical CICU on Sunday, and then transferred to cardiac rehab, likely within a week. Did either of them have any questions? No? Then he'd see Gil again in the morning.

Silence hung in his wake, only the soft sound of machines in the room. "Well, I suppose I'll go," Lydia said. "I know the kids will be glad to see you."

"Sorry to interrupt." A nurse was at the door. "Mr. Carson, there's a phone call. Do you feel up to taking it? It's Elle, from your office."

Lydia's head snapped around. "Alisha?" she asked.

"No, she said her name was Elle."

Elle? Someone who worked for him had the name she'd used at the lake? And why would anyone from the office call? They knew by now that Trevor was in charge. She looked at Gil, who didn't look at her.

"Uh, no," Gil said. "Tell her I'll talk to her—to them—later. By the way, when can I get my phone back?"

"Your wife can bring it in for you next time she comes," the nurse said, and was gone.

Elle, Lydia thought again. It seemed Trevor had mentioned all of the employees' names while they were at the bank, and none was an Elle. She bit her top lip, hard, as the irony of the realization struck her. Elle—short for Marielle. The audacity of that bitch.

And Gil, she saw, knew full well who was calling. That's why he wanted his phone back. With one fiery glance at him, she turned and left without a word.

***

Lydia was in no hurry to return the next morning. While her bed sheets laundered, she packed and did some housework for Audra. At her own house she unpacked, and set Ned's lake painting in various places until she found one she liked, where she could notice it from several vantage points. She stood and stared at it before she left, Paul Simon's words again undulating across her mind like a plane's banner: "Michigan seems like a dream to me now ... It took me four days to hitchhike from Saginaw ..." It had been four days since her return to Tampa, and the lake seemed like another lifetime. She put on her sunglasses and locked the door behind her.

"Well, look who's here," Gil said. "My sleepy headed wife." A nurse was in the room, and smiled at her as Gil spoke. "Guess she was jealous of me lolling in bed and decided to do the same. You look nice this morning," he told her.

She didn't respond. The nurse did, first telling Gil he was to finish the rest of his lunch, then turning to Lydia on her way out. "Good news. Dr. Androvsky confirmed your husband can leave SCICU tomorrow."

"You do look nice today," Gil repeated. "What time do the kids get in?"

"Jim texted. He's at the airport. Waiting on Sara. She should be landing soon."

Gil frowned. "You mad at me? Did I do something? What?"

Did you do something? she wanted to scream. "No."

"Okay, if you say so. Say, did you bring my phone?"

It was in the bottom of her purse, where it had been since she'd picked up his personal belongings. "Sorry. Forgot it."

He pressed his head back against the pillow. "Damn it. I really need to call the office."

"There's no one there. It's Saturday."

"Shit," he said under his breath. "I keep forgetting I've lost a whole fucking week."

"Be glad you didn't lose your life," she said, finishing the sentence in her mind: the way I've lost mine.

He rolled the lunch tray over the bed. Neither of them spoke. While he ate, Lydia stared through the glass wall, watching the quiet comings and goings around the unit.

Time dragged. Neither had much to say. Gil asked an occasional question, talked a bit about getting out of the hospital, getting back to work, he hoped it wouldn't be long, the office was in a bind. *In a bind*, Lydia thought, *interesting way to put it.*

Her phone pinged. She reached for it and looked at the screen. "The kids are on their way up. I'll go out and meet them. I'll see you tomorrow."

"You're not coming back in with them?"

"No. Only two visitors allowed at a time."

"Oh, right. Remember to bring my phone. I really need it."

I'll bet you do, she thought as she walked away.

Lydia was at the elevator by the time its doors opened. Sara and James spilled out as rapidly as their greetings, and it felt so good to feel her children's hugs. Sara pulled back with a grin. "I *love* your hair. It looks so good. You look *much* less Republican. You ought to keep it that way. Makes you look like a totally different woman."

"Save it, Sare," James said. "Where's Dad's room? How is he?"

A handful of people could be seen inside the SCICU waiting room. Lydia walked past it, preferring to keep their talk private. She told Sara and James everything she could—the details of the heart attack, the surgery, and his condition, all the things she had kept from them on the phone. Both of them were visibly shaken.

"But he is well enough to be moved to a regular room tomorrow? They're sure?" James demanded.

"Yes. Now go in and see him." She pointed at their carry-on bags. "Let me take these. I'll wait for you in the food court."

James flashed a glance at his watch. "We want to stay as long as we can. Until either he or they kick us out. Why don't you go on home? Maybe get some rest. You look like you could use it." At Sara's elbow jab to his side, he barked. "Ouch. She does—what's wrong with that?"

"No squabbling." Lydia leaned forward to kiss each of them on the cheek. "Now go on in. I'll see you at home later."

***

The house seemed to express displeasure at being disturbed when she entered. So different from the emptiness of the lodge, which seemed anticipatory, dog-eager to see whoever was coming in the door. Rolling the kids' bags to their rooms and then unpacking the last of what she'd taken to Audra's, she hoped the house would feel different, perhaps more like home, with all three of them in it. On her way to the kitchen her eye caught Ned's painting of the lodge. She decided she wasn't ready for Sara and James to see it yet or to explain, and carried it to her bedroom.

As she prepped dinner, she turned on the community radio station, hoping some lively music would help. But even that didn't dispel the deadness of the house. She became aware that it had been creeping in for years, so slowly that she hadn't noticed it. She wished she could open every window and let cool lake air in to vanquish it. Yet death could not be vanquished, and there was no lake, and it was stifling hot outside. The house felt like a tomb.

The kids showed up around six, weary from travel and the emotion of seeing their father. She sent them off to freshen up and unpack, and had drinks waiting to carry out to the shaded deck. There, and over dinner, they talked of inconsequential things. Lydia was fully aware of the elephant in the room. Out on the deck again later with a nightcap, after darkness had fallen as suddenly as a final curtain, she took it by the tusks. "I told your father I'll withdraw the divorce. Or at least postpone it for now."

Hours later, lying in bed, she played it all back. Their visible relief. She'd expected that. She wasn't surprised that Sara had gushed on about how that would help her daddy recover, how awful the divorce had made her feel, how their marriage had always been so *good*, how whatever had happened could be worked out, couldn't it? How, as soon as her daddy was out of rehab, she'd be down from Chicago as often as possible to help care for him. The brush of the evening breeze touched Lydia's neck then—a touch of death again poking, mocking her.

James, however, launched into full professional mode, grilling her like the estate attorney he was. He insisted on going into Gil's office, where they dug through files for paperwork he wanted to review. When he sat down at the desk to work, it struck Lydia how alike, yet unlike, his father he was. It struck her how well she knew her son and yet now, how little. "I'll bring you another drink," she said. "Then I'm going to bed soon. I'm tired."

Her body was exhausted but her mind would not shut up. While James had been satisfied with many of her answers about finances and insurance, it became apparent there was still a lot to be done. Not including preparing for Gil's return home. Not including what that meant for her job—the next semester was now six weeks off. She pushed that thought aside. What she couldn't push away was the choking sensation that came with the thought of having to care for Gil, nursing him back to health. After all he'd done to her. She rolled over and jammed another pillow under her head. *Tammy Wynette be damned*, she thought, *and damn me for standing by my man.*

Coffee was ready and breakfast set out by the time Sara, and then James, rose. He said he'd worked until about two and had more questions but they'd wait. Both were in a bit of a hurry to get back to the hospital. They each had afternoon flights and wanted more time with Gil first. At the door, she handed James her car keys. "Wait. One more thing," he said. "His phone. Dad wants me to bring it."

Ah yes, the damned phone. She retrieved it.

***

Gil was talking on it when she walked into his semi-private room on the cardio rehab floor late that afternoon, and she nodded to the man in the bed nearest the door. Gil's voice sounded tired, but was smooth, and then something feral passed across his eyes when he saw her. "Uh, gotta go. Visitor… No, they're on their way home. My wife's here … Yeah, sounds good. Talk to you tomorrow." He laid the phone face down on the bed and rested back on the pillows.

Lydia sat down on a gray, utilitarian chair and crossed her legs. "Nice digs."

"Right up there with the St. Regis." The bland beige walls did nothing to enhance Gil's appearance or of the man in the other bed, making them grayish shadows like those cast through the window.

"When did you get here? I went upstairs first. I didn't know they'd moved you."

"They moved me soon after the kids left. They get off okay?"

"Far as I know. They'll text us both. More to check up, I'm sure, than check in. Sorry to have interrupted your call. Who were you talking to?" She tried to keep accusation out of her voice.

"Oh, Trevor. I wanted to check in, see if he needed anything."

"He's got everything under control?"

"Seems so. Might bring some stuff in for me this week."

Lydia crossed her arms and leaned back. "I see." The foot of her crossed leg tapped the air.

"Look, you don't have to be here if you don't want," Gil said. "Why don't you just go. I'm tired and you look pissed."

"Sorry. I'm tired too." Lydia stood and shouldered her purse. In her head she added, Tired of all you've put me through.

"Yeah … Well, come back tomorrow. Maybe we'll both be in a better mood. And bring my laptop? I'd like to get a little work done if the Nurse Ratchets here will let me."

Lydia noticed but ignored the look of curiosity on the other man's face on her way to the door.

***

Morning coffee was brewing and Lydia was coming out of the bathroom when her phone rang. It was too early for calls. But not too early if something had happened at the hospital. Should she hope, or worry? She grabbed the phone off the kitchen counter and flipped it over. Trevor's name was on the screen. She answered it without a hello. "What did you do, sleep at your desk all weekend? We don't need you having a heart attack too."

"Nope. But I hope you slept better than I did. I didn't wake you, did I?"

Lydia put the phone on speaker so she could pour her coffee. "No. What's up?"

"I got in about an hour ago and remembered, again, that Gil's car is still in the parking garage. I totally forgot to ask you to bring the keys on Friday so we could get it back to your house. I didn't want to bother you over the weekend, with your family in town."

"Thanks. I'd forgotten about it too. It's been the least of my worries. But you're right, I should get it out of there. I'll pick it up this morning. So, you okay?"

"Tired. No rest for the wicked, you know." *Oh, I don't know*, Lydia thought, as someone who was truly wicked was certainly having a rest, even if it was in the hospital. "Spent the weekend going over everything here," he said, "and it's a god-awful mess. I don't know what Gil's been doing or why, but there are client projects I knew nothing about that haven't been started. No wonder those folks are pissed. And some of the operating funds have been going into a vendor account I can't identify."

"Did you ask Gil about them?"

"No. Figured I'd better come up to speed first."

"Didn't you talk to him yesterday? I thought he said you'd called."

"No. I didn't want to do that until I cleared it with you, that he knew you'd put me in charge. Does he?"

Interesting, Lydia thought, *another lie, already another lie.*

"You still there?"

"Yes, uh, yes. I guess I misunderstood him. But no, I haven't told him yet. I plan to today, now that he's out of ICU and the kids are gone. Do I need to come in, pick up anything for him, when I'm there for his car?"

"Nope. I'm still making a list of stuff to ask him about. The more I dig, the more I answer for myself. But like I said, I'd rather wait until I know he's up to it. Tell him I say hi. We all do. Tell him we hope he gets out of there soon."

It took several minutes for the ride-share driver to wend through the parking garage before Lydia spotted Gil's SUV. It had been ages, at least a year, since she'd driven it. She drove cautiously, unused to such a large vehicle, and was extra careful taking the tight turns in the hospital garage to find a space she felt comfortable parking in.

Gil's laptop bag hung heavy on one shoulder, her purse weighing down the other, and she gripped both their straps like a hiker on expedition through the long corridors to the elevators. When she turned the last corner, a crowd was choking the passage between the two banks of four lifts. She moved in close enough to see an out-of-service notice taped to one. The floor indicator lights of the others moved slowly when they moved at all. The weight on Lydia's shoulder was growing intense before a murmur of relief whispered through the impatient group. A single rider stepped out when the doors opened, jostled by the people jockeying to get in. Before Lydia was near, the car was packed. She had no choice but to wait for the next one. She lifted the straps from her shoulder and dangled the bags in front of her, the laptop case resting on her toes. Working relief through her shoulders at least gave her something to do as others around her sighed or complained.

When the next car arrived, it too was jammed by the time she got on. Trying not to press against those behind or beside her, Lydia shuffled around to face the front. The elevator across the hall opened and its riders spilled out. A woman caught Lydia's attention, someone who looked familiar, but the doors of her car closed before she could crane her head for another look. Where did she know the woman from? Maybe she didn't. *You live long enough in South Tampa*, she thought, *you start recognizing people from passing them in the stores*. That's probably all it was. Or, as her mother used to say, it was middle age: "Middle age is when everybody you see looks like someone you think you've met before." But there was something about the woman …

“Excuse me, it’s three,” a voice called from the back. “Who pushed three?”

Lydia jolted to awareness, murmured “Sorry,” and stepped out. As the elevator doors slid shut, she stared at their blankness, still thinking about the face she’d seen, before taking a deep breath and walking to Gil’s room.

“Morning,” she said with a nod to the man in the first bed. Gil wasn’t in his. She set her bags on the chair in the corner.

“Morning.” The man’s voice was croaky. “He’s in the john. You’re his wife, right?”

Lydia nodded without looking at him, hoping he’d get the message she wasn’t interested in small talk.

“Too bad you wasn’t here five minutes ago. You just missed his sister.”

Lydia turned to look at him. He was flicking a remote through channels on the silenced TV suspended opposite his bed. “His sister?”

“’Cording to him.” The man’s eyes stayed on the TV. “Said she’d driven up from Amelia Island. Good to have family close enough but far enough. Still, pretty far drive to stay such a short time. If I made that drive, I’d’a stuck around longer.”

Lydia’s grip tightened around the bag straps. Gil didn’t have a sister. That’s who that woman was—The Slut. That’s why she’d recognized her, from the pictures she’d seen. Seething, Lydia was about to hurl the laptop onto the empty bed and leave. *No*, she thought, *screw him*. She shouldered both bags again and left the room, the floor, the hospital, to the car, her anger at their audacity growing with each stride.

The SUV’s tires screeched as she shot into traffic, and horns blared from two drivers she’d cut off. Cold rage roiled through her as she sped across the bridge from the island. Her phone was ringing again. It had begun to ring before she’d reached the parking garage. She hadn’t answered it then, and she wasn’t going to now. She knew who it was, and she was damned if she was going to talk to him. She pulled the car onto the first side street she could and slammed to a stop, her knuckles white against the dark steering wheel. Breathe, damn it, some part of her mind commanded. Breathe, and for god’s sake goddess up. Her hands dropped to her lap and her head fell back on the headrest.

The phone had kept ringing, stopping, and ringing again. She pulled it out of her purse and turned it off, then drove slowly along side streets all the way to the house, trying to figure out what to do next.

The kitchen clock read a quarter to noon. *Screw it*, she thought, and pulled a bottle of vodka from a shelf. Out on the patio, she didn't care about the heat. She squinted against the harsh brightness of mid-day. The neighborhood was silent, everyone at work, the only living things being herself and an ibis, bobble-heading for food in the neighbor's back yard. She stared at it, at its methodical, steady movement, interested in nothing more than what was before it, not angry about the tiny lizards it had missed or wondering if the bugs were better on the other side of the yard. Doing nothing but taking one step at a time.

One step at a time. She watched the bird for a long time, her drink untouched, until she knew what step that would be. She picked up her glass and went inside. In her office, she pulled down the cash box, taking out the envelope with the thumb drive and the cell phone she'd used at the lake. On the kitchen island, she opened her laptop and looked up a phone number. She dialed it. A frustratingly long, automated response came on, listing a menu of options before offering a company directory. She punched the number for that, then tapped in the first three letters of a name. She quickly dug for a pencil and paper when the auto-response announced an office extension number before routing the call.

A man answered. "Jon Wharton."

"Mr. Wharton. My name is Lydia Casselberry. We don't know each other but our spouses do. My husband is Gil Carson. You may not know—"

"I know Gil." He interrupted; his voice quiet, hesitant. "What's this about?"

"I'd like to talk to you. But not over the phone. How soon could we meet?"

"Gil Carson," he repeated. "I think I know what this is about." There was a long pause. "I'll clear some things from my calendar." Another pause. "How about two-thirty?"

"Today? Absolutely."

"But not at my office. There's a coffee shop ..." He gave her directions and agreed to meet her at a table outside.

Lydia turned her regular phone on again. Three voicemails from Gil, the first curious, the second concerned, the third angry. And a text, demanding: WTF are you? WTF happened? It took her a second to realize the first W was for where, not what. She texted back. Sick. Sudden & bad. Had to find bathroom. Home in bed. Turning the phone off again, she tossed both phones in her purse, and left the house.

Once past St. Petersburg, traffic was light until she reached Sarasota. She arrived at the coffee shop early and scoped out the patio, but the only single men were too young to be Jon Wharton. She went in to order a frozen coffee, then chose a patio table at the edge where she could watch. Not too many minutes passed before a well-dressed man about her age came out and looked around expectantly. When Lydia stood, he approached with a quizzical expression. "Mr. Wharton?" she asked.

"Yes. You're Lydia? Please, call me Jon." He set his coffee on the table, shook her hand, and removed his suit jacket before sitting down. He stared at her, pain in his eyes. "They're having an affair, aren't they? I had a feeling but couldn't prove it."

"Oh, it's more than an affair." Bitterness sparked Lydia's words. "But I'm curious. What made you think they were?"

"I wasn't certain. Either that she was cheating on me, or that it was with him. But I could tell something was up, from the way Marielle's been acting over the past couple of months. Then one day working at home I answer the phone and a man asks for her. She wasn't there, and he wouldn't leave a message. I was pretty sure it was your husband's voice, though."

"You know him?"

"We've met several times. In fact, it was Marielle who introduced us, two or three years ago, and first suggested my company should hire his agency."

Lydia gave a short rueful huff, thinking, *What a brazen bitch*. "I'm not going to sugarcoat this. They have been having an affair. For a long time. But it's a lot more than that."

As Lydia talked, he stared into his coffee cup, turning it around and around in tiny increments. She didn't tell him every detail, unable to deliver the cruel news herself. He asked a few questions, his voice quiet, his pain evident. When she finished, they sat in silence before she spoke again.

"I was going to mail this, anonymously, about a week ago." Lydia reached into her purse for the thumb drive and slid it across the table. "In fact, I was about to do that the day I got word Gil was in the hospital."

"Hospital? What happened?"

"Major heart attack. Major surgery. He's still there." She paused again. "Your wife called him while he was in cardiac intensive care. She used a different name. They didn't talk—I was there—but I knew it was her. I'm pretty sure they talked yesterday, though. Gil was on the phone when I arrived, got very nervous, and quickly hung up. But the kicker is, she was at the hospital this morning. I saw her leaving. I recognized her from pictures on that." She nodded at the thumb drive lying like a symbolic coffin between them.

He sighed and shook his head. "So, that's why she was out of the house at six. Said she had an eight a.m. meeting in Naples. She went to Tampa instead."

"I had filed for divorce," Lydia said. "His getting the papers seems to be what precipitated the heart attack. But afterward I told Gil I'd put a hold on it until he recovered. This morning I changed my mind. I'm divorcing him as soon as possible. After you see what's on the thumb drive, you'll understand why."

She stood up to leave. "I don't know what you'll decide to do with what's on there. I can't say I much care. Except you seem like a nice guy. I'm sorry about this … No, I'm not. I am sorry to hurt you, but your wife and my husband have hurt us both long enough. They deserve whatever they get. I promise I won't contact you again. I doubt you will sleep well tonight. I'm sorry about that too."

Before driving home, she used the restroom. When she tossed the paper towels into the trash, she dug the flip-phone from her purse and shoved it to the bottom of the bin.

She slept better than she had expected to, but was up long before light. By five, she had her coffee and was at work on the plans she'd thought through during the night. She packed Gil's casual clothes—he wasn't going to need his suits for weeks—and personal belongings in his luggage and two yard bags. She loaded it all into his SUV in the garage. With more coffee and the classical radio's soft sounds around her, she took care of the tasks to be done at the computer. At eight, she was on the phone. After making her calls she texted Audra, asking to meet for dinner. At nine, she was out of the house.

Gil's glassy-eyed roommate was again scrolling the soundless TV channels when she walked in. Gil stared at the window, not noticing her, and it took a moment to realize his Bluetooth was in his ear and he was listening to his phone. She planted herself at the foot of his bed and slung his computer bag onto it.

Startled, Gil gave her half-smile and pulled out the earpiece. "Hey. You're feeling better, I hope. Suppose it was something you ate?"

"No," Lydia said, thinking, *Something I saw*. "We need to talk. About after you get out. Is there someplace we can do that? In private."

"Sure. There's a common room, or the outdoor walkway. Hot as it probably is, I wouldn't mind getting outside for a bit. But they won't let me walk that far. Ask somebody to get a wheelchair."

"Sure."

The wait, short as it was, seemed interminable. Gil tried to make conversation, telling her about the podcast he'd been listening to, asking what she'd been up to, but she saw it for what it was: his playing the dutiful, interested husband. As if everything was normal, back to the old usual between them. When the orderly had Gil settled in the wheelchair, she pushed it through the halls to the walkway exit. There were benches set far apart, and she wheeled him near one in the shade, then sat down.

She stared at him. "I called the attorney this morning."

"Good. Great." He exhaled, as if relieved. "I really do want to work things out, Lyd. I know you're hurt. But that's over. It was over the minute you found out. I promise. I'd like us—you and me—to get couples' counseling. We can start as soon as possible, once I'm out of rehab. You can get past this. We can, I mean."

"I didn't call the attorney to put a hold on the divorce. I called to tell her what your offer is."

"You … what? My offer? You told me—"

"What I told you went out the window, or should I say out the elevator, yesterday. I saw her. Your supposed sister. This wasn't just an affair. I know more than you think I do. I know *everything*. The email account you share with that woman. The website where you two have been finding so-called play dates. How you two travel all over hell and gone for your sex parties. And I know about the hidden bank account you've been socking money into. What were you planning to do with that, Gil? Certainly not share it with me, since you've been lying about our finances now for years. And if you don't want your son and daughter—hell, the whole damned world—to know, you will not contest one thing in what I told my attorney the deal is."

All color drained from Gil's face as she spoke and she wondered if he was having another heart attack. "I … I don't … I don't know what you're talking about," he stammered.

"You damn well do. I have computer files of everything. So does my lawyer. And now, so does Marielle Wharton's husband. I wasn't sick yesterday. I went to see him, gave him a thumb drive with it all. He had an inkling you two were playing footsie, but didn't know for sure. Now he knows as much as I do. But I doubt I know everything. I've reached the point where I don't care."

Gil's face turned ashen and his breathing was ragged. "Shit," he whispered. "You're the one who sent all that stuff to my clients, aren't you?"

"Stuff? What stuff? I don't know what you're talking about," Lydia lied. "I'm serious. Either you agree, or I tell Sara and James everything. And, golly, somehow, word will spread to Trevor, your clients, maybe everyone you know. So, you sign the agreement my lawyer sends and I let everyone think it's an amicable divorce. You don't?" She shrugged.

He said nothing, not looking at her as she glared at him and waited. She counted to seventy before he spoke. "So, what is this offer I've supposedly agreed to?"

"Three things. First, you sell the agency to Trevor for half its assessed value and you split that with me. You've decided to retire. Due to your health. Trevor already has full control. I used my power of attorney to give it to him Friday, so he could pay the staff and keep the agency going. It was supposed to be temporary. But that was before I heard you talking to that bitch and then saw her leave here yesterday. Two, you give me half of all your financial assets. Including," she stressed, "what's in the hidden account. Third, we sell the house and split it fifty-fifty. Oh, and there is a fourth thing. You pay all my legal fees."

Gil squirmed in the chair. "Jesus. Are you kidding me?"

"No. I told you; I am deadly serious. You have until tomorrow morning to agree," she said. "By the way, you won't be going back to *our* home when you get out of here. The locks are being changed this afternoon. You've a reservation at the extended suites near here for after rehab. I've packed what you'll need and it's in your SUV. You'll still be able to get into the garage, so you can pick it up or have someone do that for you."

"Jesus," he muttered again. Shock was vivid on his face as he spit, "That's extortion."

"Oh? I'd say it's a bargain. All the time in the world to golf and go on all those 'play dates' of yours, anytime, anywhere you please." She handed him his car keys and garage door opener from her purse and stood to leave. "Call me by morning. Either agree or don't. Your choice. I'll have someone get you back to your room."

She leaned down, her hands grasping the wheelchair arms, and whispered into his face. “When you fucked with me, you fucked with the wrong woman.”

***

Late in the afternoon, Lydia picked up her phone. As it rang, she dangled the set of new house keys to give Audra at dinner, enjoying the sharp silver glint of their metal in the window light. She clasped her hand around them and smiled when she heard a voice.

“Max? It’s Lydia. I was wondering, is there any chance of my taking you up on that dinner this Saturday? Yes, yes, I’m coming back to the lake, at least for a few more weeks ...”

Acknowledgments

This book itself would have remained undone but for the urging, support, and advice of so many others. For each and all of you, I am so grateful.

First, to the others of the Sopris 7: You were the ones who inspired me to bring this story to life. To Lettice Stuart for hosting the retreat where the first words were penciled, and to Anita Hecht, Marion Johnson, Stephanie Kadel-Taras, Pat McNees, and Paula Yost for your positive reactions to the very raw first pages written then—it was you who gave me both the permission and the courage to stick with the long process that lay ahead.

To Tex, for providing an insightful first critique. To Rick Crossley, Jerry Greenfield, My Haley and Arsenia Walker, Martha LaBare, Jayne Lisbeth, and Iris Pastor, for graciously giving your time as first readers. To Francie King, for help with the final polishing. And to Sally Goldin and Vera Rosenbluth for further advice.

To John Dunn, Bernadette Hogsett, and Christine Mele, APRN, for providing insights into areas of expertise that are theirs, and certainly not mine.

I thank you all.